MW00330045

THE F
GERONTAS

The continuing voyages of HMS SURPRISE

To Don

A glass with you sir !

Alan Lawrence

ALAN LAWRENCE

I went out aboard the boat,
Because a desire was in my head
And spurned the love I left behind,
Though she pleaded we should wed;
And I took the shilling of the King
Whilst great guns were flaming out;
I fought with Nelson at Trafalgar
And caught a splinter flying about.

When I was laid upon the deck
I waited long but no help came;
The ship aflame and become a wreck,
A familiar voice called out my name;
It had become my long lost love,
With comfort and sweet names
Who held me in her arms and cried
Then faded in the smoke and flames.

Though I am old with voyaging,
Through endless seas to far off lands,
I wonder oft if she will wait
For my embrace, my anxious hands;
To join together in our home town
And share in love with me our fate,
The silver years as we grow old,
The golden years to Heaven's gate.

Long lost love
by Alan Lawrence
after W. B. Yeats'
Song of Wandering Aengus

THE FIRESHIPS OF GERONTAS

The continuing voyages of HMS SURPRISE

The Sun had set (ah, men of Greece, a Sunset for you!)
And the Moon was no more to be seen,
No more to be seen the clear Morning Star,
Nor the Star of Eve that shines in its place,
For these Four held council, and spoke in secret,
'The Sun spins round and tells them, spins round and says
'Last night when I set I hid myself behind a little rock,
And I heard the weeping of women, and the mourning of men
For those slain heroes lying in the field,
And all the earth soaked in their blood -
Poor souls all gone below in their country's cause.'

Yannis Makriyannis
Greek freedom fighter
1797-1864

A tale of the struggle for Greek independence by
ALAN LAWRENCE

Mainsail Voyages Press Ltd, Publishers,
Hartland Forest, Devonshire

www.mainsailvoyagespress.com

THE FIRESHIPS OF GERONTAS

The continuing voyages of HMS SURPRISE

This *second* edition is copyright (c) Alan Lawrence 2016 and 2017. Published by Mainsail Voyages Press Ltd, Hartland Forest, Bideford, Devon, EX39 5RA. Alan Lawrence asserts the right to be identified as the author of this work in accordance with the Copyright, Designs and Patents Act 1988. The reader may note that this book is written by Alan Lawrence. It is not authorised, licensed or endorsed by Patrick O'Brian's family, agent or publishers. There is no association with any of those parties.

ISBN-13   978-0-9576698-5-7

Story text typeset in Times New Roman 11 point.
Printed and bound by CPI Group (UK) Ltd, Croydon, CR0 4YY

All rights reserved. No part of this publication may be reproduced, stored in a retrieval system, or transmitted, in any form or by any means, electronic, mechanical, photocopying, recording or otherwise, without the prior permission of the publishers. Specifically, the author and publishers DO NOT consent to the scanning and/or digitalisation of this book in part or in whole by AMAZON or GOOGLE or any of their subsidiaries or associates, nor by any other entity or individual, which this author and publisher consider would be a flagrant breach of the copyright attaching to this book. This book is sold subject to the condition that it will not, by way of trade or otherwise, be lent, re-sold, hired out or otherwise circulated without the publisher's prior consent in any form of binding or cover other than that in which it is published and without a similar condition being imposed on the subsequent purchaser. A CIP catalogue record for this title is available from the British Library.

Cover painting by Ivan Aivazovsky: 'The Battle of Sinop at night';
Photograph courtesy of www.russianpaintings.net;
Cover comment by David Taylor, Cheshire;
The Reef Knot graphic in this book is courtesy of and
copyright (c) United States Power Squadrons 2006

The continuing voyages of HMS SURPRISE, the series

The Massacre of Innocents   *(first edition 2014, second edition 2017)*

Freedom or Death   *(2017)*

was originally published split within the lengthy first editions of the preceding and succeeding titles, both of which have been abridged for the second editions

The Fireships of Gerontas   *(first edition 2016, second edition 2017)*

The Aftermath of Devastation   *(2017)*

THE FIRESHIPS OF GERONTAS
The continuing voyages of HMS SURPRISE
A FOREWORD BY THE AUTHOR

Whilst contemplating writing my first book in this series a few years ago I was abstractedly mindful of that famous quote of the Earl of St Vincent: *"I do not say, my Lords, that the French will not come. I say only they will not come by sea"*. It's quite a witty quip and may conceivably in its delightful hauteur, no doubt born of justifiable great confidence, have provided an element of inspiration for the quotations of another First Lord of the Admiralty and conceivably Britain's most charismatic Prime Minister, Winston Churchill, over a century later when in the early 1940s Britain faced another megalomaniacal peril. In my own rambling contemplations *(I had undoubtedly been enjoying my grog ration)* the splendid quote transmuted to become relevant to my own musings on the sublime sea stories of Patrick O'Brian: *"I do not say that there will be no further tales of HMS Surprise. I say only that they will not be written by Patrick O'Brian"*. That rather silly mental trifling, in a very minor way, helped shape my own conviction that I should, to the best of my own modest abilities (being a first time author), endeavour to perpetuate his literary magic myself, for surely there were other like-minded souls sorely lamenting the end of his exquisite series. In striving to do so I was always conscious that it was *"Mission Impossible"*, for O'Brian's stories of *HMS Surprise* were so far ahead in quality in comparison to everything else that I had ever read in fiction that I held few illusions that I would succeed. I say few but not quite none at all *(the second half of that grog ration no doubt)*, and hence in a flight of wholly reckless optimism I set aside my reasoned and well-founded hesitations and embarked upon the voyage. Perhaps I should better say the *cruise,* for it has certainly been most enjoyable.

In this *second* edition of this book the story describes the hugely significant sea battle of 10th September 1824, when the Greeks defeated an Ottoman fleet (greater in number than that which Nelson defeated at Trafalgar) in the Bay of Gerontas *(modern day Gulf of Mandalya)* in a battle which finally thwarted Ottoman efforts to capture

Samos. It ends with the hurricane which devastated many south coast ports, towns and villages of Britain on 22nd November 1824.

In this factually-based story of my own series I have endeavoured to endow it with a trifle of Patrick O'Brian's essential and complex essence and I have strived to attain his rich eloquence, customarily replete with diverse linguistic faux pas and rife with humorous conversational and other ambiguities together with his remarkable ability to fascinate with an infinity of detail. The reader will be the judge of whether I have succeeded.

This tale cannot be a story about those wonderful characters, Jack Aubrey and Stephen Maturin, Patrick O'Brian being disinclined towards authorised sequels, and quite obviously it isn't written by the genius himself, but it does have *HMS Surprise (38)* within a rich plethora of accompanying nautical background detail and a general ambience not unlike that of his own superb books. Strictly stated, the ship of my stories is the historical successor to O'Brian's *HMS Surprise (24)*.

In any event, the conclusion of writing this book brings to my own mind considerable pleasure when I observe that *the barky* is afloat once more upon the literary waves and with her crew of many fascinating individuals: interesting characters all and generously bestowed with a well-distributed sprinkling of many of those familiar traits reminiscent of our old friends Aubrey and Maturin. I do hope that it brings similar satisfaction to many other O'Brian fans. To use the metaphor of flavour: soused hog's face and a capital sea pie are greatly different dishes, but I am sure Jack enjoyed one as much as the other.

I would like to express huge thanks to my *cultural attaché* on Kefalonia, the remarkable and warmly personable Elaine Vallianou, for her unstinting help in all matters relating to the island which touch upon my books. I have not the least doubt that her considerable and greatly varied research contributions have added significantly to the historical veracity of my writings in that respect. I also thank Geoff Fisher for the cover finalisation, Ivan Gorshkov for the Ivan Aivozovsky cover photograph, Don Fiander for permission to use the reef knot graphic, and Larry Finch and Margaret Muir for general advice. I am very grateful to Don Seltzer, Roger Marsh and David Hayes (webmaster at *www.historicnavalfiction.com*) who have all provided *considerable* technical help and to my Sally for unstinting support. Mention must also be made of *"Seamanship in the age of sail"* by John Harland. It is a thoroughly remarkable reference book, a veritable treasure chest for anyone striving to understand the operation of ships of those times. At the end of the book there is a glossary of contemporary words occurring within the story with which the reader new to the naval historical world may be unfamiliar.

Several of Mark Twain's memorable and witty quips are uttered, generally with minor amendment, by Lieutenant Pickering, ship's wag.

There are a great many books about historical conflicts, both factual and fiction. As an extreme generalisation it is true to say that few of them examine in any depth the deleterious effects on the men *at the sharp end*: those determined, brave souls who experience close combat, many of whom become wounded in doing so or experience the loss of dear comrades. These are men (and women) who for the most part must and do continue to persevere with considerable bravery throughout the very worst of life's experiences, both during and after the traumatic events they encounter. This story, though fiction, strives to touch upon this oft neglected issue of warfare and the painful burdens of the enduring aftermath. This book is dedicated to all those who served in the 1982 war in the South Atlantic - on both sides of that bleak, wintry conflict.

Give you joy, shipmate! Come aboard! Voyage with HMS Surprise! Share her crew's reminiscences in familiar old haunts and revel too in their exciting new adventures. Come aboard! Swiftly now, there is not a moment to be lost!

Alan Lawrence   *April 2016*

THE FIRESHIPS OF GERONTAS
The continuing voyages of HMS SURPRISE
HISTORICAL & METEOROLOGICAL NOTE

There have been two recorded hurricanes in the British Isles: the first, of 1703, was described by Daniel Defoe in his book *"The Storm"*; the second, of 22nd November 1824, is much less well known, but contemporary accounts are very vivid:

"We had the highest tide at Salcombe that was ever remembered by the oldest inhabitant, sweeping everything off the quays. Two vessels wrecked off the Start..."

From a Plymouth resident, *"the lowest parts of the town were inundated"*. The new breakwater then under construction there suffered 200,000 tons of stone washed away and 22 vessels were sunk in Plymouth harbour. Also at Plymouth the *Colonist* was swept onshore; all the crew were saved. It was reported that *"the winds blew at times from WSW to SE"*. The *Coromandel* was wrecked on the western end of the new breakwater;

At Poole, *"the tide had risen to such an astonishing height as to overflow all the quays."* The houses there were inundated to between 1.2 and 1.5 metres (4ft to 5ft);

At Melcombe Regis (Weymouth) the quays were awash, the seafront houses flooded and boats were driven into the centre of the town (a SSE wind at 4am on the 23rd);

At Chesil Beach (at 5am-6am and a SW wind - *the hurricane eye now closer*), an onlooker reported the sea at and over the very top of the long stone berm, which would usually be 6.7 metres (22ft) clear at high tide! The normal maximum of a hurricane surge is about 5 metres. At East Fleet, behind the Chesil lagoon, the sea came inland *"as fast as a horse can gallop"* (35mph), demolishing the nave of the church and sweeping away five houses. Chiswell village on the Portland isthmus was destroyed, 80 houses were damaged or washed away and 28 inhabitants drowned in a destructive half-hour. The Chesil Bank was lowered by 20 to 30 feet;

Also at Chiswell the West Indiaman *Colville* of 400 tons was wrecked off the village with all aboard lost and the *Ebenezer* sloop of 90 tons was washed straight over the Chesil Beach and isthmus from the west, and was later relaunched in Portland harbour to the east!

Another ship of unknown name of 500 tons sank off Portland with no survivors.

The London trader *Unity* was driven ashore under cliffs near Lyme Regis; her crew were rescued. Also at Lyme Regis the Cobb was breached at 4am on the 23rd.

In the far west, the Cornish harbour of Porthleven was destroyed, and at Polperro 19 fishing boats were totally wrecked in the harbour, its walls requiring rebuilding;

In East Devon at Budleigh Salterton, pebbles on the beach which were swept east blocked the mouth of the River Otter;

At Sidmouth a naval officer described the wind as *"stronger than the West Indies hurricanes"* and *"all the cottages under the cliff were washed away... the rising of the sea so sudden."* The Chet Rock, formerly 40 feet high, was wholly swept away. The actual atmospheric pressure was recorded here as 29.49 at 8am, falling further to a low of 28.25 in the evening of 22nd November. On the evening of the 22nd the wind was consistently from the south but by 6am-7am on the 23rd (and the hurricane wind at its worst) the wind was coming from the south-south-west;

At Fleet the *Carvalho* was lost and a Danish brig driven ashore;

At Brighton, the toll-house for the new pier was destroyed;

In Dorset the tempest had abated by noon on the 23rd.

For historical veracity I researched the 1824 hurricane to find everything I could about it so as to better understand its track as it blew in from the Western Approaches. The south coast of Cornwall, Devon and Dorset and on into Hampshire was worst hit. Contemporary observers reported winds initially from the south-south-east, then directly south and finally from the south-south-west later in the tempest. Present day comment I found suggests the fierce winds *veered* from SSE to SSW, but this is a simplification: the more substantive reason appearing to be the rotation of the hurricane winds about its eye. Winds from these directions are experienced within the lower right or south-east quadrant of the hurricane, relative to the eye: its winds in the northern hemisphere rotating counter-clockwise. The eye of the hurricane is of relatively small diameter, 20 to 30 miles across, whilst the strongest winds are experienced immediately outside the eye wall, remaining particularly strong for a radius of about 60 miles, weakening beyond that with greater distance from the eye. The relatively few precise historical facts we have of the 1824 event combined with the behavioural aspects of hurricanes suggest the track of the eye crossing very close to or directly over the Scillies and moving east-north-east at about 20mph, the lower half still largely over the coastal waters of the Channel and the eye being consistently over land after landfall near Lands End. This track implies the hurricane would have gradually lost its (water) source energy as it shifted east, eventually crossing Kent and thence into the North Sea.

The 1970 Hurricane Scale developed by Herbert Saffir and Dr Robert Simpson (then Director of the U.S. National Hurricane Center) defines a Category 3 'Extensive' hurricane as one with central air pressure between 27.91 and 28.47 inches. The 1824 hurricane would seem to accord with this rating. The scale defines wind speeds as 111 to 130 mph and the sea surge as 9 to 12 feet. In more recent memory, Hurricane Katrina of 2005 was also a Category 3 'Extensive' hurricane as it made landfall.

A hurricane in the British Isles is an exceedingly rare event. Formed in and fuelled by the much warmer waters far to the south-west, in the Caribbean usually, the hurricane has lost much of its force as it blows into the much cooler waters of the north-east Atlantic and the British Isles. A contemporary captain such as Pat O'Connor, being so far from the tropics, would therefore be presented with the most significant decision of his sea-going life, one to make without a great deal of understanding; indeed, likely with a lack of comprehension of what was about to be inflicted upon him and his ship. Make the wrong choice in such circumstances and the result was inevitable: Davy Jones' Locker.

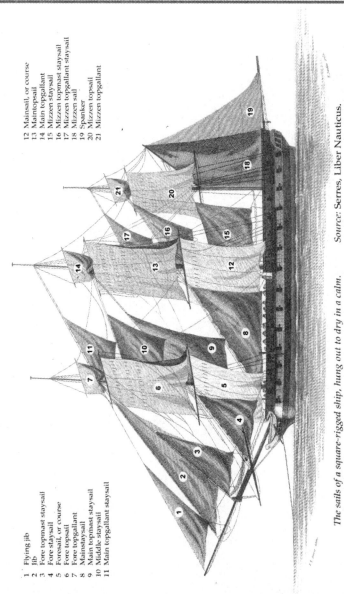

1 Flying jib
2 Jib
3 Fore topmast staysail
4 Fore staysail
5 Foresail, or course
6 Fore topsail
7 Fore topgallant
8 Mainstaysail
9 Main topmast staysail
10 Middle staysail
11 Main topgallant staysail

12 Mainsail, or course
13 Maintopsail
14 Main topgallant
15 Mizzen staysail
16 Mizzen topmast staysail
17 Mizzen topgallant staysail
18 Mizzen sail
19 Spanker
20 Mizzen topsail
21 Mizzen topgallant

The sails of a square-rigged ship, hung out to dry in a calm.   *Source: Serres, Liber Nauticus.*

Chapter One

Thursday 9th September 1824   17:00   *Colones, Samos*

Nearly three weeks had passed since the arrival of letters and orders from the Admiralty for the rather battered and damaged frigate *Surprise,* moored a cable off the Colones quay. The close proximity facilitated contact with the shore and receipt of the provisions that Lycurgus, the island's Magistrate, sent daily in grateful thanks for *Surprise's* crucial assistance in defending the island in the prior month. A ferocious serious of battles had been fought in August to defend Samos against a Turk fleet intent on invasion. It had resulted in several deaths and many more casualties within the frigate's crew. The wounded had all been returned to Cephalonia in the English-ruled Ionians, conveyed aboard *Surprise's* tender, the schooner *Eleanor.* The frigate, although ostensibly owned by her captain and sailing under a letter of marque issued by the provisional Greek government, was in fact covertly operating under Admiralty orders: His Majesty's Government, though unwilling to strain diplomatic relations with the Ottoman powers, was minded to favour any emerging new government for Greece, and the British Foreign Secretary, George Canning, was himself something of a Philhellene.

For once the frigate was the solitary vessel at the port, all the armed Greek merchant brigs which constituted the Greek navy had sailed to the south, beyond Agathonissi in search of the anticipated return of the Turks, Admiral Khosref believed to be sure to try again to capture Samos with a greater Turkish fleet. No one imagined that the Turks would give up, having already sacked and ravaged the two smaller islands of Kasos and Psara. In both those disasters *Surprise* had also sought to defend the two islands, but had necessarily fled when confronted with greatly superior enemy numbers. Thankfully she had been more

1

successful in the case of Samos, arriving fortuitously in the vital hour to decoy away Turk warships from their troopship charges, the arriving Greek warships inflicting severe losses on the unescorted invaders. In distant Constantinople the angered Sultan had subsequently summoned reinforcements in the form of his Egyptian vassal's powerful and French-trained fleet, and they, under Ibrahim, were now known to be at sea and sailing to join with and to support their Turkish overlords. A few days ago, on the 5th, so merchants' reports had stated, the Greek admiral, Miaoulis, had engaged inconclusively with the frigates of both Khosref and Ibrahim in the channel off the islands of Kos and Kappari, the Kos fort's battery firing at long range at the Greek brigs.

Surprise's captain, Patrick O'Connor, had paid that news little mind, anticipation of his own greatly deteriorated ship's approaching departure for England now preoccupying the thoughts of all on board. The dutiful crew of *Surprise*, bouyed by their captain's announcement that they really were going home, the Admiralty having ordered her recall, had laboured long and strived hard, as best they could without benefit of shipyard stores, to restore the many and varied damages the ship had suffered in the several and ferocious August battles in defence of Samos from the Turk invaders, and she was once more as ready for sea as she could be without recourse to the slip, although the two shot holes in her hull had been rectified with temporary repairs only. *Surprise* had escaped substantial damage when she had participated unsuccessfully in June and July in prior skirmishes during the Turk invasions of Kasos and Psara, but the fact that she had been unable to prevent the violent sack of those islands had proven dismaying for all of her crew. Her surgeon, Doctor Ferguson, had found the exceptional number of casualties during the Samos battles extremely distressing to deal with.

Pat was sitting in the great cabin eating supper. He was accompanied by his friend, Simon Ferguson; by Duncan Macleod, recently promoted to commander and Pat's First officer; by Abel Jason, sometime purser and presently sent from England as an Admiralty messenger; and by Tom Pickering, his senior lieutenant and the ship's wit. There was a mood of relief about the table, a realisation that their task was done, that they would not engage in any more bloody battles, would lose no more men. Despite this lifting of apprehension, of tension they could not quite bring themselves to accept that their obligations were ended, that they really were going home. It was plain that the war was not over, and to Pat's mind the Admiralty recall sat uncomfortably with the unfinished business which was that war. He knew just how valuable a contributor the relatively powerful *Surprise* had been alongside the armed merchant brigs which were the mainstay of the Greek fleet, and whilst he felt that they undoubtedly would manage without her, without his own men to help, he was minded that the Greeks would surely persevere and ultimately prevail; yet, despite this, he remained in two minds about the recall, for he would never personally countenance letting down his allies. It was plain to him that his men were ready to go home, so many - dozens - having been wounded, and worse - the deaths of a number of his men were exceedingly painful to him and to everyone aboard the barky, for all had served together for long years aboard *Tenedos* before *Surprise*. Pat took a long draught of his wine, ignored the bitter taste, the execrable quality of it and allowed his thoughts to wander towards contemplation of something better to be brought aboard, perhaps in Malta or even Minorca on the way home.

Noon long past, the sun was beginning to slip into its descent towards the Samos horizon, casting a diminishing light and warmth through those unbroken glass panes in the stern gallery which had survived the fierce engagement with two Turk vessels off the island of Candia in the previous year when *Surprise* had first arrived in Greek waters. Many other panes remained boarded up, no glass or glazier having been found in all the time since to repair them. Despite this, despite the frequent gusts of cooling wind draughts - very pleasant in the heat at the top of the day - the cabin remained warm and was, particularly at mealtimes to which Pat customarily invited one or more of his officers, something of a refuge from the day to day concerns of the war.

'Freeman, this is an admirable supper,' said Pat amiably to his black steward, a liberated African slave. Both his stewards were fussing about the table; the second one was Murphy, a compatriot of Pat's, both being men of County Galway. The toad in a hole was cooked to perfection, the ingredients were fresh and palatable; the meal was delicious, and it registered as such with them all, being greatly in contrast to the ceaselessly dismal food of recent weeks.

'Aye, laddie, so it is; I dinnae collect anythin' better from Murphy afore ye joined us,' Duncan Macleod joked in his oft near impenetrable accent of the Isles, for he hailed from Lewis and was a man without the least of social pretensions. Murphy was refilling the glasses, and he frowned darkly. 'Pat, there surely cannae be any need of the twae stewards noo, and perhaps Murphy will return to the for'ard mast!' Duncan, in fine good cheer, laughed loud and long; Murphy scowled.

'Pat, I refer to your recent instructions from the Admiralty,' said Simon. The surgeon hailed from Tobermory, Mull; he was a highly educated man, trained in Edinburgh and a great student of the classics; he was an inseparable friend of both Pat and Duncan. Pat's mood sank instantly in reluctant anticipation of a return to further exhortation by Simon to a subject he did not much care to contemplate, for disagreement verging on argument was sure - an insistence upon a return home was undoubtedly Simon's direction. 'I collect their Lordships referred to *diminished clarity to the political situation*. What, would you suppose, do they mean by that? And what particular signification might it hold for us, for our own prospects?'

'Mr Jason, would you care to enlighten us?' Pat looked across the table, Jason usually possessing an informed view.

'You may collect that the Greeks have struggled with two calamitous burdens until early summer: the first being the Turk and the second an internecine struggle.'

'An internecine struggle?' murmured Pat in a low voice, shocked, his mind striving to find even the smallest reminder of the events.

'Surely that is the greatest disaster to afflict any state - *civil war* - as we ourselves found to our enduring cost, for much ill sentiment lingers still,' Simon interjected.

4

'Civil war... why, I collect no recent news of such,' remarked Pat, his astonishment lingering. All looked to Jason for further explanation.

'The rebel Kolokotronis surrendered Nauplia to the government in June, bringing the civil war to an end,' Jason explained. 'Mavrocordato in Messalonghi has managed to stay outside the struggle, and so has presumably said little or nothing about it to you. We may presume that news of the end of the civil war had not reached London when the Admiralty despatch was issued.'

'On my life,' Pat exhaled deeply, 'a civil war... and whilst we are here fighting the Turk for them. *Damned foreigners*... for sure it is time to go home.'

'In the first place,' said Pickering in a droll voice, 'God made idiots - *for practice* - and then politicians.' A low laugh echoed about the table.

'I am entirely of your way of thinking, Pat,' said Simon with undisguised determination. 'This wretched place is certainly no Arcadia.'

'How is it beyond the ken of so many leaders to set the proper course? Eh? I ask ye,' Duncan's deep voice boomed across the cabin.

No reply to that profound question forthcoming, Pickering spoke again, 'When I was a young mid of fourteen, my captain - not you, sir, I hasten to say - was so ignorant I could hardly stand to be in his company...' Puzzled faces all, everyone staring at him and waiting for what they knew must be coming, Pickering hastened on, '... but when I got to be a junior lieutenant... I could not believe how much he had learned in five years!' The expectant gathering dissolved into hearty laughter, Pat raising his glass to Pickering with a wide smile across his face.

The thoughts of all at the table returning to Pat's so deeply felt and succinctly expressed intent to return home, and Simon's corroboration, no one spoke further, all ruminating on the situation, *Home, blessed home* very much foremost in their thoughts. Eventually all except Pat departed, his officers going below to join their colleagues in the gunroom. Pat leaned back in his chair and sipped the last of the coffee with great pleasure, luxuriating in the mood of relaxation. His mind finding a rare measure of contentment, he took up his 'cello and determined on an attempt upon a lead for Bocherini's cheerful *String quintet in C major,* a great favourite in the cabin; but to his considerable dissatisfaction even the merest of familiarity with his instrument would not come and so he paused after several attempts upon the succession of single long-drawn notes of the bell simulation of *Ave Maria,* setting down his instrument. With a deep sigh of exasperation, he resigned himself to sloth with the rare thought that perhaps that did, after all, have some small merit. He settled within his cot for a nap, quickly falling asleep.

A little later, as Dalby rang four bells of the first Dog watch, Pat stepped gratefully up to his quarterdeck to take in the evening air. Clutching his telescope in one hand, a flask of Greek brandy in the other, he determined to further recuperate whilst spending an hour or two indulging his interest in astronomy, for the time and peace of mind for such had been so greatly lacking in recent weeks. It was a sweet evening, the heat of the day enduring as pleasant warmth and the air near still save for the merest hint of a northerly breeze. He leaned back on the curved broad transom rail above the stern, watching a glorious sunset over the island, his eyes absentmindedly catching sight of a schooner arriving from the south, working hard against the so slight but adverse wind until, eventually, it tied up alongside the near quay, Pat allowing his gaze and curiosity to slip away from it. He stood in silence, in private contemplation, enjoying the familiar scents of the salt air, the aromatic warm tar, the odour of the hemp of the rigging, his mind basking in the simple pleasure of the nautical twilight with just the Colones lights twinkling on the ripples of water near the shore. Above the town and to the west over the island streamed the few remaining vestiges of clouds in long, thin wisps, reflecting pink on the undersides, the ethereal nature of them in some ways, he felt, akin to the fragility of his own thinking, his uncertainties. He savoured intense pleasure in the quietude, with only the tiniest of sounds from the rigging, the breeze faintly shifting the tied bundles of canvas on the yards, rustling the many and varied hanging ropes, the noise not really registering in his mind. He turned around and stared up into the eastern celestial expanse; the moon had not yet risen over the peak of distant Mount Samsun. His eyes studied the brightest of the emerging stars. He swept the sky with his gaze, staring through his glass and marvelling whilst taking in the majesty of the star-studded infinity. He turned about once more: Mercury was hanging low in the western sky and many stars were now becoming visible even in the last lingering presence of the post-sunset twilight, fast fading but still holding back the absolute black clarity he awaited to the west. In the continuing evening warmth, his unkempt hair just ruffled occasionally by the gentlest remnant of the northerly *Meltemi,* he strived to relax, to slow his mind to a crawl, to attain a tolerably restful state, but rude and unwanted interruptions, recollections and memories - which he could not dismiss - returned constantly to breach his incomplete mental wall, preventing the relaxation he so much sought, and eventually he resigned himself to pondering the recent events and the present situation. He strived to turn his thoughts to the morrow, to a future without such as the painful and personal losses of recent months; he directed his mind towards contemplation of a more harmonious time, his welcome thoughts of family drifting in and out of his mind, but sadly he found only a cursed inability to focus solely on that which he so much wished for. Intermittently, between thoughts of *Surprise's* essential purpose, he did manage to relish the precious tranquillity, a rare and fragile moment without any danger or disruption whilst time slowly slipped by, his mind reaching for, grasping the so rare and very blissful short minutes of pleasant musing when he managed to cast aside all thoughts of conflict, precious short spells with consternation absent, past horrors thankfully forgotten.

The sea swell was small, *Surprise* rising and falling gently without any roll, the motion repeating itself, up and down in graceful slow movements, Pat oblivious to it. He ignored the single bell at the change of watch and the staring interest of his men near the wheel until, at eight bells at the end of the last dog-watch, the final vestiges of sunset being long faded away, he was accosted by Abel Jason, venturing upon his captain's sacrosanct starboard side of the quarterdeck. Pat's striving for solitary relaxation was broken, but he did not mind in the least, for he had failed to find it in the form he so much wished for: consternation and worry were determined fellows. Furthermore, *Surprise* was anchored in a safe haven and Royal Navy convention, it seemed, had long been abandoned in numerous ways as the year had passed; and in the evening thus far he had, despite the peaceful nature of his deliberations, failed to find that clarity of mind which he had sought in his silent examination of the stars. He was an accomplished astronomer and the sky's sparkling panorama was greatly familiar to him, the expanse holding a sense of majesty; yet on this occasion, the brutal clarity of his perception of its enormity made him feel utterly insignificant and without value in that moment of the rude realisation of it.

'Mr Jason,' Pat spoke pleasantly to the new arrival on the quarterdeck. Indeed, he felt a degree of relief in the company of a companion, even an uninvited one, in that stark moment of his feeling of personal inconsequence.

'Good evening, sir. Please forgive me if I am intruding,' Jason's face illustrated his own disquietude.

'Never in life. I bid you come join me, please.'

'I had decided upon taking the fresh, the cooling nocturnal air, the gunroom so uncomfortably warm; and the conversation down there, cordial as it was, turned to homecomings. I could not dispel my concerns; indeed, my anxiety that such thoughts were a trifle optimistic... premature perhaps? Are they groundless, tell? Will I cast away my worries?'

Pat could offer no immediate answer to Jason's question; indeed, he realised that it had revealed the reason for his own unsettled mind, his inability to completely relax. Instead he proffered his telescope, 'Look, look there, directly above and a trifle to the west, *the west*... above the town, over there, our summer friends: Deneb... and Vega. There... and below them Altair; they form the triangle you will see.'

'Ah... yes, there they are,' Jason's tone of voice expressed his interest. 'I see them plain, such luminosity; their clarity is striking, even amidst the inspiring multitude of their fellows... so many, hundreds of them, perhaps a thousand or more.'

'Why, look east now; I doubt we see less than ten thousand,' murmured Pat without the least condescension. 'In less than half an hour, the moon - it is but one day past full - will subdue our gazing save for the very brightest of stars.'

'I have always found there is something greatly reassuring in the majesty of the heavens: a temporal infinity, an eternity, a scale beyond mere mortal comprehension. Is that not so? Does it act upon you in that way, sir?'

'Indeed it does, Mr Jason, indeed it does,' Pat's quiet reply was thoughtful, assured; perhaps there was a small advantage in being truly insignificant. A further five minutes passed before he spoke again, 'As to your concern, for that our patience must answer; a day or two more, not longer, and we will leave this place.'

He studied Jason unobtrusively. Many years beforehand, during Pat's South Atlantic command, he had served as purser aboard *Tenedos*. Jason had been an admirable purser, but then she had paid off in Chatham, Pat's officers all departing for their precious few prospects of post-war service elsewhere. Jason had been more fortunate than most: his linguistic abilities had brought employment as a translator for the Admiralty and his present position as aide in that respect for Pat's mission. The years had, Pat thought, caught up with him, for Jason looked old; the thought had never previously occurred to him. His scrutiny of his companion, Jason staring again through the telescope, revealed a man of perhaps near sixty, short in stature, with still a good head of pale grey hair, near white; immaculately shaven and plainly dressed. He was blessed with the greatest of intelligence and willing too to turn his hand to any task, for he had assisted in the bloody surgical operations during and after the recent battles, the surgeons being overwhelmed. 'A capital shipmate,' Pat concluded his thoughtful diversion, 'a man with his heart in the right place.' He had not the least doubt about it.

For near half an hour longer they stood under the inspiring celestial panorama, their occasional and cordial but subdued conversational exchanges lapsing into silence as they stared in awe, the stars shining bright over Turkey and Greece in their procession through the heavens, both men gratefully taking stock in many ways within the so rare occasion of absolute quietude. Not the smallest extraneous sound had disturbed the evening's peaceful oasis in life's violent journey, but then, just as the great, lambent moon emerged in its near full splendour over the Turk mountains to the east, there came the unwanted intrusion, the jarring thump against the hull of a small boat coming alongside, and all focus on the brilliant majesty above was rudely swept away. A loud, enquiring shout from the watchman brought an acknowledgement from the visitor and the end of Pat's precious relaxation. It was Captain Zouvelekis, come back aboard. The Greek, a Kasiot refugee since his island had been invaded by the Turks, had served aboard *Surprise* for some months in the capacity of liaison officer with the Greek admirals. He had remained ashore with his Greek compatriots after the end of the battle against Khosref's fleet. He stepped in haste up to the quarterdeck, his demeanour one of great anxiety, which was alarming to every man he passed by. Pat and Jason stared at him in expectant curiosity, a dawning sense of foreboding settling upon them. In a state of considerable excitement, Zouvelekis wasted no time with formalities, 'I beg pardon for my intrusion, Captain O'Connor, at this late hour. I am come with a message from the schooner just arrived at the quay. I bear a message from Admiral Miaoulis.' Pat simply nodded and the Greek continued, 'His vessels are engaged with the Turk, to the south... and their numbers are so great, so very great that he begs leave to request your assistance... your *immediate* assistance.'

From Jason there was a sharp intake of breath, prompting Pat's glance towards him, the magnitude of the shock plainly revealed by the look of horror on Jason's face. Coming from anyone else the solicitation might have prompted the most cautious of reply; uttered by Zouvelekis and originating from Miaoulis there was no prospect of any prevarication or any evasion in Pat's mind, for he held both the Greek officers in the highest respect. He placed his arm gently on Zouvelekis' shoulder, 'Please, let us go below. Will you care to tell me more of the situation?' They stepped down the companionway and into the deserted cabin, the dim light from the cabin lamp glowing in muted welcome. An enervated Murphy hastened in immediately, solicitous of his captain's needs and plain curious as to why Pat was holding a meeting at this late hour, his captain in the past few weeks of recuperation having usually retired by this time to his cot. 'Murphy, light along a pot of coffee, if you will,' murmured Pat in a subdued voice. The enormity of the Greek request, the fundamentally changed prospects for *Surprise* and his men were entirely filling his mind, and it raced frantically with the magnitude of the daunting implications. 'Please, Captain, be seated,' he said to his visitor with trepidation and a rising feeling of unease.

Zouvelekis sat down reluctantly, a man plainly in considerable anxiety, and he continued his message, 'The schooner so recently arrived in haste from our fleet, which is near Ataki, brought this report. In the face of overwhelming Ottoman superiority, Admiral Miaoulis with all of our squadrons intends to retire this evening to the line Lapsa, Farmakonissi, Gulf of Gerontas - to its northern shores. The Admiral is, of course, familiar with the *Meltemi* and its behaviour generally. As you will yourself recall, it is a northerly wind, blowing in the arc between north-west and north-east, rarely present in the morning and at the peak of its strength in the afternoon, the *early* afternoon.' Pat poured and passed a glass of the Greek brandy, the bottle still on his table, to Zouvelekis who gulped a large draught - thankfully it seemed, for his demeanour was still exceedingly agitated - before he continued, 'By holding our squadrons in that line, it will take Khosref many hours to bring his fleet north from the strait at Kos, and so we may use such time as we are afforded to best prepare our position and our tactics. The afternoon *Meltemi* will afford our fireships better prospects of success, prospects which are customarily absent in the calm of the morning.' Pat nodded his understanding and the Greek resumed, 'That, sir, is the Admiral's plan. Our numbers are many fewer than the Turk, now united with his Egyptian vassal; our ships are smaller, our guns lighter. With your frigate, our chances of halting Khosref before he is able to reach and

11

bombard Samos are undoubtedly better...' Zouvelekis faltered, the essence of his report concluded, and he simply stared at Pat for a long minute before his whispered plea, grave anxiety and deep despond plain in his voice, 'Will you help us, Captain?' The request was made: plaintive, desperate even. The combined Turk and Egyptian fleets represented the most formidable foe that the Greeks could ever encounter.

Greatly perturbed, shocked even, all dreams of home so rudely and abruptly shattered, Pat stood up; he paced across the cabin in silence, his mind frantic with private contemplation of many and varied factors: the dreadful state of his ship, his tired men, their return home postponed; how would that be received? He turned and looked at Zouvelekis for a long minute, his thoughts awhirl in computation of the position that Zouvelekis had explained; he was absorbing the huge significance for his ship and his men, weighing the so fundamental change of their intentions, painful duty pressing heavier upon him than he could ever recall. Finally he turned towards Zouvelekis. Murphy was still an onlooker, his face frozen in mute apprehension. Pat nodded very slowly before uttering his reply, quiet, resolute, '*Surprise* will aid you, Captain; we are with you...' a long pause as if reconsidering the implications of what he had just declared; '*We are with you*,' he offered again in quiet confirmation. Murphy gasped and hastened out of the cabin.

Zouvelekis rose, seized and shook Pat's hand with an iron grip; he could find no words in that moment, his relief and his gratitude simply overwhelming him. A frozen minute in time elapsed, the two men feeling the onset, the weight of huge obligation, before Pat stepped back to his table and looked at his chart, examining it for several more minutes, Zouvelekis looking on, not daring to speak.

Pat spoke at last, his mental calculations issued aloud, 'Lapsa is eight leagues away, and we too have little wind, as you doubtless remarked coming out from the quay. I doubt we will make three knots bearing every sail she carries, and so our passage will assuredly be slow, very slow. At least we are blessed with a near full moon. We must leave immediately; there is not a minute to be lost.'

Zouvelekis, still speechless, nodded; his gratitude was so palpable, so plain in his face. Murphy sidled in with the coffee pot, setting it on the table, and he began to pour, all the while listening intently. 'Murphy, there is no time for that,' cried Pat, to his steward's evident dismay and astonishment - coffee never before having been refused. 'My compliments to Mr Macleod, and let us pipe all hands on deck. Cut along, lose not a moment!' His sense of urgency rising, he shouted, 'And Murphy... you may care to run!'

The bosun's rousing, shrill and unexpected pipe whistle a minute later brought every officer and every man of the crew hastening from their cots and hammocks, those men still awake striding from their assumed leisure to a gathering on the gun deck, to loud speculation, minds everywhere in growing trepidation, the clarion call sitting ill with their general preoccupation with thoughts of home.

Pat stepped out from his cabin, his stomach churning in his resumed anxiety, his mind whirling in formulation of how best to break what would doubtless be unwelcome news to his crew: men who, a few hours ago, were celebrating the joyous prospect of the voyage home; men who now faced a return to likely and imminent battle and against huge odds. It would be, he had no doubt, the most bitter of news. He paced exceedingly slowly, his mind in consternation, towards the middle of the gun deck; his thoughts were racing; he was keenly aware of and absorbing the tiniest detail of everything all around him, his mind shocked to complete clarity of observation, his eyes registering the shifty glances towards him of many men as he stepped by: old hands who were customarily as steadfast as ever could be, *Tenedos* veterans included. He sensed, no more, the confusing perception of time itself being slowed, near stopped; everything about him was shifting infinitely slowly. Another slow step forward. All the crew, officers and men, a hundred, two hundred, were standing all about the gun deck, the furthest being far away near the galley stove. One more step. The crew gazed aft in expectant silence, looking to him with faces filled with curiosity, with concern, plentiful unsettled expressions all about. Many a man stared through narrowed eyes; here and there an intensely suspicious demeanour was evident, though it could not be said that anyone exhibited the least hostility. The anxious crowd, for that is how Pat perceived the mood of the gathering, were looking too at Zouvelekis, the Greek officer one pace behind Pat. A last step and Pat halted. Every man present was staring at him and at Zouvelekis, the Greek standing alongside Pat; doubtless all were wondering what tidings their visitor had brought and how it would affect them; their fears were rising, all hope frozen amidst their darkest thoughts: their voyage home - was it now to recede, to fade into some distant future?

A darker and more unwelcome question crossed Pat's mind as he steeled himself to speak, cognizant of the likely magnitude of the approaching Turk host, 'How many of them would ever see their homes and families again?' He reined his thoughts in; he coughed; he looked up with a silent stare and swept his gaze across the front rank of his men. 'Mr Macleod,' he commanded in a stern voice, 'Pray let the hands be called aft if you please.' From the corner of his eye he noticed Simon, with Jason, both leaning on the capstan; Simon's face was one of deep concern, a picture of great anxiety; such was the overriding image which registered in Pat's mind even amidst the surging, alarming thoughts pressing hard upon him.

Simon stepped quickly through the throng and to his side, whispering, 'Listen, Pat, if you will. I must tell you this. It cannot wait a private word in the cabin... there is a deal of discontent amongst the men.' The unwelcome tidings had spread already throughout the ship, Pat realised. It was not unexpected. 'You are to understand that they are not happy,' Simon persevered. Pat turned his head away: it was not what he wanted to hear. He had discerned from many men's faces - and the demeanour of several of them - an evident strain, a tension, significant disquiet amongst the crew. This was his conclusion in just the brief duration of walking out from the great cabin: something afoot, a noxious draught brewing. There were few secrets aboard a crowded frigate, and such as there were rarely lingered long in an ambience of furious gossip. Simon persevered, stepped closer, strived to continue his warning, 'A vexation is upon them... the men seem displeased.'

'All hands aft!' bawled Duncan, cutting off what more Simon intended to say. There was a general shuffling of feet and the men pressed towards Pat. Despite the warmth of the evening Pat felt a cold frisson of anxiety overcoming him, accompanied by an onrush of loneliness. It was for him alone to break the news, news which many would receive as the very worst of tidings: black news, unwelcome news, the destroyer of hopes, the end of all thoughts of home, a longer absence from loved ones: wives, sweethearts and children. He looked about him, to many familiar faces in the throng, and he sensed the great unhappiness within the assembly, an unease born of sensing disappointment, a disquiet rooted in fear of an imminent change for the worse - very much for the worse; and the resentment for all those things was exaggerated by liquor, for several of the men he looked at exhibited anger and the near ones smelt heavily of drink; doubtless smuggled aboard on the Colones supply barque with the water. It was not that the Surprises were unaccustomed to being away from home or that any man shirked his pledge to fight, and to fight hard, for that was what every man had signed up for. No, it was the accepted imminence of their departure for home being so rudely shattered that seemingly had not been well received: they knew. Of that Pat had no doubt, he could see it in their eyes. It was also concern for their wounded comrades; every one of those unfortunate men was longing to see their precious kin once more; in some cases for the final time, the condition of several being fragile, their prospects poor, life itself so uncertain.

'Silence fore and aft!' shouted Duncan, and the uneasy babble of scores of men faded but did not cease entirely.

'Lads... lads,' Pat began his desperate plea, 'Captain Zouvelekis has brought news of Khosref's fleet.' The hubbub persisting, he raised his voice, 'It is approaching Samos once more... coming together with the Egyptians.' A very small diminution in the babble of scores of voices, he pressed on, 'They are expected within days... and every Greek ship is called to repel them.' This did not appear to impress the Surprises in the least and the background noise of loud voices broke out once again: rising, louder, discordant, the tone of anger discernible amongst the groans of deep dismay. The mutterings of discontent were plain to Pat's ears, though at least he did not gain any impression of personal hostility. He glanced towards Simon: the surgeon had become a picture of unhappiness.

'Silence fore and aft!' shrieked Duncan again, but the noise continued, only a very little quieter; at the front of the assembly endemic whispering persisted whilst at the back there was no response to the call whatsoever.

'HOME!' came the far shout from near the galley, 'HOME!' taken up by others, scores of feet stamping the deck with a repetitive accord with the shouts. Simon's feelings sank to new depths, Pat was overtaken by a wave of heartfelt dismay.

'Take that man's name!' Duncan screamed, 'Silence! Silence!' Pickering seized up and beat loud on the drum, "BOOM, BOOM, BOOM" and the men to a great degree quieted, the protest diminishing. Seconds passed and the noise withered, though not to silence; the angry mood of the gathering was one of festering dismay, of despondency; gloom had overtaken everyone present including all the officers.

Pat had immediately recognised the danger presented in delay and prevarication; 'LADS, LADS,' he shouted as loud as he could, 'HEAR ME.' The atmosphere calmed a little more, the resumed raucous shouting declining again to general murmurings of discontent, of grumbling, but glares of hostility were becoming evident even from some of the older hands.

'HOME!' came again a solitary call from forward, from the vicinity of the foremast.

'I ain't here to make a speech,' Pat shouted, feeling his control of the men about to slip away. 'Hear me, shipmates... HEAR ME,' he cried out, his own consternation plain to all in his voice. Perhaps it was recognition of that which saved the situation, which held back anarchy, the mutiny so palpably close.

Men so long inured to the constant dangers of life at sea, to the greater dangers of close combat in the slugging matches of ships and great guns, men accustomed to the violence of battle, the offensive bloody toll of killings, the ever present proximity of death in all its forms develop a great capacity to endure, to persevere. For without such accommodation wars must be short, but such tolerance is not without its limits, and every man recognises the fundamental moment when such finality is upon him, when he can no longer endure; when anything, *anything at all*, is preferable to continuing; when he has reached the acutely pressing moment when he has had enough, has done all he can, the tortured mind shrieking "enough and no more". Many of the Surprises had long reached that point, had recognised it in several and varied ways, but they had soldiered on. Many men had remained buoyed up by the support of their veteran comrades throughout the agonies of the Greek summer - so many of their shipmates killed and wounded - but now those same men burned with a need, a longing within every vestige of their tormented souls to go home, to be reunited with their precious kith and kin. They had been too long away, too long immersed in violence, and a return to such, however brief, was not something they cared to further contemplate. Pat, with his decision made to return once more to the fray, was therefore in considerable difficulty, which he knew only too well. He took a deep breath, raised both arms, and as the angry voices of discontent settled to something quieter within his audience, a degree of empathy for their captain in his own consternation lingering and his men willing to hear him out, he resumed his appeal very gently, in quieter voice, 'Lads... I ain't one to bark about the bush... and it must be ten years we have been shipmates... on *Tenedos* before and now *Surprise*... ten long years it is...' He paused to let this sink in, the murmurings of the men, of the discontented gradually dying away; the sentiment of pride had registered with many, Pat's opening striking a chord, and for a great number allaying to a significant degree their sense of an injustice about to be perpetrated upon them. Recognising the favourable registration his words had received, he continued in the same vein, 'We have seen some hard times together... and we ain't come here to line our pockets... to fill our boots with filthy lucre...'

'Just as well,' thought Simon. Taken aback by the dire substance of the unexpected development he was deep in the very depths of his own despondency. He was aware that not a man had received much more than a guinea apiece in pay since leaving Falmouth and that in several instalments for rare spells of shore leave. He stared closely at Pat's face; his friend's expression was resolute. He was plainly a man of considerable moral stature, as had always been recognised by all aboard the frigate, yet his eyes, Simon believed, gave away his consternation, his anxiety. In the apparent reception of his words, this no longer came out in his voice which, whilst carrying the tone of long-endured weariness, now disseminated conviction and moral rectitude, and conveyed a measure of reassurance, even when the price demanded would likely be high and surely measured in blood.

'We have all of us seen what has happened on Psara and on Kasos,' Pat continued, a little of confidence growing, 'Do you remember the burning... the damnable killing? DO YOU? Do you recall the boats, the swimmers, the drowning of fleeing souls?' The briefest of pause, 'I DO... I SEE IT NOW... 'tis clear in my mind, so it is.' Five more interminable seconds of pause, barely a whisper now audible from the men and a little of sympathy plainly gained, Pat resumed, the sense of rectitude, the moral compulsion to not stand aside loud in his voice, 'Will we stand by while Samos is sacked, eh? Will we stand by while wives are made widows... and children orphans? EH? WILL WE? I don't care to see that ever again myself... DO YOU? Would you see this in Falmouth Town? What would you have me say to YOUR wife, eh?'

'For sure there is nothing like candour for any appeal,' observed Simon, his own feelings remaining so very low. The change during the further pause after Pat's last words was very noticeable, the effect electric, sobering, immediate and powerful; the conveyance of his natural presence to his men had brought them to an uncomfortable silence whilst some measure of command authority and respect had plainly flooded back. 'Truly remarkable,' thought Simon; Pat's resolute determination and honest sincerity had resonated throughout his words to the crew. 'The man is uncommonly blessed with infinite fortitude and resolution. I pray they will listen.'

The fragile silence perpetuating, Pat persevered, 'Lads, I tell you now, though the barky be ordered home, as ye know, and there ain't anything I would like more... my mind is CLEAR! I am staying... I am staying to help these people. Damn it, I ain't happy, NO... but it ain't the end of the world. A few days more... ONE OR TWO DAYS to help the Greeks once more... and then we will be going home... HOME! I PROMISE YOU... D'YE HEAR ME?'

'I do indeed,' said Simon to himself, 'if we survive.' A momentary reflection and he added, 'Forgive me, what a flat I am become.'

'Does every man hear me? Shout if I ain't made myself plain. At the back there... a few more days; that's all... and then we are Falmouth bound... FALMOUTH... a few more days... and I don't ask more than that.'

A low chorus of 'Aye' rippled through the men, some louder than others, though in the background the babble of discontent lingered, though it was much diminished.

Pat's face was visibly deeply florid to all who stood near despite the tan of many months. His breathing was laboured, coming in short breaths. A subdued half-minute passed, still dark murmurings from a few of the men audible, and Pat pronounced in a low voice, 'If there is any man here who does not want to sail with the barky... sail again with me... If there is any man who will not stay to fight with his comrades... he can GO ASHORE.' Pat left that stark offer in the air for another half-minute to sink in before he resumed, 'I cannot say fairer than that... IS THAT PLAIN?'

The rebellious mutterings died away and absolute silence abounded; the moral dilemma, the fundamental choice was indeed sinking in.

Pat switched his words from an ultimatum to a timely appeal, 'Lads, I need you... the people of this island need you... to hold back sack and murder. ARE YOU WITH ME... are you with me, SURPRISES?'

'AYE,' came back the general response, still subdued and not without a hint of reticence, a residual grumbling audible in some quarters.

'ONE AND ALL?'

19

'AYE,' the shouted reply resonated with a little more warmth, with an audible degree of greater conviction, with a return of the crew's former commitment.

'ARE YE WITH US?' Duncan shouted at the top of his voice.

'AYE!' came back the roar of the men, now in unison.

'Thankee lads,' this was spoken without shouting, Pat's voice failing him, become hoarse, his throat sore, dry. 'Go to your duties now, it is the busy day we have tomorrow,' Pat's tentative grasp of a sense of welcome deliverance was plain to all those standing close about him in his heavy exhalation of breath, his words finished, nothing more said. His nerves shattered, he trembled but strived to let no man see it. To his huge relief there was no resumption of muttering, of protest; the motion had seemingly been carried. Doubtless with reluctance, doubtless with disappointment, but carried it was; and Pat was left quite overwhelmed with the nervous reaction within himself. He was suffused with a sensation that he did not belong here, a feeling that his service as an officer of the Royal Navy seemed somehow to lie in the past and he was now remote from it as if it was merely a distant memory. He was a trifle old-fashioned at heart, but the old days were gone, now mere memories; and the proof of that was in the brutal developments of the evening, and he was left feeling utterly debilitated and downcast. The realisation of that led his mind to ponder if not to question the validity of his present appointment and his entitlement to expect that he should carry his men with him. Even as Simon put his hand gently on Pat's arm, he sought to cast out from his mind a vague recollection of the regrettable Spithead events of years long gone by, and it was some further minutes before he gathered his thoughts to focus on the present, reflecting that ostensibly every man aboard was in reality somewhat outside His Majesty's military service: *Surprise* had been ostensibly originally engaged for hydrographical survey, though he doubted there was a single soul who believed that; and hence he did not know where an overt mutiny might have left him. Eventually his mind steadied, the trauma ebbed, the worst moment was past; the endemic high quality of his men was prevalent; the malcontents, such as they

20

were, would doubtless be prevailed upon by their comrades. *Surprise* was united once more in her purpose, and Pat felt the restoring tide of ease within his hugely unsettled and churning stomach, his mouth remaining painfully dry, his throat burning; the acid bile lingered.

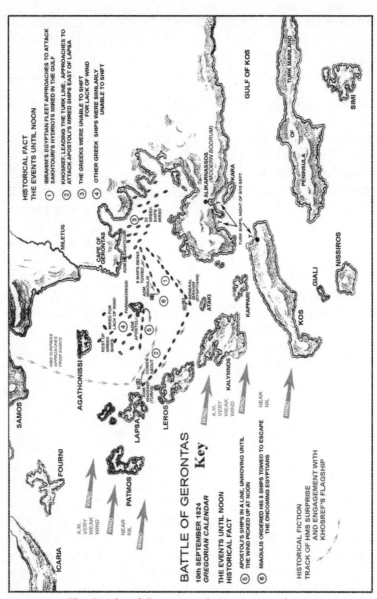

The Battle of Gerontas, the events until noon

Chapter Two

The pale light of the brilliant moon, high overhead in a cloudless sky and just one day past full, had long washed away the spectacular star-filled darkness of the prior early evening and now illuminated *Surprise's* sparkling phosphorescent silver wake, barely the gentlest of ripples on a near glass-smooth expanse which extended to the far limit of visibility. To the east, in the extreme distance and behind the larboard quarter a glimpse of the barest of shadows afforded the men at the tops a perception, no more, of Cape San Maria emerging from blackness. The grey sea surface was undisturbed by any trace of a swell, nothing of such discernible, and the air all about them was cloyingly still, exhibiting only the gentlest of breeze, the temperature clement, the night clinging to the last vestiges of the prior evening's lingering warmth. *Surprise* had hoisted every stitch of canvas she possessed and was flying her full complement of studdingsails, topgallants and royals, but despite such a press of sail she made a bare three knots in the meagre wind, such as it was, near abeam from starboard; and the ship's movement over the water was hardly noticeable, no strain at all on the yards or braces and not a one of any gull present to disturb the quietude. So slowly, like some *Flying Dutchman*, she ghosted south with one point west in near total silence save for the creak of her masts and rigging, hardly a soul remaining on deck and her passage near surreal, eerily so in the moon's bright diffusion.

On the hushed starboard side of the quarterdeck, the nearby helmsmen mute save for the occasional whispered murmur, a contemplative Duncan Macleod allowed his thoughts to wander. Despite his earlier forebodings during Pat's briefing of what disasters the day might bring, the odds against them being so very great, his mind would not allow him to dispel the so rare sense of rest, contentment even, which he had so much enjoyed during the recent days of preparation for *Surprise's* return home. Clutching in his mind for that which he knew in his heart was rapidly slipping away, he gazed at silver moonlit reflections from the tiniest of wavelets abaft *Surprise's* passage, mere ripples but beguilingly hypnotic, the atmospheric tranquillity presenting a scene of great beauty, creating a sense of profound calm, fragile though he knew very well it was; and so the occasional artist within him strived to record every detail in his memory for later reproduction: *were he to survive the day* being the sobering thought in his momentary anxiety. The peaceful scene seemed so greatly incongruous in the light of their new purpose, and that stark thought recurred again to once more jar his composure.

Since several days Duncan had begun to contemplate home, his tiny cottage on the bleak and windswept moor of Lewis. Despite the imminent prospect of spending six long, cold and dark months upon the island in winter, to his profound surprise and satisfaction it now held a restored appeal, one which he had not felt for many a year. He reflected on past times there, happier times in his younger days growing up at Rodel in the south of Harris, and he forcibly displaced all thoughts of what today or tomorrow would bring by indulging in fond memories of days gone by, sweet recollections, the long days of sunshine in his youth; those most precious and swiftly-passing of years. His parents both long deceased, his mind wandered to recollections of his closest relatives and then to the more notable but distant ones. His great-great-uncle, Alexander, had also been a seafarer and had built his home, a new house, in the tiny Harris harbour of Rodel on his retirement as captain of an Indiaman. Meeting the great man, who was celebrated throughout Harris, was his first distinct memory at the age of two. He had visited the house in all the years through his childhood, many a summer day being spent there with his Macleod clan cousins as youngsters. The settlement was a delightful waterside retreat to which he had oft returned with his Irish wife, Kathleen, to paint landscapes and seascapes, for such was their mutual passion. Indeed, they had been married there in the tiny Saint Clement's church, so prominent on the bleak hill above the tiny harbour, the church standing fortress-like in its prominence, and in its isolation so

24

much a bastion of precious sanctuary, a silent place, a haven in which to indulge in the most personal of reflections, to weigh those deep introspections of the soul, the precious time for such so rarely recurring in his own turbulent life; lamentably so, he reflected.

Duncan Macleod was not a religious man, but he determined in that particularly sobering and profound moment in his introspective recollections, so vivid an instant of crystallised thought, to return to Rodel as soon as possible - for private contemplation; perhaps even prayers might be said. Time passing in gentle quietude, his mind's general memories of past happiness progressed to a sense of specific delight in a glorious vision of the sure and warm welcome he would find on his return home and of the joy he would bring to his relatives when delivering the glad tidings of his promotion; but then came the heart-wrenching return to reality, the disquieting recollection, the extinguishment of all warmth in his thoughts in the bleakest of instants as he remembered that in Rodel itself there was now hardly a soul still living: his uncle, the absentee estate owner, had evicted everyone from their homes in a swift clearance in the year 'eighteen whilst Duncan had been serving aboard *Tenedos* in the South Atlantic. Indeed, his own former home had been burned down, the event prompting his move to a modest croft on Lewis, inherited from another relative. A wave of nausea washed through him, engulfing his thoughts of the tragedy, his boyhood community of a hundred and fifty hearths destroyed; and in his bleak despair he bit hard on his lip and he determined that he would never again miss any opportunity to find and visit as many of his relatives as he could whenever he was returned to the island, returned to his *home*, for it was still such, as diminished as it might be, and he clung to that precious thought.

On the other side of the quarterdeck, Simon Ferguson was engrossed in his own solitary introspection. He turned, sensing a companion leaning alongside him on the rail: Abel Jason had appeared. The overriding perception striking Simon was one of an unhappy man, riven with uncertainty, beset with a deal of fragility even. 'Jason, what are you doing so far from your cot in the wee hours?'

'Precious sleep eludes me, colleague. I have lain awake for hours, with a deal of contemplation of what the day may bring. I had hoped we were bound for home, blessed home... and then the call came, to battle once more... for so it seems, and I confess that sits ill with me.'

'There's a great deal to be said for contemplation,' Simon temporised, Jason known by all his companions to be a man who could never be accused of verbosity, a man who usually said little and only that which was of substance, of import, 'and doubtless the uncertainty is a strain... the apprehension... for sure it is. Will I prescribe laudanum? The merest trifle will serve, in the order of thirty drops. What do you say?'

'Oh no, no indeed; I greatly fear the day will call upon the utmost of my resources, the very utmost. That is to say... I am in contemplation of the prospects for my attendance at your side... in the cockpit... and I would not care to attend were I... were I, in any capacity - will I say - disadvantaged,' Jason's voice tailed off and he stared hard at Simon, in silence and plainly waiting for some pronouncement of reassurance.

Jason's remarks struck Simon hard, a chord resonating loudly in his mind and prompting his departure from his own customary reserve, sparking a confession, 'I admit, Jason, that I am sorely set back myself, so I am, but here is our place, our duty... with our shipmates, those precious souls who in the very worst of circumstances will require of our attendance... and that... and that, I give you, is a comfort of sorts, an uncommon relief, for I have no other, dear colleague. But come, take heart, for you are tolerably accustomed to the necessities of the cockpit; I collect your help, your attendance when we served together on *Tenedos*. You have not forgotten?'

'No, how could I? The events of that day and night inflict distress upon me even now.' The evident dismay in Jason's face underlined his words, 'I was most painfully reminded of it when attending the wounded during the recent Samos battle. I had come to terms with... indeed I had welcomed the declared, the imminent prospects of home.'

Pat O'Connor, unable to sleep, bleary-eyed, had been leafing through his log, writing up the events of the recent days. He had finally reconciled himself to wakefulness and had strived to slough off tiredness with plentiful strong coffee in the cabin. A whole pint of a particularly bitter brew drunk, 'Murphy's dregs reheated, no doubt,' so he thought, he determined to set out on an informal inspection of the ship. He stepped out through the coach, deep in personal rumination as he slowly paced along the gun deck, glancing at the faces of men as he passed in assessment of their morale. The three weeks of recuperation since the jubilation of victory over Khosref's fleet and the distressing burials of his men had served them all well, of that he was sure, no doubt at all. The call from the Greeks was immeasurably easier to deal with in his mind than had it come two or three weeks previously. During Marston's funeral oration he had been near breakdown and had refrained from visible tears with only the greatest of difficulty, his own considerable distress so near to overpowering his personal control, his mental reserves utterly expended, his morale very fragile, as doubtless was that of many others; yet, as he reflected, an occasional nod here and a single word of greeting there to the score of men he passed close by on deck, he concluded that his men seemed to be once more the veteran crew of Falmouth's departure day, all to a man busy in their duties, a low audible banter everywhere about the ship, and for that he was deeply grateful and immensely relieved. His announcement of their return to fight the anticipated Turk fleet had not been well received, and it had been an unpleasant quarter hour after he had broken the news before anything resembling the crew's customary professionalism had returned. However, Simon had not spoken a word to him since the beat to quarters the prior evening, leaving the cabin in dark displeasure; and Pat feared a rift, the call once more to arms so very unwelcome to many aboard, most visibly to his dear friend.

Still on the quarterdeck, a disturbed Simon remained with a plainly agitated Jason. The sudden, unexpected and hasty weighing for a likely return to action and that coming just a bare few days before the long-anticipated departure for home had hit him hard, a veritable mental hammer blow. His heart sinking, his mood had become deflated and vexatious; he had not cared to speak with his captain lest he say something which both would regret. 'Home... I should like it of all things,' he whispered.

Throughout the prior evening Jason had strived valiantly with conversation to lift Simon's spirits; the lack of response, near nothing, by way of reciprocation leaving him only with frustration, his own mood sinking. As a last resort for both of them, he had resorted to pursuing Simon, staring over the rail, with questions. 'I beg your pardon, colleague; will we remain on deck... or perhaps it would be better that we retire, to try once more for sleep?' No reply, Jason persisted, 'Will the captain endure awake all night?'

Simon, cross-grained as he was, sighed but did not reply for some time. 'I dare say that is likely; doubtless he is considering of our situation,' the belated response offered eventually, his face filled with gloom. He added after a further long pause, 'Plainly it is his duty to go to the aid of the Greeks, to reach them before they engage with the Turk. It could not be otherwise. He is... he is a conscientious soul.' A further minute passed, Simon deep in thought, until he murmured, 'Thank you for your benevolent interest; I admit that I am moderately low in spirits.' The noise of men, of movement all around broke the introspective spell, and Simon looked about him: the Surprises had begun to carry up powder from the magazines and shot from the hold, roundshot being stacked in the racks near each gun. He reflected for several more moments, his thoughts firming to their conclusion, 'I must strike this lamentable despond from my mind.'

Gunners the length of the ship busied about drawing the loaded charges from all the guns - extracted in case of moisture having reached them - and the guns were reloaded with fresh powder cartridges, their tompions restored to keep them free from damp and spray, it being many hours before anyone expected to actually see the enemy. Canister and grape, rusty bar shot too, on Pat's order were hauled up from below in some quantity. In the forward and aft magazines, men worked to fill more cartridges with powder. It being likely that any engagement would be some time away, the hammocks had not been piped up,

28

were left *in situ* to be tied up at the dawn; but everywhere splinter-netting was being rigged overhead and the bosun's men set to, chaining up every yard to its mast, fearful of spars falling during battle and inflicting injuries on the men on deck. Below, the armourer and his boys hung screens over the ways to the magazine in case of any explosion flashing its ire and igniting the powder stores. The walls of both magazines were clad in soft copper to preclude any spark and their doors were always kept closed during any action, fresh charges being passed out through small apertures covered by cloths. The boys, though they were hardly such, were the youngest of the crew - every man a veteran - busied about spreading sand over the gun deck so that gunners, hauling out their primed two-ton charges through their ports, would not slip when the deck became wet or bloodied. Others brought butts to the guns: one to hold a precautionary slow-match in case of misfire of the flintlock and its priming powder being cast out, the gunners generally welcoming the reserve of a match. It was the old way and *Surprise's* veteran gunners did not care to wholly discard it. A second butt was filled with drinking water to slake the thirst of hot, weary men with no time to leave their station; and the third for the wet sponge, to soak the barrel after firing and before loading its next powder charge. Slush, begged from the cook, was splashed over all the gun trucks' axles to aid their movement.

Pat came up from the companionway and paced across his quarterdeck, seeing his First, breaking the persisting train of Duncan's recollections of home on Harris. 'Duncan, there you are. Good morning to you.'

'Good morning, sir.'

'I confess I am a trifle dismayed,' Pat murmured absently, 'Contrary to my belief of weeks ago, my swim yesterday revealed she is fouled with weed. I suppose a year and a half in these warm waters and despite the copper we may suppose 'twas always likely it would be so. I regret to say it is likely that may cost us a knot or two.'

'I dinnae feel so nimble myself, these days,' Duncan replied. 'And we dinnae care to hear anything from ye rogues,' he added to the nearby helmsmen, the bosun and the duty lieutenant who were all smirking at his remark.

'Man was made at the end of the week... when even God was tired,' offered Pickering with a smile.

'Mr Pickering,' said Pat, not caring for humour, 'Let us see what can be done in the line of extra shrouds in case any are torn down when firing starts,' adding, 'We make no claims to be a smart ship. Perhaps we will rig several spare blocks at the crosstree for every mast in case any are shot away. Mr Sampays... we have no want of cordage... let us tie spare breeching ropes to every gun.'

'Aye aye, sir,' the lieutenant and bosun hastened away.

Slowly, as the small hours passed, *Surprise* made southing. As the first twilight lightening of the sky appeared, the eastern stars paling, her preparations for battle were completed; only the partitions for Pat's cabin remained to be taken down. Most of the crew remained at their guns and stations, the sense of urgency and curiosity about their situation and prospects dispelling for many a man the natural urge for sleep. A very few, old hands, veterans of many a campaign, returned to their hammocks to gain what rest they could.

The sun poked its first bright rays over the Turk mainland off the larboard beam, the island of Agathonissi astern and Lapsa directly ahead, the islands' bulk still apparent only as shadows as the near darkness slowly and, it seemed to Pat, reluctantly yielded to the emerging new day. *Surprise* was making little more than two knots and the wind had dropped to the gentlest of west-north-westerly breeze.

'Deck there, ships off the larboard beam,' came the excited shout from the lookout, 'a dozen... brigs,' and a few minutes later, 'Greeks... GREEKS.'

Pat climbed wearily to the maintop and nodded to the watchman, a gruff 'Good morning, Billings,' uttered as he squatted down, 'Where away?'

Billings nodded, 'Aye, mornin' sir,' and shifted to the platform edge. 'Look there, sir,' he pointed.

Pat took out his glass and stared intently, 'Ah... I see 'em.'

30

The Greeks, recognisable as the armed merchantmen they generally were and flying Psariot colours, were becalmed without wind, sails slack and no movement from any of them. A little further south-east appeared a picket line of eight more Greeks, hardly more than black specks and stretching west from south of the small island of Farmakonissi, indistinct in the weak dawn light. Miaoulis had brought his ships north, as his messenger had said he would. Pat gazed in every direction through his glass for fifteen minutes, still something of a haze directly to the south, the blighted clarity making observation difficult without any clear horizon and the far line of approach of any Turk squadron quite invisible. 'Take my own glass, Billings. Guard it well. Lose not a moment and shout if ye see the least sign.' A growing sense of trepidation sitting ill with him, he slowly descended, determined to return to his cabin for first breakfast.

As Pat reached his table, Dalby rang four bells and the hands were piped to their breakfast. He sat, exhaled deeply, his face filled with worry, his mind disturbed with recurring thoughts of so many of his men lost - killed and wounded - and he took a deep draught of his coffee and gazed at a plentiful spread of food. His face brightened as Simon stepped in. 'I beg pardon for interrupting you. If you will forgive me, that is to say forgive my contumelious gravitation of yesterday, I venture to ask if I might join you,' Simon's tone was conciliatory. He sniffed the delightful aromas in the air, a weak smile on his face, 'Might I beg for a slice of toast? Would there be a tint of that fortifying coffee left, at all?'

'With great pleasure,' Pat's voice too betrayed his profound relief in Simon's gesture of small rapprochement, nothing more said or needed. 'Murphy... Murphy there, more coffee and soft tack too.' Pat looked to his friend and to the bountiful quantity of untouched food, 'Here, could you eat a brace of chops, an egg or two?'

Pat's offer appeared to go unnoticed, Simon taking coffee and sitting in the opposite chair, speaking without further ado, 'If you are minded to think that I have offered you less than my customary support these two weeks gone, I beg your forgiveness,

31

brother. Do not suppose for one moment that my allegiance, my fidelity is lacking. You are to consider that there is much that sits ill within my own mind at present...' Simon's voice tailed off, his thoughts in some confusion, and he simply stared at Pat.

'There is nothing to ask my forgiveness for,' said Pat without hesitation, looking hard at his friend. A long minute passed in silence, Pat considering the real question that Simon had asked. He set down his fork and stared down at the table, his hands now clasped together, dwelling on his thoughts for a few seconds longer before he looked up again to gaze square into his friend's eyes and he replied, very quietly, 'To be sure, I find myself tolerably disheartened to remain here when we are without a score and more of our lads, every one of them wounded so... but we are pledged to support the Greeks. I could not... I could not in good conscience ignore their plea. I... that is to say...' he stopped.

'It would not be Patrick O'Connor speaking were your intentions to be otherwise. I concede you are in the right of things. Please, go on.'

'Thank you. I am troubled by...' Pat stopped, momentarily incapable of continuing. His heart rate and breathing accelerating, and his nose tingling, he reached for his handkerchief.

'Troubled? What troubles you, my dear?' Simon prompted softly, sensing that his friend wished to say more. 'Bless you, it is decent and benignant in you to share these intimate considerations with me.'

Pat blew his nose; he paused as if to gather his thoughts, to bolster his resolve before he spoke again, 'I doubt... I know I will never lose the black memory... it sits so powerful with me... of that infernal day when we... when we buried so many of our men over the side.' He swallowed the remainder of his coffee, the small diversion intended to conceal the pain and distress he felt overtaking him.

'I am very sensible of your frank intimacy, and in that matter you are entirely of my own way of thinking.'

'I oft cannot shake it from my mind, awake and asleep.'

'For sure there is a great deal to be said for reflection... and doubtless times when it will prove of the utmost value... but it does not on every occasion serve us well. For sure such bitter thoughts will long endure in our memory, and when they do we would do well to deliberate on other matters, ones with more pressing claim to our attentions.'

'Well, Simon, here we are, and I am puling miserably, lamenting our losses... and what is in my gift to do about it, eh? Precious little.'

'At such times as the present, for myself, I insist I consider of those others of our men who are presently wounded, and my mind is tasked with devising all I can do to help them...'

Pat interrupted, 'I am sorely vexed that our casualties were so high... I... that is to say... could I have done better? There it is, damn it, I've said it plain.'

'Although I am surely no great philosopher, brother, nor indeed could I claim to possess any of the credentials of a naval strategist, but I will venture the honest thought that whilst we have... regrettably... lost a deal of our comrades I do not believe that any captain could have done better in preserving the lives of those of us more fortunate souls; of that I have not the slightest doubt.'

Pat blinked several times and stared at his friend, deeply grateful for the generous words, their significance so valuable to him, but in the turmoil within his thoughts he could find no reply.

'DECK THERE!' the far shout of the lookout carried plain into the cabin.

'Excuse me,' Pat remarked, leaping to his feet, his tone urgent, alarm showing plain in his face and anxiety flooding his thoughts. He stepped in great haste from the cabin and rushed up the companionway steps.

'Ships... Turks... TURKS! Off the larboard bow,' came the alarming and long anticipated alert from the watchman. 'There be dozens... SCORES OF 'EM!'

Pat stared south at an indistinct white murk, his anxious gaze sweeping slowly from left to right and back again, but from the deck nothing could yet be seen of any ships. He hauled himself again in haste to the maintop. From there, plain through his telescope, ahead at twelve miles distance, close off the eastern shore of Leros and unmistakeable in its magnitude was the Turk fleet: dozens of ships, scores of them. Pat gasped, 'On my life... that is a damn great fleet!'

The morning light was still weak, the sun low; in the mass of ships it was difficult to make out one from another. In the van and plainly visible, a two-decker led the fleet, a seventy-four at the least. Her consorts in long line behind her were just distinguishable in the haze and were similarly rigged with the maximum of canvas they could bear. Pat strived to count all the ships, his tally passing fifty, but the more distant ones were mere specks, their sails blurring into a homogenous mass. It was an impressive show: nothing of the ilk had he ever seen before even at the peak of the French war; certainly nothing of the magnitude of this fleet had ever put to sea in all that long conflict. He sat watching and admiring it for an hour, striving to assess their measure as they tacked, whilst counting dozens more ships becoming increasingly distinct from their fellows, the eight bells at the end of the morning watch barely signifying. The oncoming armada was close-hauled, the wind much adverse for the Turks who, standing off and on, tacked at half-hour intervals to make the smallest of progress towards Lapsa. 'They are doing well not to miss stays as they come about in this light wind,' he marvelled, murmuring his thoughts aloud to himself and to the lookout sitting next to him. He judged the distance and rate of closing, gauging the separation to be eight miles before he descended slowly to the quarterdeck, his mental focus on tactical considerations uppermost in his mind.

Simon had followed his captain from the cabin and observed his ascent and descent. 'What of the enemy, brother?' His voice betrayed his nervous anxiety.

'Lord, it is the prodigious fleet of the world,' Pat declared. His words did nothing to alleviate Simon's concerns, nor those of anyone else in earshot. 'It will test our mettle, for sure,' Pat murmured, 'This day will call for exemplary valour, I have no doubt of that.'

Simon's own valour, however, was a quality of which he was exceedingly doubtful at the best of times. 'Oh dear,' the succinct words escaped him, alarm flooding his thoughts.

'If we had but a tenth of that fleet, why I venture we might...' Pat stopped, becoming aware of the widespread apprehension on the faces of all on the quarterdeck.

'Is it so very great a magnitude? Is there a significant preponderance in comparison of our Greek allies, tell?'

'I have never seen the like,' Pat replied more quietly.

'I am a child in sea-faring tactics, I readily concede; I make no claims of competency in that arena, but - I merely throw this out - I had supposed that perhaps this may be one of those entirely justifiable occasions - undoubtedly rare I grant you - when we may without any hint of opprobrium attaching consider flight rather than fight? What do you say to that?'

A wan smile passed fleetingly across Pat's face, 'What a fellow you are. Would you have me cut and run before the first whiff of powder smoke?'

'Forgive me, brother; I wholly concur such has a most unpleasant ring to it, there is no doubt at all, but on the other hand prudence too has its merits: it is of the most virtuous of all our several inclinations, would you not agree?'

'There is no doubt of that, old friend,' Pat laughed, 'but let us not leap to a hasty verdict, eh? Our Greek friends truly have vast fighting abilities.'

'Vast? I dare say you are confident in their competencies; able mariners they are, no doubt. Please to describe their achievements in similar circumstances.'

'Oh, prodigious achievements, splendid ones... You may consider of the famous battle of Salamis, a crushing Greek victory. Themistocles, so it was. I do have a tolerable grasp of history, eh? What do you say to that?'

'Commendable, and I will say I am fully persuaded of it; indeed, but I collect that particular event may have been some considerable time ago, if my recollection is not fallacious. Was not Themistocles a contemporary of that admirable philosopher, Plato?'

'Eh?' Pat looked slightly uncomfortable, edgy; perhaps reflecting that his historical grasp on this occasion might be less well-founded than he had believed. He persevered, 'And there was also Lepanto. I venture they sailed from Cephalonia too, so they did,' this in an injured and defensive tone of voice.

'I collect on that occasion they sallied out in galleys; was that not the case or am I very much mistaken?'

'Well, then I speak under correction, but for sure they dished the Turks that day.'

'Indeed they did, and I hardly like to mention this, but was it not two hundred and fifty years ago?'

Pat, in a sharp and dissatisfied tone, raised his voice, 'The Turk ain't generally reckoned to be much of a mariner, as we have seen at Samos. We wiped their eye then, and size ain't everything; no, not by a long chalk.'

'Doubtless that is the case,' Simon murmured in resignation, his thoughts taking the most unwelcome turn, coming back to memories of the ship's dead and wounded of the Samos battle. The stark recollection prompted him to persevere once more, 'Surely it is not in your contemplation to hold firm against the approaching behemoth, the odds being so greatly adverse?'

'Why, I collect in an earlier Greek conflict... I can't recall exactly when, but a long time ago it was - perhaps I never was much of a fist at history - a mere five hundred Spartans stood firm against the Turk... the *Persian* horde.'

To this latter comment and Pat's vague grasp of much of history, Simon wisely decided to offer no corrective reply; he earnestly hoped that the men at the helm had a similarly incomplete understanding. He contented himself with a loud noise of agreement which he endeavoured to make sound as firmly corroborative as possible in hope that such might in some small measure sound suitably reassuring to the helmsmen, for in truth he did not feel that way in the least himself.

'We hold the weather-gage,' declared Pat, 'in this northerly wind.' Simon's persistent inabilities when discussing everything nautical oft bewildered Pat, but he did at least have, in only the simplest, the most fundamental principles some understanding of the movements and consequences of the wind acting upon the ship, and he therefore also realised it would equally become a hindrance if *Surprise* was ultimately to retreat in the face of the advancing enemy leviathan, and were Pat to order a turn about, perhaps because of damage incurred, then escape would be far from assured in what would become an adverse wind. It was an exceedingly worrying prospect.

Most of the crew had eaten their breakfast and near every man stood gazing to the south and east, waiting. At this distance the Turks were still not visible from the deck, though one or two of the men claimed sight of specks, far mast tops. The Greeks, much closer, abaft and abeam, remained visible but indistinct in the haze and against the glare of the rising sun.

Pat nodded to Duncan, 'Mr Macleod, we will beat to quarters.'

'Aye aye, sir. Mr Pickering, beat to quarters, clear for action!' The resultant, rousing drumbeat was superfluous, every man was already at his station.

'Mr Macleod, let us wet the sails, all of them, and keep them so. That may gain us a half-knot... and we will leave the hoses rolled out and ready. I am fearful of fire in the caulking, the day so hot.'

'Mr Sampays, fire engine to wet the sails!' shouted Duncan, Pat's order acknowledged by Pickering and the bosun, both men nodding emphatically.

'I am fair clemmed and will take my breakfast,' announced Pat eventually, '... whilst Mr Tizard still affords me the luxury of a table and before the galley fire is put out.' The carpenter had been busy in his absence while he had been aloft, striking down the wooden partitions between the great cabin, the coach and the gun deck; rolling up the black and white chequered deck-cloth, all packed away to the hold. 'Prematurely,' Pat thought, though he said nothing. Only Pat's table and one chair had been left, on Murphy's insistence, to be taken below after Pat had breakfasted. Murphy had removed virtually everything else from the cabin, though a cabin it was now in name only, his table being visible from everywhere on the gun deck. Pat determined on showing the men perfect normality and calm. He shouted for coffee as he ate his burgoo and then called loudly for toast with marmalade, ensuring his requests were plainly heard at least as far forward as the main. In truth the eating was a struggle, for his stomach; indeed, his whole body was tensed with a degree of apprehension that he had never formerly felt before an action. He supposed it was the adversity of very great odds, together with the uncertainty that endured when he considered of their allies, many fewer than the Turks, whilst their ships were also of a significantly lesser size. Freeman and Murphy, sensing the small gesture of theatre, busied about him, ostentatiously replenishing his coffee and removing his empty bowl. At the mizzen mast just forward of the cabin, the gun crews, staring aft towards Pat's table, waited to seize their moment, to prepare their four guns within the cabin.

Forward, on the gun deck, Pickering and Codrington paced up and down looking at every piece, speaking to all the gun crews, offering words of encouragement, of jest; proffering too the odd reminder of preparation of some missed minor point: insufficient sand about the gun or its train tackle a trifle too slack or too short; all the while assessing the men's preparedness, their morale. On the quarterdeck, Macleod did likewise with the carronade crews. All, to the officers' minds, seemed fine, normal; an air of confidence abounded throughout the ship which was founded on long experience. From *Surprise's* quarterdeck, the closing Turk flagship and her immediate consorts could now just be seen, hull down, royals and topgallants in sight, the tops'ls briefly appearing as *Surprise* rose on the small swell, the wind a little stronger. The Turks were perhaps six miles distant, the gap closing slowly, barely perceptibly. At the guns, many of the Surprises chattered amiably; others were silent, pondering the forthcoming day. Every man was stripped to the waist, hair tied back; heads everywhere were adorned with a cloth wrapped about them, another tied around the neck: both to mop the anticipated sweat when the hot work began. Hardly a man had not seen an action in the French wars and all had fought in the battles against the Turk galleys back in July of the prior year, and with their Greek comrades had turned back Khosref's first invasion of Samos in August. They knew what was coming; they understood their role, their officer's expectations of them, and they were unperturbed and phlegmatic about it.

Dalby rang one bell and Pat stepped up to his quarterdeck; the carpenter and his men rushed in to remove his table, followed by gunners with a score of men keen to ready their guns: *Daniel Mendoza* and *Billy Warr* on the port side, *Bull Horns* and *Mighty Fine* opposite.

'Put her helm up one point, Mr Prosser,' ordered Pat flatly, the master himself at the helm. 'We are to close on Lapsa, off the cape there, afore we turn to port.'

'Aye aye, sir.'

The majority of the Turk armada was coming into plain sight, four or five miles south-south-east of *Surprise*, off the north-east cape of Leros island. With all the canvas the Turks could carry, Pat had calculated that they made barely two knots, close-hauled; the weak wind was a little north of west, the huge armada beating against it with frequent and short north-westerly tacks to make the most minute of westerly gain. Pat presumed that they had engaged on such tiring and repetitive manoeuvres for many hours to approach thus far from the Kos strait, doubtless straining the cohesion of the admiral's line to the very limit. 'Miaoulis has chosen his strategy well,' Pat mused, save that he too was greatly hindered by the wind, the *Meltemi* customarily a north wind, but today, unusually, being so westerly. He hoped that it did not prove to be a fatal mistake. The Turks had no longer any certain need to tack, would do so perhaps once more, Pat thought; but then they could sail directly north on a bowline, passing to the west of Agathonissi and so directly to Samos. It would still be slow, but the way was clear; for the majority of the Greeks, both of the Hydriot squadrons, remained motionless, becalmed in the Gulf of Gerontas: the door to Samos had been left wide open. Would those few Psariots in *Surprise's* wake come to her aid? How long could she persist against the horde before being destroyed? Should she bear off, one against so many? It would not be considered disgraceful. All these questions and more pre-occupied Pat's thoughts, his final question lingering: what could *Surprise* usefully do without she was smashed, burned and sunk?

'Another hour, gentlemen, I doubt the Turk will be longer,' Pat announced to his companions.

'Oh dear,' exclaimed Simon who had ventured, with Jason, across to the windward side to join Pat and Duncan. Ahead of them the hammocks were being brought up and affixed within the netting, the men still busying themselves even now with shot and powder charges for every gun; though without the slightest indicator of haste, an air of confidence, of experience pervading.

'Simon, there you are,' Pat's greeting was cordial, giving away nothing of his own anxieties.

'Pat, I do not care to be presumptuous in matters I can hardly deny are completely outside my province, naval strategy is surely one such, and I confess my sagacity is limited generally to matters of a surgical nature; but plainly as we look over there to... to larboard would it be... *to the left*... upon my word we are mightily outnumbered. Beg pardon, but please be so kind as to describe your intentions,' Simon's anxious enquiry was uttered in a near whisper.

'Oh, the Turk there... yes, *to larboard*; he is greatly hampered... and striving to make the slowest of progress towards Samos.'

'For want of wind?' Simon interjected.

'You smoked it,' Pat laughed loud, a small release from tension; the helmsmen too sniggered, which reached everyone's ears.

'Your soul to the devil, Patrick O'Connor!' retorted Simon.

'There's precious little that escapes your eye.' Pat marvelled at Simon's weak nautical understanding after so many years at sea, and on this occasion he could find no better reply. The nearby helmsmen were still grinning broadly.

'Oh, I would not say that; I graciously concede my ignorance of seamanship. I have no illusions that few know less than I about all such matters within your nautical province.'

'Never in life, Simon. You are a good-hearted soul, there is no doubt. I beg your pardon for my rudeness.'

40

'It cannot be considered amicable.'

'Forgive me, I am speaking like a scrub. For sure I am cursed snappish this day.'

Simon put his hand on Pat's arm, 'Allow me to say you are no diplomat.' The helmsmen, the hour before combat always a trying time to endure, welcomed the diversion but turned their faces away, biting hard on their tongues to hold back a pressing tide of laughter, an escaping titter reaching Pat's ears, the sound stinging him to embarrassment.

'I never thought I was.'

'It is of no moment, brother.' Silence returned, all staring at the approaching Turk fleet.

'One hour, Patrick O'Connor... one hour longer until we look again into hell,' Pat whispered to himself. It always seemed the longest hour in the world, the anxious hour before an action. He shouted over to Clumsy Dalby at his station near the bell, 'Dalby, fetch our colours from below... two Greek flags,' adding to Macleod, 'I am minded that we will fly them at the main and the mizzen, in case one is shot away.'

'Aye aye, sir,' Dalby hastened below to fetch them.

Pat sniffed the air: it was the customary dry seasonal wind, a land wind, the *Meltemi*; it came from afar and originated on the hot and dry central Anatolian steppe, and he knew that as the day progressed it would certainly blow stronger, 'I believe the wind is freshening; what say you Mr Macleod?'

'Aye sir, that it is. Cast the log!' he shouted.

'Two and a half knots,' the cry came back from the younger Pennington after what seemed an eternity, *Surprise* so very slow.

'We will take in stuns'ls... and furl royals and t'gallants, Mr Macleod, and strike down the royals and topgallant yards,' ordered Pat, and immediately changed his mind, 'No, let us leave the yards up until we see if any blow develops. The royals and t'gallants... I venture we may have further need of them... that is if this precious puny wind does not strengthen.' Duncan barked the orders and the men hastened aloft.

Dalby returned. 'Colours, Mr Macleod,' cried Pat, 'mizzen and main, if you will.'

Fifteen more minutes slipped by. 'Three knots,' Pennington bawled: the wind was indeed freshening.

'Mr Macleod, we will not clew up her main and fore courses, but let them be reefed up; we may need to shake them out quickly if what little there is of this wind fails us,' Pat was focussed on the final preparations for battle, the gap rapidly closing, or so it seemed. The leading ships of the Turk fleet, scores of them now in plain sight, were still tacking with all the canvas they could bear. The leading ship, the flagship, looked beautiful to a sailor's eye even as she threatened, and the Turk line behind her was quite splendid, magnificent even.

Pat stepped down the companionway steps and called all the men to him as he stood forward of the main, looking down the length of the gun deck. He shouted for all to approach him, to come from forward and aft, and to leave their guns. They gathered around him, behind him, in front of him, men from above standing at the waist and looking down, all staring, all with enquiry written plain on their faces. 'Lads,' he cried, 'I will tell you what I have in mind. Khosref's flagship is nigh upon us... his squadron in line astern of him. We must be canny: to become closely engaged in a slugging match will not help us. We will not board any ship this day. We will hold off and keep our distance as we fire. We will not seek to kill their crew but to knock away masts, spars and sails; we will strive to cut shrouds and stays, for such will slow the Turk. Mr Codrington,' Pat looked to his Second, 'I collect there may remain a score or two of chain shot in the hold. We will haul it up and hold it ready for the occasion when it may suit. Lads, set your guns to fire high, load 'em with round shot... we will load with chain and bar *only* if they get close - within two cables, though I plan to stand off at five so we can haul away if needs must.' He looked to the faces of his men and was gratified to see no overt fear, no anxiety visible in their demeanour; rather a calm preparedness prevailed, a readiness for what they understood was coming. 'We are only one, and will expect to be hard pressed if we find ourselves amongst this fearsome armada. With so many fewer men since... since Samos... every man must stand ready to fight both sides of the ship at the same time. Is that clear?' Nods all round. 'We ain't

42

got enough men... so many men wounded, and every man must be ready to stand in for any of his comrades who are stricken by shot or splinter. Am I plain?' More nods. 'Go to your quarters and stand ready; another hour or less and we will see their mettle.' His words, he was pleased to see, were well received; a growling chorus of 'Aye aye, sir,' was returned with gusto, lifting his spirits and pushing back his own doubts, the numbers against them so daunting. The Surprises returned to their guns, every man now possessing to some degree a sense of understanding of the only role *Surprise* could play, of the limitations she would bear, the risks she would face; all these minutiae greatly helping their own state of mind, facilitating their personal calculation of risk and their prospects, and they were grateful for it.

'Out tompions!' shouted Macleod, the command echoed by all the lieutenants. 'Run out the guns!' The command was followed by loud rumbling and screeching as the two tons of metal of each of the great guns was hauled out to project from their ports, every one shotted and primed, all ready to open fire.

For the next hour, time itself seemed suspended, the men at the helm near motionless, no change in course or sails asked for, nothing of turbulence in sea state or wind to insist on such. Pat and Duncan gazed from the quarterdeck at the approaching Turk fleet. Silence abounded all about the ship, the men preparing themselves for battle and perhaps, the more meditative, even to meet their maker. Every man with the smallest of excuse had congregated about the officers, crowding the quarterdeck: all the men curious, anxious; the prospects so hugely adverse; for who could consider that a single frigate, though it be *Surprise* herself, could long withstand the impending titan, now looming large; the formerly far press of canvas closing, so immense, so intimidating.

The bright sun, not a one of clouds anywhere in sight, was noticeably rising in the eastern sky, its heat already fierce; every man was sweating profusely, doubtless with anxiety as well as warmth; more so the officers, encumbered as they were in their best uniforms of dark blue long coats with gold decoration, white breeches and silk stockings, all their vestments pressed to

43

perfection by Murphy that morning. Pat positioned himself on his quarterdeck within the shadow afforded by the mizzen to gain some small respite from the torrid oppression. He wore his old and favourite tricorne hat, considered by many officers to be a relic, for the bicorne had long been generally adopted. He considered it to be his lucky hat: lucky because it had kept him alive in all his battles, for that was how he saw things.

Simon and Jason hesitated about going below; the slow pace of closing had lulled them into immobility and enduring curiosity. Not usually finding themselves in any position to see what was happening, for they were customarily below in the hell that was their lot on the lower deck in battle, they had absorbed the rising sense of foreboding which was becoming prevalent on the quarterdeck, the odds against them so very great. Half a dozen men, the best shots with the musket, had already clambered aloft: so much the better to watch the spectacle that was the Turk armada. All were carrying two firearms with two score of cartridges and shot. Behind the great guns, the men stood: attentive, confident, waiting. Plentiful shot filled the racks; the aroma from the burning slow matches, smoking in their tubs next to each gun, drifted along the prepared, tidy deck. The quarterdeck with its carronades was similarly ready, the gunners waiting in anticipatory silence, customary whispers from one to another wholly absent on this occasion, the men perhaps daunted by the Turk numbers; for even the most experienced veterans amongst them had never seen the like of the approaching fleet.

Along the sides, in the netting above the bulwarks the hammocks were strung up. The quietude abounding on the deck was eerie, oppressive even: expectant silence, absolute save for the ever present gull; just the quiet creak of the rigging and the occasional slap of canvas flapping in the wind's frequent but feeble gusts. The usual sound of wave against hull was wholly absent, the frigate's speed so slow, only the tiniest of ripples at her bow, her closing progress almost dreamlike in its infinitely slow pace.

Simon, now standing square with his friend, whispered so as not to be heard elsewhere, his voice filled with anxiety, 'I am generally no friend of speculation, as you know, but would it be

44

aberrant to ask, Pat, will we stand long against such a tumultuous host, tell? It is tolerably daunting.'

Pat was gazing full at the Turk flagship. He could not understand why Khosref had not struck down his royals or hauled up his courses to the customary reduced canvas, to "fighting sail" as it was termed, and Simon's tremulous query, whispered as it was, did not register with him for some moments. 'Eh?' he started from his ponderings and looked at his friend with a hint of irritation. 'Questions and answers, Simon... questions and answers,' he said, rather obliquely, finding his friend's interruption a little taxing in his absolute concentration.

'I only throw out the plain enquiry, for all love,' an irritated Simon frowned; 'Never mind me.'

'I collect you once said it is not a civilised form of conversation,' Pat relented.

'If I may be allowed to offer the most general of observation then; we are only one, brother, and over there, approaching, is a vengeful horde about to assail us. David at least faced only one Goliath,' remarked Simon testily; his dread, his fear plainly audible in his tone of voice which wavered plaintively.

'It had crossed my mind,' Pat said absently. 'Yes, yes; I am fully persuaded of it.' Seconds passed and he added, quietly, 'I am reminded of my grandma.'

'I am concerned to hear it - *your grandma?* At such a time? Surely not?' The near helmsmen, greatly interested, their attention gripped by the exchanges, stared, unsure themselves of what they had heard and its relevance.

'*Cleverness is better than strength*, I collect she said that... in our days of difficulty, in our hardships; and when I was a boy there were plenty of those times, to be sure.'

'That is an admirable notion; indeed, it is, but I am not wholly with you. You do not mean to stay and fight the Turk, so; I had supposed that flight was the more prudent answer, cut and romp directly, or am I much astray?' The helmsmen looked doubtful, shifting about uncomfortably.

'Good heavens, Simon, is this an infernal committee?' The irritation was plain in Pat's voice. 'Do you think I am some rum

45

cully come fresh from Roundstone, that I am a poteen-swiller from the Connemara bog? What, fight a seventy-four with her broadside weight of metal near thrice ours and with three score or more of her armada in train? No, we will hold our distance for as long as we can, perhaps fire a broadside if we can place the barky on her bow or quarter, before we must turn away and flee.'

'You foresee this outcome, our emergence unscathed?' Simon did not intend to relent.

'I could not swear to it, but the hare cannot long challenge the whippet. Doubtless you have remarked that.'

'Would it be uncivil to say that I venture it is conceivable; indeed, it is likely that the sensible hare, the hare in full possession of his cerebral faculties... would flee without the briefest of delay?' This bringing no response, Simon continued, 'I offer no counsel, no, nor do I care to sound discontented, but were we to stand long against them I doubt I will have space enough below for all the wounded we must surely expect... or buckets enough to fill with all the bloody body parts I will cut off.' This was offered in the tone of deepest dismay.

'Never be so concerned. I dare say a very few shots at his rigging might serve us well if we can bring down a yard or two, perhaps even a mast; now there's glory for you. I can do nothing more; indeed, there is nothing more Nelson himself, the great man, could do. We are but one ship, and I dare say the Turk will not thank us for outstaying our welcome; we will not lock horns with the bull. No... it will bring no discredit upon us when we must flee.'

'I am very sensible of your intentions. Will I say I cherish your very words... and I am greatly relieved to hear them. Indeed, I have hopes that my bowels may endure the whole of the day without affording embarrassment,' whispered Simon.

'Cut and romp?' remarked Pat absently.

'I had always supposed that it signified to bear off and away in great haste. Is it not a commonplace expression in your nautical parlance?'

'Yes, yes, of course,' murmured Pat. 'An admirable phrase, so it is.'

At that moment the lookout cried down, 'On deck, deck there... half the Turk line is bearing away... EAST!' Everyone gazed east, looking towards distant Farmakonissi. It was just possible to make out the masts of a half-dozen or so of brigs, south of the island.

'One moment, Simon, if you will,' said Pat, his eyes sore and in that moment feeling deeply tired. Turning, he said, 'Murphy, be so good as to bring coffee. A man has pressing need of a strong draught in times like this.' He stepped forward quickly and climbed again to the maintop, hauling himself past a surprised Billings, taking back his telescope in passing and continuing up to the crosstrees. When he had settled aloft, he gazed east, striving to discern why half the Ottoman fleet had turned away in that direction. His eyes fastened on the nearest Greek brigs, directly east, and he was amazed. Eight of them, the lead he recognised as *Kimon,* the flagship of Miaoulis, were being towed; their crews were all pulling hard in their boats. Behind them, though it was hard to discern in detail, were another dozen or more of brigs, shifting so very slowly in the breeze on a southerly track. 'Miaoulis!' It was the reason why half the enemy had switched to their north-easterly course: they sought to strike the Greek leader whilst his ships were in the lee of Farmakonissi, unmoving and so very vulnerable. Miaoulis had split his own fleet, half shifting with what little wind they could catch to the south, doubtless to turn south-westerly as and when they found it possible, and his own Second Hydriot squadron was rowing, *rowing* to position themselves to block Khosref's route to Samos, but they would never arrive in time, for there was no prospect at all against the generally westerly breeze, for that was the size of it, though freshening as it was. Pat's mind saw the situation as it was developing with brutal clarity. 'By God!' he exclaimed to himself: Khosref would not linger to fight *Surprise*; rather he was determined to sweep her aside and lead his Turk fleet on, on to Samos; doubtless this time to bombard the town of Colones to dust, no Greek ships present to stop him. His cohorts, the Egyptians it was, Ibrahim's short pennant visible at the main, who were sailing to attack Miaoulis, the Turks left with a free hand to press on: except for *Surprise* in Khosref's direct path, and the Spezziots, few that they were, in their line between *Surprise* and Farmakonissi, but still greatly hindered by the westerly. He gazed back, astern, off the larboard quarter to the Greeks previously milling about, without wind, behind - north of - Farmakonissi. He looked upon the brigs that *Surprise* had left in her wake an hour or more ago: Psariots they were, Canaris and his men. They were moving, shifting slowly, south-westerly, the wind scant on their starboard side, sails shivering, *but moving towards Surprise*! They were coming to her aid, as now were the Spezziots - their task much harder, their course near directly into the wind: for them it would necessitate many and frequent short tacks, but they too were coming, all closing in support of *Surprise*. The relief poured through his mind like a flood tide: *Surprise* was not alone! He hastened down to the quarterdeck, all about him gazing in query, in anxious expectation.

'We ain't alone, Simon,' he gasped, regaining his breath; for he had descended as fast as he could, without pause, and he had over-exerted himself a trifle, bloodying his hands in his descent. 'The Psariots, the Spezziots; they are both in our lee.'

'I am heartily gratified that such is the case. You mean we may survive this day?'

'I dare say we shall; our Greek friends are coming. *We are not alone*,' Pat repeated, his voice firmer, louder as he strived to project confidence.

'Will that be soon, would you think? Pray tell me the general view, if you please,' Simon's anxiety was plain in his voice.

'Calm yourself, old friend; you will collect that it is of great importance that we retain the weather-gage,' Pat, realising Simon would not desist, began to explain his thinking.

'Great importance?' exclaimed Simon.

'The very utmost.'

'You have often mentioned that.' The helmsmen could scarcely restrain their mirth. Pat had noticed their increasingly unsuccessful efforts to conceal their sniggering, and he scowled at them.

'I will endeavour to explain, if you will attend,' said Pat with exasperation. 'It is for us to slow Khosref until the Greeks can reach us. Only *Surprise* bars the door to Khosref reaching Samos, and we must turn them away or at least delay them.'

'How do you intend to effect this?' Simon, uncomfortably aware of the helmsmen's humorous interest, spoke in a lowered voice, 'What measures are open to us, a solitary vessel? Pray tell?'

'We will start her sheets and slow the barky a very little to encourage Khosref in his chase, and then we may hope that an exchange of fire, a very short exchange of fire that is, may persuade Khosref to turn away from his course for Samos to continue his pursuit of *Surprise*.'

'Sure, it is a plan,' said Simon, his voice resonating with doubt and suggesting he believed it was one to which he attached small merit.

Indeed it was the simplest of plan and wholly incomplete: no thought allowed, were it to succeed, for an escape from the obviously many pursuers, save for the eventual conjunction with the approaching Greeks who were still deep within the bay and coming from near Cape Gerontas, sailing very slowly with short tacks against the weak wind. 'We must pray for a trifle more of wind,' said Pat.

'Do you not set too great a store on what we may hope to achieve with... with this... this *caper*, as you might term it? Are we so enticing a prospect? Us it is, our beloved *Surprise*; one ship, one very small ship, and we are presently all alone,' Simon's words were plaintive, despairing even. 'Will the Turk follow us or bear down directly for Samos?'

'For sure, there is no telling which.' His nerves and his patience failing him, his attention wavering, Pat gathered his breath and in the loudest voice he could manage he shouted so all staring at him could hear, 'The Psariots and Spetziots are coming up astern of us, the Hydriots too from the east.' Faces all about showed plain their understanding, their relief.

Simon, still doubtful, took a deep breath; he shivered, the familiar cold sensation coursing through him as he anticipated the inevitable blood, and he whispered, his voice resigned, his anxiety so evident in his reply, 'I am no accomplished mariner, I only throw out the enquiry: when do you suppose firing will begin, tell?'

'We shall be busy in half an hour or so, I think,' said Pat.

'I merely air my rumination, frightening as it is. I have... perhaps ill-conceived as it may be... I have a sense that alone, as we are at present, we can do little against the horde.'

'Presently we will see what can be done and what cannot.'

'I don't doubt it,' mumbled Simon to himself.

'Well, here is coffee for 'ee, sorr,' announced Murphy at that instant, the can in his hand, the offering so timely, so very welcome, 'an' the galley fire is out.'

'Thankee, Murphy,' Pat nodded to his steward and wiped his bloodied hands down his coat.

'Bejasus!' muttered Murphy, horrified and failing to conceal his dismay, his immediate demeanour a disapproving scowl whilst with difficulty he managed to choke off his righteous reprobation until he shifted away, muttering dark oaths in his discontentment.

Simon gazed all about him, studying the faces of the men on the quarterdeck. The imminence of an action rarely presented such an opportunity for him, for he generally hastened below to prepare his table and instruments. He stared at Pat: his captain's demeanour had shifted from the customary nonchalance he displayed in days long gone by, before an action, and he had assumed an air of complete concentration. Simon could not determine if it included confidence; that was much harder to discern, and with the odds against them being so very great perhaps such was not to be expected; but Pat most certainly exuded a command authority, a conviction and purpose, and this was transmitted to the men about him, all of whom demonstrated not the least uncertainty or anxiety. He himself was filled with the greatest of such, but he could not speak further of it with his friend for there was now an aura of distance, of significant separation between them, Pat's mind computing every facet, every nuance of their situation to the exclusion of all social exchanges, speaking little save for his commands, and Simon knew it would remain that way until the end of any battle.

Pat gazed through his telescope at the Turk flagship: she had made one final north-westerly tack, as he had suspected she might. 'She must soon come about; she cannot long hold that course without she fetches up on the rocks of Leros,' he muttered to all in hearing. 'Another quarter hour and it will be too late for her to turn. Do you follow me, Simon?'

'Of course, my dear,' said Simon, not inclined to suffer further embarrassment, 'if a trifle imperfectly.' He resigned himself with a sigh to getting nothing more out of Pat.

Pickering and Codrington stepped up to the quarterdeck to make their reports: all guns and crews were prepared and ready on the gun deck, heavy charges packed all round for distant firing, the guns loaded with roundshot. 'Thank you, gentlemen. I believe our friends over there will wear in the next few minutes, and we must follow her change. We will strive for a parallel track.'

All the lieutenants nodded their understanding. Simon simply stared, open-mouthed, for the audacity of Pat's intentions confounded him still.

'Mr Pickering, the starboard guns are to open fire on my command. Mr Macleod, tell the men plain - hold fire with the carronades. I do not plan to get so close that the Turk will be within their range of accuracy, and there is to be no showing away by the gunners. If the Turk hauls closer than five cables we will likely be lost.'

The remark served as a jolting reminder to Simon, increasingly uncomfortable on the quarterdeck and Pat no companion at all. He turned to Pickering and said, in a tone of quiet resignation, 'Mr Pickering, are we likely to be going to heaven or hell this day?'

'Which one matters little to me; for sure I have friends in both places,' Pickering replied, smiling. Pat, overhearing, simply stared.

'Where will the end of this day find us, Pat, eh? To be or not to be,' muttered Simon testily, 'that is the question.'

'Hamlet?' asked Pat, pleased to recognise the phrase and smiling now, 'the Danish one?'

Simon, humour quite beyond him, stared blankly before he retorted sharply, 'No, the dead one.'

'Come, Simon,' said Pat, 'a whiff of powder, an exchange of shot, a broadside or two, and we shall flee like the fox before the hounds.'

'I am sure of it,' replied Simon, though his voice belied a total absence of conviction. He turned back to Jason, 'Plainly, Jason, our contribution up here is of little value. It may be that our own endeavours will better serve our colleagues in preparation for the conflict and its inevitable casualties. Come, we will go downstairs... to our station.'

Chapter Three

All along the length of the ship, the Surprises stared intently at the Turk flagship. By now everyone saw plainly that her course and that of *Surprise* were converging, but who would turn first? The Turk faced the rocky shore of Leros fine on her port bow; *Surprise*, in theory, could pass by the south-east point of the island of Lapsa and continue on towards Leros, towards the strait between the two small islands, a passage little more than four miles in width and with dangerous outlying rocks obstructing much of it nearer the islands' shores. If *Surprise* did continue so and the Turk did not come about but simply slackened stays and slowed, then a near stationary engagement would develop. Pat did not think this likely: no captain would choose to become stationary if their adversary could still manoeuvre, for such would mean becoming a target, to be fired upon at the pleasure of the enemy, and, more significantly, the flagship was followed by dozens of her consorts all in her train. No, the Turk must make her final turn to steer north; she could not delay at the head of her long line of trailing squadron, and so she must come about very soon, in the mere minutes left to her before she ran out of sea room.

As the imminence of action pressed upon them, there was near complete silence throughout *Surprise*. Every man awaited the commencement of firing, longed for it, impatience and anxiety proliferating, fear held in check, imagination suppressed; for every man had seen battle beforehand, had experienced the brutal and bloody nature of it, and none expected this day to be any less so. All expected the Turk to imminently make her final turn, to adopt a northerly course which would take her and all her companions far past the Psariots and the Spezziots, all of whom were struggling against the westerly wind south of Agathonissi and who could move west with only the slowest of progress. The

Greeks coming to *Surprise's* aid might never arrive in time. Pat's positioning of his ship, presently all alone and increasingly looking to be a forlorn hope, was intended to block the Turk fleet's onward passage to vulnerable Samos. In this the Greeks were essential; if, that is, the weaker and fewer Greek ships, aided by *Surprise*, were capable of holding Khosref off, or at least enforcing a course change, away from Samos; but all that was far from sure, the Turk fleet being far more powerful.

Pat studied the Turk flagship through his glass. Khosref would be able to use his lower guns, for the wind was weak indeed and the sea state such that his lower ports were all open, ready; the most clement of weather presented no danger of heeling ships flooding through open ports on their leeward side. At every ship's bow the wake alongside was barely discernible and the confluence of *Surprise* with the Turk fleet seemed to be happening at the slowest of snail's pace.

'Which ship is she would you think, Mr Macleod?' asked Pat, adding, 'for the log.'

'Och, I am nae familiar with the Turk fleet but I collect she may be the *Necm-i Şevket,*' said Duncan, recalling an Admiralty report sent to him by Melville, 'but dinnae ask me to translate that.'

'A most prodigious fine ship. What does she carry?'

'She is a third rate, an eighty-gun ship. Doubtless she boasts of 24-pounders... perhaps even 36-pounders.'

'Quite formidable,' murmured Pat, dwelling momentarily on the daunting thought that a well-aimed and close broadside from such a heavy armament would rip *Surprise* to shreds, smash holes all through her and kill scores of his men. 'I have no aspirations to sink, take, burn or destroy her, Duncan, eh?' His weak jest and fleeting smile went wholly unanswered, unappreciated, for his First knew too well that the Turk was a formidable foe: her broadside weight of metal was greatly in excess of that of *Surprise,* and the frigate could not conceivably stand against her for longer than the briefest of engagement without she would surely be destroyed. Ship handling of the highest order was the only means of survival, to keep *Surprise* away from any possible Turk broadside; together with the skill and experience of Pat's gunners the two factors together might yet preserve the frigate.

Silence reigned everywhere: on the quarterdeck, on the gun deck, fore and aft. Every man gazed at the approaching Turk behemoth in contemplation, trepidation now general. Even the least intelligent of the Surprises was wholly aware that the frigate had no chance of surviving anything more than a passing encounter, could not conceivably endure a sustained enemy barrage. Men throughout the ship pondered what their captain might do, what he *could* do when faced with such an unequal opponent. In the enduring silence the occasional small rustle of the feeble wind through the rigging and a rare slap of canvas were the only noises; there was a complete absence of any sound of water, *Surprise's* progress so infinitely slow, near dreamlike. The inevitable intrusion into this near surreal moment came from the lookout: he bawled loudly down to announce what every man on deck could plainly see: the Turk flagship was changing her sail plan.

Pat, taken up with his concentration on Khosref, had already observed her change of sail. 'They are taking down royals,' he remarked, '... reefing courses too.' It was to be expected before an engagement and represented nothing of great significance, and then he saw the long awaited turn commence: signal flags flying aboard the Turk and a gun to reinforce the message. 'She is turning... coming about, as we expected; her course is now plain for Samos,' he exclaimed. 'Mr Macleod, prepare to wear ship.'

Anxious long further minutes passed as the Turk, her sails filled after her laborious turn, gathered a little speed and shaped her new course, north-north-east, the distance from *Surprise* reduced to a mere one mile. Behind the flagship, dozens of frigates and corvettes turned to follow. It was a well-executed turn, the line maintaining its cohesion: impressive, and bringing a wind improvement for the Turk, for if *Surprise* were to remain parallel she must near turn back on herself, though with too some ultimate gain of speed, wearing with the westerly wind being more favourable to her even as the whole Turk fleet gained momentum on their new course.

'Mr Macleod,' said Pat; 'We will come about now, if you will. We will close the Turk... our course is east, if you please.'

'Aye aye, sir,' cried Duncan. The critical moment was upon them; the pipes wailed *"all hands about ship"* as *Surprise* made her turn downwind. Quickly she turned, harder and harder to port, a perfect transition, her speed picking up steadily as she adjusted to her new course, east, wind astern, settling to her fresh direction and converging rapidly with Khosref's own course, both ships sailing large. She still held the weather-gage, the weak westerly wind veering with a little more northerly in it, for the small advantage that represented.

The Turk fleet as a whole was sailing faster now, their own turn through the wind completed, and they were holding a north-easterly course, so much more favourable for them than the former north-westerly short tacking. Pickering and Codrington had returned to their stations on the gun deck. 'Any minute now,' was the thought in the mind of every man. The Turk was closing on *Surprise's* starboard quarter, their courses close to being parallel, the diminishing separation reduced to only three-quarters of a mile. Nearer, nearer still, the Turk loomed large in everyone's vision. An expectation of imminent roundshot flying all about them crossed Pat's mind, for the anxious waiting could not last much longer. Closer came the Turk flagship, nerves all throughout *Surprise* on edge, the tension huge and rising. Pat drank the remainder of his coffee, now cold.

'BOOM!' The sound was distant: the Turk bow chaser had opened fire. 'Let us pray to all the saints that he does not change course again; we must hope that he does not choose to cross our stern and range up a-larboard,' Pat described his principal concern, 'for such would leave us floundering even as he gains ground towards Samos.'

The Turk was so close now that every man aboard *Surprise* could see her guns projecting from her ports. Doubtless they would be heavier guns than *Surprise* herself carried, certainly 24-pounders, perhaps greater. The ambience aboard remained eerily silent: not any sound at all from the men, a constant low hum in the rigging with the freshening wind coming from abaft the larboard quarter the only noise which broke the absolute silence. Even the customary sound of orbiting gulls, for once, seemed absent. The Turk chaser was being reloaded and slowly so, for after the first shot several minutes previously it had not fired again. 'We may hope all their gunners are as tardy,' remarked Pat. 'Note the time, Mr Macleod,' he added, staring at his own Breguet repeater, its hands indicating ten-thirty precisely. Khosref was not intending to turn again: that was becoming plain and such was a huge relief, the Turk's wake and line remaining straight, removing that particular threat which Pat had much feared, the rising certainty of that becoming clear. His flagship and *Surprise* were now parallel on their eastern course but perilously close at only a half-mile of separation; it was a little too close for Pat's liking. 'Mr Prosser, come up a point to larboard,' he ordered, the small course change a gesture, no more, towards a more comfortable though near imperceptible (to the Turk) divergence. 'I venture five cables is as near as we will hazard. Our eighteens will be effective enough at that range and our targets are her sails not her hull.'

'Aye aye, sir,' Prosser's reply exuded his customary confidence.

Two miles directly ahead of Khosref were the Psariots, and at a similar distance, on his starboard bow, lay the Spezziots. Together they counted a score of vessels, brigs for the most part. Khosref had bypassed the majority of the Greek fleet, the Hydriots still being becalmed in the far reaches of the Gulf of Gerontas. *Surprise* alone lay immediately between the Turk fleet and Samos, and were the still distant Psariots and Spezziots to fail to close to her support she would be the last resort, the solitary ship left to fight Khosref's fleet or to flee before it. Fine off *Surprise's* starboard bow, Miaoulis's eight brigs remained under tow, yet still two and a half miles off, Pat estimated. It would be another thirty minutes before *Surprise* could expect the least assistance, and that assured the most uncomfortable half-hour in the lives of every man aboard was now pressing upon them. 'God help us,' said Pat to himself.

Surprise and the Turk flagship were now neck and neck, the wind veering to blow with a little more northerly in it, but still essentially north-west, a further freshening discernible. The change in wind direction had not made progress for the Turk any slower: she was sailing large. However, the gap between her and *Surprise* had been steadily - and stealthily, Pat wondered - reduced to six cables, well within firing range of the powerful Turk guns. The master steered *Surprise* to keep the gap at least at that distance even as the Turk, Pat believed, with great subtlety adjusted her own course to close up. 'Were I to be knocked down, Mr Prosser, and you to be waiting on Mr Macleod, you are to maintain our separation... *five cables and keep never a yard less*. Is that plain?' Pat asked, touching a finger on the wooden wheel for a second before he spoke his next words in a low voice, intended for Prosser's ears only, 'Any closer and her broadside will surely destroy us... we could not long endure.'

'Aye aye, sir, plain and clear; five cables and never a yard less,' came the steadfast reply; the co-helmsmen, who had all been listening closely, nodded vigorously, Pat's caution plain, his reasoning perfectly understood by all.

'Our situation is tolerably delicate,' Pat expounded to Duncan, 'even were we able to hold off Khosref's flagship, and that is a mighty tall order I make no doubt; the Turk has plentiful support directly astern and but five or ten minutes away. Against the flagship herself, we have the smallest of prospects; against all her near consorts we have not the slightest of chance. We cannot hope to do more than discourage him until our friends arrive. Let us pray that they do so and swiftly. Were Khosref to direct his frigates astern of us, we will likely be lost: his frigates, certainly his corvettes, may well shift a knot faster than the barky can manage these days - with the weed on her bottom so.' Pat continued his analysis, 'It is the frigates and corvettes I fear; we can always run before the flagship.' Behind Khosref's flagship the procession of frigates, of brigs, of corvettes and others seemed unending, so many; the number so daunting, an impossible challenge for even the very best, the most skilful of single frigate captains. 'At least we are all - us and Khosref - running towards the Greeks,' he murmured to himself. 'Let us see what we can do to keep it that way.' He looked to his men in assessment of their feelings. 'We would not want the fellow to think we are shy,' he shouted aloud, Duncan catching the meaning of his words. 'Mr Macleod, we are flying a Greek flag as ensign at the mizzen. It is a trifle beyond our present standing and I have no knowledge of the customary Greek standards, but I collect we still have the the long blue pennant given to us by the lads at the Dock after her refit; let us cut that short and we will fly it at the main... below the Greek colours, if you please; that will serve to confuse the Turk and keep his attention.' He smiled as Duncan grinned, his understanding plain: a broad pennant, signifying command of at least a squadron, would surely guarantee the sustained Turk interest; no commander with such a superiority of firepower would shy away from such a prize, particularly in the evident absence of any supporting ships.

'Murphy,' cried Duncan,'... away with ye, below; swiftly now, d'ye hear. Fetch the blue pennant, the sixty-footer.' Murphy nodded and disappeared down the companionway steps, reappearing within five minutes, the much-prized pennant brutally cut short. Barton himself seized it from Murphy's obvious hesitancy, for the steward had not hoisted any flag on a halyard for some time, years even. Within five minutes the pennant streamed out atop the main, fluttering forward and to starboard, towards the Turk; the signal clear, bold, challenging. The so unexpected sight brought about a resurgence of conversation all along the decks; the men, nervous and tense with anticipation, were grateful for the welcome distraction and speculating loudly on *Surprise's* very apparent and new senior standing.

Every man on *Surprise* nervously awaited the order to open fire and looked to his immediate officer. Every gunner tinkered with his aim, peered along the length of his gun, raised or lowered his barrel a trifle with his handspike, or commanded his men to heave its truck a little to the left or right with their long bars. Eventually they settled, a great tension general to them all, gun captains looking out of their ports; all ready, time suspended, every man making his own calculation of how long the present inactivity would endure.

Those Surprises studying the Turk flagship in that moment were alerted by tiny red-orange flashes erupting along her hull:

visual alarms. At last, the long awaited and hostile guns had opened fire; the bright, flickering flames one by one winked out, the distant guns in turn immediately spewing out huge clouds of dirty grey-white smoke, such a cloud of it that it concealed momentarily the Turk flagship save for her mast tops which projected above the clouds of lingering murk from the explosions, the wind so ineffective and still little more than a fresh north-westerly breeze. BOOM, BOOM, BOOM, the barrage persisted; BOOM, BOOM, BOOM, the rumble of firing reached the ears of the Surprises a little over two seconds later, as did the sound of the shot, its distinctive noise of passage somewhere between a whistle and a hum, flying high aloft and far above their heads; the barrage of noise ending the long wait, dispelling the silence, shaking minds all about the ship from the accumulation of tension. The general anxiety remained; indeed, it was raised to new heights, each man striving to deal with it as he thought best: for some it was another check on their gun, for others a glance to the sails. Gun captains scrutinised their men, peered at their slowmatch and blew hard on it to convince themselves it was still burning. Pat looked again at his watch and noted the time. Though he had twelve master-gunners aboard, experienced veterans of the years fighting Bonaparte -which was some small comfort to him - his fears would not be dispelled, the magnitude of the challenge so great, the disparity of force so overwhelming. 'God between us and all harm,' he whispered to himself.

On and on went the distant firing for twenty seconds: a dozen explosions, a score, two dozen and more; the roaring thunder ragged, some shots merging with the noise of their fellows, others distinct, until all the Turk's portside battery had roared its mighty anger and spat its venom. Pat gazed cautiously up and about *Surprise's* masts, looking to the sails and rigging: he could see no damage from the Turk's broadside. 'We may presume that she fired on the roll,' he remarked to Duncan. 'Lay me closer, a cable towards her... no more, for a starboard broadside, Mr Macleod.'

'Aye aye, sir; Mr Prosser, bring her over to starboard, a cable more and nae closer.'

As the wheel was hauled over, the frigate - within minutes - converged perceptibly with the Turk flagship. Pat paced forward to the waist, one hand on the rail, waiting... waiting... until he judged the range at 1,000 yards and he sensed *Surprise* herself returning from her own gentle roll to larboard; he drew a deep breath, raised his hat high, and - bringing it down in a swift, slashing gesture - he shouted 'FIRE!' at the top of his voice; the shout was so loud that it was painful to his larynx, and he thought it must hurt his throat for evermore. 'FIRE!' shrieked Duncan; 'FIRE!' screamed the lieutenants on the gun deck.

The readied starboard long guns roared almost as one, no gunner waiting for a rolling broadside, fourteen 18-pounders on the gun deck all opening together, the explosion deafening, the cacophony of noise overwhelming the senses; vast long streaks of red-orange flame erupted all along her length, her broadside of deadly missiles flying on their way. The deck shook as if by an invisible hand, the hull vibrating violently for several long seconds, thirty tons of guns ferociously recoiling, their trucks squealing like a whole herd of stuck pigs, her yards and masts quivering with the instant and huge strain imposed upon them, the rigging everywhere shaking as if gripped by a huge hand, one enraged. Smoke poured out from the guns in bilious, thick white clouds; an impermeable blanket settling before the eyes of the Surprises, nothing at all of Khosref's flagship visible; fortunately drifting away from the ship within a few minutes. It was a benefit that had been denied to the Turk crew whose own broadside must have plunged their men into a choking, foul and sulphurous miasma as it was blown back aboard.

Surprise's quarterdeck carronade crews, equally desperately keen to begin firing, had been ordered to hold their fire; the range was too great for their guns, for they were accurate at ranges less than three hundred yards and their absolute maximum range was a thousand, though with little prospect of any accuracy or penetration at that distance.

All about *Surprise* was loud noise and frenetic activity: every man of all the gun crews was cheering, gun captains pressing their men to faster endeavours, shouting, screaming exhortations, 'SWAB! POWDER! WAD! SHOT! WAD!

HAUL! HAUL THERE!' Along her length the guns, their hissing hot barrels swabbed and reloaded, squeaked on their trucks as they were hauled back to project from their ports, ready to fire again, the crews working like demons, pulling like men possessed, the single urgent thought resonating in their mind being to fire their gun. 'Stand back... BACK! FIRE!' the loud shouting everywhere, endemic. The second barrage erupted, less uniform than the opener: *Axeman* fired first from near the bow, then *Pure Poison*, *Old Nick*, *The Nailer* midships; great fiery explosions, thunderous roars erupting on and on down to the aftermost gun in the great cabin, *Mighty Fine,* until all aboard were near deafened and the whole ship was subsumed once again in the stinking cloud of gunsmoke, the air reeking of burnt powder, irritating the throat and nostrils with its acrid, tingling sensations, all along the deck men coughing and spitting.

Pat had counted aloud the seconds from *Surprise's* first broadside. He had reached a hundred and five when the roar had erupted again. The Turk flagship eventually fired her own second, three minutes after her first, 'A trifle slow,' Pat's dry comment to Duncan. The Turk's success was two deep thuds on *Surprise's* hull, the strikes going unnoticed by men sweating at their guns, but the low bass reverberation remarked with concern by the officers on the quarterdeck. Had the balls penetrated? Were any men killed? This second time, most of the Turk's shot had flown low across the water: a series of splashes, white fountains, visible to the watchers; falling short, sinking; leaving *Surprise* almost unscathed bar the two low hull strikes. Pat, expecting the carpenter to deliver a damage report any moment, peered through his glass, waiting patiently for the smoke to clear in order to assess the success of *Surprise's* own broadsides. He had no great expectations of major success, for a thousand yards was the very limit of effective range, of assured damage and accuracy except for the luckiest of strike, but he did not dare go closer with such a numerical and weight of shot disadvantage. *Surprise's* stand could only be a limited demonstration, a holding action pending the arrival of the Greeks. Even then they would be sorely disadvantaged, the Greek brigs possessing much lighter guns. *Surprise* fired her third broadside, the great grey clouds of acrid, reeking gunpowder particles adding to Pat's difficulty in assessing the strikes of his gunners. He coughed painfully himself. Slowly the smoke cleared, and men the length of the ship peered with acute curiosity to see what damage they might have inflicted. The distant smoke about the Turk had also entirely disappeared, blown away by the wind; it was gusting a little stronger, Pat noted, and still veering towards the north: it would slow them all a very little, particularly the Turks, and that small thing was to be welcomed.

Whilst the gunsmoke had persisted, the Turk had turned to larboard and edged closer in the fog of the guns, the gap now noticeably diminished, little more than four cables - close, too close for comfort. 'The crafty old fox,' mused Pat.

'Yon Turk's creeping closer,' declared Duncan.

This had been noticed too at the helm, for Pat felt the beginnings of her own gentle turn to larboard, Prosser mindful of his instructions, no command necessary. Pat nodded to the master by way of approval.

'You can't trick an old dog,' said Pat to himself, 'particularly one so long in the tooth.' He looked through his glass again and he could see that all along the larboard side of the seventy-four her gun ports were absent any guns: the Turks were reloading. *Surprise* was about to begin her roll to leeward, and her own battery fired concurrent with the mouths of the Turk guns re-appearing in their ports. As the smoke from *Surprise's* fourth broadside dissipated, the next winking red flashes appeared from the Turk. Until this moment, the damage to *Surprise* was insignificant: just the two hull strikes which, the carpenter had confirmed, had not penetrated. However, the slight lessening of the range was a benefit to gunners in both ships: the Turk shot struck hard on *Surprise's* hull, on the bulwark; shattering a two yard length at the waist into scores of dangerous flying splinters. Fortunately no one was standing in that place: the gunners forward at the bow carronade were fifteen paces beyond the strike. On the quarterdeck, crowded with its carronade crews, with the helmsmen, Pat and Duncan too, all were fifteen paces back from the strikes and splinters. Above the waist, a number of shrouds and ratlines were severed; the lower parts of the main topsail had been torn in two places; the yard of the main topgallant had broken in half near the mast and tumbled down, one end held at the mast by its chain-tackle, the outer end swinging, its canvas ripped away and sagging. The lower shot strikes, this time, had smashed through the hull and into the gun deck: the crew of *James Figg* were all knocked down by splinters, the shot ricocheting after splitting the gun's truck to strike *Hurricane* on the port side before it exited the ship, smashing through the larboard hull side, huge energy propelling the shot. *Hurricane* had been near pushed round, snapping its train tackle; two of its gun crew were also knocked down, both men wailing in pain with broken legs, their agonies heard even above the firing of the near guns. A half-dozen of men rushed to help carry their stricken comrades below, their agonised voices - wails and screams - audible until they had descended the companionway, trails of blood left behind. Men from the larboard battery stepped across to take their places. Others strived to tie down *James Figg* and *Hurricane,* for a loose cannon represented an almighty danger: near two tons shifting about, uncontrolled with the roll of the ship, was a very unwelcome hazard indeed.

Codrington and Pickering paced up and down through the choking filth of the smoke all along the gun deck, shouting encouragement and directions, 'Fire high... fire high! HIGH!' They attended every gun in turn, substituting a fresh man here and there for a wounded or injured one, shouting for powder and shot distribution to the men feeding the guns, bawling instructions for aiming whenever passing a readied gun and offering words of encouragement generally as they paced by.

The smaller, only three men carronade crews, wholly desperate to begin firing and the Turk approaching to within their extreme range, or so they perceived, had also opened fire, and now laboured hard and furiously to reload the heavy 32-pound shot, a strike from which would guarantee infliction of the most severe damage. The lessening of range greatly aided the quarterdeck carronades, the "smashers" as they were called, for they fired a far heavier shot than the 18-pounder long guns, but were accurate only for a much shorter range. They were also faster to reload and the crack of their higher-pitched discharge rang out more frequently than the lower bark of the long guns below them.

'Aim for her tops!' bawled Duncan amidst the near continuous roar from *Surprise's* guns and carronades, every piece firing individually, no command necessary; men everywhere struggling with the burden of shot, reloading furiously, hauling their guns out, no man impeding his fellows, gun-captains' signals immediately understood, no words necessary save for encouragement with the huge exertion of hauling the heavy guns out when readied to fire again; 'HEAVE!' the common exhortation, 'HEAVE!' the gunners and all their men bawled before levering with all their strength themselves on handspikes to aim their guns; the crews leaping aside before the detonation of firing and the violent and forceful recoil of heated guns on their trucks, kicking back with huge force. The half-dozen men sent aloft with muskets were shooting at the very limit of their range, more in hope than expectation for the smoke rarely permitted them sight of any target and that only fleetingly, a thin crackle of their intermittent firing occasionally audible on the quarterdeck between the roaring discharges of the great guns.

'FIRE!' shouted Macleod, overlooking the waist, the command reiterated down *Surprise's* starboard side; 'FIRE!' screamed Pickering; 'FIRE!' echoed Codrington; the two lieutenants paced all along the length of her gun deck, jumping aside every few yards as the great guns recoiled with great violence and energy as the powder ignited. Gun to gun the officers shifted, the barrels everywhere scorching hot, now too hot to touch, the gunners labouring amidst the noxious smoke of discharge and the sweat that all were soaked in; heaving and hauling their pieces out, time after time, through their ports, recharged, reloaded; 'FIRE!, FIRE!', the enduring and frantic cries endemic along her length. All about them flew Khosref's incoming shot: for the most part whistling above their heads, but also striking the ship: the occasional strike smashing bulwarks, steps, rails; SMASH!, CRACK! Showers of jagged wooden splinters were flying through the air for the first time on the gun deck. From all around came the shrill shouts of wounded men: wailing, loud shrieks; long screams from men in their agonies, their fellows too busy about them to attend; others of the larbowlins hastened everywhere to haul more of their stricken comrades below, down to the cockpit, to Simon and Jason.

The choking smell and acrid taste of powder had become endemic throughout the ship, had long seeped below and melded with the noise and vibration, the intermittent thudding of shot strikes on the hull creating a low, dull resonance throughout the ship's timbers, a huge dislocation of dust showering everywhere, covering every man. The surgeons were starkly aware, indeed frightened that if the gap closed up then a fury of grape would also pour across to inflict greater casualties and more fearsome wounds.

BOOM! BOOM! *Surprise's* great guns continued to return fire, now kicking back more violently after every shot such that even their trucks were lifted from the deck, the guns so hot, their men leaping aside despite their own energies being reduced; the hurricane of noise had long simply overpowered the senses, overwhelmed any aspirations of looking about to gain any notion of the general action; every gunner simply concentrated on firing his next shot to the exclusion of everything else.

Codrington and Pickering continued to stomp along the gun deck, from bow to stern behind the starboard battery. Other than exhortations of encouragement, there was little of substance for them to do save urge the removal of an injured man; all the crews were fighting their guns furiously, without a moment lost; the gun captains were shouting brief commands, the men preparing their pieces in short order and hauling them out again. A quick sighting, an intent but momentary gaze when possible through the bilious white smoke in assessment of their prospects for striking a good target, a rapid glance at the pendulums from which they could gauge where the ship was in her rolling oscillations - the sea calm, little swell, and her roll very gentle - and the gun captains, judging their moment, pulled on their lanyards to snap gun flintlocks all along her length, and the guns boomed out again, spitting long jets of flame and flinging their heavy shot, the guns leaping back on their trucks, ejecting burning wads into the air, the heat-radiating barrels burning careless fingers. From several of the crew came loud cheering as their own particular gun struck the Turk, the momentary clearing of the choking smoke smog giving them a rare glimpse of their success. The noise of the barrage was so powerful, so overwhelming of the senses that it far exceeded anything any man had ever heard off the ship; the violent roar was deafening, an assault on the ears, the manic activity all-consuming for every man. The battering of his own senses, aural and visual, was so tremendous that it was difficult for Pat to be sure, but he observed that *Surprise* was firing far faster than the seventy-four, and he concluded that the Turk gunnery was lamentable: her shots were for the most part flying overhead; admittedly some, a very few, were striking the hull, but most were flying above, occasionally glancing from masts and yards with a resounding smack, a few holes appearing in the sails; other shots skipped and bounced across the water before falling short and sinking. He could not be sure but he believed that *Surprise's* own shots were striking home near every time, and the Turk must surely be enduring prodigious substantial damage.

Thick powder smoke had enveloped the Turk flagship once again and little could be seen of her. On his quarterdeck Pat's mind shifted to nearer focus and he turned all about him, looking once more in careful assessment to see what damage had been inflicted on *Surprise* herself. That there must be significantly more damage than the broken main topgallant yard he did not doubt, for *Surprise* had now been struck hard a dozen times by heavy shot, and aloft the fore topgallant yard was also smashed, its sail brought down, enveloping men on her foc'sle where several men were toiling to clear the fallen canvas away. A 24-pound ball had torn away a huge section of the hammock netting, smashed away the handrail and near all the prominent starboard companionway structure. Another had hurled a flying hail of splinters towards the aftermost carronade crews, four men struck down, the deck substantially bloodied.

'Dear God and Saint Patrick preserve us,' whispered Pat to himself, his fear rising as fast as his spirits were sinking.

At the wheel, Prosser and his men were watching the enemy closely through occasional gaps in the thick smog, ensuring that the Turk did not close further, four cables the closest she had succeeded in getting; and the Turk helmsmen, following *Surprise's* own course changes, had subsequently maintained the narrow gap. At such range, closer than Pat had wished, the murderous fire, the damage, the wounding and the killing was unavoidable and would remain fearsome; and neither the Turk nor *Surprise* could long endure it. His observations of the gun deck and his quarterdeck had revealed to him that a constant contingent of men carried their wounded mates below in a steady stream, though it was, thus far, fortunately far fewer wounded than he had feared. He recognised all the gunners he could see at those near guns, and none of those crews were fighting with substitutes, but the situation would be grim indeed were it to persevere beyond more than a very few more minutes: five or ten minutes in this parlous situation against a *French* line-of-battle ship and *Surprise* would be burning and sinking, of that he had not the least doubt. It was only the lamentable Turk gunnery performance that held abject destruction in abeyance, but that would not preserve *Surprise* for much longer.

Perhaps it was the roll of the seventy-four or perhaps the Turks had shifted their aim, for their next broadside came in low, the 24-pound balls thudding into the hull and bulwarks, sending more jagged splinters flying all over the quarterdeck, one of them striking Duncan down, his loud shriek of pain heard by all about the helm and the carronades. Barton nearest, stepped away momentarily from the helm to attend him. The master, Prosser, seizing the wheel himself, ordered one of the carronade gunners to help him, and they heaved him up and carried him away and down the larboard companionway steps.

All about the decks men were being struck down, falling in pain, in agony, blessed unconsciousness claiming the more fortunate. Blood streamed towards the scuppers in an unceasing flow, rivulets all along the gun deck and on the quarterdeck becoming a red tint smeared over all with the passage of hundreds of bare feet, the men still racing in their commendable but increasingly desperate efforts to ready and fire the great guns as fast as could be. The captain of the near carronade, Collins, fell backwards at Pat's feet, whirled around and thrown down by a ball grazing his shoulder. He looked directly at Pat from the deck for an instant, their eyes meeting before he collapsed unconscious. His mates dragged him away from the carronade slide and pushed the loaded gun forward and fired. In that moment, Pat looked about him once again and saw two more men lying prone on the bloodied quarterdeck, unmoving; both of them were old *Tenedos* veterans and men of Falmouth, much blood puddling all about their bodies before flowing away with the heel of the ship. One man, Enys, was conscious and staring at the heavy crimson flow from his chest which was deeply perforated by a large splinter protruding through his lower ribs, his clothing sodden red. 'Oh God, help me, help me,' his plaintive cries tailed off as his life ebbed away with his blood. His mate, Wynn, came to his aid, tearing off his own shirt for a makeshift bandage to wrap around his comrade to stem the flow, but then came an inaudible whisper, a sigh, and the gravely wounded Enys expired, his shocked tiemate gently shaking his comrade's head for some sign of life. The other man, Harkett, had lost his lower left leg, taken off by shot, and blood streamed out from the ragged stump. He was screaming and shaking in fitful convulsions; a half-minute more and his screams became moans, his breath coming in short gasps before he lapsed into the relief of oblivion.

Standing forward of the helm, Pat realised that little time was left to him to escape complete destruction: *Surprise* could not long endure against this great ship, poor as the Turk gunners were. A strike on a mast or one cutting through her sheets and she would be lost, immobile, no prospect of moving away from the hell that the bombardment had become. He had no choice at all, and he shouted at the top of his voice over the huge din to the master standing at the helm who caught his eye, observed the great anxiety in his countenance, heard the desperation in his voice, 'Mr Prosser, I venture we must shift her away, north-east bound... as quickly as can be. Put her helm hard down... we must bring her as close to the wind as she will stay without she is in irons.'

'Aye aye, sir; helm hard down it is,' cried Prosser, shouting the order to the helmsmen with vigorous gesticular reinforcement.

Pat paced forward to gaze over the rail and down to the gun deck, studying his gunners for several minutes. The frigate's guns were firing still at a creditable rate, scarcely slower than the first three broadsides within the five minutes he demanded. Everywhere, men were furiously reloading and hauling their guns out through their ports with great exertion; others, running, brought powder up from the magazines and shot from the hold; the gun-teams were sponging, loading, ramming, hauling out and firing their charges with determination, skill and self-evident confidence borne of long experience. Along the gun deck, amongst the horror that it had become, Pickering and Codrington busied about still, exhorting the gunners on, shouting encouragement, looking to the ready shot and charges. Turning back to look aft he noticed Duncan's absence, though his cox'n had returned. 'Barton, what has happened to Mr Macleod?' he shouted over the overwhelming din.

'Carried below a minute or two ago, sir.'

'How is he? Pat stared at his cox'n, the bile rising in his throat.

'Struck down by a splinter; his head it was, sir.'

'May God protect him... and help us,' Pat's heart sank to a new low.

Notwithstanding the overpowering size of the immediate opposition and despite being vastly outnumbered - more Turks coming up astern of Khosref's flagship - *Surprise* was excelling herself; her veterans of many years were surpassing any and every expectation that Pat had ever held of them; to a small degree quashing his rising and burning fear of being overwhelmed, and in that moment he felt a great frisson of pride within him. Although her firing was no longer simultaneous broadsides, the guns being out of step after the second or third discharge, there was no let up from the fast cyclical repetitions of firing that Pat expected his gunners to achieve. Within the din, amidst the obscuring smoke of powder, he could not be sure, but looking down from the waist at number twelve, *The Smasher*, they were even now firing a shot in one hundred seconds; and looking behind him on the quarterdeck the carronades were firing faster. Pat had no doubts that his men were by far the superior gunners, for the enemy firing was undoubtedly far, far slower. Furthermore, the aim of his gunners was also much better than that of the Turks: much of their shot striking and sinking into the intervening water; presumably the gunners were firing late during the windward roll.

His eyes stinging in the foul air, he gazed with difficulty through the distant white clouds of gunsmoke to try and see the state of Khosref's ship. It was near impossible: the bilious, stinking swathe of murk was impenetrable at such close range; the haze was filled with unburned, stinking gunpowder particles and tiny fragments of charred wood chips; the air stank too of dust, sweat and blood. If *Surprise* did not haul away, if they did not further open the gap within the next five or ten minutes - no longer - he doubted he would have any ship left to command. He was sure that *Surprise* had given better than she had got, the Turk gunnery being woefully inaccurate, and he was in no doubt that his men and guns must have mauled the Turk severely. He was sure her rate of firing had diminished, and he wondered if she might be preparing to close and perhaps try to board. His anxiety leaped to new heights with that thought shouting loud in his mind. He peered again through the murk of the smoke: to his immense relief and jubilation, and that of every man on deck for not a one staring had missed it, he could see that the Turk's mizzen topsail was toppling and the mizzen sail crumpling, the mizzen mast itself broken below the gaff, all of which was collapsing; slowly at first, its stays and shrouds striving to hold it, but cut through or tearing away with the huge weight of timber and press of sail they could not hold back the inevitable. Within fifteen seconds it was all fallen over in a huge heap of total disarray; mast, yards, gaff and sails all collapsed all over her lee side, her quarterdeck guns inaccessible to their crews and control at the helm severely compromised. All observers on *Surprise* were euphoric, the enemy so substantially damaged, the ship visibly and swiftly slowing to a halt.

At the present separation, never a great distance but it had opened again to a safer half a mile, Pat could not hope to gauge the Turk's casualties, but he thought that, his firing instructions to his men to aim for her rigging and such being seemingly so successful, they might be light. Yet her firing he noticed, even on her weather side which was not obstructed by the toppled mizzen debris, had fallen off considerably.

'I think she is stopped,' shouted Duncan who had re-appeared from the undamaged larboard companionway and who now stood behind Pat near the aft carronades, great excitement, not to say delight resonating in his voice, the adrenalin of battle running swiftly through his veins, his face bright red, his breath coming fast. Blood from a deep splinter scratch poured down from his head all over his face, his head wrapped in a towel, his collar sodden in the crimson flood; his every gesture, his every shouted word was so animated, so expressive.

'Are you all right, Duncan?' asked Pat, much relieved to see his friend, noticing his head injury and his generally dishevelled state.

'Aye sir, 'tis but a trifling scratch, bloody for sure,' Duncan grinned, 'I cudne see a damned thing and took a wee moment just now to find my towel.'

Pat peered again through his glass just as CRACK, the first carronade fired; CRACK, the second was near concurrent. The enduring BOOM, BOOM persisted still in the background cacophony that was the gun deck. Despite *Surprise* leaving the Turk off her quarter in her turn away, the great guns were keeping up their spiteful hail, levered round on their carriages as far as they could be to still bear upon the target, but near all the Turk guns had fallen silent. How long before the Turk could clear her debris? Would Khosref then strive to catch *Surprise*? Was the frigate's turn away obvious to him? And what of his compatriots? It was a minute, two minutes, an eternity of time and passing so slowly before Pat eventually spoke, his words meant only for himself but audible to all nearby, his overwhelming relief so evident in his voice to all at the wheel, 'She is stopped, so she is; and with her mizzen lost she cannot pursue us whilst we are to windward of her... thank the Lord, thanks be to Mary and Joseph. She has lost way... thank God... thank God.'

Pat's relief was short-lived: from the top came cries of panic, shrill and loud; audible only because the firing had slackened, 'BOW THERE, STAND ASIDE, SHIFT, STAND BACK!' and in that instant there was a huge crash as the fore topmast tumbled to the deck, the men aloft the main alerting all below to its fall beforehand; the unlucky two men on the foretop crosstrees having abandoned their muskets in haste, in panic, and having scrambled half way down the ratlines were lying on the deck, unmoving - fortunately having chosen the windward side, the leeward rigging gone into the water, the shambles dragging along *Surprise's* starboard side.

Great swathes of top rigging, canvas and broken spars enveloped the forward guns, all of which ceased firing, as did many amidships as men rushed forward to help their comrades.

'Avast firing!' shouted Pat.

'Fore topmast's gone, sir, broken above the cap... smashed down,' shouted Codrington, hastening up the companionway steps.

'How strange is that?' mused Pat, his mind reeling from the crash of the fore topmast and racing to consider the implications; Khosref's flagship's mizzen was down and near the same thing - albeit it was her fore topmast - had happened to *Surprise*. He shifted to the lee rail and looked forward to see a swathe of collapsed canvas all about the foc'sle, over the bow and trailing down her side.

'Mr Tizard and his men are attending,' a weary and somewhat breathless Codrington added.

'Very good, Mr Codrington. Mr Prosser, let us bear off, leave this place; put her helm down; we will open a trifle more distance before the Turk returns his attention to us.'

'Aye aye, sir; helm down it is.'

Forward, men laboured frantically to clear the wreckage; cutting ropes with their knives, slashing away with axes at those remnants of the broken topsail and topgallant yards still on deck, much having gone into the water, and striving desperately with anything at hand to make space for the affected gunners to reach their guns. The Turk flagship was mired in her own debris off *Surprise's* starboard quarter; the intermittent firing from her bow chasers had become desultory, inaccurate. *Surprise* maintained her own fire from all her starboard guns aft of midships; none of the gunners and neither of the lieutenants had heard Pat's command to cease fire. A final discharge erupted before the angle became too great for the guns to bear.

'Murphy, my compliments and regards to Doctor Ferguson, and pray enquire of our casualties. Davies, Beer... bear a hand there, handsomely now; these men are to be taken below, to the cockpit.' Pat shifted aside to admit passage to his men carrying the wounded; he stepped on to something indeterminate; he shifted once more and glanced down to his feet; he was standing in a red pool of blood, Harkett's severed and crushed lower leg next to his boot.

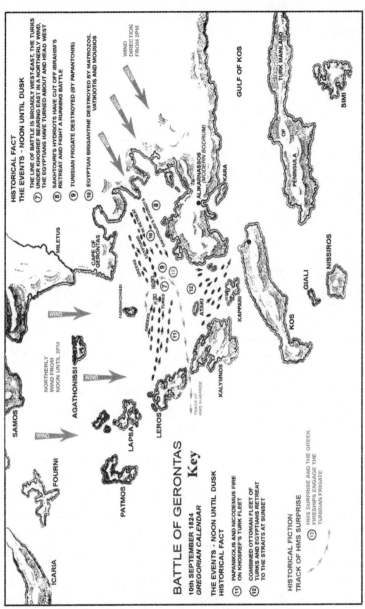

The Battle of Gerontas, noon until dusk.

Chapter Four

Friday 10th September 1824   11:30   *South of Samos*

Surprise, the weak wind off her port quarter and steering two points north of east, was now shifting much more slowly with her fore topmast lost, rolling more heavily as a consequence. The Turk line was sailing two points south of east, and the growing divergence, small as it was but now a mile, was bringing increasing relief to all aboard the damaged frigate. Ahead, perhaps a mile and a half off, were the eight brigs of Miaoulis, no longer under tow but moving a point south of west, the strengthening and more northerly wind propelling the opposing forces faster towards their inevitable confrontation. Off *Surprise's* larboard quarter the Spezziots and Psariots were trailing a quarter mile behind her and had opened fire on the nearer of those aftermost Turk ships in Khosref's wake. In the far visible distance, perhaps five miles off *Surprise's* starboard bow, the Egyptians and the far Hydriot squadron under Sakhtouri were also closing on each other. The Hydriots were east of the Egyptians and looked to be steering south-west to a position which would leave the whole of the Turk-Egyptian fleet encircled.

However, aboard *Surprise* not a solitary soul contemplated the strategic position of the various squadrons of both parties, every man seizing the welcome respite. For the moment, the men of *Surprise* enjoyed a welcome albeit likely brief respite in which to take stock, to tend the casualties and to do what could be done with the downed fore topmast and the broken main topgallant yard. The distant Turk squadron remained clearly visible, in line astern of their flagship, none seemingly shifting to take advantage of *Surprise's* partial immobility; perhaps pre-occupied with skirmishing Psariots and Spezziots. Many of the surviving men from the quarterdeck carronades had gone forward to where the carpenter and his mates were sawing away aloft to take down

76

the remnants of the damaged topmast. Fortunately that was broken above the lower cap, well above the level of the fore course yard - which appeared undamaged and could still serve if all the severed rigging about the mast could be cleared. The fore topmast staysail had collapsed but the fore staysail, however, remained intact, its stay still supporting the foremast. It was all far from ideal, but the men of *Surprise* bent to with determination to remedy as best they might the damage and deficiencies.

At the stump, about four feet above the lower cap, two men worked to hook new top-blocks and to reeve in two hawsers to aid hauling the smashed wooden detritus out of the way. Others strived feverishly to cut away those braces, bowlines, back-stays, bob-stays, fore topmast shrouds and rigging which had been rendered useless by the damage and which now cluttered the deck, to toss fallen blocks and bitts in the netting and on the deck over the side, and to haul away the dangling remnant of upper fore topmast towards the rail. Further aft, others toiled, sweating in the boiling heat as the sun approached the top of the day, to cut away the shattered and dangling half of the main topgallant yard.

The two injured topmen, the musketeers, both with broken limbs and plainly concussed, had been taken below. Everywhere all about the gundeck, the foc'sle and the waist the tangle of shredded canvas and rope appeared insuperable; the jibs and the fore topmast staysail had all collapsed, their canvas hanging over the bowsprit. *Surprise* had lost a great deal of her motive power, certainly much of her leeward manoeuvrability, and she remained extremely vulnerable.

'Mr Macleod, when the men have cleared away we will shake the reefs out of her courses. Will the foremast, its shrouds cut so, hold firm the main topmast stay? Would you think so?' Pat was considering how best to augment his much depleted spread of canvas and manoeuvrability. The fore staysail and perhaps a spritsail both set would surely help.

Duncan's bright blue eyes glowed through the black-engrained powder all over his face. Most of the blood formerly flowing from the gash on his head had been wiped away, though a trickle still ran around his left eye and over his cheek, which he wiped periodically with his hand; he blinked frequently to clear his eye. His hat had blown away during the battle, and he looked wild and bandit-like in his demeanour; yet despite all he had suffered, his spirits remained high, 'I will go for'ard and see for myself, sir.'

He descended the companionway steps and made his way along the gun deck. Fortunately there was only the gentlest of roll to hinder him, for in truth he felt his strength greatly depleted and his head was dizzy; he passed by the guns amidships and came to the tangled debacle nearer the bow. The Surprises were still working manically all along the decks, cutting and chopping. Those tired gun-crews he passed, firing having long ceased, were in good spirits; one or two of the more vociferous amongst them still bawled after the Turk, shouting the most caustic and vile of profanities - challenging her to come back to the contest; though doubtless such was wholly insincere, exultant bravado. Others, more fatigued or perhaps more sensible, nodded or smiled weakly at him as he paced along the deck, grateful for some small moment of recuperation. He spoke words of encouragement to all as he stepped by, offering a wave of his hand here and an encouraging nod there to many a man in passing, every recipient pleased and grateful to be acknowledged: his popularity with the men was well-founded.

Pat paced across his quarterdeck and stared off the starboard quarter towards the long line of frigates, brigs, brigantines and corvettes following the Turk flagship. Thankfully all appeared to have turned with Khosref to keep their station and none had seized the opportunity to break their line to attack *Surprise* in her disarray. Most of the Greek brigs were now interposed between *Surprise* and the Turks, firing endemic along their lines. 'Perhaps they cannot see our fore topmast down as we are bearing away?' Pat wondered, for she was now bearing directly north-east, Farmakonissi off her larboard bow; sailing six points off the wind, as close as she could sail to it in her effort to move as far from the Turk fleet as quickly as could be. The last few stragglers of Spezziots and Psariots together were now passing over her track and would soon also interpose themselves between

Surprise and the rearmost Turks whose line still stretched a mile or even more back to the north-west, towards Lapsa. The desperation and urgency had, thankfully, eased in Pat's mind with the lack of Turk pursuit. He turned to the master, 'Mr Prosser, ease her half a point; let us not venture too close to the wind. Mr Pickering, shake out her courses.'

Murphy appeared on the quarterdeck to pass a towel to his captain. Pat stared at him, enquiry burning in his thoughts and showing plain in his face, a stern demeanour of anxious expectation plain in his eyes. 'Well, Doctor Ferguson is busy as a dozen bees, sorr; Mr Jacob is 'elpin' out,' Murphy reported. 'Fer sure there's a deal o' work down there... Bedlam ain't in it.' Correctly assessing his captain's patience to be non-existent, Pat's face screwed up to the most hostile of stares, he accelerated his report to its conclusion, 'Enys and Harkett are dead, sorr. There ain't no more deaths reported *yet,* but three or four o' the lads are wounded... *very* bad.'

'Thank God, so few deaths, thank God,' Pat could not refrain from the words, Murphy's news bringing an overwhelming, surging flood tide of relief to Pat's racing mind. 'Thank God,' he continued to repeat to himself, over and over.

'We'se got a score o' wounded... splinters fer the most part, an' a couple o' lads 'as got broken legs or arms. Doctor Ferguson sends 'is best wishes an' 'opes fer a quieter hour, so 'e does,' Murphy concluded. Pat simply nodded, could not reply, his dry and sore throat constricted with the relief of so few deaths and his anxiety.

'Two knots,' bawled the linesman; *Surprise* had slowed significantly. One bell rang out and one of the topmen shouted down, 'Turks are turnin' south-east... SOUTH-EAST.'

'That will suit us admirably,' murmured Pat with a rising feeling of relief. He stepped over and took a deep draught from the scuttlebutt, tipping a second tin over his head, gratefully wiping his sweaty, smoke-encrusted face before replacing his hat.

Duncan had returned to report. 'What's left of the fore topmast stump has been brought down, the rest has been cut away and gone over the side... and the lads have cleared away the jibs'ls. For the most part the canvas is taken below. The carpenter is minded the foremast stay will hold firm... as will the main topmast stay. I believe the main topgallant yard can be fished, but that isnae soon as the men are working at the fore; Mr Tizard says he will try directly. The sailmaker swears that the tears in her main tops'l can be fixed... sewn, aye, but nae here.'

'Very good, Mr Macleod; put the men to the braces and tell the helmsmen to shiver the sails; we will creep away towards Cape Gerontas. It will give us an hour or two to make what further repairs we can.' Pat was breathing a little easier with the growing distance from the enemy line and the Greeks lying between *Surprise* and the Turks, in parallel with them as if akin to a shield for the barky. Firing was vigorous all along their line and a further general but indistinct roaring of guns could be heard from the far south and east: the Hydriots and Egyptians were engaged.

Pat took another long drink from the scuttlebutt before scrambling once more up the rigging on the main, determined to see for himself the relative positions, directions and, as far as possible, the intentions of all the parties. The topmen shifted aside as he clambered through the top and Pat hauled himself all the way to the cross-trees where he squatted and stared all about him through his glass. Khosref in his flagship was, thankfully, at least a mile off and heading south-east into the Gulf of Gerontas, his squadron's line unbroken in his wake. Pat heaved a great sigh of relief, it was something of a release: it was plain to see that *Surprise* had succeeded in his intention of turning the Turk fleet away from its direct course for Samos; that had most likely saved the island. A half-mile off the larboard side of Khosref and his near consorts in the Turk line was Miaoulis' Second Hydriot squadron where general firing had broken out all along the Turk van. Three quarters of a mile to the south of *Surprise*, the Psariots and Spezziots likewise were exchanging fire with the last of the Turk line, the Turks still a half-mile off the Greeks' starboard beam. The near and distant booming of many hundreds of guns firing could plainly be heard from every direction; the winking flashes of the far Turk guns were visible between dense, voluminous and expanding clouds of dirty white gunsmoke: the most prodigious exchange of fire Pat had ever experienced, could ever have conceived was furiously underway. He had never before seen or heard its like. For a few minutes he marvelled at the scale of it all, his eyes absorbing the sight of score upon score of ships firing upon each other, but he could no longer make out through the widespread fog of smoke where the Egyptians were, or the First Hydriot squadron under Sakhtouri. He presumed that they were both still fighting each other much further to the south; indeed, the horizon in that direction was totally obscured with a layer of white gunsmoke; much of it blown there by the strengthening, now northerly wind from the battle against the nearer Turk squadrons. To his great relief, *Surprise* appeared to be in her own forgotten backwater of the battle flow: safe at present, ignored by all and free to make what repairs she could. He started wearily down towards the deck, then stopped on the rigging to stare all about him: all his lieutenants were actively absorbed in directing repairs; the barky could manage without him for ten minutes. He decided upon a visit below, to the lower deck. He was seized by a pressing need to see for himself how his surgeon and the wounded were faring.

As Pat reached the gun deck he was accosted by Codrington and Pickering, both anxious to make their reports. There was nothing of fresh concern for Pat, and he merely nodded his acknowledgements to each in turn whilst considering the situation generally. A sense of hunger came over him, 'Mr Codrington, tell cook he may light the galley; dinner is to be prepared and served as soon as it is ready. I venture we will be here, near adrift for an hour or two whilst the carpenter fixes what can be done. Mr Pickering, a ration of wine is to be issued; doubtless every man will welcome a glass to whet their appetite.' His lieutenants nodded their confirmation, his words bringing grateful nods from the men in earshot; Pat's orders would certainly be welcome throughout the ship. He looked down and espied Duncan's bicorne hat, blown away off the quarterdeck and fallen into the waist. He picked it up and passed it to one of the hands, 'Boscowen, pass this to Mr Macleod with my compliments.' From somewhere he found an attempt at a smile;

he paused and stared all about him to the men standing nearby, all of them looking to their captain, and he added, 'We would not wish to see him ill-dressed.' His feeble jest brought a pleasing tiny glimmer of relaxation to tired men; many of them grinning, he was pleased to see; his tiny ray of humour, of relief had broken the high tension of the past hour, had brought a reconnection with the essential spirit and essence of the barky.

The carpenter passed by with his men, all clutching their axes. The deck was clear of debris at last. The fore topmast and its yard were all gone, thrown over the side, and the shattered fragments of the main topgallant yard similarly so. The bosun, Mr Sampays, and his men had settled to work at the fore crosstree, and were soon working furiously on lashing another preventer-stay from it to the jib. Broken fragments of wood continued to fall, blown down by the gusts in the wind; some were caught by the netting, though much of that had been torn down too as the yard fell; other timber pieces intermittently thudded to the deck all about them, making the work dangerous in the extreme.

Pat, gathering his courage and with considerable trepidation, stepped down to the lower deck; he peered through the dim light towards the bow where the surgeons worked. He paced forward very slowly, in great dread of what might be revealed; he looked to his right and to his left; he stared at a half-dozen wounded men on each side, all of them slumped on the deck and semi-conscious at best. The ambience was more restrained than he had feared and anticipated; certainly there were the customary moans of the wounded, doubtless many in considerable pain, but the wails and screams of despairing men in their agonies, as had been the case in prior battles, were absent, greatly to his relief. Jason accosted him as he reached the fore hatchway, 'Captain O'Connor, sir, how goes things, how are you?' His voice was measured, anxiety near absent. 'Pray forgive me, sir, but you are looking exceedingly pale.'

'Oh, I am tolerably well; thankee. How does Doctor Ferguson fare, tell; how are the men, the wounded?' Pat's own subdued voice was recognisably filled with apprehension.

'We have concerns for Symons,' said Jason. 'A Turk ball struck the shot rack near his gun, smashing it, some part impacting his chest and breaking many ribs; his breathing is laboured, doubtless painful were it not for the laudanum... and his pulse weakens. He spits considerable blood. I regret that Doctor Ferguson has doubts that he can endure.' Pat grimaced and took a huge intake of breath before the slow release. Jason resumed, 'Enys is gone, before he was brought below, Harkett soon after. Doctor Ferguson fears Tremayne will not live long, his blood loss so great. There are a dozen other men with splinter wounds; the most severe of them are treated, cleansed and bound. Doctor Ferguson is presently attending the lesser wounded, and there are eight fractures to set and strap after that. The men have all been given laudanum and are quieted, their pain subdued... thankfully.'

A silent Pat, speech beyond him in that moment, received Jason's report with a tremendous surge of concern which washed through his very being like a wave. He was aware of his racing heartbeat and acutely conscious of the blood rushing to his head, colouring his face which was suffused with heat. After a deep exhalation, his shoulders sinking, he replied very quietly, 'Thank God that there are so few deaths... Thank you, Mr Jason. I am extremely obliged to you, infinitely obliged. May God and Saint Patrick protect them all.' He turned about, not wishing to reveal in his demeanour further of his anxieties; indeed, his distress, and he paced slowly away, his head down. His raging fears of many more deaths were assuaged; his deep dread was receding to a more modest concern, and that was a great help to him in that particular moment.

Back on the gun deck, Pat looked about the resting men, scores of them seated around their guns, all drinking their wine, eating bread with lobscouse. None had gone below to eat on the customary lower deck whilst the surgeons were at work. He nodded to everyone whose eye he caught in passing, indicating that they should not rise, and he stepped up to the quarterdeck with a gathering sense of relief. Macleod, his face wiped clean and his hat restored, no longer looked like some wild, raging pirate. Pat gazed all about the ship: *Surprise* remained alone in her own several square miles of sea, in a relative oasis of peace. It was doubtless temporary, but no immediate threat was apparent. To the south hundreds of guns were firing still, the distant noise clearly audible, the battle continuing. Pat, deep in thought and assessment, merely nodded to his First; his mouth was very dry, a desperate thirst pressing upon him, and no words could he manage.

'Well, sorr, coffee's up,' announced Murphy. It was very welcome tidings indeed. Pat gulped several large draughts down from the flask: strong, bitter, hot, wonderfully hot. It was reinvigorating and cleared the enduring, unpleasant taste of powder in his mouth which had irritated his throat so. He nodded his appreciation and gratitude to his steward, and he swallowed another mouthful, saying nothing further whilst he took mental stock.

Five minutes passed in contemplation of the general situation before Pat could speak without revealing his own distress and uncertainty, his receding anxiety giving way to a ravening hunger. 'Lord, I would be the happiest man in the world with a slice of cold beef,' he exclaimed. 'Cut along, Murphy, and see what can be found in the line of a sandwich.'

Forward, it looked as if the carpenter and his men had largely rectified what they could: the last of the swathe of rope, spars and canvas was all cleared away; the foremast still supported the fore course and the fore staysail remained largely undamaged save for a hole from a ball shot. Above the fore crosstree, the main topsail stay supported the rarely used staysail which had been brought up from the sailmaker's loft to bring a small aid to augment lateral headway at the fore. *Surprise* appeared capable of sailing once again. 'Well, sorr, here be cold mutton sandwiches,' said Murphy, clutching a small wooden tray.

'Thankee, Murphy; obliged... obliged,' Pat found his voice again and seized a sandwich. He bit hungrily into it, nodding his gratitude to his steward.

'There isnae any hull damage, sir,' Duncan provided his report; 'The mizzen and main are untouched, save for tears to the

84

main tops'l. A few yards of cut rigging are to be replaced, but 'tis the for'ard sails where we be hardest hit. There isnae anything left atop the fore course and nae jibs, as ye know. The main stays'l is hoisted up.' Pat simply nodded gratefully and continued to chew his sandwich, all the while considering the situation, weighing the ship's capabilities and what she could achieve against such odds.

Pickering arrived on the quarterdeck within a half-hour to report, 'The bosun and his men have respliced the starboard mainsheet, sir; they have repaired three severed main shrouds, the fore preventer stay, four main halliards and braces, the main bowline, the mizzen staysail halliards and the larboard main brace.'

'Very good, Mr Pickering; my compliments to Mr Sampays and will he rig a spritsail on the yard; at least that is still there.'

A further anxious half-hour passed; *Surprise* was drifting, braces all slack. The weary bosun - he was exhausted - looked up from the waist and nodded to his captain who was staring down from the rail. A feeling of relief was general, every man pleased that *Surprise* had mobility once more.

'Well done, Mr Sampays,' Pat shouted down to the gun deck, waving his hat in salute.

'I venture she is ready to shift again,' declared Duncan, nodding in emphasis.

'Thank you, Mr Macleod,' acknowledged Pat, brightening. 'Let us make our course south-east, and we will see what is happening with our Greek friends. Doubtless they are busy and will welcome our return, our help.'

'Aye aye, sir.' Duncan moved away to shout his orders to the bosun and to Prosser at the helm, rousing scores of weary men all over the ship from their rest. He bawled out to the men to pull tight the braces, and her yards were hauled round to the wind. Jubilation! Another minute passed and a thin cheer erupted from all about the decks as *Surprise* began to gather way. The wind, whilst *Surprise* had effected her urgent and temporary repairs, had veered further round in its arc and now blew a strong northerly, bringing her bow round as her rudder turned, hard over. With no jibs it was a slower turn than customary, the helm control and her course resolution at the bow somewhat compromised, the staysails only partially ameliorating the loss of her jibs. The main topmast staysail held up and filled. Slowly, so very slowly, she gathered headway, the wind off her larboard quarter, and on she moved, gaining a little speed, south-east bound towards the distant battle.

'How does she feel, Mr Prosser?' Pat asked of the master at the helm.

'She wants to turn by the wind, sir, and she rolls. I can hold her with the wheel down a peg; 'tis no calamity.' Pat nodded his understanding.

'A most creditable effort of the carpenter and the bosun,' declared Pat to Duncan, his mood lifting with *Surprise's* control largely restored and her casualties being far less severe than he had feared. The sand in the glass ran out; Dalby struck four bells. On the quarterdeck Pat gazed all about him in assessment; he noted the much strengthened wind, driving *Surprise* swiftly on towards the smoke-laden conflict between Turk and Greek, still some miles to the south and east. 'The wind remains advantageous for the Greeks,' he mused, Duncan listening, 'but a retreat, if required, would face the dangerous converse: the need to work against it whilst likely remaining under fire for a prolonged spell.' As *Surprise* closed on the furious conflict, the unceasing din of distant gunfire began to register ever louder, reinforcing a rising awareness of its scale. Pat pondered the choices open to him: he could stay on his south-east track into firing range of and remain parallel with Khosref's fleet, which was heading for south of Farmakonissi and towards the distant centre of the Gulf of Gerontas, the Greeks to windward of the Turk line; or *Surprise* could turn directly south, passing straight through that conflict, crossing the Turk line, going further south to where the Egyptians were battling against Sakhtouri's First Hydriot squadron in the southern waters of the Gulf; or finally, *Surprise* could stay near the coast of Leros where Khosref's stragglers, the last of his line, might still conceivably break away and bear down towards Samos; but which one of three was he to choose? The combined Ottoman fleet, if wielded effectively, far outmatched all of the collective Greek squadrons with their many fewer and much smaller ships; ships equipped with guns of lesser calibres; and so *Surprise*, even damaged, represented the most effective single asset available to the Greeks; but how should Pat decide to deploy his ship? Miaoulis to the east could offer him no direction: no signal was visible at such distance and the clouds of white gunsmoke, though much dissipated, did not help; indeed, his eyes, red and sore, tingled and smarted incessantly with the constant irritation of spent powder particles, noxious and foul-smelling. The northerly wind afforded him the luxury of choice, and Pat chose to stay on the present south-easterly course. Another mile, ten minutes, no more and *Surprise* would be in the midst of the melee once again, in close support of the Greeks and engaged in the fierce conflagration.

'Deck there... on deck!' one of the topmen hailed, 'Fireships ahead, starboard bow; a mile, three of 'em... four... FIVE!'

Pat peered through his glass, the nearer individual ships and all close developments were in plain sight from his quarterdeck. 'Miaoulis has sent five fireships against Khosref,' he said to Duncan, every ear on the quarterdeck straining to hear his words.

The Psariots under Canaris and the Spezziots under Androutsos, both a half-mile fine off *Surprise's* starboard bow, were hard pressed against the Turk stragglers; that was plain. The Greeks, with the weather-gauge, were preserving a separation, as Pat had, and the firing was taking place at a range of between a half-mile and one mile, Khosref's line maintaining its course for convergence with the Egyptians to the south-east of them. The second Hydriot squadron under Miaoulis was a mile directly ahead, firing on the north or port side of Khosref's van, and it was there that the fireships, five of them, were evident. The Egyptians, as far as Pat could make anything out through gaps in the widespread smoke, were at a distance of four or five miles further away to the south-east; they were surely fighting Sakhtouri's First Hydriot squadron, both opponents mixed in an almighty jumble of command confusion, signal instructions near impossible in the smoke, so slow to clear in what was still the most modest of winds.

'Mr Macleod, will you take a look through the glass?' asked Pat, pausing to rub his tired and sore eyes.

'I can see all of the fireships gone through the Turk line, sir; save for a Spetziot close alongside a Turk brig; I think she may be tied alongside, but at this range I cannae be sure,' reported Duncan, his eye, that one absent the still-flowing blood trickle, screwed to the telescope. 'The Greeks are taking to their boats. I widnae like to be boarding them myself, the enemy frigates all about them... brave, brave men.' At that moment the Greek boats were below the maximum down inclination of the near Turk guns who could not fire upon them, but that could not be expected to last. There was also no sign of any Greek brigantine turning to cut through the Turk line to their rescue, a daunting and hazardous manoeuvre.

'We will aid those men,' cried Pat. 'Mr Macleod, waisters to the braces; there is not a moment to be lost. I mean to bear off as quick as can be and steer through the Turk line.'

'Aye aye, sir. Waisters to the braces!' bellowed Duncan. 'Helm up, Mr Prosser.'

Surprise turned a little to starboard to run south-south-east, the wind on her larboard quarter, gaining speed after her prior dawdle, for that was all it could be termed; she was bearing directly to cross the Turk line a half-mile ahead, Khosref's squadron still steering south-east.

'Mr Macleod, we have need of every knot!' shouted Pat with a degree of anxiety, 'We will boom out all those of her stuns'ls that she can still carry.'

'Aye aye, sir,' replied Duncan, passing the orders to the crew standing forward of the wheel and shouting down to those below in the waist, the men hastening to the rigging.

'Mr Pickering, we will double-shot the guns with ball and bar-shot, and the carronades are to be loaded with grape. Pass the word: after firing the present loads, the guns are to be reloaded with reduced charges... all with ball but half of them with grape too and the other half with bar-shot.' Pickering nodded his understanding and Pat continued, 'It will be close range work and such will smash more splinters when the balls strike. We will give them a bloody nose.' Pickering nodded with a grim face and hastened away.

Aboard the Turk ships, the realisation that *Surprise* was turning to cross their line had registered, and with guns swivelled as far as could be there began a desultory firing with long range shots skipping across the water towards *Surprise*. If Khosref's fleet changed its course, then any gaps for *Surprise* would vanish and she would find herself abeam one, two or even three enemy frigates or brigs; if that happened, she would be well within their firing range and likely would suffer heavily. 'Will Khosref hold his course? What was in his mind?' Pat asked himself with burning trepidation. Khosref's squadron was running south-east under topsails alone, courses all along the line clewed up. Presumably he was intending to split the two slow-moving Hydriot squadrons and join with his Egyptian allies. Pat reckoned that all the Turk followers would remain rigidly in line astern, behind their admiral even as *Surprise* broke their line; for that was the reputation of the Ottoman navy: to display any initiative at all in the presence of their admiral was to court reprobation, perhaps even dismissal or worse. It was known that the Egyptian commander, Ibrahim, had bastinadoed captains for less and had hanged one who had dropped his anchor in two hundred fathoms, losing it and much of its cable.

Surprise was making her way faster through the water, gaining a little more speed every minute until she reached, Pat believed, a steady six knots, the main topsail canvas increasingly flapping its loud complaint, torn as it was. 'I hope that sail will serve a trifle longer,' he thought whilst casting anxious eyes in the direction of his concern, 'and that we will not have to get it reefed or furled.' He turned to his First. 'Cast the log, Mr Macleod,' he cried. Duncan reiterated the order to the linesman.

'Six knots... Six and a half!' came back the shout.

Surprise was bearing directly for the gap in the Turk line. 'BOOM!' the bow chaser of the Turk frigate behind the gap opened fire, the shot whistling across the bow. There were no longer any jibsails nor any fore tops'l to tear or further damage, the small consolation occurring to Pat. On *Surprise* advanced;

she was near fully into the gap, and still the Turk did not change course. Even a point or two of change and *Surprise* must be battered, the range a bare quarter mile.

'Quickly now; hang trailing lines out for those men from the fireships in their boats,' bellowed Pat to Duncan, tension swiftly rising all about the ship, 'It is their only chance.'

'Aim high, lads, HIGH!' bellowed Pickering and Codrington on the gun deck. 'FIRE!' *Surprise's* starboard battery opened fire, the fourteen guns firing roundshot the short range to smash into the Turk frigate's sails: tearing lines, cutting through canvas, smashing yards and splintering through her bulwark. Her fore topsail ripped its length from top to bottom, torn away at its base, the two halves flying wildly apart, the braces ripped away by the bar-shot. Three holes appeared in the Turk fore course and another three shots smashed through her side. It was the most splendid display of accuracy as had ever been achieved, *Surprise's* gunners peeking swift glances through their ports, busy as they were in reloading.

The Turk captain, recognising his danger, *Surprise* set to rake his ship from bow to stern on her next broadside, began his turn to the south, to present his own beam and provide his gunners with a target. It was too late. 'That will not do,' declared Pat to all present nearby, adding in a voice resonating with considerable experience, 'That will never wash, not by a long chalk.'

The Turk fired those few of her guns nearer her bow which could target *Surprise*, and a feeble handful of shots whistled across, none falling short in the extreme close range, three striking the bulwark to send a flying shower of splinters across midships and two cutting holes in *Surprise's* mizzen topsail. Thankfully none of her men were injured. *Surprise's* starboard battery fired again almost as one, the distance little more than a hundred yards. The projectiles, a fiercely effective mixture of ball, grape and bar-shot, all aimed high. The Turk masts and rigging were savaged, her foremast was shattered below the course yard, tumbling backwards, smashing down upon the main in its fall. Blocks and splinters rained down upon the Turk crew, tearing away the overhead netting. The Turk in one destructive minute was bereft of all motive power, all progress swiftly halted; the ship had become a sitting duck as she came to a halt, her own turn incomplete, mired amongst the debris of her fore mast. *Surprise's* third broadside, a killing swathe of shrieking shot and screeching grape, swept the Turk quarterdeck. In the briefest of moments, through a gap in the gunsmoke, Pat saw her captain struck down and others of her men on her quarterdeck knocked down; her wheel had been smashed away from its mounting, the upright stand a broken stump. Smoke enveloped all once again and he could see nothing further until, ten seconds later, it cleared momentarily; he could see her quarterdeck near devoid of men, very few remaining after the hail of grape and all in plain confusion. The smoke closed in over the dreadful scene. *Surprise* fired another broadside once more to strike her opponent again terribly: smashing her gunwhale along much of its length, shattering her bowsprit, destroying her bow chasers' trucks, the metal of those guns hurled backwards, their tackle ripped away; the near raking fire travelling the length of her deck, killing and wounding dozens of victims in its irresistible path, an unforgiving hurricane of metal death.

Pat had no intention of lingering, a dozen more Turks were coming up astern of the smashed frigate, and hence *Surprise* maintained her southbound course, continued her passage through the Turk line. The corvette behind the frigate veered away from the obstacle in her path, bearing away in a sharp course correction, her captain plainly not wishing to engage such a fury as *Surprise* had shown herself to be. The Turk corvette slowed substantially as she strived to pass to the north side of *Surprise*, but the wind, still feeble, was against her. She turned within four points of the weak wind, but she would not stay and fell off; her manoeuvre had failed; in irons and drifting, her bow collided with the stricken Turk frigate. Aboard *Surprise* the men cheered until they were hoarse.

Pat allowed himself a grim exchange of nods with Duncan; their fleeting satisfaction was interrupted by *Surprise's* larboard battery firing at the stern of the fleeing Turk brigantine which had simply maintained its own course despite *Surprise's* attack on the following and now severely damaged frigate. The broadside simply crushed the top of the Turk's transom, obliterated every window in the captain's cabin, smashed the mizzen to pieces, and all unfortunates standing on her quarterdeck were struck down by the barrage of grapeshot, swept away like fallen leaves in an autumn gale. More great hurrahs erupted from the Surprises.

A hundred yards directly ahead, the Greek fireship was near alongside the Turk brig; near, but no longer attached because the brig had succeeded in drawing away, shifting a little to the east. The *bourlota* had been abandoned whilst it was still attached to the brig; it was blazing furiously and drifting due south, its Greek crew having taken to their two boats. *Surprise* bore down on them, the master steering *Surprise* to pass between them. As they came near alongside Duncan shouted to the men standing in the waist, 'Away the lines! Throw, throw! AWAY!' The grateful Greeks seized the ropes and hastened to tie them to their boats, *Surprise* not slowing in the least. The lines were allowed to run out, the boats being towed fifty yards behind, until Pat could see she was in no immediate danger from the Turks in the rear of Khosref's line: all such were manoeuvring to pass the disabled frigate and showing no inclination to close with such a formidable adversary as *Surprise* had so powerfully demonstrated herself to be.

In the steaming gloom of the lower deck, amidst the noise of the creaking of the ship's timbers and surrounded by the pitiful wails, pleas and cries of the wounded, Simon and Jason, dripping with perspiration and assisted by Freeman, toiled valiantly, no pause for even a moment. The next patient was brought to the makeshift operating table of sea-chests lashed together, to the side of which, on another chest, was a red-sodden cloth laid out with numerous and varied saws, scalpels, dressings, splints, gags, retractors and other surgical accoutrements, the steel instruments all bloodied. Plentiful more blood saturated the unfortunate casualty's lower clothing, much of which had been cut away and hung in red rags. He was conscious and gulping down the proffered rum, between the swallows of which his face was contorted into agony, and from his lips escaped constant gasps of pain, the patient valiantly striving but failing to suppress his screams when he moved the merest fraction. The surgeons, striving to ignore the aural barrage all about them, had determined there was no frothing, no evidence of blood at the mouth; they hoped and prayed that there was no wound to the lungs. The air stank; the malodorous stench was hugely oppressive; the temperature was in the eighties and the humidity was such that the clothes of everyone present, whether working or wounded, were sticky and sodden through and through with sweat, those of the surgeons streaked and soaked with copious blood. The deck was strewn with foul swabs, was slippery with much more blood; not that Simon gave it any mind, preoccupied as he was within the exposed lower body of his patient. A large incision swiftly made, the skin was cut away and peeled back below the ribs on the right side of the man's body to gain sight of the area of liver where the penetration had occurred. A grapeshot or splinter, Simon could not yet determine which it was, had penetrated the liver or severed a vessel attaching to it. At the side of the operating table, Freeman held a candle low, just above the wound, to improve the poor light. Simon peered intently, Jason constantly swabbing away the blood. 'Thankfully the wound is below the lung, which is spared,' Simon murmured. All about them lay more men, wounded or dying; from many of whom in the greatest of distress poured forth sharp shouts of pain, shrill wails of anguish and loud cries of supplication.

Simon wiped the sweat dripping from his brow with a bloody hand, a red smear instantly streaming across his forehead. He stared intently at his patient's gashed lower chest, only dimly illuminated by the weak light of the lantern hanging to the side which was augmented by two brighter candles, closely held by Freeman, an acrid burning smell never far from his nostrils. He ignored the tickling irritation and looked to his assistant, the merest nod offered, and he began: the knife cutting swift incisions, the flesh folded back, the forceps wielded by Jason with infinite caution, a gentle pressure to hold the artery aside as Simon's probe inched delicately in search of the invader, his hand instantly withdrawn a fraction as the booming, reverberating thuds came thick and fast, the hull struck by smashing shot strikes, dust falling all about them.

'You, sir!' shouted Simon, exasperated, to a man leaning back nearby against the hull side, bawling for assistance. 'Desist, be quiet. You have a broken rib or two, no more, and plentiful others, a score at least of sound ones; whilst here are men with greater difficulties. Have a care for your shipmates and be silent.' The shouting ceased. Remarkably, the immediate patient at hand, Hammett, was conscious. He had drunk the half-pint of rum provided to him, and the gag was tied within his mouth. Simon, leaning over the table, his back arched, his head a few inches above the wound, peered intently in the flickering light, the close candle wobbling in Freeman's hand as the ship rocked on the swell, the boom of the guns above and the reverberations of shot strikes all about a persistent backcloth. He worked on for fifteen intense minutes, offering the odd word of support to Hammett who was in considerable pain but listening. 'Hammett, when we are finished here today I venture you may be excused your customary duties for some weeks to come... and you will be a man of leisure; what do you say to that, eh? No, no, say nothing; I beg your pardon. I see the strap will present you with some difficulty there. What a card I am today, eh? Hah hah!' Hammett gasped and groaned in reply. Simon worked on grimly, his eyes never wavering from the wound, probing as gently he might in the damaged area. The copious blood obscured his view, making his task extremely difficult. His hands paused for the briefest of moments as another ball smashed into the hull. Hammett wriggled and gasped in great pain, prompting Simon to pause. 'I beg you to hold firm, Hammett; two inches of steel slipping the merest trifle will do you great ill, and I am struggling with the violence of movement that this accursed vessel inflicts upon us both.' Hammett gasped and nodded his understanding. 'Hold firm, take courage; I will not be long.' Hammet could offer no further corroboration of his understanding or his courage, the struggle was proving to be beyond what final vestiges of strength were left to him and he lay back quite still.

'I am minded we have little time here, Jason; hold back the flesh... there, more, pull... a small splinter. I see it now, an infernal piece of oak no doubt. Thank God, I believe the blood vessels may remain intact; Freeman, the fine pincers, quickly... Jason, hold firm... a moment more; I have it... there; it is out as best can be. Quickly now, the needle, Jason, the needle; thank you... let go the skin now; wipe away; plentiful vinegar if you will; I can see nothing; Freeman, the candle, the cloth; wipe if you will... hold,' five anxious minutes and Simon murmuring his directions until, 'hold... another half dozen ligatures may serve.' Ten more feverish minutes, sweat dripping from Simon's brow to the cloth above the wound and the desperate urgency of the operation receding, Simon breathed more easily. More to himself than to his patient, he spoke with some little relief in his voice, 'Hammett you may be grateful she is an oak ship, blessed English oak... and not teak as are her Bombay sisters... when the accursed infection is sure to set in.' But Hammett had long since passed out. It was another minute before Simon spoke again, 'Jason, the lint... you may bind around the wound.' Whilst Jason applied the bandage, Simon felt Hammett's pulse, all the time staring intently at the face of his patient. 'His pulse is steady and thankfully he does not exhibit the pallor. I have hopes that he may endure... if he escapes the accursed shock.' He stepped away from the table and passed his hand over his forehead, irritated by the burning sensation to which he could give no mind whilst holding his instruments. 'By God, I have singed away my eyebrow.'

'Make way! Make a path there!' loud shouts from a pair of men carrying in great haste a severely wounded man. They were rushing towards the surgeons, all care for anyone along the way discarded, even giving little of attention to their burden, speed being the sole consideration, the wounded man unconscious and in a dire state, nothing of his face free from blood, his hair matted in it, the loss very great judging by his red-sodden shirt. The bearers halted, their despairing rush over, and the patient was delicately hoisted with the utmost care to the makeshift table by the immediate surgeons' aides taking over the task. It was a grisly and appalling sight: brain pulp smeared all over the head, not the least vestige of a recognisable face visible through the gore and blood.

In an instant, Simon's spirits sank to new depths as he stared in horror at an obviously inoperable head wound, not the least prospect for saving the wounded man. The back of the skull had been impacted by grape and a quarter at least of the brain swept away in the strike, the patient still breathing but mercifully unconscious. In the bleak seconds of scrutiny and distressing diagnosis bitter despair surged through the surgeon, quashing every other sentiment with the realisation of how helpless he was to offer the slightest of care. The wound was catastrophic. How the patient had lived even until now was a miracle. Simon's stomach turned, choking bile rising within his throat, speech far beyond his gift in the distressing realisation of a hopeless prognosis. He swallowed hard, looked to his helpers, his face a picture of bleak despair; he looked away from the casualty, tore his eyes away to look down, to the deck - anywhere, anywhere else at all - struggling hard to hold his distress and his tears at bay; he closed his eyes and simply shook his head.

Chapter Five

A half-mile to the south of the Turk line, in a peaceful oasis away from the battle, Pat ordered the mizzen yard backed, and *Surprise* quickly hove to; the lines were hauled in and the rescued Greeks were taken aboard. On the quarterdeck with Duncan, Pat gazed all around them: to the north, Khosref's Turk line, still progressing south-east, was engaged with Apostoli's Spezziots and fighting too against the Psariots and Miaoulis's Second Hydriot squadron; to the south, the Egyptians, the van of their line deep within the Gulf of Gerontas, were firing on the First Hydriot squadron under Sakhtouri, his ships a bare two miles off the southern shores of the Gulf.

'Will ye look there, sir; a brace more of fireships,' Duncan pointed to the north-east. The Greeks were striving to manoeuvre their smaller warships to maximum advantage whilst preparing to send their fireships at any likely targets. The still relatively weak wind made any approach for the fireship crews highly dangerous, for the Turks had plenty of time to aim and fire their guns at the slow *bourlotas*, and evacuation from the blazing fireships in small boats was hazardous indeed.

'Admiral Miaoulis has chosen well his position, I venture,' observed Pat, gazing through his glass at the Hydriot pennant flying atop *Kimon,* the admiral's brig escorting the fireships, all sailing due south and directly into the Turk host. 'The wind is veering further, Mr Macleod; I sense it is becoming easterly. That man is the tactician of the world, so he is,' Pat marvelled at the Greek commander. 'The Turk has been beset by wind against him all this day.'

'Aye, sir, I will agree with ye there. I will endeavour too to suggest Miaoulis has also had the help of the frigate captain of all the world.' Duncan grinned and licked away the resumed blood flow around his lips, wiping his cheek with his sleeve. 'I do believe Khosref widnae have turned away, would likely have sailed straight on to Samos, had ye not shot down his fore topmast.' Heads all about the wheel nodded, not a man in any doubt of the veracity of Duncan's statement.

'Thank you, Mr Macleod,' said Pat, a grim smile on his face, 'but enough of this banter. On, on; south, south we will go. We too must profit by this wind. Let us strive in our path to aid Sakhtouri. We will see if we can get ahead before Khosref makes his turn, for he cannot linger in the Gulf, the easterly wind against him now. For now, for a brief moment, I will go below to see how our surgeons... and the wounded are faring.' Summoning all the fortitude he could find, Pat stepped down the companionway to the gun deck, nervous anxiety rising within, his mind racing, nerves a'flutter in the pit of his stomach. He offered an encouraging smile and a nod to the crew of *Hell's Mouth* as he passed by, stepping with some trepidation down to the lower deck. He paced slowly forward, his eyes registering the bloody trails just visible in the gloom and his ears assailed by pitiful groans and gasps of pain from men lying on the deck. He halted short of the surgeon's bench, staring in assessment and steeling himself for any particular calamities that Simon and Jason might reveal.

'Here, drink down this draught; in one now, take it all down and presently the pain will recede,' said Simon to Penrose whose broken arm was being strapped about the splint by Jason. 'Now, Penrose, there is no further task for you to do this day; you will sit and rest. There is nothing more beneficial than sleep for you now, if you can find it.' Penrose nodded gratefully, his pain evident in his grimace as he was helped to stand and assisted to a low slung hammock, two men helping to ease him into it. 'Gently there, have a care with that arm,' said Simon to his helpers, his eyes not leaving his patient, one more successfully treated, to his considerable relief. 'Freeman, you may kick that rat,' Simon shouted; the rodent, forced out of the hold by the rising bilge water, had seized on a large fragment of flesh on the deck which had escaped the bloody bucket; a half-dozen of its fellows scuttled about in the shadows. A score of casualties lay all about the surgeons, the most severely wounded in an opium-induced comatose state; others were hovering on the edge of unconsciousness or simply sleeping the sleep of shock-induced exhaustion from loss of blood or concussion. Subdued groans and quiet exclamations of pain came intermittently from the distressed men. Swathes of bloodied bandage dressings covered heads and were wrapped around chests, arms and legs. Of one man's head only a nose and a mouth were visible. It presented a most alarming and distressing picture for Pat, but thankfully the frantic earlier hour was over, the manic desperation of it in the past, the most severely wounded patients stabilised, blood loss halted and the excruciating pain of the worst of the casualties diminished. It was a great tribute to the surgeons: Simon with Jason in support. Both were now looking all about them, as if awaiting the next casualty. That their long-awaited short moment of respite had come was dawning upon them. Pat, his attention shifting from the wounded, stared at them both. Their hair was soaked and dripping with sweat which ran across their faces, down their necks; their blood-spattered shirts were similarly sodden. The odour, heat and humidity in the lower deck was suddenly overpowering to Pat, no draught of fresh air at all in the gloom. The darkness was relieved to only a limited degree by the hanging Argand lamps, casting their weak light. One hung low above the surgeon's table which was also illuminated by the remaining stumps of near-finished smouldering candles. A nauseating stench of blood and vomit permeated the air. Overlaying those abhorrent smells in the excruciating heat and stifling clamminess was the distinct smell of fear: the fear of men who still awaited the surgeon's knife or who wondered, deep in their hearts, whether they might reasonably expect to survive, or whether death, thoughts of which were always put firmly out of mind, was now in close prospect. The heat was overpowering, the air thick, dust and smoke lingering, swirling in the poor illumination of the lamps. The candles and lanterns consumed the oxygen, leaving the air foul, rank; everywhere men coughed and spat. A little way from the surgeon's makeshift bench were a half dozen buckets: in one was an arm, in another a lower leg; a mass of dark, bloodied flesh lay puddled in a third with what looked like a liver, and beside it a foot, or something resembling a foot, for it was crushed and near unrecognisable as such. It was as much as Pat could do not to vomit, and his hand came involuntarily to cover his mouth as he felt the unpleasant gagging sensation. He swallowed hard to choke back the muscular rebellion and stared at Simon: the surgeon's eyes were red hollows ringed with black candle smoke, both his eyebrows singed from the proximity of the candles as he had operated; he was wiping his arms on a bloodied towel. 'Is there any help I can offer you?' asked a dismayed Pat tentatively. 'Anything at all... the least thing?'

'Oh for a hot bath,' murmured Simon vacantly; he sighed deeply, 'with warm towels... oh for a warm towel... *we can but dream,* eh?' The surgeon appeared to pull his thoughts together, to emerge from a semblance of something indefinable, some hiatus resembling a daydream, a complete preoccupation with other thoughts. 'I would give my soul for hot coffee. Might there be a prospect of such, for Jason and I, Pat, for all love?'

'I will send Murphy, directly... with not a moment lost,' whispered Pat, horrified at what he had seen and grateful for the excuse to leave the scene. Without further ado he seized and shook Simon's bloodied hand; he hastened away, not looking either back or down to the human bundles of distress heaped the length of the lower deck.

In the backwater of their temporal and spatial oasis amongst the all-surrounding battle, the men of *Surprise* discussed their situation: being surrounded on all sides by Turks and Egyptians, their allies the Greeks outwith the enemy ring of guns all about them, and they speculated about what the afternoon would bring. BOOM... BOOM... time after time the distant firing of great guns persisted without let up. A half-mile to the north, it was plain that the Turks had avoided the two Hydriot fireships, for such had passed by and disappeared into the smoke; their attack had seemingly failed.

Some of Miaoulis's brigs were following the disappearing fireships, south-west bound. In that direction the vast clouds of gunsmoke, slow to clear, made for great difficulty in seeing let alone understanding the general situation. To the south of

Surprise, that Sakhtouri's Hydriots must be hard pressed no one had any doubt at all, for the Egyptians had been trained by the French and so were reckoned to be better sailors than the Turks.

The cook having doused the galley fire during the frantic activity of the battle, the men's dinner was simply bread with Greek cheese, served with their wine. Every man stayed at his gun and the boys served out the plain but welcome food all about the ship. It was the shortest of respite, *Surprise* closing inexorably on the whirling mix that was the Egyptians mingled with the Hydriots, the nearest ship still a mile to the south. Dalby rang four bells. *Surprise* was sailing large, reefs let out of her courses and stuns'ls boomed out; on she pressed, her direction south-west, sailing in and out of great swathes of gunsmoke, bilious great clouds of it laying on the water, until she neared the furious southern mass of the battle. From all directions thundered hundreds of guns, the sounds eerily reverberating around the great bay of Gerontas. Smoke obscured most and occasionally all of the conflict. Emerging from one particularly dense and drifting bank of it, Pat looked all about in every direction: three-quarters of a mile off the larboard quarter a frigate was flying the pennant of an admiral, her course westerly, converging with *Surprise*, her colours unfamiliar. Duncan suggested, with a rather less than convincing declaration, that she might be a Tunisian. She was sailing directly towards two Hydriots, as was *Surprise*, and both the enemy's bow guns were already firing at the Greeks. The appearance of *Surprise* out of the smoke bank must have presented the most unwelcome shock to the Tunisian captain and his crew, the confrontation with *Surprise* immediately thrust upon them. It was most certainly also an unexpected encounter for Pat and his men, *Surprise* already mauled by two engagements. The south-westerly direction of the Tunisian suggested that the Egyptian fleet had already turned about, the easterly wind against them, and that they were now sailing west, the fundamental change of their course presenting a perilous armada to port, to starboard and also astern of *Surprise*.

A half-mile in the wake of the Tunisian admiral and to the east, the Tunisian's own squadron, a brig and another frigate, were firing at four harrying Hydriot vessels; they were armed brigantine-rigged merchantmen, the mainstay of the Greek fleet. The older two had seen better days, that was obvious to any onlooker: their sails were worn and patched, their hulls lacking in care and attention, and it was plain that they were prepared as fireships, but they had seemingly missed their chance.

'FIRE!' shouted Codrington and Pickering. *Surprise* and the Tunisian opened fire on each other in the same instant, the range closed to less than half a mile. *Surprise's* entire larboard broadside exploded in a single thunderous detonation that shook the ship violently from stem to stern, deafening again every man on deck. Frantically the men worked to reload until, after a bare minute and a half, the ear-splitting, stunning crescendo of noise that was the simultaneous discharge of every long gun on the deck was repeated, the barrage overwhelming the ears once more. Every gun crew toiled manically to reload and fire as fast as they could, the uniformity of the opening broadside within mere minutes dissolving into constant repeated roaring from the guns, the air filled with smoke, with swirling gunpowder particles, the sun's light quite dimmed through the murk, bright red-orange flames shooting from *Surprise's* guns flashing through it. CRASH! THUD! The Tunisian's violent ball strikes on the hull were loud, reverberating; the thunderous roar of her guns reached the ears a second after the strikes; a hail of sharp splinters flew all about the gun deck, three more men knocked down. From the main and mizzen tops the men were firing their muskets, more in anger than in hope, for the distance was a little too far for assured success.

A minute passed, the two combatants closing inexorably to a bare cable of separation and the Tunisian frigate coming within the range of the carronades. Pat, in huge anxiety, alarm ringing loud in his head, for he had not planned on any close engagement, turned towards his gunners about the quarterdeck, all of whom were staring at him and awaiting his order. 'FIRE!' he screamed. Now the sharper crack of the carronades could be heard above the lower roar of the long guns. Orange flames jetted out all along *Surprise's* larboard side, the air filling again with stinking white smoke clouds, visibility difficult but not so bad that the Surprises could not see their shots strike home, the distance so short; the enemy mizzen gaff was smashed away from its mast, its sail tumbling down on the aftermost part of the quarterdeck; her fore topsail was torn in several places; a jib was ripped away from its tie to the bowsprit and flapped listlessly as it hung down from the foremast; certainly a great nuisance for the gunners below it. All along the gun deck the Surprises' cheers rang out, every man delighted with the obvious success of their gunnery.

Closer still, the two frigates approached each other, the Tunisian nearing *Surprise's* beam and no more than three hundred yards of separation; the firing of both ships was constant, the ball strikes of the two frigates near instantly heard and felt after the detonation of the powder, readily apparent to both crews: the gap become ever smaller, the combatants so close together that even the poorest of gunners could not miss. Huge white splashes appeared constantly from balls striking the water as the Tunisian gunners fired on the roll, some ricocheting upwards to strike *Surprise's* hull; 18-pound balls smashed away long splinters; several shots penetrated through *Surprise's* thick timbers just above the waterline; others struck gun ports and bulwarks, sending scores of jagged fragments flying through the air, killing and wounding many more men as they were toiling at their guns; *Hell's Mouth* and *Bill Stevens* fell silent, their injured crews incapable of more. One gun captain sat back in shock against the hull side clutching his chest which had been torn open, leaving bloody ribs exposed; another sitting man pressed his hand over a leg artery spurting blood; a third could not sit at all but lay on his side, a huge splinter projecting through his buttock. The gun captain of *Damnation* lay quite still, prone on the deck, bleeding, unconscious; another man's gaze was fixated on the stump of his own leg, a red stream flowing over the deck; a gunner, both arms broken and quite incapable of rising from his misery, sat staring all about him in agony and despair. Two of the crew of *Heaven's Gate* had been hurled over the side, a ball strike on their gun breaking the barrel off its truck and flinging the gun round, knocking all its crew away in every direction, the unfortunate two in their daze encountering nothing to keep them aboard, the hull either side of the gun port long smashed by prior strikes and much of it broken away. Robert and George Collins, Falmouth brothers and *Tempest* gunners, sat back against the cold galley holding hands: Robert with both knees broken and George with a large splinter through his upper arm. Their gun captain, Bill Jenner, lay near their feet with a fractured skull, unconscious within a pool of blood. Pickering and Codrington hastened up and down the deck, hauling an injured man aside from his gun, substituting another man, shouting, screaming orders with greater intensity.

In the relative quiet of the cockpit below the waterline, Simon and Jason, hugely overwhelmed by the renewed flow of incoming casualties, toiled desperately, frenetically, their burden frightening in both its bloody gore and the magnitude of the numbers wounded. They heard the constant boom of the guns and felt the deep thuds as heavy balls struck home on the hull, the jarring reverberations oft precipitating the hasty withdrawal of the knife as the lanterns were jolted, their weak light flickering, showers of dust falling after every strike. Simon, desperately fatigued, too long standing over the unceasing stream of his patients, one after another with never a break before the next man was before him, could feel the stream of sweat pouring down his back, over his face, running down his chest, his shirt sodden and everywhere sticking to his skin. He had sensed his strength ebbing for the past hour and now his legs were beginning to tremble. Thankfully that had not overtaken his arms, hands and fingers, at least not yet, but he wondered how much longer he could persevere before it would. 'Jason, be so good as to take the arm, if you will; it is about to come off... just one further cut to severe the tendon here... there, it is done.' The patient, biting down hard on the stick tied between his teeth, passed clean out. 'Freeman, please to remove and empty the bucket.'

The surgeons could not keep up with the already waiting casualties and yet more were brought below, a constant rush of shouts from the men carrying them, agonised screams from the stricken, wounded men, in great pain and frightened; more and more victims coming, until it seemed that all the lower deck was filled with the unfortunates; yet the firing continued, unceasing, and Simon knew that he was desperately tired. All about him lay men in their agonies, in their blood and in their soil: unwashed, stinking; some calling for water, others shouting, pleading for help. The air was hot, foul, malodorous with the smell of fear, of sweat; the vile stench was overwhelming, the straw laid to mop the blood and other wastes a sodden pulp underfoot. The difficulties Simon faced were exacerbated by his frayed nerves, and his dry thirst taxed him hard, but there was not a moment to pause, to take the most minimal of refreshment; with determination he called upon his last reserves of strength - physical and mental - and pressed on in silence save for an occasional grunt of instruction to his helpers, a mute nod to signify to them to lift the next patient to his makeshift table, and an ashen shake of his head when a man expired; the death of each one directly before his eyes sending a huge burst of despair surging through his very being, the copious sweat flowing all over his face merging in the last hour with an unceasing stream of tears as his fortitude crumbled, seeing shipmates he had known for many years dying before his eyes, his attention - miraculously - still holding up and his every thought dedicated to each successive sufferer in their agonies under his knife, striving, praying that he might save each man in turn.

'I cannot do anything for this man,' declared Simon with a sigh of infinite regret, his voice hardly more than a whisper, staring hard at the corpse lifted on to his table, an ear straining for a heartbeat yielding nothing: one or more projectiles had torn bodily through the lungs of the unfortunate. 'He is gone beyond my care, God rest his soul.' Simon stood for long seconds, immobile, as if willing life to return, a huge flush of sorrow and angst gushing through his breast as he relinquished the wrist that he had been holding in desperate but futile search of a pulse. He coughed, spat into the bloody bucket, stretched out, wiped his eyes and face with that part of his apron that was not so much bloodied, picked up the bloody crowbill, and he bent again to his grim task, the next man already on the table amidst the spreading pool of blood.

A strong gust of wind and the smoke surrounding the two frigates cleared, drifting away to the south in a rising, blowing cloud and revealing to both captains the general situation: the Tunisian had closed to a bare two hundred yards to leeward of *Surprise*; she was abeam and the two ships were fast converging. Pat's heartbeat pounded loud in his head, twice the speed of usual, panic near upon him. 'What to do?'

The smoke from the next discharges again filled the gap between the two frigates, so dense that hardly anything could be seen for nerve-wracking minutes, the burnt white particles eddying in the weak wind across *Surprise's* decks, gunners the length of the ship coughing and spitting. From the tops, the musketeers continued to peer over and into the murk, striving for a glimpse of the enemy deck before firing; so close now that in the momentary gaps as the gunsmoke shifted and cleared they could plainly see the officers on the enemy quarterdeck, and that was where they directed their firing, the musket accurate at one hundred yards.

The Tunisian suddenly put her helm down and hauled round to starboard, to windward, beginning her slow turn, her men hauling on her braces to adjust her yards, her sails now shivering as she slowed, striving as if to pass behind *Surprise*'s stern and so to rake her. Though the rate of firing was brisk, both ships hammering the other hard, the movement of both ships was slow, allowing Pat time to consider his tactics. He needed none; at once he decided he would turn south in order that *Surprise* could fire her own broadside in reply and then shift away in the opposite direction, but the opposing manoeuvres would first rapidly hasten their convergence and only then bring about a hasty divergence. If such could be achieved, Pat recognised it as the only prospect of salvation; for at this late stage in the day, he knew his ship could not endure much longer, her men exhausted, her powder low. He would have time enough to fire her larboard battery twice unless she turned again. He would then seek to continue *Surprise's* turn and cross the Tunisian's stern, if *Surprise* did not again lose any of her sails and be knocked about first. Nearer, nearer, on came the Tunisian; she was a paltry hundred yards off *Surprise's* larboard quarter. The quarterdeck carronades fired, the erupting roar of the flame, the proximity and immediacy of the violence and noise of the barrels smashing back in their slides and the explosion of filthy, choking smoke exacerbating Pat's rising sense of alarm, loud bells of such ringing in his mind, his shouted words to Duncan a spoken amalgam of vigorous and concurrent thoughts, 'For sure the iron is hot and we are in the fire here!'

Captain Zouvelekis, the Greek liaison officer, standing on the quarterdeck near Pat, a most polite individual and usually a man who spoke little, suddenly seized Pat's arm and shouted manically and unintelligibly in Greek, a shrill scream of 'BOURLOTAS! BOURLOTAS!' In the face of Pat's uncomprehending stare the Greek waved his arm and pointed in the opposite direction, away from the Tunisian frigate which had wholly occupied the unwavering attention of all aboard *Surprise* to that moment; he shouted again with all his voice, 'FIRESHIPS! FIRESHIPS!'

Pat whirled round, horrified, 'Oh my dear God!'

In that instant came the fright of their lives for every man looking about on both ships: the two fireships from the northern battle had emerged out of the great swathes of white smoke. One was astern of *Surprise* and fine off the starboard bow of the closing Tunisian frigate, the distance between them no more than a hundred yards; the second was approaching *Surprise* herself, off her own starboard bow. Both the *bourlotas* were fiercely ablaze on their decks, the bright flames amidships spreading forward towards the bow and beginning to creep aloft on the masts. It was a sensational shock, both to the Surprises and to the Tunisians. Most of the fireship crews had taken to their boats, in short tow behind them; the few souls still visible aboard were a dozen men standing ready and holding firm to haul on the braces plus the helmsmen, four men on each and all striving valiantly to turn their charges a little more to the south-east, towards the Tunisian. The nearest of the burning hulks was closing quickly to the fore of *Surprise*, the Greek helmsmen frantically striving to turn away, desperately hauling down on her wheel. Pat abandoned his intended course change, to leeward, in less than a second and with all his voice screamed, 'Put the helm down, hard a lee!' and Prosser with his panic-stricken helmsmen heaved at the wheel with all their might. The nearest fireship had come closer and was a mere thirty yards before the bow, the other one was still astern, no danger to *Surprise* and fifty yards off her starboard quarter; the close proximity of the first was such that the crackling sound of the fires aboard her was plainly audible. The ongoing barrage between the frigates diminished as every gunner on both ships felt the immediate hard rudder, for the Tunisian had sharpened her own turn and was now bearing north. Every gunner on both frigates within minutes saw his target shifting to near beyond the limit within which he could swivel his gun.

'Hands to the braces!' shouted Duncan, though not a man heard a word of it, the roaring tumult of firing unceasing, overwhelming.

The tensest, the most frightening two minutes Pat could ever recall in his life and *Surprise* passed a bare ten yards astern of the nearest fireship. Those Surprises at the bow would later swear *Surprise's* bowsprit had passed over the Greek's stern. Pat coughed and spat: the pungent hot tar smell of the fire smoke was strong and quite distinct from that of the discharge of the guns. He gazed with infinite respect at the helmsmen on the fireship who were still struggling at the wheel. He raised his hat in salute, staring, struck dumb by the bravery of the Hydriots: near alone, masts and yards all above them alight with dancing, flickering flames; the last remaining men of her crew bravely struggling even now to reverse her helm and turn their vessel back towards the Tunisian frigate; a dozen more men were hauling hard, pulling desperately on the fireship's braces.

'Hands to the braces!' Duncan tried again, for the firing had largely ceased, the thunderous barrage suspended as both frigates were beyond the arc of swivel of each other's guns save for the light stern chasers, and no one gave them any mind.

The Tunisian admiral was a very frightened man: that fireship astern of *Surprise* remained fine on his own larboard bow, perhaps no more than forty yards ahead and fast converging. He kept his helm hard down, continuing his turn;

north-east the only choice open to him to avoid the fast-closing, blazing Greek furnace, whilst the second *bourlota* was perhaps sixty yards off his larboard quarter, *Surprise* between the two and still a great danger. He could do nothing more to get away from the floating, flaming fireballs. His turn continued as an anxious further sixty seconds went by, becoming sharper, tighter, the gap opening from the more westerly fireship which was herself turning, her course a point south of east but safely left behind and representing no immediate danger to the Tunisian; but then, his helmsmen awaiting orders from their still shocked officers, the frigate came up a little more east and she slowed as her bow came closer into the wind. The ship was moving only very slowly, the weather leeches of her sails beginning to flutter, shiver and shake as she found herself all in the wind; her way fell off rapidly until... disaster... the ship was in irons, without motion and the helm unresponsive. The nearer fireship was closing rapidly and the Tunisian could do nothing more. Her crew gazed in horror at the approaching catastrophe, a fireball roaring and spitting its burning venom from exploding tar barrels. Twenty-five yards, fifteen... she came alongside with a thundering, jarring CRASH! The masts of the *bourlota* were well aflame, much of her sails blackened with great burnt-out holes in the canvas; flames were burning all about the ends of the yards, leaping from ship to ship. The Tunisian's gunners were horrified, had long ceased firing; all aboard were anxiously looking to the falling, burning spar and sail fragments, in great fear lest they set alight the pitch of the frigate's deck.

In the meantime, Pat had ordered *Surprise* to turn back on her track, and she had worn south to sail east, closing towards the distressed Tunisian frigate and the fireships, all of which now lay a cable and a half ahead of her bow. Far beyond them the followers of the Tunisian squadron were engaged with the pursuing Hydriot brigs. As *Surprise* closed once more with the Tunisian every eye on deck was fixated on the action of the fireships, for nothing like it had they ever seen before. The second fireship had taken advantage of the frigate being stopped, floundering in irons, and with a long south-easterly tack had come about and was returning on a north-westerly one - how her crew had managed it was a miracle, their ship subsumed in many and varied fires. Despite roaring flame all about her she closed on the Tunisian, whose firing had much diminished. Closer, closer, on came the second Greek fireship until, her motive power failing as her sails flamed and crisped, she too came alongside. Her own deck was covered in exploding, dancing flames, violent fire surging up her masts, her sails alight, flames roaring and dancing along all her yards, sparks setting aflame the canvas of the Tunisian.

'I venture she is done for,' whispered Pat, in awe at the roaring, raging inferno that was the entanglement of the fireships with the frigate, all firing by the Tunisian ceasing. Scores of *Surprise's* crew stood all along her side, watching in something akin to shock; the barky was slowing, her yards no longer best braced, her sails near slack, her men staring in anticipatory horror at the rising conflagration of the fireships and the Tunisian.

Surprise drifted closer, hove-to; she was little more than a cable away from the burning frigate, and even at that distance the crackling of the savage fires covering the Greek fireships and spreading from aloft to engulf the frigate's yards and sails could be heard. In only minutes, it seemed - every Surprise shocked and spellbound - the Tunisian was wholly ablaze. Many of her crew were leaping from her deck into the water, others were trying to launch her boat at the stern; the two fireships both alongside were preventing her remaining boats being lowered from amidships. The Surprises gazed, awestruck and in horror, for fire at sea was the nightmare of every mariner. The frigate's sails were blackening, ever larger holes becoming apparent; her canvas was shrivelling and crisping; the fire was raging atop every mast and yard, melting pitch sparked and blazed all over her decks; even the clothes of several of the men leaping in panic into the sea were also aflame, the scene one of unmitigated horror to every onlooker.

'Do ye care to shift away, sir?' asked Duncan. 'When the fire reaches her magazine...'

The Greek fireships' crews were pulling as hard as they could in their boats and with all their might to escape the conflagration a mere hundred and fifty yards behind them, rowing frantically towards *Surprise*. The Surprises were all lining her deck, shouting at the Greeks, exhorting them to pull harder, faster. Closer they came, a hundred yards, fifty, the Surprises passionately urging them on. 'PULL, PULL!' dozens of men shrieked wildly in their fervour to see the Greeks row further from the burning wrecks before they exploded, for such an end was sure; the *bourlotas* were all primed with several powder trails to their well stocked magazines.

'When she explodes...' Duncan persisted.

Pat had since five minutes determined that the Greeks, the bravest men he had ever encountered, would be rescued from the water. The Surprises had quickly slackened the main topsail sheets, slowing her to a near stop, the frigate only drifting; lines were cast out to the two Greek boats as they neared alongside, the blaze just a cable and a half away. The guns of the Tunisian were cooking off and exploding their remaining loaded charges at random; all of her crew had leaped overboard in their haste and panic.

'Mr Macleod, take those men aboard directly and send them below; a pint of wine for every man.'

The grateful Hydriots were hauled aboard, slowly and with great difficulty, every man exhausted and unable to speak more than a brief and unintelligible word; their boats were tied astern, and men everywhere hastened once more to haul on the braces and tie the sheets until *Surprise* picked up the slowest of way once more, to the south again, her speed little more than a crawl from the burning conflagration. On her quarterdeck, *Surprise's* officers, every one of them, stared astern as the gap opened; a desperate minute passing, only two cables of separation achieved, no more; another anxious minute and the gap had become three cables, but then came the cataclysmic, ear-shattering, vast explosion as the powder within the Tunisian frigate's magazine detonated. The ship vanished in a blinding bright flash, followed instantly by a deafening enormity of painful pressure, a physical slam of violent sound: thunderous, assailing the ears in an instant and bringing pain to many; a billowing black cloud enveloped the scene in moments, the light all about darkening, all sight of the frigate gone.

'OH MY GOD!,' shrieked Tom Pickering, standing near the helm, 'Every man jack, hundreds of them, all gone in an instant.'

Surprise heeled alarmingly; her sails filled and, some would later swear, stretched before recoiling, the braces and sheets under the most violent of tension; the ship heeled instantly and violently with the dense air surge; flying fragments and splinters, heads and plentiful limbs, even whole bodies all passed overhead; detritus of all forms smashed against her hull and rigging, much of which was indeterminate plunging from the sky on to the deck and splashing into the water all about them, and then she righted, whipping back with the blast wave passed by, every man grasping for something of support in the extreme roll. The shock endured and utter silence reigned for several minutes until eyes blinded by the fierce light of the explosion readjusted to lesser light.

'South west, Mr Macleod; we will make for the passage 'tween Leros and Calymnos; that is our course,' shouted Pat.

'Aye aye, sir; Mr Prosser, put her helm up,' Duncan shouted, 'Mr Pickering, hands to the braces, south-west it is.'

Pat, the shock of the almighty obliteration easing a very little and relief flooding through his every fibre, swiftly determined his intentions, 'We will not linger in this place. Khosref and all his fleet must turn back, turn south with the wind so. I venture it is too late in the day for him to press on to Samos, and I would not care to remain across his track.'

'Aye, I venture there isnae any reason to linger; our day is done, nae doubt of that,' said Duncan with unmitigated relief.

Within minutes *Surprise* came round to her new course, gaining speed, pushed by the *Meltemi* which was veering north-easterly and remaining very favourable to those Greeks engaged still within the Gulf, although the noise of gunfire was generally more subdued than at its former peak. To the north-east of *Surprise* the battle in lesser form still raged, but a steady flow of the smaller of the Turk vessels, corvettes and the like, now passed ahead and astern of her; all were heading south, departing the day, no party wishing to approach too closely or engage with any other. Pat was extremely anxious to shift away from any potential adversaries, *Surprise* being so greatly damaged, her speed so much reduced. He was standing at the taffrail staring all about him through his glass, scouring all points of the compass for any conceivable convergence of enemy ships, indeed any ships at all until, a half-hour gone, the welcome sense of the violent day approaching its blessed end began to settle upon him; he felt a much needed release of the acute tension he had endured all day, allowing him to begin to unwind, not to say relax; for such was very far from his mindset, still a turmoil of thinking, precautions, necessary vigilance. He was, so soon after the engagement, somewhat surprised and taken aback to see Simon emerge from the companionway and stumble on to the quarterdeck. Pat stared, shocked: Simon's vestments were soaked in blood; his shirt, his breeches, his apron all daubed with dried rusty-red patches and wet with brighter red streaks over all his clothing. The surgeon, so obviously exhausted, his face white and bloodied, stood stock still for some moments; the tension within him was very evident to the observer. His head bowed, he sucked in deep draughts of the fresh salt air and then stumbled hesitantly aft to stand next to Pat, his fatigue and discomfort readily apparent to every man about the deck, all staring at him.

'You look uncommonly fagged,' offered Pat, not unkindly, Simon visibly palpitating. The surgeon turned and stepped away in haste and leaned over the rail, obviously in great distress; the helmsmen were looking back, staring at him; and then he vomited, his throat wracked by wave after wave of coughing. Barton, witnessing his misery, arrived in haste and pressed upon him a flask of weak wine. It was one which was kept at the wheel for the helmsmen in times of hot weather. Simon gratefully drank great gulps. Pat and all the helmsmen looked on with infinite concern and waited patiently for him to recover his composure and speak.

'Thank you kindly, Barton,' gasped Simon, returning the flask, his hand shaking. He turned and stared at Pat, his whole body trembling, his eyes wild, his words faltering, 'I do not remember... to have experienced... such a day ever before. I have

113

seen... I have seen... horror upon bloody horror... downstairs. I cannot collect ever... ever... feeling so overwhelmed... crushed. I am at a stand.'

A shocked silence registered upon all in earshot, the men at the helm staring in disbelief, and Pat simply nodded, wondering how best to respond: never before had Simon appeared on deck whilst there were surely still casualties to treat below.

'How is it... below?' said Pat tentatively to his friend with nervous hesitation.

'There remains much to do... and Jason, precious rock that he is, remains with the wounded. Freeman is there too... and he will not leave them. However, Pat... I can endure no longer... my knife in a shaking hand is a danger to my patients.'

Pat placed his hand on Simon's upper arm. 'No, I should certainly never accord with that,' he said gently but emphatically. 'Simon, the battle is over and the black dog is with us all, with every man aboard. That is ever the case.'

Simon stared into infinity, striving to gather his composure, his anxiety such that his voice trembled, 'I am sorely vexed... I strived so... I did... for all of those men... but so many poor souls have died... died under my knife this day.'

'Simon, dear friend,' Pat's words were softly spoken, his tone of voice unshakeable in his conviction, 'No one could have done more for those men, of that I have not the slightest of doubt.'

Simon found tears welling up in his eyes once again; he blinked hard, frantically, as if such might dispel them, but despite his efforts they streamed in a copious salt flow all down his cheeks. He found his words only with considerable difficulty, his voice halting and filled with sadness, with despair, 'I would not let up... in my efforts... to save the last one... Yescombe it was... Yescombe... I grieve so that I could not save him.' The tears rolled on and on and he brushed his face with a grimy, bloody hand, smearing his cheeks with red and black streaks, a coppery smell lingering all about him.

Pat's heart sank in an instant, his own fragile spirits washed by a gushing wave of cold despair: Yescombe was another of the

Tenedos old guard. He could find no words before Simon resumed, his voice firming, no longer any trace of trembling, 'For my own part I find I am in dire need of air... bountiful fresh air, before I am overcome... I can do no more - *God forgive me.*'

Pat, his own painful feelings pressing hard upon him, choked back his own anguish and stared at his friend: Simon's tribulations were plain to all in sight, the shocked helmsmen staring, no thought for anything else. 'No forgiveness is called for, not at all.' Pat spoke in a low voice, firm but gentle, 'Do not think such thoughts for even a moment.'

Simon looked up from the deep abyss of his despair to stare at Pat; he blinked several times to clear his eyes; he wiped his cheeks again. His voice trembling, he resumed in little more than a whisper, 'I can no longer endure the faces of men who know they are about to die... men who are long familiar to me... men for whom I can do nothing... their cries and pleas... their imploring eyes... their tears of resignation when they know... they know...' Simon stared blankly at his friend, burning pain radiating from his face.

'Simon, there is not a single man amongst the wounded who is not profoundly grateful for your care, your attentions,' Pat stared directly at his friend, his tone pleading. 'There is not a one on the barky who is not glad that it is you who will attend them if they are struck down. Your mere presence is a great comfort, an immeasurable help... a Godsend to the men.'

'What stuff! Humbug!'

'I beg you,' Pat persevered, 'Take a precious moment to gather your thoughts, your strength... for we are all at a loss without you... we are so, all of us.'

'I could not attend sweet Mary if Jesus himself called upon me... I cannot go back down there... I am quite finished.' Another bout of coughing and Simon stared into the distance over the side. 'May the Lord forgive me.'

Although they stood at the rail, far back from the wheel, and it was unlikely that their private words could be overheard at the helm, Pat, gathering a measure of his own strength, fragile as it was in that moment, spoke very quietly to his friend, 'Never in

115

life... *a stumble is not a fall*... my dear old grandma again, so it is. Those unfortunates below are in pressing need of you, of your ministrations, your *personal* ministrations, so they are. Simon, for all love, may I trouble you to return to them? It will greatly comfort the men, all of them.' Pat whispered, 'Indeed, it will greatly comfort me, so it will.'

'Doctor Ferguson, sorr, if ye please,' pleaded Murphy with some anxiety, emerging from the companionway, 'Mr Jason sends his compliments an' begs yer attendance below.'

'Would you do me a kindness?' said Simon after a long minute, clutching Pat's arm and his despair subsiding a very little, 'Tell me, is that the end, Pat, the last of our conflicts? I can endure no more. There is a limit to all things, and for sure I have found mine this day. Another hour and I will be fit only for weeping.'

Pat, without further ado, seized Simon about his shoulders with both his hands and stared directly into his shrunken, yellowed eyes - deeply bloodshot - and both his eyebrows burned away. 'Nonsense. You are tired, soul, in a sad way; and I am heartily sorry for your distress, so I am; but we are going home, brother, *going home*. God and Mary be with you. Look to our men if you will.'

'I will cling so to that precious thought,' Simon whispered. 'I beg your pardon... I beg your forgiveness for my fleeting incapacity... but now... now I must return downstairs,' and with that he was gone, Murphy in support and clinging on to his arm.

The tumultuous day was fast nearing its end as *Surprise* approached the two islands, a league ahead. More and more of Khosref's fleet were becoming visible, southbound off *Surprise's* starboard beam and quarter, although considerable distant firing was continuing and plainly audible to the north and east. At one bell of the first dog-watch another huge explosion was heard to the north and a second at two bells, both undoubtedly the detonation of magazines, and at three bells the receding trickle of Turk ships became a flood, all far astern of *Surprise* and none caring to approach to challenge her. At four bells, Pat, nervously cautious and still greatly attentive on his quarterdeck, was grateful to reach the narrow passage between the two Greek islands of Leros and Calymnos. There was barely light and time enough left in the day to take *Surprise* through the dogleg channel, the sun already well down in its descent to the horizon, barely a finger above it. The western sky was effused with bright, pink light and the east darkening by the minute. Pat gazed over the rail, his racing mind of the day slowing substantially as utter fatigue encroached upon him and the infiltrating sense of anti-climax of the past hour extended its benevolent reach to every part of his sweat-bathed body; his shirt was sodden and stinking in its acrid reek, though he was utterly oblivious to that. He turned his head as he became aware of his First standing next to him, but no words could he offer.

'D'ye think that would be the end of the day for us now, Pat?' asked Duncan, wearing no hat, his head swathed in a very bloody bandage.

Pat directed his gaze square to his friend and placed his hand on Duncan's arm before he delivered his reply, spoken after a long minute, 'With the blessing, I believe we are done. Why, I doubt we have powder and shot enough for any further engagement.' He breathed deeply and sighed. Duncan simply stared at him in silent thought until Pat swallowed hard in a fruitless attempt to lubricate the driest of throats, and he added, 'I was thinking just now of Simon. He is tolerably distressed. For sure it has been a foretaste of hell... for him and for me too. How do you fare yourself, Duncan? How are you? Could anyone have asked more of us this day?' His prevalent feelings of bleak despair would not allow him to say more, and neither did Duncan reply, lost in his own contemplations.

Surprise entered the channel, no ship in pursuit and none in sight. On she sailed for another twenty minutes, a tired fox which had escaped the bloodlust of the baying hounds, the dusk silence utterly beatific after the bloody violence and unrelenting horror of the frantic day, the weary Surprises allowing minds and bodies to slip from tense awareness to relaxing and soporific rest, the wine ration being dispensed even as all remained at their stations, still in readiness at their guns. Another quarter hour and *Surprise* turned to port at the channel dogleg. 'House your guns,

117

gentlemen,' Pat, now looking down at the waist, croaked his order as best he could to his lieutenants, his voice failing him even as they and many of his gun captains congregated below on the gun deck, many blackened faces looking up in query, exhausted men everywhere gazing at their captain. 'Well done, lads... well done,' cried Pat. 'I dare say our day is ended, our race is run.'

Surprise emerged to the west of the islands just as the sun's magnificent, blazing red orb was beginning to slip away below an infinite expanse of flat water, with nothing which could be termed a wave to disturb a scene of absolute serenity, the sense of peace and calm in such utter contrast to all the prior desperate and fearful sensations of all the hours since the dawn. Pat's eyes were adjusting to the general lessening of the late afternoon light and his stare had shifted from the gruesome discovery of half a severed hand enmeshed in the hammock netting to fix upon the sunset ahead; his tensed hands gripped the waist rail, relaxation not having reached them yet; his voice was little more than a murmur to his First, 'Prodigious hellish day, Duncan,' a momentary pause, 'Nip and tuck it was against the Tunisian, nip and tuck, a close run thing. I do not care to think we shall see its like again.'

'Aye, and I hope not,' Duncan's reply was soft, a near whisper, absolute relief the overwhelming sentiment of them both.

A long pause followed before Pat spoke again, his words whispered, a mere murmur, 'I am with you; I doubt I could endure such again.'

'Aye, myself too; there isnae doubt of that,' Duncan nodded, his own thoughts entirely concurring.

Surprise moved gracefully on the near still water, only the tiniest of swell, hardly noticed by anyone aboard, just the smallest of heel to the lee side and the sound of the water along her hull barely discernible. The occasional creak from the rigging heralded a return of normality, of routine, whilst all around the light was fading from its former brilliance. The two friends stood companionably at the rail in reflective silence, as if in search of mutual reinforcement, both gazing into the far distance, the sun half-way in its descent into the water ahead of them.

'What has become of us, Duncan?'

His old friend could not find any reply, and so they stood together for a considerable time in introspective silence, staring; neither man feeling inclined to return in that profound spell of reflection to the customary routines of the ship. Both ignored the call to supper, their minds remaining overwhelmed, their weary bodies incapable of movement, both mute in private contemplation; whilst slowly, infinitely slowly, the last remnant of the huge, blazing fireball sank down through the darkening blood-red sky, melting into the water and gracefully slipping away to disappear in its entirety below the horizon, yet brilliantly illuminating for thirty more spectacular twilight minutes the whole of the western heavens in a richer and deeper red, the spectacular panorama filled with endless and backlit horizontal ripples of cloud, near black in colour and so much resembling ragged waves; the whole stunning sunset to its close and eventual darkness presenting so appropriate a final climax for the day of naval Armageddon.

Chapter Six

Surprise sailed on for hour after hour through all the hours of darkness, the languorous waning moon illuminating her unwavering passage: steady, south-west, unfaltering, a constant six knots. The *Meltemi* wind, with great good fortune, though diminished from its vigour of the prior day had remained consistent: a gentle and temperate wind off her starboard quarter. All aboard felt a huge mental and physical deflation, a slower tempo; one of such great contrast with the frantic desperation of yesterday: relief, blessed relief, minds slowing, bodies recuperating; every man taking personal stock after the debilitating shock of the day from hell. A distressed Pat, in some small state of trauma, had not left his quarterdeck at all during the prior evening despite his encroaching awareness of hunger, preferring contemplative solitude, gazing for hour after undisturbed hour at the frigate's wake in the moonlight, standing in the enduring warm air, no man caring to interrupt him. He had deliberated on the prior day's events to the exclusion of all else, turning decisions and events over and over in his mind until, with great reluctance, he had relinquished command at midnight to Codrington, pressed to do so by his insistent, concerned lieutenant. He had retired to his cot with the most generous measure of Greek brandy after picking at a hot mutton sandwich presented to him by Murphy, for the huge tension he still felt many hours after *Surprise's* final engagement would permit him to eat nothing more, and he fell asleep after eating only half of it. He had slept fitfully, uncomfortable, unable to shake the unpleasant taste of burnt powder from his mouth despite the brandy wash. His disquieting thoughts endured, precluding deep sleep and rest. Questions burned in his mind: had he erred in any of his command decisions and, if so, had that led to greater casualties? His tired brain weighed his orders of the prior day again and again, reflecting on the three engagements they had fought, his thoughts slipping into angst and discomfort when they returned to painful reminders of the consequent casualties, as was always the case after actions. He could not recall ever suffering so many men killed and wounded in all his prior commissions, and that burden languished on his mind throughout all the small hours as he drifted in and out of brief spells of near sleep, listening to the lantern swinging and creaking on its mount with the roll of the ship, deep slumber proper entirely eluding him. He was not so much concerned for the damage to the ship, for such could be repaired: the Falmouth shipwrights could deal with her restorations, of that he had no doubt; and her recall home was timely given the considerable damage and casualties, no further conflict would she engage in. In his disturbed state whilst striving to dispel his oft-recurring distress, he clung fiercely to that last thought, reassuring to the modest degree that it was and bringing him some small measure of relief from his torment, allowing him to eventually drift into the slumber of utter exhaustion. It seemed but a fleeting moment before the ringing of six bells brought him wearily out of a long bout of returned semi-consciousness and out of his cabin, barefoot in his nightshirt. He stepped wearily in his fatigue up to the quarterdeck as the dawn sun emerged from its weak aurora over the horizon behind the taffrail, bright in a clear sky bereft of the smallest vestige of cloud and extinguishing all the eastern stars. Santorin was a league off the larboard beam. He shivered as if to try to shake off the fog of his fatigue and gazed all about him: there was no other vessel in sight in any direction, and looking astern the unwavering wake stretched arrow straight into the distance. *Surprise* was heeled gently to larboard with fore course, main-top and mizzen alone driving her. The fore topmast had been lost in the battle. It had been discovered some hours previously that the main course yard too had suffered a ball strike and was severely cracked near the mast. The fracture had declared itself with loud creaking and squealing when under the tension of the sail, and Pat had decided to furl the course to lessen the strain upon it, to preserve the yard and the canvas. At least the maintop staysail and the spritsail to some extent substituted for the lost fore

121

topsail, and both were aiding the helmsmen to hold her steady on course.

'Good morning, sir,' said Pickering, looking at Pat's face, so obviously tired, his eyes bloodshot, deep red within dark grey sockets, the greying of his red hair more readily apparent in its unkempt dishevelment. 'How are you?' he added, concern in his voice.

'Oh, tolerably well; thankee.' Though his words strived to project confidence, assurance and stability the distinct tone of his voice, one of doubt and hesitancy, suggested otherwise. 'Nothing that Murphy's coffee will not remedy.' Pat strived for a smile, unsuccessfully, 'A prodigious fine morning, so it is. How are the men, the wounded?' The question was asked with nervousness in his voice, concern, fear even. His throat remained painfully sore. 'Doubtless the shouting and the powder of yesterday,' he thought, moving his tongue all about the dryness within his mouth; he coughed and spat over the side, 'Excuse me, damned throat.'

'At eight bells, when I spelled Mr Codrington, Dr Ferguson had retired to his cot. All the men were as comfortable as could be, so said Mr Jason. Freeman has attended them all through the night, fetching coffee for the surgeons and tending the casualties with weak wine and with wet cloths for hot brows.'

Pat nodded cautiously, a few more minutes passing in silent, shivering reflection before he turned about and returned to his cabin. Murphy entered near immediately, bearing the priceless pot, the aroma of the coffee offsetting the still present reek of spent powder; the precious liquid was never before more welcome than in that particular moment, for coffee was Pat's personal remedy, his grateful panacea for many ills. 'Well, will 'ee be ready fer breakfast, sorr?' asked Murphy emphatically, his concerned gaze correctly assessing his captain's demeanour: in need of sustenance of several kinds. 'Ready d'reckly... in a minute or two,' he added, his tone softening.

Pat stared at him in silence, neither Pat's eyes nor his ears wholly registering Murphy's message. 'Thankee, Murphy,' he nodded absently. He washed his face in the bowl within his quarter-gallery; he felt a little more awake; for the first time the feeling of hunger pressed upon his conscious thinking. He finished dressing as his steward returned.

'Burgoo's 'ere,' Murphy's firm declaration was underlined by a delightful aroma, the well-filled bowl a most pleasurable and welcome sight to Pat's hungry eyes, 'an' more fresh coffee is a comin' up, sorr.' A brief hesitation and Murphy added, with some trepidation, 'Mr Jason's compliments an' can 'ee come in to speak with 'ee?'

Pat's heart sank, fearful of what further unpleasant tidings Jason might bring; the burgoo, so keenly anticipated, was forgotten in an instant. 'Please ask him to come in, Murphy, directly. Thankee.' Pat's stomach turned over, the acid bile rising in his throat as Jason entered the cabin. The sight of his volunteer assistant surgeon confirmed Pat's worst fears; indeed, it was horrifying: his smock and trousers were stained with blood, a great deal of it, dried for the most part, and his clothes were so much soiled that the off-white original colour no longer signified. A silent Murphy stared from the cabin door in utter dismay. Pat strived to recover his composure. 'Please, Mr Jason, sit down; will you take coffee?'

'Thank you, sir. I most surely will, though I believe I have already consumed a quart since Dr Ferguson halted in the small hours, too tired to remain awake. He is resting, and well deserved rest it is. Please forgive me if I am troubling you; I am come to tell you of our casualties before I myself must strive for an hour's sleep.'

'Murphy, the coffee,' said Pat softly.

Jason looked uncommonly calm thought Pat, even as his own heart seemed to be thumping so loud, pounding, his breath coming in short spasms. He nodded, could summon no words to suit the moment, expectant, his own feelings of anxiety and tension so very high. Murphy, listening carefully, poured the coffee, hardly taking his eyes off the visitor, spilling much over the table - which no one noticed. Jason resumed, 'There are thirty men wounded... and doubtless you know of the two who were lost over the side... and collect the six deaths of yesterday.' Pat blanched and set down his coffee in hope that neither Jason nor Murphy would see his hand shaking. Jason continued softly, 'The wounds, that is to say the splinter wounds of every man... are dressed and all the fractures are splinted...' Jason sensed the burning trepidation, Pat immobile, staring, and he concluded in haste, 'Doctor Ferguson is minded that three or four more may not see the morrow... the most severely wounded... and five or six more do give cause for concern... The others, he believes, will fare well; that is to say in every case if there is no infection. It is devilishly hot below...'

Pat, in his anguish, heard nothing else; he had never in all his career at sea inured himself to the surgeons' news of distressing wounds and casualties, hence the simple report in its few words overwhelmed him, every ounce of his energy and strength deserting him in a tremor that passed throughout the whole of his body, from his head to his legs; his anxiety was so great that he could not move momentarily, could not reply, and he simply slumped back in his chair in shock. He exhaled deeply, wrung his hands together so hard that it was painful to himself until he relented his grip. He blinked and pulled out his handkerchief, blew his nose even as he wiped his eyes and his cheeks. He strived to halt or at least conceal the warm tears beginning their desolate flow, and he stared at Jason for some moments, finally nodding his understanding. A silent minute more passed, the salt stream reaching his lips, and slowly he rose from his chair and stepped round to Jason's side of the table. Jason, in some small uncertainty rose to stand before him. Pat seized his hand in an iron grip for a long half-minute until he stood back, and he whispered the only words his tired mind could find, 'Thank you...' More coherent speech remained quite beyond his powers for a few more seconds until he recovered his composure. 'Thank you, Mr Jason... I will see another windsail is rigged this hour... without delay,' another pause, 'I am infinitely obliged to you, to Doctor Ferguson... God and Mary and Saint Patrick be with you all below,' he murmured.

Three bells of the first dog-watch rang, and Pat sat with Simon, awaiting the others of his guests, his officers, for a very late dinner become supper in the cabin, the morning and afternoon having passed with all aboard busy without pause in recovering from the shambles left at the end of the prior day.

'You look exceedingly worn, pale, brother,' remarked Simon with sympathy. 'Why, in the broad daylight, you might be taken as a man out from the Marshalsea after the longest of sentence,' a long-absent sliver of humour was creeping into his observation.

'Why, I have never been so tired in all my life. This morning I confess I was so damn... excuse me... so low in spirits I did not know what to do, was at a stand.' Pat rubbed his eyes.

'Have you slept at all, tell?' asked Simon, Pat's self-evident fatigue suggesting not.

'Precious little, to be sure; tossing and turning, dreams, awakenings, hours dozing without sleep proper; I feel like a boar with a sore head.'

Simon studied Pat for a few seconds before his reply, noting his friend's downcast demeanour, 'Well, let us see what can be done. Do you refer to a bore of the tedious kind? One who will not hold our interest at the table, or such as the porcine variety? The wild one perhaps, *sus scrofa*, or was it a bear was intended? I beg your pardon but will you be plain?' Simon strived with humour to lift Pat from his obvious dejection before his lieutenants arrived.

'Eh? You are the wit, for sure. It may be that my lights are not the very brightest today,' muttered an irritated Pat, Simon's attempt at mirth beyond him. 'Murphy... Murphy there.'

Simon reverted to his professional medical tone of voice, 'It is undoubtedly the long spell of duress and the anxieties of the recent days. Your pallor is ghastly pale. You will allow me to prescribe a modicum of tincture of laudanum before you endeavour to sleep this night. For anxiety and insomnia ten drops will answer the case uncommonly well. On occasion I myself have recourse to its remarkable benefits.'

Pat stared doubtfully, 'Well, I don't know about that.'

'I must insist. Perhaps I will whip up a raw egg in rum for you?'

'Never concern yourself. Let us look to tomorrow; 'tis sure I will sleep like a lord once the barky arrives in Argostoli; there is no doubt, no doubt at all.'

'Be so good as to show me your tongue.'

'We will pay no mind to that,' snapped Pat. 'Ah, Murphy, there you are. Pass the word for my officers.'

'It is the damndest thing: I have long steeped my thinking in the most excellent treatise of Samuel Sharp, more latterly the studies of Cheselden, and consequently... I may say... with some degree of confidence... I can take off a mangled limb, tie off a bleeding artery, suture and stitch up the most ghastly of wounds... and dress and splint a fractured limb; all of which can be accomplished in a matter of minutes, as I have oft practised; yet... yet there is precious little - indeed, there is nothing at all - that I can do for the troubles of the mind or the heart; I should be very happy was it not so. Perhaps a trifle of purging is timely, is required?' Simon added, another tilt at jest.

'Enough of that,' said Pat, neither the surgical references nor Simon's humour appealing to him in the slightest. 'I am obliged to you for your concern, but I do not care to dwell on such matters, if you please; enough, Simon.'

'Brother, please do not speak of obligation between us, for such is the death of amity, of sincere friendship. For the moment then, perhaps a generous brandy will serve, will answer the case. After dinner we will press Murphy to part with one of his precious bottles... and we will share the divine liquid to its soporific conclusion. My colleague, Doctor Tripe at the Dock, swears by the beneficial powers of a generous tint for the ills of the soul.'

'I should like it of all things,' said Pat, quietly; 'I beg your pardon. I am sorry if I have spoken chuff, but I find I am awakened miserably hipped this morning, and I cannot shake it.'

A loud knock on the door from his steward to announce Pat's guests interrupted them, Murphy ushering them to their seats. The steward poured wine, dispensing the last of the Greek supply; the officers sat in silence, awaiting their captain's initiation of the conversation, as was the old tradition.

Four bells rang, *"ding-ding, ding-ding"*, the familiar sound signalling a small beginning to a returning precious routine, so thoroughly welcome to all, reassuring as it was. Despite this, the ambience around the table, Pat's guests settled and awaiting the meal, was muted, though not oppressively so: it was more akin to a deeply felt sense of relief, blessed relief, following their departure from the dangers of the conflict; abundant relief that their contribution was over, that they were homeward bound, at least as far as Argostoli could be considered to be home. They knew very well that their combatant endeavours were over, without the least doubt; they understood, and that thought was wholly prevalent in their thoughts, burning fiercely in all their minds to the near exclusion of all else. Indeed, the precious realisation helped many a man to hold firm, to withstand the intolerable strain, and the modicum of restored hope preserved their sanity. *Surprise* was no longer a combatant, could not be in her present state of considerable damage, and must ultimately return to home proper, to Falmouth once preparations were completed. In the meantime, the ship must be repaired as far as possible and the wounded of the battle would all be disembarked and taken to the house in Metaxata. All these thoughts of small consolation, so valuable, so precious, were tightly clutched by the violently subdued minds of the still shocked men around the table, and they were all, every man present, profoundly and abundantly grateful for them.

'Well, the dinner ain't ready yet, sorr,' declared Murphy, fussing, setting out with a degree of pride clean white cloths and sparkling cutlery. 'It'll be 'alf an 'our, so says Wilkins.'

Pat nodded. He looked all about him in assessment of his colleagues, all politely awaiting his words. He stared at Duncan, his head swathed in bandage; looked to his lieutenants, so obviously wearied; to Jason, self-evidently mute in reflection; doubtless the enforced silence of undeclared shock; and finally he gazed at Zouvelekis, the Greek sitting in blissful contentment; no doubt rejoicing in another Turk defeat. He recognised on all faces that which he felt so strongly himself: profound relief. The master, Jeremiah Prosser, alone of his officers remained on the quarterdeck, still at the helm with Barton and two others. Murphy had insisted on a change to fresh clothing for all, to the heavy broadcloth of dress uniform, his long-laboured complaints that all the officers looked like the cast-offs of a prison hulk ultimately prevailing over even Simon's grudging reluctance; and that was, as Murphy perceived things, another aid to precious normality. He had insisted on washing all their stained clothes himself, and though it was neither Monday nor Friday he had rigged drying lines across the deck in the waist. He fussed about the table, basking as he saw things in the reflection of the fresh-polished, shining silver all about it, enjoying the formality and immediately refilling any of the glasses that had been depleted by even the tiniest of sips. Freeman remained below, in self-imposed absence, still tending his wounded charges from whom he would not shift; for all the men had welcomed him aboard after his perilous escape from slavery, had taken greatly to his constant commitment to serve his officers and to his irrepressible demeanour of goodwill to all aboard the barky. The present distress afforded him his long-sought opportunity to return to his shipmates some demonstrable and heartfelt reciprocation of their extended comradeship, so precious to him in his enforced exile from his African home.

'Murphy,' Pat looked to his steward who had been muttering to himself for some time whilst setting down little dishes of Greek olives and bottles of sherry, of gin and wine of several sorts, his apparent disgruntlement catching Pat's ear in the beginnings of a small intrusion into his own emerging contentment. 'This is an admirable table, the napkins, the cutlery, so it is... and I venture you were in the right of things... beating about the right tree there... the clean, pressed uniforms - a capital idea. You have my best thanks.'

'Hear hear,' came the loud endorsement from all at the table.

'Well, thankee sorr, yer 'onour,' Murphy positively flowered, a hitherto unseen broad smile on his face, and that no grumble would be heard from him for at least the next half-hour was assured.

Pat was beginning to feel somewhat restored himself from the shock which had lingered all throughout the morning; the prospect of his return home was as welcome as anything could be, but it seemed to him that the table, in contrast to the relative informality of recent months, appeared to have lapsed into Royal Navy convention, no one initiating any subject and all awaiting their captain's lead. 'Gentlemen,' he began quietly, 'I am minded to think that we are missing our friend Mr Marston...' A long pause followed with blank, staring faces of curiosity from all. 'That is to say *not* in his medical capacity; no, no, for that we do not lack; we have the sterling services here of Dr Ferguson and Mr Jason...'

'Hear hear,' the emphatic sentiment echoed around the table.

'No indeed, and you all have my heartfelt thanks... my heartfelt admiration and thanks...' Pat was plainly searching for his words. He looked all about the cabin to each of the waiting faces, kindly faces, and his mind slowed, his racing thoughts settling, subsiding.

'Hear hear,' louder, hands beaten on the table all round.

'Jason and I are very sensible of your kind words,' said Simon, his own mood rising, near beatific, precious Argostoli coming closer every hour.

Pat resumed with firm resolution, 'I venture this moment calls for another word of thanks... to the highest authority and, heaven knows, with better words than I can find. It may be that my own knowledge of the scriptures is not so very accomplished... and... and I am afraid I am brought by the lee... I can't recall exactly the prayer I had in mind...' He looked down, quite deflated. Pat was a traditionalist at heart and a greatly pious man; he held a deeply natural affinity for those biblical passages exhibiting messages of benevolence and of custom, but rarely did he trouble to consider the writings and meanings within those of the scriptures which held little appeal to him, and consequently there was not a great deal of specifics retained within his recall without he was able to refer directly to his bible in the moment of his enquiry.

A long pause and a solicitous Jason interjected, 'Would it be one of the Psalms... sir... that you allude to... Mathew perhaps it is?'

'I dare say, in the good book in any case...' another pause; Pat wracked his tired mind for his intended prayer. Failing, he continued, 'I am perhaps a trifle out of my depth here... Were Marston with us then... then we would hear something more significant. For that, Marston is our man, none better... he is truly familiar with the Book... a great man in the ecclesiastical line...' He looked down as if in contemplation.

'Hear hear,' again from all present, more quietly.

'For myself, I find it oft takes days to devise an impromptu speech,' offered Pickering, striving to bridge Pat's silent minute of reflection.

Pat looked up at Pickering momentarily; he smiled, nodded to his lieutenant and finished very simply, 'Thank you, Lord, for our salvation these past days.' The short prayer was repeated by all as Murphy entered with the meal, Old Jim Lamb pressed to help.

'By your leave, sorr; here be the dinner.'

'Steady there, Murphy; have a care with that tray; lose not a whet of that... Solomongundy, ain't it? Set it down, there, alongside the plates; handsomely does it, and rouse out a brace more of bottles, anything will serve... and be so good as to find the cigars.' The tray was filled with a hearty mutton stew, the meaty aroma of which brought salivation to hungry mouths.

'Murphy, Jim, pray pause for a moment; the Captain is desirous of our attention,' said Simon, looking to Pat who was poised to speak once more. The stewards stepped back from the table.

All seemingly still waiting on his words, Pat gazed at the friendly, expectant faces around the table for a long ten seconds before he spoke again, 'I find I am devilish hungry, but before we begin - you will forgive me - I will offer another prayer, gentlemen; one which I have *never* forgotten; one which was always spoken at my parents' table... *that* memory will always live with me. For myself, I have no doubt it will suit our purposes this day most admirably.' The attention of all riveted upon him, the cabin brought to silence, Pat continued, 'An old Irish prayer, if you will.' An acknowledgment from all before the

130

table hushed again and Pat began to speak, very softly, his respect and his comfort in a long cherished memory plain in his voice, his demeanour seemingly strengthening even as he uttered the sincere, the profound and heartfelt words, 'Thank you Lord for this food and drink. May it restore our strength, our tired limbs, our weary minds; may it fortify our souls and bring warmth to our hearts... Amen.'

Pat's prayer brought stirring words of endorsement from all at the table, 'Hear, hear.' Duncan spoke in reply as the hubbub died away, 'Fine words, sir, none finer. Give ye joy of thoughts of home, of days with your bonnie lassies and young Fergal. All are awaiting ye and will be with ye in a day or twae, nae more, nae longer. A drink with ye, sir,' Duncan raised his glass, 'May the wind be always at your back and the sun warm on your face; aye indeed. Sláinte!'

'Why, I take that very kindly, Mr Macleod, more so than I can say. Thank you. I am obliged to you,' said Pat with feeling, humbled by his friend's so self-evidently heartfelt best wishes.

'And I will offer my own prayer too, if ye will?' Duncan continued quickly before anyone could interject, 'A wonderful wee tait from the great man himself, Robbie Burns it is.' He raised his voice, perhaps anticipating a vociferous interjection from his friends, accustomed to his poetic idiosyncrasies, though none came, 'Some hae meat an' cannae eat, an' some wad eat that want it; but we hae meat an' we can eat it; an' sae the Lord be thankit. Hoorah!'

'A capital prayer, indeed, Mr Macleod' said Pat, laughing now, as were all, 'and our meat will make me very happy, so it will. Allow me to help you to a... *a wee tait*... of this mutton,' he said to laughter, his spirits lifting, more jovial comment around the table. 'By God it smells good. How is that head of yours, tell?'

'Och, 'tis a scratch, nae more; thankee. A cursed shard of the rail; there isnae much left of the damned thing.'

'May I venture to suggest, Mr Macleod, when next under fire that I loan you Byron's steel helmet; it is still in my dunnage,' said Simon, laughing loud, his mirth echoing heartily around the table, the mood beginning to relax more, 'and will you oblige me with the wine, if you please.'

The meal thereafter passed pleasantly by until, at its conclusion, all satiated and enjoying a rare cigar, Pat addressed his companions again, 'If we remain favoured with this so beneficial easterly wind I calculate our present six knots will serve us well and we may fetch home to Cephalonia late on the morrow, perhaps a trifle before midnight. More likely the wind will shift to its customary north-westerly when our progress will become infernally slow, but I dare say Monday will then bring our arrival.'

'Hear, hear,' a loud echo from all at the table.

Pat's mind was returning to blessed clarity, to the demands of the present, yet he recalled well the exigencies of the past thirty-six hours and he decided upon the necessity for a well-deserved gesture, shouting to his steward outside the door, 'Murphy, there; pass the word for Freeman.' His second steward arrived within minutes, knocked on the cabin door and entered, nodding to all at the table, his face impassive; doubtless wondering why he had been summoned. Pat strived but failed to put him at ease immediately with a hearty greeting, 'Come in, come in, if you will.' He rose from his chair and approached an exhausted Freeman, the man plainly near asleep on his feet. Pat took his arm gently. 'You are a capital fellow,' he said, leading him to the table. 'Please, sit down; here, right here,' indicating his own chair. Freeman, somewhat nervous and plainly confused, sat down, infinitely cautiously, his eyes darting all about him. Pat filled and passed a wine glass to him, Murphy looked on, staring open-mouthed in complete disbelief, for such things simply did not happen in his navy. 'Gentlemen, will you raise your glasses and join me in a toast to one of our most deserving of shipmates... to Freeman! God bless you and our best thanks to you!'

'God bless you!' the chorus was shouted with great gusto around the cabin, every man present aware that the steward had not left the wounded at all since the first man was carried below had stayed with them, resolutely tending every man.

Freeman, greatly relieved, beamed with joy, utterly overcome, understanding that his contribution was acknowledged; the deep pleasure he felt was evident in the broadest of smiles, 'Thankee, massa.' Simply overwhelmed by the recognition of his officers, by the warmth of their thanks, he gratefully gulped down his wine in one and could say no more.

'Here, will you take a plate of mutton with us?' Pat insisted, piling up the most generous of servings before his steward. Freeman needed no encouragement, nodded and began to eat wolfishly, Pat refilling his glass. 'Gentlemen, I think I will stretch my legs for a minute or two and take the air before we will enjoy another cigar.' The table rose as one, Pat pressing a still anxious Freeman back into his chair, 'Stay, please; eat up, you look fair clemmed. Murphy, bear a hand there, man; you will attend your shipmate until he has eaten his fill.' Murphy was speechless, dumfounded; such had never happened before in all his years at sea, *someone from for'ard sitting at the Captain's table*, and he could find no words; he simply nodded, dumbstruck.

On his quarterdeck, Pat, standing behind the helm and contentedly observing every facet of his ship, heard the three bells of the last dog-watch as he looked all about him, noting the wind; unusually it was persisting still as a north-easterly. *Surprise* had left Cerigo in her wake an hour previously, the island indistinct but just visible in the evening shadows, the ship throwing a discernible bow wave and making, Pat thought, perhaps six knots. The day was approaching its close, the sun low down on the starboard bow, a quarter hour of sunlight remaining before the imminent sunset. The perfect sky blazed pink with not the smallest trace of cloud. 'Mr Prosser, be so good as to bring her about, north by west, if you please,' Pat ordered pleasantly, his world more nearly resembling something normal. 'Let us pray to all the saints that this kindly wind persists.'

'Aye aye, sir, north by west it is.'

Pat smiled and continued, 'I am most uncommonly pleased to be homeward bound,' all at the helm nodded vigorously, 'and I have the greatest wish to see my dear wife again; with the blessing as soon as that may be. Lay her course for Cephalonia, Mr Prosser, and for all of our people in that place.'

'Aye aye, sir,' the master's emphatic reply was accompanied by beatific smiles from every man present at the helm, all listening most attentively.

In more customary circumstances, the weather so clement, Pat would have hoisted royals and likely boomed out stuns'ls too, but the true extent of the damage remained somewhat uncertain: perhaps more, hitherto unrevealed, would yet become apparent. Not wishing for any calamity to overtake them in the night he had contented himself with reduced canvas with which *Surprise* had been running sweetly at a creditable rate, the wind off her starboard quarter, hour after pleasant hour, the constant creak of her timbers aloft and the squeak of her rigging reminding all on deck that a degree of normality had returned and an ambience of safety, of security was upon them once more. Even so Pat longed for a little more, yearned for an extra knot or two. 'Let us see what we can do to preserve her speed, for with her turn we will be close-hauled for the remainder of her passage, of that there is no doubt. Set the mainsail, if you will,' he said cheerfully. His words served only to produce a look of alarm verging on horror on the master's ruddy face.

'Reefed, sir? Beg pardon, but that fished yard is mighty weak; I fear it will never do; it will not stand a press of sail; it will carry away,' said Prosser, grave doubt plain in his voice.

'No, no reef. Shake out the reef. Let us put our confidence in Mr Tizard's repair... and the barky. In any event we will not mind a broken yard, if it eventuates, for we are not pressed by any Turk or likely to be. I fancy we will rig topgallants and stuns'ls in the morning and crack on at best speed. Carry on, Mr Prosser; never mind about a spar carrying away; do not be concerned so. I am minded to reach home, blessed home, and without the loss of a moment.'

'Very good, sir, no reef it is,' said Prosser, whose confidence had its meagre limits, who had harboured no aspiration of hoisting the slightest of more sail, certainly neither topgallants nor stuns'ls, and who was very concerned indeed, though he was now smiling himself, weakly and without a great deal of conviction, but his own apprehensions had been lifted a very little by Pat's encouraging sentiments.

The wind had not remained kind to *Surprise*, the adverse *Maestro* blowing from the north-west for much of the day and bringing low-lying dark grey cloud, portending rain, before it faded to a mere zephyr as the afternoon progressed towards the approaching sunset. It had been two more days of long tacks and just the last hour of daylight remaining when she approached the entrance to the Gulf of Argostoli, all of her commissioned officers on the quarterdeck, a rising sense of anticipation endemic to all on board. With the fading of both the light and the wind, *Surprise* had spread all the sails she possessed so as to get into the Argostoli bay before the dying of the sun.

'Why, Doctor, there you are,' said Pat, Simon stepping up from the companionway. Both men exhibited the demeanour of the greatest physical debilitation, of weariness and fatigue: their faces were unshaven, their hair unkempt, their clothing shabby and soiled. Yet for all that, the imminence of homecoming and their awareness of it held up a fragile equanimity, a thin satisfaction that a trifle more of comfort, of safety was near at hand. Even so, anxiety was not wholly dispelled. 'Is all well below, tell?'

'Admirably so, indeed it is. There is an expectancy, I say no more, of a plentiful, a generous - will I say *liberal* - ration of wine this evening amongst the men; and there has been much talk of going ashore, of enjoying ale and fried bacon once more...' Pat's eyes narrowed and twitched, his face coloured, and Simon resumed before he could interject, 'I am striving for a modicum of small jest to lift the spirits a trifle, my own particularly, but I am aware that you refer to the wounded. I regret that three more have died and I fear for another eight: they are sinking fast... and God's kingdom beckons. The others are recuperating as well as can be expected. Certitude is hard to find, but there is no sign of infection, of gangrene; that damned corruption of the flesh, though 'tis early days before we might expect to see that cursed affliction.'

'I am heartily glad to hear it. Is there anything more to be done, tell? That is to say, is there anything I can do... the smallest thing?' asked Pat, an overwhelming rush of concern filling his thoughts.

'Since the first Samos battle and our wounded laying aboard there is the most foul stench below.'

'I am dismayed to hear it.'

'I regret it becomes ever more vile by the day,' Simon grimaced, 'I venture the fifth circle of hell will smell sweeter.'

'The fifth circle?'

'The cesspool of the River Styx: the wrathful will struggle there until eternity. I would hope our stay will be tolerably shorter.'

'It stinks so? I ain't ever had occasion to hoist sail on that particular river.'

'I dare say, but can anything be done, tell?'

'Oh, forgive me; we will open the sweetening-cock and see if the pump will serve to freshen the shingle of the ballast. Doubtless it is become filled with... with *Admiral Brown* and it is in need of changing, but we cannot do that here. The Dock did not care to remove it for more kentledge and new iron water tanks when she was refitted, as was done for *Diamond*; an unnecessary expense... so they said... *damned cheeseparers*. Are they... our people... are they in good spirit? How are they coming along?'

'All are significantly cheered by the prospect of our arrival here. When will that be, tell?'

'Oh, not above an hour now. I dare say we will let fall her anchor before three bells... before the light is gone. Give you joy of our arrival. How happy I am to be here. I am hellfire yearning to get off the barky myself, to see Sinéad and the twins. It would give me the greatest pleasure was you to accompany me, and I believe we may step ashore together presently. Ain't that prime?'

'I should like it of all things, no doubt, but I will most certainly remain with the men. I have prepared a list of medications and dressings that Jason will take ashore. It is my most fervent hope that Marston will return with them. That is to say, if his duties with the men already here permit of such.'

The warm wind blowing from its more customary north-westerly direction, the frigate's approach to the inlet necessitated making frequent short boards until, close-hauled, she passed the islet of Vardiani to larboard and was through the entrance. The sun was now low in the sky above the Paliki peninsula, its light weakening, the air noticeably cooling. Within little more than a half-hour she was through the narrows and ready to make her turn, southbound for the final mile to Pat's intended deepwater anchorage, two cables off the town quay: the short distance from it would facilitate the transfer of his men and stores to and fro.

'Mr Macleod, put the helm up, if you please,' said Pat pleasantly.

Keen and willing hands served her in near silence as *Surprise* turned sharply to starboard so as to enter the sheltered anchorage behind the low, wooded promontory on which the town was situated. She progressed only slowly down the wide gulf towards the distant structure of Colonel Bosset's Drapano Bridge, the protected inlet all about them surrounded by low hills, Argostoli town to starboard and the odd building visible between the trees on the port side. Slowly the ship glided along at a near imperceptible speed, the feeble wind no longer even stirring the hanging shards of her cut rigging, the last vestiges of the ambient temperature of the cooling late evening lingering still, the sense of warmth recovered a very little as the sun, invisible for most of the day through the dense cloud, made its brief, near momentary farewell appearance. Pat glanced west: the last of the sun, bisected by thin wisps of cloud, was sinking low over precisely where the tips of the Argostoli and Paliki peninsulas overlapped; the sky was filled with wide horizontal swathes of purple-tinted cloud, illuminated on the underside with orange reflections; on the water silver glimmers of light sparkled on the tiniest of wavelets all the way across the inlet and the gulf to Paliki, now in dark silhouette. In the moment of his held gaze, the glorious sunset in its splendour became a timely welcome; indeed, in a satisfying way it was one which so appropriately signalled the end of their costly endeavours, the timeless and uninterrupted routine of the sun at the end of one more day in uncounted millenia bestowing a re-assuring certainty, and that thought cheered his spirits and warmed his heart.

However, there was no welcoming signal gun to greet them, and within moments *Surprise* came to the place of Pat's intended anchorage, twenty fathom water on the far, eastern side of the inlet. To any shore observer she looked to be in a pitiful condition, shabby, the unmistakeably smashed state of so much of her sides so very plain to even the least nautical of landsman, and so obviously battle damaged: cut rigging, missing hammock netting, plentiful tears and holes in her sails, and shot holes roughly plugged in her sides. Indeed, she resembled a rather forlorn-looking survivor of a heavy conflict, for her many and varied deteriorations including several missing gun port covers and others dangling precariously from a single hinge could not by any stretch be confused with storm damage or the dilapidations of an uncaring crew. That she was a military ship of some standing was also obvious to the layman, a frigate being a most rare arrival in Argostoli; but those of her crew who could be seen standing on her deck resembled the most bedraggled of street urchins, including all standing on her quarterdeck, for not a one wore any uniform at all. Indeed, the officers, if they could be perceived as such from the quay in the gloaming, were as ill-dressed as the men, all of whom were gazing over her shattered and smashed rails across the bay to the town. Of course the casual glance could not perceive the severe wounds inflicted upon her crew or the grievous deaths she had suffered, but anyone of a naval background and with the smallest of imagination could conceive of the ferocity and desperation of the engagement she had so obviously fought, with the terrible slaughter which must have occurred, and would imagine well enough the accompanying rivers of blood which surely would have flowed all over her decks.

'Mr Macleod, clew up, heave to; I think this place will serve us admirably,' said Pat, his own spirits rising strongly. 'We will lay off a half-mile from the quay, away from prying eyes, the barky being damaged so. Let us anchor ship out here.'

'Aye aye, sir,' Duncan replied. He turned and bawled in full voice, 'All hands to anchor ship! Clew up there! Look lively now!'

'Mr Macleod, anchors away; best and small bowers, alongst if you please; we will be here some time.'

'Aye aye, sir.'

'Why, there is *Eleanor,* and she has already put off from the quay,' exclaimed Pat in some little surprise, the schooner already approaching from Argostoli's quay. She came near alongside within fifteen minutes. The able bodied of the Surprises, all in jubilant spirits, stood on deck, on the waist, on the forecastle, infringed even on the forward parts of the quarterdeck; not that Pat minded in the least. All waved exuberantly to the Eleanors, the schooner's crew equally excited and working quickly to bring her as close as close could be. Her boat was lowered and swiftly rowed across to *Surprise.* Reeve climbed aboard to greet his captain, and loud shouts of excited greetings, of anxious enquiry were exchanged between the men of *Surprise* and *Eleanor.*

'You were sighted from Metaxata late this afternoon... young Miss Brodie with a glass,' explained Reeve, beaming, '... all the youngsters running, *running* all the way from their home to the port with the news; aye, so they did. Why, here they are now.'

Brodie, Caitlin and Fergal climbed aboard from *Eleanor's* boat, Caitlin rushing to embrace her father, Brodie likewise to Duncan. Nothing was said for several minutes, the men hugging tight their daughters; wild, excited joy abounding from the girls. Fergal shook Simon's hand, 'How do you do, sir? The ship... the ship seems fearfully damaged, if I may say so. Is all well, sir? That is to say, may I offer my help if I can be of any use, the tiniest of use?'

'That is an exceedingly generous offer, young man, indeed it is. Would you have the great kindness to accompany my colleague, Mr Jason, ashore? Will you guide him about the town? It is of the utmost importance that we find supplies with which to replenish our medical stocks, all of which are considerably depleted.'

'Of course,' Fergal nodded; he looked away anxiously, to his father, his sister become free of Pat's embrace, 'If you will excuse me, sir.' He stepped towards Pat who, shunning his proffered handshake, swept him up unceremoniously in a bear hug, clutching him fiercely for a minute or more before setting him down, Pat's hands on his shoulders, Pat's face creased in overpowering emotion, staring at his son, his words pouring out: greetings, questions, all a-jumble in his unrestrained joy.

The decks everywhere were filled with Surprises conversing loudly and in great excitement with the half-dozen Eleanors who had come aboard. 'You look uncommon happy, if I may say so, my dear,' said Simon, all about Pat looking to their captain for his orders; though Pat himself was still taken up in the moment, subsumed within the joy of arrival, the intense pleasure of his children being about him, his mind enjoyably diverted far from thoughts of organisation.

'How agreeable it is to be returned here. What is it, Murphy?' asked Pat pleasantly.

'Askin' yer pardon, sorr; will 'ee be wanting yer supper d'reckly or is 'ee goin' ashore?'

'Going ashore? I should like that of all things, I would so. I long for the company of my wife, a glass or two of red wine with supper, and oh for a warm bed,' Pat turned towards Simon, 'but I must... and 'tis with considerable regret... *must* accord with Doctor Ferguson's position. I will remain with the ship and the wounded. There is a deal of things to be done here. Why, I imagine it will not be long before we see the authorities enquiring of our purpose here, her damages so plain.'

'I must beg leave to disagree,' Simon spoke with a considerably stern tone of voice, one which would not brook the slightest objection. 'Will I suggest that your dear wife, Sinéad, will most surely rejoice to see you,' he offered, Pat's face a transparent picture of painfully conflicting obligations to his wounded men and to his family, '... and doubtless too Mr Macleod's wife, dear Kathleen, does most dearly wish to see him. You are to consider that there is no pressing call for either of you here. Mr Pickering and Mr Codrington possess the necessary familiarity with our present circumstances, and our necessities will better be served with you ashore if you are able to furnish Jason with the medical essentials that our men must have. I say *must have*, Pat, and without the loss of a moment.'

Eleanor moved off from *Surprise* on the final peal of eight bells in the twilight, every Surprise waving vigorously and with the greatest of envy to the first contingent of starbowlins going ashore, their fading voices drifting back, the sound of laughter evidencing a benevolent rekindling of spirit - long downcast, the schooner swiftly shifting away from the frigate and closing the small distance to the quayside. Pat and Duncan gazed back to the ship in dismay verging on horror; they stared at the many gross damages more plainly visible from *Eleanor's* deck: missing gun port covers, gaping holes in bulwarks, long lengths of rail smashed away, hammock netting gone, lengths of cut rigging trailing down her side; and then there was the dreadful mess which was the sorely depleted and partially shredded remaining rigging still in place, no fore topmast above the fore course, the main course yard damaged and serving with a deal of rope lashed around the fracture; the ship looking for all the world like a shabby example of a slothful crew. 'Dear oh dear,' observed Pat, his attentions fully returned to his ship and hating all that he saw, 'What a lamentable state she is in. I am sore pressed to think of any other ship I ever served in looking as sorry as she does now.'

'Och, havnae concerns, sir; all of that isnae beyond the skills of the men with a few weeks to do nothing else,' Duncan strived to put the best face on the horrible spectacle.

'Would that were altogether true. The two holes in her hull leak water at a foot an hour, and that is held at bay only with the constant attention of the pumps. Only the yard with a slip can remedy that, for I would not care to careen her here.'

Eleanor tied alongside the quay within minutes, the last vestiges of dusk light holding back the totality of darkness, shades of copper lingering in the western sky and an armada of stars emerging to the east, more insignificant lights flickering from windows all along the quay. Every one of the Surprises leaped gleefully off the schooner, the men jubilant to be ashore in a friendly port; each man clutching two silver sixpences and three silver piastres to spend: uncommon wealth as they saw things. As the throng of jolly men cleared, disappearing into the streets of the town in smaller groups, Pat and Duncan with Murphy clutching their bags, peered along the length of the deserted quay, staring, their attention attracted towards the far end a hundred yards away; and there they beheld amongst the long shadows cast by the buildings three figures walking quickly towards them, stepping ever faster, waving vigorously as mutual recognition dawned; now running, all shouting, louder and louder.

'Give ye joy, sir, of your homecoming, 'tis the bonnie lasses, Kathleen and Sinéad, with Marston.'

Tuesday 14th September 1824   *Argostoli*

Pat and Duncan, with Murphy, returned to the town from Metaxata at mid-morning to find an excited throng gathered on the quay, *Eleanor* alongside and awaiting their return. The crowd was chattering loudly, hands everywhere pointing to *Surprise* as they debated the so obvious substantial damage. Pat kept his head down and his path to *Eleanor* direct, stepping briskly to the quayside and boarding her without a word to anyone, Duncan and Murphy firmly but politely easing several men with more determined curiosity out of their path.

'Cast off directly, Dalby, if ye will,' shouted Pat. He stared in dismay at *Surprise* as *Eleanor* closed on her, 'On my life, Duncan; how are we to explain this when Napier comes calling?'

'Never fear about that. I understand he is away to England.'

'Your secret source here?'

'Och nay, 'twas Captain Cazzaitti, the harbourmaster. I spoke with him just now, whilst ye was with the ostler.'

'I doubt it will be long before Captain Kennedy will be out to see us in Napier's absence, and I am short on any credible explanation for her present state; doubtless too word will reach Sir Frederick Adam, High Commissioner in Corfu, and then there will be all hell to pay. We will be besieged by commissioners, governors, diplomats of all kinds... and there will be ructions at the Admiralty. I see it plain, and that will be the end of us in His Majesty's service: no return and half-pay forever... ten bob a day and penury, eh? Forgive me, Duncan; we are surely on a lee shore this time.' Swiftly aboard *Eleanor's* boat, a gloomy Pat murmured, 'Larboard, Dalby.'

Back aboard, Pat immediately went below to see his surgeons. Stepping carefully and with great trepidation he paced the length of the lower deck; he peered intently to where Simon, Marston and Jason were all engaged with the wounded. Much of the forward half of the lower deck was filled with the recent casualties. The youngsters - Brodie, Caitlin and Fergal - were helping the surgeons, the deck illuminated by the dim light cast by the lanterns. The air was vile to the nose: filled with the coppery smell of blood, the stale odour of sweat, the acrid smell of urine and the stench of the soil of men unable to shift in their injuries. All of this was deeply unpleasant despite the windsails erected to bring the draught down from above, these proving to be utterly ineffective with the ship moored and the near absence of anything save the smallest of breeze. The temperature was already in the mid-seventies: warm, but not as excruciatingly hot and intolerable as the summer peak, and flies buzzed all about the men. The surgeons were attending two men undergoing further operations: both were suffering amputations, a leg in a bucket and an arm coming off even as Pat stared in dismay. He did not care to step closer, to disturb his surgeons; his bile was rising and his spirits sinking equally fast as he caught a deeply unpleasant whiff, no more, of decay of the flesh. He retired swiftly to the fresh air of the gun deck to speak with the carpenter about the greatly evident damages.

Mr Tizard climbed down from the foremast stump and paced aft to report as soon as he saw his captain. Pat's anxiety was plain and unrestrained in his face as he nodded, and the carpenter began his report without prompting, 'Good morning, sir. There is a powerful plenty of work to do... a want of timber to furnish a new fore topmast; the old one, smashed at the sheave, was thrown overboard in our haste.' Pat nodded again; he hoped it offered some encouragement. 'We have neither any fore topsail yard nor any t'gallant mast or yard. All went over the side. I doubt the main yard will long endure, such as it is, in more than a fair breeze...' The carpenter paused in uncertainty, as if the report was too bad to endure more.

'Pray continue, Mr Tizard,' said Pat, striving to conceal his deep concerns and no little anxiety. 'Let us hear your full account.'

'There is little or nothing suited of timber which would serve for repairs, nothing left of such as the best of the nordic spars; all have long been used... four of her gun port lids are missing, blown away... and the bulwark on both sides has took plentiful shots too.' The carpenter halted, sure that his report was too grave to continue.

The bosun intervened to add his own concerns to the depressing litany of severe destruction, 'I doubt, sir, we have enough of rope to remedy the rigging save we take all from one mast to serve the other, and plainly that will not serve. There is precious little of the Riga hemp left below.'

'Thank you, Mr Sampays,' Pat frowned.

The carpenter interjected, 'The cutwater is damaged by a ball strike, two frames 'midships are splintered on the starboard beam, and I fear for the sternpost for it surely too took a strike at the top rudder hinge. The starboard cathead is splintered, and we could not hang her anchor off it for it will surely break away; the bowsprit is damaged beyond the figure piece, and the figure head is missing. There ain't hardly a piece of the starboard companionway left; the mizzen topsail sheet bitts are smashed away - the helmsmen were blessed with plentiful luck that day... so close...'

'Is there anything else, Mr Tizard?' Pat was despairing of the lengthy damages' report.

'And the two holes below the water ain't pretty.'

'So, we have a want of timber for repairs... and no cordage... and if such were forthcoming, how long would it take to rectify these matters?' The dismay was plain on Pat's face, quite unconcealed.

'Three of my carpenters are wounded, sir. I have precious few men left with any competency with the adze and the slick...

that is... to aid me with the making of masts and yards. I venture three weeks afore I would swear to her state, maybe a month... if we had the timber.' Tizard halted, Pat's ashen stare enough for him.

'Well, pray do what you can, and we will see what might be found in the line of timber. Dalmatia is scarcely further than a hundred and fifty leagues, and there is the finest oak to be found in all the Mediterranean.' Pat's reply was by rote for nothing else of substance could he find in that instant; indeed, the ship's finances were so parlous as he knew only too well that he could see no prospect of purchasing enough of Dalmatian oak to fashion even the shortest of oar, though of this he could not speak.

Tizard remained silent, for in his own despondency he gave his captain's vagaries no credit whatsoever. 'There's five guineas for each of your men if we can sail before November,' Pat added in small encouragement, offered with a weak smile.

'Very good, sir,' the weary carpenter replied, albeit his gloomy tone suggested otherwise.

Pat returned to his cabin and shouted for Murphy, the steward entering immediately. 'Will you ask my lieutenants to attend, compliments of course, and Captain Zouvelekis. Thankee, Murphy; and bring plentiful coffee for all, if you will.' He stared out of the lights, the unbroken ones; for those shattered in the engagement many months previously had never been repaired. He gazed across to the port, reflecting that *Surprise* in her present pitiful state was in plain view to all. Doubtless that would be remarked by Turk agents within the town and reported in due course to their masters. Perhaps it was best if she remained within the Ionian Protectorate waters until she was repaired as best as could be, but where to find suitable timber for masts and yards? The majority of the trees of the island, as far as he had seen, were plentiful olives, though he did recall seeing likely suitable firs on far Mount Aenos; their trunks would be rich in pine oil and they would bend a long way before breaking. However, it was wood which, without many months to cure, to pickle within a saltwater mast pond, would remain soft and fissile. Although it might serve for a yard of the smaller kind, such as the topgallants, he doubted it would serve to repair the main yard; and as for a fore topmast, heaven knows; he did not.

'Come in, gentlemen,' Pat shouted to the voices outside his cabin. 'Pray be seated. Here is coffee.' The gathering settled around the table, Murphy pouring. Pat resumed, 'I find that Mr Tizard is minded that repairs will take some weeks, weeks during which the High Commissioner will surely take an interest in us, the damage to the barky so noticeable from the shore. We must prepare to leave as quickly as may be. If we do not then perhaps we will be impounded or at the least be asked to leave.' He sighed, 'She is not fit to sail let alone fight, and so we will return home as soon as we can effect repairs...' Pat paused for a thoughtful moment, adding, 'and the surgeons give leave for our wounded to be transported. We have more than a score of them ashore in Metaxata where my wife and Mrs Macleod are tending them. All those men will be well, with the blessing. We have another near three dozen of casualties here on the barky. I must say I do not know how things look for those men below; there has been no occasion to speak today with the surgeons, for they are plainly busy down there, but I fear not all of our men will survive.' The strain and worry of their situation was showing plain on Pat's face.

There came murmurs of concern from all present before Pat resumed, 'Captain Zouvelekis, I regret our association... your most valued association with us... must end. You know of our recall, and we will return to Falmouth, to England for the winter when we leave this place; but before that we are in dire need of a fore topmast and a mainyard or seasoned timber for such. Would you have any knowledge of whether such might be procured on this island, or for that matter from anywhere at all?'

'I have a cousin on the island, sir, in trade. I shall speak with him. There are several ship owners who risk the embargo with the mainland with whom he is associated, and he will better answer than I.' The Greek nodded in emphasis, adding, 'I too will regret your ship's departure, Captain O'Connor... gentlemen... as will many others. You have been the most magnificent friends of Greece.'

'Thank you, Captain; perhaps you may find the occasion to report our departure to Miaoulis,' Pat murmured. He pressed on, striving to dispel the general sense of gloom with thoughts of activity, 'In the meantime, gentlemen, our efforts will be directed to repairing what we can do with pressing and immediate repairs, and preparing to shift the wounded ashore to Metaxata where the ladies will help our surgeons. Mr Macleod, please to arrange horses and a carriage or a wagon at least to carry them. I will speak with the surgeons directly; I will be grateful if you will stay with the men when they arrive in Metaxata. Mr Codrington, you are to seek out from the town what materials the carpenter desires and can be found. Mr Pickering, you are to stay aboard and supervise the repairs. Mr Reeve, you will remain on *Eleanor* to shift men and materials between the town and the barky, and to furnish us with such fresh food as the cooks require. Mr Tizard is minded that we will be in this place for three weeks or more. However, if the authorities take too close an interest then it will be imperative that we leave directly before we can be impounded on Adam's order. Thankfully Napier is not here, and we will pray that news of our presence and damage might not reach Corfu for a week or two.' Nods all round and the cabin was vacated by the visitors. A disconsolate and weary Pat was alone at last, grave concerns pressing upon him. He shut his cabin door firmly and sat down in his chair. He sighed deeply, as if in so doing his exhalation could dispel all the worries of the world. His mind was fogging. He closed his tired eyes.

Chapter Seven

Eleven of the Surprises had died aboard, three before reaching Cephalonia. A particularly virulent infection had ravaged the other eight men, all amputations and too weak for evacuation to the refuge which was the Metaxata household. Most of the wounded of the Gerontas battles had avoided infection with their timely removal from the ship as soon as the outbreak had become apparent; only those too severely injured to be moved had remained aboard, and all eight of them had died, their skin blackening as the ghastly blight inexorably progressed to its inevitable conclusion. The wounded men had lingered in pain for near three weeks after the Argostoli arrival until, to the deep angst and dismay of the surgeons and despond becoming general to all on the ship, they had slipped away, one or two expiring each day amidst the vile stench of gangrene permeating the lower deck. The windsails and lower temperatures had done little to dispel the foetid reminder that death, heart-rending death was upon them, salvation by amputation not a remedy available to the surgeons for a second time. Day after intolerable day the sailmaker was summoned and the dead sewn into old and worn sails, two shot at their feet, the bodies accumulating in the cooler air of the hold pending burial every third day and before the rats could tear through the canvas.

Simon had persevered during their last days, rarely shifting from the sick-bay and personally administering substantial doses of the replenished laudanum supply to all in their last hours, to men far gone and long past the caudle sustenance which for days was all that many could manage to take in. He remained hugely distressed by their deaths, chafed mentally on his inability to save their lives and had withdrawn into solitary reflection, rarely entering into discussion at table unless pressed, his morale sinking, his mind falling deeper and deeper into a malaise of catastrophic introspection, shying away from all social intercourse to the extent of taking solitary meals within his medical storeroom.

Throughout the gangrene outbreak the malodorous air below had become so offensive that none of the hands would sleep on the lower deck, all preferring the gun deck despite the cooler nights. The officers dismayed too, the flimsy partition failing entirely to check the stench before it drifted aft to their tiny cubicles. Only after Marston had officiated at a deeply depressing funeral service for the last of the dead, conducted aboard *Surprise* before *Eleanor* had carried them to their lonely burial at sea some ten miles off the west coast of the island, did the air on the lower deck begin to freshen a little.

Simon was particularly set back: every day he had looked to his eight patients, and all of them had preserved some measure of comprehension before slipping away into unconsciousness. Before doing so, all had voiced their concerns, their fears and ultimately their understanding that precious life was slipping away; every day the sands of time of their life were diminishing inexorably. They knew that; they understood, and as the end neared they embraced a measure of detachment, of resigned composure, passivity. As their final hours approached they spoke with Simon; they expressed their wishes as best they could for him to transcribe them, to be passed to their kin. For every patient lost he had felt less and less able to cope with his inability to save them, becoming increasingly depressed with the death of each one. In the relative quietude of the ship, outside the heat of battle, the losses had been much harder for him to come to terms with, and as the days passed by he had sunk into an overwhelming sense of disappointment, into self-reproach, down into the deep pit of depression; he had engaged less and less with the others of the crew, his close friends particularly, for he did not know how to enter into any dialogue without he was swiftly become overwhelmed, and that onerous burden he had not wished to inflict upon his friends.

The wounded survivors in the meantime had been shifted far from the ship and were accommodated within tents in the benevolent fresh air of the spacious garden of the Metaxata house, the far more pleasant environment subsumed within the heavy scent of honeysuckle, fragrant zephyrs also drifting from the adjacent orange and lemon groves. They were attended there by the surgeons with Jason; the wives, the girls and Fergal all helping, Freeman too. Freeman had become something of a celebrated hero within the crew. He was revered by all, both sick and fit, for his unstinting attendance at the side of men too weak to do anything more than sip their wine and eat bowls of fresh burgoo which he made constantly. Forty-seven wounded Surprises were recuperating at Metaxata, including twenty-three wounded recovering from the August battle to protect Samos, and a daily wagon delivered fresh supplies of foodstuffs from Argostoli.

Everyone aboard *Surprise* and all at Metaxata had sought, unsuccessfully, to lift Simon from his increasing despair. Both his immediate colleagues attending the wounded, Marston and Jason, had been coldly rejected, given short shrift, though why this was Simon never made plain to anyone. Pat had felt wholly out of his depth; his many invitations to the cabin for dinner or to supper had been consistently ignored and often brutally rebuffed.

Duncan it was who emerged to help Simon come out from his personal withdrawal, to escape from his private tragedy. Perhaps it was the Scots brotherhood that persuaded Simon to open his ear to Duncan's solicitation, to his appeal; perhaps it was his fellow Scot's gruff, blunt manner which pierced the psychological barriers and bridged the chasm of separation which Simon had increasingly maintained. It was something entirely innocuous which acted as catalyst, a discussion at the dinner table, all of Pat's officers present for the formal dinner he insisted on hosting on the first Sunday of every month. A cordial prior hour, no prospect of any further military engagement and the most generous dispensation of libations - Greek wine in the main - had created a relaxed ambience at the table, at least for all save for Simon, and jest in good humour flowed plentifully.

'This is precious tough eating, Murphy,' said Pat, chewing hard on his mouthful of meat, 'a trifle dry, and I venture it ain't pork.'

'Goat, sorr, 'tis local goat. Fresh killed, off the mountain this morning; so said Panagis...'

'Panagis?'

'The butcher; 'ee swore it was fresh... 'ee did so.'

'I venture it must be an old goat, eh? Must we look to the duff for a bite to enjoy?'

'Kin of yours, Murphy? A very old goat? Ha ha!' laughed Duncan.

'Well, Pete... *the butcher* that is, 'ee said if there ain't no rain then them goats don't drink fer months.'

'Not like you, Murphy, eh?' said Pat with a huge smile.

'Six months an' nothin' to drink, so 'ee said, an' no rain this summer.'

'I venture ye cudnae manage that, Murphy,' cried Duncan, 'six months without so much as a wee dram... and nae grog, eh?'

'An' 'ee said it had silver teeth...'

'Silver teeth, that would catch your ear, for sure,' shouted Duncan, laughing aloud.

'Well,' an indignant Murphy began, his reply stalling, nothing of substance or wit coming to his aggrieved mind.

'And will we suppose it had wings too, eh,' cried Pat. 'Ha ha! Silver teeth indeed; all my eye and Betty Martin!' The table dissolved into raucous laughter, Simon the sole exception. That he was deeply disturbed his friends were painfully aware, and a burning, deeply-felt concern was common to all, though none had any glimmer of what might be done, many prior approaches having been bluntly rebuffed in all the prior days. 'Enough of such cant, Murphy,' shouted Pat over the general laughter.

'Pat,' said Duncan when the merriment had subsided and Murphy had left the cabin in great ill-humour, 'I havnae found the time for many a month to paint. This talk of mountains... I would dearly like a day or twae on the hills to paint. With your consent I plan to spend a trifle of time away, with the brushes, with the paints. I venture when atop the Black Mountain I will gain the most splendid of view.'

'Of course, take a few days, Duncan. There is nothing pressing here at present. Take a glass, you may espy the silver-toothed goats too, ha ha,' Pat laughed again, the mirth reciprocated all round the table except for Simon, silent, immersed in private introspection. The eating concluded, the port was passed round, Murphy returning with the cigars. The ambience was more relaxed than it had been for weeks. The cabin soon filled with an aromatic fug, and ripe figs, plentiful hot coffee and brandy were all brought to the table. Ultimately all save for Simon sat back in rare contentment; however, he remained noticeably morose in mute contemplation.

'I believe you may encounter plentiful wildflowers, Mr Macleod,' offered Marston, 'if they endure still; it is late in the year. They may present suitable matter for your art. There are also a great variety of trees, the island so verdant and exceptionally blessed in that respect. You will surely find the Holly, plentiful Eucalyptus, the Olive of course and indeed the Maple. There is an indigenous Pine and the Black Fir aplenty.'

'Och, I will have need of an authority such as yourself,' exclaimed Duncan.

'The bird population is reputed to be of exceptional variety,' Marston continued without breaking stride, gazing with great concern at Simon, an intriguing thought entering his head, 'and all the species of raptors are particularly well represented. Why, I have read that the island boasts of the most glorious populations of eagles, harriers, buzzards...' This was offered with huge enthusiasm whilst looking all about the table, '... and kestrels, hawks and falcons all abound; such a splendid variety of the most spectacular of all the avians... and here on our doorstep; 'tis surely not to be missed.' He peered discreetly across to Simon. His friend's attention was engaged, that he could plainly discern; his head was no longer staring blankly at the table or the deck; the vacancy in his gaze was gone and his eyes stared directly back at Marston who persevered valiantly, striving as never before to project interest and curiosity, '... warblers, pipits, martins aplenty... and wagtails, I venture. Of course there are gulls in abundance... and doves...' By now all at the table were staring at Marston, open-mouthed, drinks suspended in mid-air or left on the table; his well-minted penny was beginning to drop with everyone. He pressed on aloud and without the briefest of

152

pause, 'There are finches and shrikes in great plenty too. Yes, a glorious plethora of avians. Would that I could be with you, Mr Macleod.' All eyes had shifted at Marston's conclusion, inexorably and with huge expectation to Simon, who became aware of their gaze but said nothing. It was plain to all that he was thinking hard.

'For sure I am in need of a guide; there isnae doubt of that,' declared Duncan, seizing the oratorical baton without a moment lost. 'I cannae tell a warbler from a wagtail, heh heh. What say ye, Simon? Would ye do me the kindness of coming with me?'

The atmosphere in an instant became sharply expectant, every mind racing, all eyes fixated on one man, no one daring to utter a word, all waiting... waiting with huge hope, the reply so significant, time frozen, the awaited response the subject of fervent prayers unspoken, seconds passing so slowly as if minutes, the deep anxiety general, all silently urging the desired answer, their heartfelt thoughts driven by burning benevolence.

'I have no doubt I can look after the men, colleague,' declared Marston emphatically.

Simon's mind, long in deep despond, had been stirred somewhat from the far and introspective depths by the more intriguing recent turn of conversation at the table. His eyes bloodshot from lack of sleep, he turned to look to Marston. He spoke after several seconds, his voice little more than a whisper, 'You are altogether too good, my dear friend.' He hesitated as if in careful deliberation and then, his voice firming, he resumed, 'If you are minded, Michael... that is to say it is most benevolent of you if you will remain with our charges...' the whispered reply was unfinished but the intention plain, the words of such moment, so welcome; hearts all around the table soared in jubilation, even Murphy letting slip a rare broad grin. '... then I will be very happy to accompany Mr Macleod on his perambulations.'

'Murphy, Murphy there,' shouted Pat, a flood tide of relief engulfing his very being, so welcome, and in an instant alleviating his profound concern for his friend. 'Another brace of the port, the yellow label, and lose not a moment, d'ye hear?'

Simon's unexpected acceptance of Duncan's invitation had brought huge pleasure to all his friends; indeed, it necessitated that all officers leave the ship extraordinarily early to attend the Metaxata household for breakfast so as to bid the trekkers good morning and success. The household mood was hugely positive, cheerful banter prevalent in the early autumn morning: warm, bright and sunny, clear blue skies with little wind. It was the perfect day. Bearing their well-filled knapsacks, being Murphy's particular endeavour that morning, the two made their cordial farewells to everyone present and set off at eight o'clock.

Five miles of steady walking along the dusty, stone track, an infinity of cicadas chirruping a loud and constant cacophonic accompaniment and the day warming brought the companions to the beginning of their ascent, a junction with the track towards the hamlet of Mihata. The first hour and a half had been a silent walk, neither man wishing to impose upon the other. Duncan had been most careful not to do so, for Simon had yet to exhibit his customary keen interest in everything within the plant realm and had seemingly contented himself with introspective contemplation, an occasional glance directed towards any bird whose flight had crossed his path, and of those there had been precious few. A nod received with only the most cursory of acknowledgements and Duncan led off up the steep trail. Within a half-hour both men were beginning to perspire heavily with the increased effort, the route winding through hairpin turns up the steeper slope: a hundred feet of height gained, two hundred, the gradient easing as they came into the tiny Mihata village with not a soul to be seen, thirst and fatigue plaguing them both.

They paused to take stock, Simon looking with interest at the profusion of olives all about them, casting a roving gaze over the landscape, plane trees too in abundance. 'Duncan, will we recuperate here, a half-hour perhaps?' the first words were uttered by Simon, the walk proving to be more taxing than his expectations.

'Aye, that we will. Here, take a whet of the wine Murphy has packed.'

'I venture these olive trees are exceedingly old,' declared Simon after a welcome swallow from the bottle.

'Nae doubt,' replied Duncan, his voice betraying his feigned interest in things botanical, but he noted with pleasure the first indications of a rekindling of scrutiny of such within his friend.

'Why, I venture these trees have seen decades of pruning, perhaps a century or more.' A significant frisson of engrossment was audible in Simon's voice. 'Will you look to the bark?'

They sat, resting, on a low stone wall with a curious goat for company until two old ladies appeared, when conversation was attempted without success, neither party understanding a word of the other. A morose Simon, tiring of the exchanges and the friendly efforts of the women to engage with them, became withdrawn and intemperate. The women, it seemed consequentially, began gesticulating towards the road, to the onward direction. Their meaning, though not hostile in the least, was confusing. Was it a route to follow or an urge to move on? The brief and puzzling encounter was eventually concluded with smiles and handshakes all round, Simon's hand seized and kissed by the older of the two women before the trekkers resumed, following the waving hands of the women in the suggested direction. A further sweltering half-mile under the noon sun and the efforts of the women were made plain: against the backcloth of the hill behind it and directly before them stood a most imposing ecclesiastical structure, an old church. The setting was magnificent: a splendid vista to north and south, the valley and church flanked by hills to the west, whilst to the east the Black Mountain rose away from them in magnificent spectacle, vast swathes of black fir trees climbing all up its rugged flanks to a great height.

'Why, I am minded it may be the church of Saint Gerasimos,' exclaimed a pleased Simon, his revelation striking no chord with Duncan. The pair stood gazing in thoughtful assessment, and in that moment a bearded Orthodox priest stepped out from the shadows to approach them. It was fortunate that Simon was able to converse with the priest in Latin, neither of the Scots having the least ability with the Greek language.

'We are invited to see the Saint's cave, Duncan, and his sarcophagus, if you will,' said Simon, rising curiosity in his voice.

'Aye, if ye wish; there isnae haste this day, none at all,' murmured Duncan, exceedingly pleased to see the spark of a revival of interest within his friend. They entered the small church, the priest leading the way to a silver casket with the remains of Saint Gerasimos and from there to a precariously fragile ladder, as Duncan saw things, down to a cave below the church, candles flickering in the gloom providing a feeble illumination. A narrow hole in the cave wall led on, so the priest explained, to where Gerasimos had lived, hermit-like, for his first years on the island.

'I am nae going down there,' Duncan declared emphatically, '... and I doubt an infant would fit in that wee hole.'

'Let us take an hour here, if you will,' suggested Simon, 'before we resume our trek. I confess I find an ambience of tranquillity in this quiet place, a most rare circumstance this past year, and it is profoundly welcome.'

'Aye, and I venture I will seek a tint of the wine I saw outside.' Duncan left the church, Simon remaining in conversation with the priest.

A pleasant hour passed with a bottle of Robola shared, and the friends set off once again, the track becoming far steeper and the going much harder; up they struggled, up winding hillside paths more suited to a goat, the arduous route turning about itself as it meandered up the ever greater incline, fifteen hundred feet in little more than a mile, the climb strenuous; and so after four more miles, hot and weary, the friends determined upon a pause for necessary rest and refreshment.

'Look there, warblers... a dozen or more,' exclaimed Simon, 'Yellow breasts... why, it is the Icterine I believe.'

'I venture we are at about three thousand feet,' said Duncan, pausing to gather breath and gazing all down the valley to the west, to distant Argostoli.

'How far to the peak?' asked Simon, the stop a considerable relief to him, his every muscle aching or so it seemed.

'Oh, I venture 'tis two thousand feet and five miles more. That will take us another three hours... and for sure it will be dark afore then. I cannae walk more this day, auld friend; better to rest here and resume in the morning. We will camp here for the night.'

'An admirable notion,' the relief was plain in Simon's voice.

'We will watch the sunset from here. I fancy I will sketch it with yon new Seathwaite black wad,' Duncan waved his prized pencil.

'Pray let me see that.'

'Have a care, dinnae drop it, 'tis fragile. One and sixpence; a fancy price, so it was.'

'Graphite, and so hard it is; I find the wooden outer preserves the cleanliness of the hand... a most innovative instrument indeed.'

Duncan withdrew a notebook from his knapsack, 'From John Airey in Keswick. I found it in an auld Jollie's Cumberland Guide; 'tis a change for me from the watercolours and filthy charcoal.'

'An admirable device and exceedingly more commodious than any crow quill and ink,' a brief pause, 'Are we favoured by Murphy with any further comestibles, tell?'

'Och aye; havnae fear of hunger; there's cheese, bread, onions... and I have a bottle of robola and, praise the saints, a second of whisky.'

'May I beg you to pass the glass?'

'Here 'tis, take it; I hope ye may espy the birds Marston described.' With that Duncan settled to his sketching, Simon content to scan the skies for birdlife. A contented hour was spent noting numerous and varied species whilst both, hungry now, contemplated too on the imminent pleasures of the wine and food to come. As the sun descended towards the distant horizon, the frenetic sound of cicadas chorusing all around, the heavy scent of the firs and pines bestowed a most pleasant aroma upon them as the first calm for many months registered within them, the realisation of the absence of worry and hurry settling pleasantly upon both men.

'Duncan, look there, far above the monastery; here, take the glass; I believe I espy an Imperial eagle... and I venture there is a peregrine too, to the right above that peak.'

'Aye, I see 'em now.'

'May I trouble you for the bread and cheese?'

'Here 'tis. A tumbler of wine too.'

'Will you ever be minded to return to this place, Duncan, when we are at home, residing in the Isles?' Simon's question was offered as both settled in a mood of companionable relaxation, the food and the robola consumed.

'For sure I dinnae care to consider a herring boat and fishing. It disnae hold any interest for me and the pay is woeful; that is if a boat can be found. There is nothing else to do at home.'

'I confess I am contemplating my home in Mull; a small house it is, on the quay in Tobermory. Doubtless there too it is a return to a meagre living, precious little of income to be found were I to retire to that place. However, I venture the islanders, many of whom are known to me, may welcome another medical practitioner, a surgeon; and I have long considered of a far-roving practice amongst the islands; to Coll and Tiree, to Colonsay, perhaps as far as Jura and Islay, the Small Isles even; precious little access do they have to a doctor. Perhaps I may have need of a boatman, one accustomed to my personal idiosyncrasies; now there is a handsome thought, eh?'

'Here, let us enjoy a whet of the whisky; take a dram with me.'

'I will indeed; thank you, brother.' The whisky poured into the small tumblers, the friends sipped in silence for some minutes; they gazed down at the northernmost tip of far Argostoli, the town quay still brightly illuminated. Duncan estimated there was only half an hour more of direct sunlight remaining before the bright orb would redden and slip behind the peninsula and shadow would settle upon the town. 'Then it falls to me to propose the toast; what would suit? What will it be, eh? To ourselves! Is that the customary toast of the day?' asked Simon.

'Aye, that will serve. To ourselves!' the reply was firm, resolute, the chink of tumblers offering a small but cheering gesture, Duncan delighted to see Simon ostensibly cheerful once more. 'And will ye raise your glass again?' said Duncan, 'Our ships at sea! 'tis Monday.' They sat in pleasant contemplation for a half-hour, Duncan eventually refilling empty tumblers with another generous measure before he sat back to continue his sketching. Simon gazed over the swathes of black fir forest stretching into the far distance, the buildings of distant Argostoli shimmering in the late afternoon heat haze. He stared towards the western horizon, averting his eyes from the now red sun, his gaze unblinking, looking but not really seeing, oblivious to everything around him. Duncan, noticing Simon's dreamlike trance, pondered whether he should interrupt his friend's thoughts, 'Och, I wilnae.' He returned to his sketch.

Ten more minutes passed in silence before Simon spoke at last, 'In all my years I have rarely been so set back as in these past weeks.' Duncan was unable to avert his gaze and simply stared at him as Simon continued, 'I have since these few days been thinking of my dear wife, my beloved, and I picture her in my mind with the utmost clarity; bless her.' The words were softly spoken, Simon's voice wavering with the tremor of heartfelt emotion; all the time his gaze remained fixed on the distant horizon, the sun beginning to sink behind the Argostoli peninsula.

To Simon's unexpected statement Duncan did not know how to respond; he remained silent, wondering where the unprecedented subject of conversation was leading, for of his wife Simon had never spoken one word since her death in the year 'thirteen. The sun finally disappeared below the peninsula and beyond the horizon, taking with it all sense of warmth and leaving a lingering vestige of uncertainty, of something lost. In the uneasy silence upon them for the first time in hours Duncan found the loud chirruping of the crickets all about them intrusive, the sound seeming so incongruous in the moment of Simon's personal reflections.

'I have received a letter from her sister, Flora,' Simon resumed, 'It prompted my own thoughts of precious Agnes. Flora has lost her husband, an Islay man, MacDougall of Bowmore. He never returned from fishing and was presumed lost.'

'Och, tis a commonplace, 'tis sad to say,' murmured Duncan.

'She has bairns... two lassies, and no income at all, ne'er a penny piece to support them.' Duncan simply stared hard at his friend's face. The perfect clarity of the day was fading into the half-light of twilight. Another minute passed before Simon spoke again, 'I have never met Flora in all these years, being so long at sea, but I am minded to offer them my own humble abode in Tobermory.'

'That is an exceedingly generous gesture; I honour ye for it, I do... and will ye support them?'

'I have a little money set aside in the Plymouth Dock Bank, my savings since working with Cornelius Tripe there. Certainly no fortune, but I venture it will feed and clothe them for the present.'

'There is just enough left of the whisky for a toast to your admirable intentions, auld friend,' said Duncan. He emptied the bottle into their glasses. 'If ye will... to new friends! Aye, there it is.'

'To new friends!' said Simon emphatically; 'To new friends,' he repeated in a murmur.

'So, ye intend to remain in Tobermory... with Flora and the bairns? Is that the future ye see?'

'Oh, nothing do I know of the future. My thoughts are unclear, my mind all in a swither. I venture a month there and matters will be clarified... when the future may likely reveal itself. For sure I will be greatly relieved to leave this turbulent place, to fetch home to Falmouth and thence to Mull; that is perfectly plain to me. How I long for that blessed, peaceful oasis of tranquillity.'

They relapsed into thoughtful silence, a cooling half-hour passing, the cicadas maintaining their chorus and the last of the birds disappearing from the skies, nightfall settling upon them.

'Here, take a blanket,' offered Duncan, his own mind whirring now in contemplation of home; in that moment Lewis seeming far, far away, remote and bleak, and nothing more could he say.

'Thank you. The precious warmth is fading,' said Simon.

Another quarter hour and the last of the short twilight had faded into blackness save for the illumination of a waxing moon and a splendid plethora of bright stars, both men engrossed for several further hours in private thoughts whilst silence descended on the mountain, save for the constant but lessened sound of the cicadas. The most minute breath of wind of earlier in the day, sufficient only to rustle the very outer edges of the firs, had faded away to not even the gentlest zephyr, leaving nothing to disturb the residual warmth which lingered for several hours until the companions, becoming drowsy, settled at last, before slumbering fitfully through the peaceful stillness of the tranquil hours of the night, welcome sleep eventually overtaking them.

The friends awoke cold and shivering long before sun up. They sat for a dark hour in the gloom of the emerging pre-dawn twilight, stretching numbed limbs and rubbing aching muscles unaccustomed to such trekking, until the sun threw its first warming glow high into the eastern sky when, in the mountain's cold shadow all about them, they gratefully shared the last of the bread and cheese.

'Will we go on to the peak now?' asked Simon, listening intently to the emerging and loud bird song, a myriad of different calls attracting his interest.

'Aye, that we will,' said Duncan, gathering up the glass and his sketching materials. Two hours of walking in the cool of the early morning and in the absence of wind - the sun rising up before them in majestic splendour - was utterly beatific, a panacea for all the ills of the mind. In silence save for the avian population chirruping their dawn chorus, together with the whirring accompaniment of the ubiquitous cricket, they stepped onwards and upwards at a constant steady pace, marvelling at the spectacular views afforded through breaks in the firs, Simon staring at every bird in flight in a valiant bid to identify every one, few eluding his determination. At last the peak, bereft of the ubiquitous black fir, and a splendid panorama opened before them: all six of the near Ionians and the mainland too were in sight, uninterrupted views in every direction: to the south, Zante; to the east, the Morea; to the north: Ithaca, Lefkas, Paxos and distant Corfu; to the west, Argostoli town and the dear *Surprise* visible at anchor. Circling high above and all about them in uninterrupted blue flew a pair of sparrowhawks, another of kestrels; all gliding high on the rising thermals. Over the lowlands near the coast to the west flew great flocks of swallows and swifts, thousands of them. 'Migrating,' declared Simon, his eye glued to the glass as they rested, just the occasional comment reaching Duncan's ear: 'prodigious numbers,' and then, 'raptors... hunting.' Complete fascination, five minutes, ten minutes passing. 'An Imperial eagle,' Simon announced with loud delight a quarter hour later, staring towards Saint George's castle. Duncan, meanwhile, contented himself with sketching, an occasional nip of the whisky from his hip flask bringing absolute contentment. He cast fleeting glances now and then to his friend as his picture took shape. Simon remained near mute, in absolute fascination for near two hours more with the glass, his obvious great pleasure radiant in his face and reinforcing Duncan's own satisfaction in the day, until at noon they began a reluctant descent for the slow trek back to Metaxata, both in jubilant spirits, Duncan profoundly pleased to see his friend emerge from his despond of recent weeks. He prayed that such relief would long endure.

Friday 8th October 1824   *Argostoli*

In the cabin, Pat sat with Duncan, Pickering, Codrington and Reeve; their greatly subdued discussion over dinner on the demoralising slow pace of progress of repairs continuing as they consumed several bottles of Greek wine. No suitable timber for new masts and yards had been found from anywhere on the island, this despite determined efforts and men despatched to all parts. A hiatus in conversation was reached, beyond which Pat did not care to go; detailed considerations of the likely provision of materials, of canvas, even tar had all brought home the doubtful prospects of them becoming forthcoming, and that he found hugely dismaying. A tentative knock upon the door and Pat shouted 'Come in.'

'I am come from the Resident's house with mail from the Corfu packet,' said Jason, stepping in. 'It arrived today. Captain Kennedy sends his compliments, and he trusts that the storm damage is being satisfactorily rectified.'

'Eh? *Storm* damage?' said Pat, perplexed. In two weeks there had been no visit from Napier's secretary, an absence that Pat had found profoundly puzzling.

'The mail today may well be indicative of higher interests,' Jason ventured mysteriously. 'It is of course in Admiralty code, and I have completed my translation. With your permission I will read it, sir.'

'Murphy, away with ye to the galley, to Wilkins,' shouted Pat. 'Fresh coffee and cake, yes CAKE! D'ye hear? Please, Mr Jason, do continue.'

'By the Right Honourable Lord Melville, First Lord of the Admiralty. To Captain Patrick O'Connor of His Majesty's Hired Vessel Surprise: Whereas knowledge of the present duties of HMHV Surprise has remained confidential to only the most trusted of persons of the highest political standing and nothing of her particular circumstances has been revealed to any officers of the Royal Navy whatsoever the Foreign Secretary is desirous of facilitating all and every measure of assistance which the officers of said vessel may require whilst within the United States of the Ionian Islands and for that purpose has communicated such to the High Commissioner and his several Governors of the various islands...' Jason paused to allow the significance to sink in.

'Well, well, well!' exclaimed Pat, 'Melville ain't forgotten us. Assistance now! Thank God for that... and thanks be to Saint Patrick in his munificence. Perhaps now we will find a mast, eh?'

'All good things arrive unto them that wait... and don't die in the meantime,' said Pickering, smiling; though his words, as was oft the case, were considered by all to be in somewhat doubtful taste. However, the news of support, though somewhat disconnected from immediacies, offered a greatly beneficial lift to jaded spirits long imbued with adversity.

'A glass with ye, Pat!' exclaimed Duncan, morale all about the table lifting, protocol abandoned, whistles abounding and hands drumming on the table. Jason mumbled on through the remainder, the customary post-amble of all Admiralty messages, but it was doubtful anyone heard him.

In the evening, Pat and Duncan returned to the Metaxata house and, before the household assembled for their communal supper, they went about their customary tour to visit the wounded, the numbers so great that, with the exception of Mower, they were all accommodated within four marquees set up within the garden. The men were recovering well and were in good heart.

At 8 p.m. the families, with Simon and Marston, settled in the dining room. The atmosphere for the convivial meal was relaxed, the ambience warm and cosy, the table and all those present illuminated by the flickering, cheerful glow of candles. The ladies busied about bringing the food and the girls served wine. Mower had joined them for the first time from his sick bed. He was a popular figure within the household, particularly with the ladies. His still boyish enthusiasms, despite his present wounds, charmed all of them. Shot and wounded in both legs and in one arm, as well as his chest taking two tiny canister shot splinters during the August battle to defend Samos, Simon's expertise and many hours of care had saved all his limbs. He was recovering well and was pampered by both the ladies and the girls of the house. Propped at the table with bountiful cushions all about his chair, his food was passed to him by one or other of the ladies, as he invariably tired quickly at the onset of every evening. Despite his frailty he remained steadfast in spirit, cheerful even. He looked across the table to a morose Simon who was once more become withdrawn, who had picked without interest at his food throughout the meal, his face maintaining an expression of gloom, of deep discontent. Even the divine aroma of the coffee appearing after supper had concluded did not shift Simon from his desolation; for his attention, half-hearted as it was, had drifted away. The gathering as a whole was silent in that particular moment, and from the far end of the table Mower cried out, 'Doctor Ferguson, a glass with you.'

Simon, brought back to the present from deep and painful reflections by the mention of his name and his elbow nudged by Marston, looked up; he nodded gloomily, almost reluctantly; for so it seemed to the onlookers. He lifted his glass but said nothing.

'We are but fragile souls,' Mower persevered. All at the table were somewhat alerted by the words and everyone looked to him and thence to Simon's reaction; a hush descended upon the room, expectant silence. 'So flimsy in body, as I myself know too well. What do you say, Doctor?' said Mower. Simon only nodded again. 'Will I read you my poem, written whilst here?' the lieutenant pressed. A general nodding of heads and a murmur of assent arose from all present save for Simon. His voice dropping to little more than a murmur, eyes all about the table fixated upon him, Mower resumed, 'At one time, when still aboard *Surprise*, I had thought I would not recover and certainly feared for my limbs, but you have saved them for me, and I am most grateful, most grateful indeed; and it seems a timely moment to thank you... I do so with all my heart... Thank you, Doctor Ferguson.' The hushed silence all round the table lingered only for the tiniest fragment of time whilst the unexpected words registered with everyone, the so obviously heartfelt words sinking in, when the table broke into clamorous uproar: loud clapping and shouts of 'hear hear,' coming from Pat, Duncan and Marston. The ladies and girls, accustomed as they were to long hours attending the many wounded men and receiving plentiful thanks for their care, found themselves deeply affected by the poignancy of Mower's words and could not hold back the flood tide of emotion, their smiles swiftly becoming tears followed by sobbing, loud and unrestrained. Both Pat and Duncan slapped Simon on his back vigorously, though he did not speak; his reply was only another nod of his head and a wipe of his eye. Eventually quietude returned. All present looking again to Mower, he resumed, speaking very quietly, his exertions plainly taxing him still, 'It is a tale of hope, of perseverance in adversity, and that seems... to my mind - whilst here all these weeks and unable to shift from my sick bed - a great comfort and so appropriate to our particular circumstances; would you not agree, Doctor Ferguson?'

'I would so,' Simon mumbled his first words of the evening. A few moments passed before he sighed deeply and whispered very quietly, 'Pray read your poem, Mr Mower,' whilst continuing to wipe his eyes.

'Caitlin, dear; will you care to pass my notebook there? Thankee.' Mower propped the book on the table, leafing through it with his operable hand, his wounded arm limp by his side. He wedged the page place with his spoon, took a large draught of his wine; he looked once more about the table, all persons present expectant, silent, the mood of the room now quite atmospheric, all aware of a sense of something indefinable, an anticipation of something special, so personal about to be revealed to them, their heartfelt respect accorded to the author. In the settled mood and restored silence Mower began, his words spoken very quietly:

'I went out aboard the boat,
Because a desire was in my head;
And spurned the love I left behind,
Though she pleaded we should wed;
And I took the shilling of the King
Whilst great guns were flaming out;
I fought with Nelson at Trafalgar
And caught a splinter flying about.'

'I did so, did ye know!' Mower exclaimed. 'It was a grenade thrown on the deck of *Bellerophon...*' Amidst the general and enthusiastic exhortations to continue, Mower resumed,

'When I was laid upon the deck,
I waited long but no help came;
The ship aflame and become a wreck,
A familiar voice called out my name:
It had become my long lost love
With comfort and sweet names
Who held me in her arms and cried
Then faded in the smoke and flames.

Though I am old with voyaging,
Through endless seas to far off lands,
I wonder oft if she will wait

For my embrace, my anxious hands;
To join together in our home town
And share in love with me our fate,
The silver years as we grow old,
The golden years to Heaven's gate.'

Uproar ensued once more: hands beating upon the table, shouts of congratulation abounding from all, until after a full minute the hush returned and Simon became aware that all were staring at him. He blinked to clear the copious tears welling up in his eyes, his mind flooded with the most painful thoughts of his own deceased wife, her loss even now oft leaving him in a cold desolation which he constantly strived to set firmly aside. He wiped his cheeks with his hand and he looked to Mower to whom he spoke in little more than a whisper, his voice cracking with emotion, 'I commend you, a splendid work, and I thank you for reading such to me... I have found myself these past weeks greatly dismayed, so many losses have we suffered; indeed, I had begun to flounder and to sink into that so bitter trough of despond.' The room was absolutely silent, his friends captivated to the exclusion of all else as Simon continued to reveal the most personal of his feelings. 'My spirits were failing... so much so that it has seemed these past weeks akin to the fading and flickering final vestiges of the candle in the darkness all about me, yet I could not bring myself to speak of it... I could see no remedy, could not see my path... and I was floundering... bereft of any particular skill to see my way clear... nor did I care to inflict my wretched despond upon anyone else. There it is... I have always found it difficult to countenance elocution of the ramblings of the unsettled mind, but conceivably I have been in error all these years in that matter.' There was a general murmuring of sympathy from the gathering, the ladies now unashamedly crying again, and Simon, Marston's hand laid encouragingly on his shoulder, his voice strengthening a little, resumed, 'My dear friends, I shall always consider myself indebted to you for the kindly support you give me today. I do hope so very much that you will all forgive me my distress, and I will endeavour to emerge from that desolation... the loneliness...

and in striving to do so it will aid me to think of the so timely sentiments of your poem, Mr Mower... *hope*, that most precious of all thoughts. Thank you kindly... God bless you all.'

Friday 15th October 1824   *Argostoli*

The morning before the dawn was unusually cool when Pat and Duncan arrived on horseback in Argostoli after a thoughtful ride from Metaxata, the conversation between them no more than desultory. It was the day of *Eleanor's* departure and the two officers were to say their reluctant goodbyes to those more lightly wounded Surprises who Simon had decided were unfit for further or imminent service but who were well enough to return home earlier on the schooner, which was also to carry home Pat's despatches, a report of their engagements and a schedule of their damages. They had both been immersed in their private thoughts, few words forthcoming from either man during the near hour along the stony track. The eastern sky lightening a very little, they left their horses at the stables on the southern outskirts of the town and slowly walked in the weak morning twilight the last quarter mile to the quay, the sun's first rays yet to appear over the distant hills beyond the harbour. Temperatures generally had become more pleasant: the days of blistering heat had long gone but the colder night time temperatures of winter were still in abeyance. 'I venture we may see the last of a goodly number of Surprises today, Duncan,' Pat remarked absently, '... and who can blame 'em? Near four dozen wounded, twenty-two men killed... *twenty-two*... *Dear God*... the barky so badly damaged, no pay, precious few letters from home... I venture *Eleanor* may not carry them all, eh?'

'Och, I widnae be surprised to see a score of men on the quay, waiting to board, ready to leave,' said Duncan with resignation in his voice, 'For sure there's a deal of muttering below, with nae prizes and nae pay, but I cannae see more leaving. So many men prefer to remain with wounded friends... and doubtless most will stay here 'til all leave together on the barky. Nae, I think we wilnae see more than a score leaving us today.'

'Autumn is upon us and winter approaches. It is the end of any campaigning season for the Turks too. Their ships will be returning home... to the Bosphoros, to the Golden Horn. Miaoulis and his men will surely welcome the rest.'

'And the order to us to return from his Lordship... leave at the end of September?'

'He would not thank us if we foundered in the storms of the Bay in our disrepair. Better late than sorry, eh? And there is precious little for her to do at home. No, I cannot see that as significant. He will not miss us. I wonder if she will be repaired or put in ordinary much as she is. She may be sold out of the service, to be converted, to endure as a merchantman. I fancy she is too small to become a prison hulk. Perhaps we may even see her sent to the breaker's yard?'

'I widnae care to see that,' Duncan murmured, his stomach turning with the unpalatable thought. All ships' crews, officers and men alike, invariably became fond of their particular seaborne home, and he was also mindful that there were few opportunities for unemployed commanders in the substantially reduced fleet, Bonaparte and the fledgling American navy long since defeated.

'I am minded that the beach and half-pay is likely all that awaits us,' Pat's gloomy speculation reinforced Duncan's doubts.

A long pause for thought, his mind striving for a more positive subject, and Duncan resumed, 'The new fore topmast timber is come here with *Eleanor* yesterday, from Zante. Did ye not know?'

'No, I did not know. That is welcome news. Mr Tizard will be beside himself with joy, no doubt. A few weeks and all masts and yards will be restored; now there's a happy day, for sure.'

'How long afore we leave, would ye say?'

'Another month, I venture; we may hope for three weeks. Duncan, consider again for another moment, if you will: do you not think it would serve you well to return home, accompany the lads aboard *Eleanor*? Your command... *Pylades*... awaits you, doubtless Melville too. It would not do to keep the First Lord waiting. Have you thought of that?'

'Och, I am come here with ye as your First and I wilnae go home without ye. Sure, ye can order me off this ship but I am nae going. Ye know I am now a Commander, d'ye nae recall that?'

'Are you quite persuaded of your decision?'

'Nae doubt at all.'

'Well, so be it. For the present, let us thank and bid farewell to those men leaving... *our lads*. I doubt we will see their like again.'

The two men walked on, immersed in their contemplations, in the quietude of complete silence; through dusty, deserted streets, the town still sleeping, until they turned at the final shabby street corner to enter upon the promenade which ran along the length of the harbour. They looked up and across the bay to the distant hills. The air hung heavy upon them, no breath of wind disturbing the stillness. All along the tops of the far hills, above the crest of the range, a colourful ribbon of glowing orange announced the imminence of the dawn; a deeper pink shade, near red, lingering still in the lower places between the peaks. The spectacle was inspiring, uplifting even; so much so that they halted to absorb it for several minutes, gazing in silence as time passed, until the brilliant orange orb, throwing a shimmering light whilst rising so very slowly, broke entirely free of the earth's grasp to the south of Mount Aenos in a stunning and splendorous announcement of the new day.   With considerable reluctance Pat and Duncan allowed their returning natural curiosity to intrude upon the brilliant panorama; they turned their gaze away from the wide vista of the inlet and the dawn over the eastern hills to look towards their much anticipated inspection of the quay and the expected assemblage of those wounded men of their crew who were departing. One hesitant pace more, a short second step and both halted abruptly. They stared, not a word uttered by either of them: fifty yards ahead *Eleanor* was tied against the seawall in her usual place, but the quay, in the calm of the morning and in the low sunlight which now brightly illuminated everything all along its length, was utterly deserted.

The day of departure was very nearly upon them. Tizard and all his men had responded with zeal when news of the promised five guineas had reached them, had vowed to work double-tides. Indeed, they had toiled for exceptionally long hours to earn their promised bounty; so much so that the ship's masts and yards were restored as best as could be with the replacements made with the Zante timbers; though the main course yard repair, fished with much strapping, was not anything that any respectable shipwright would care to put his name to. The rigging was once more in fine fettle and new gun port lids had been installed in place of those lost. There was much that still awaited the Plymouth ship-repairers, for of time there had not been enough to attend to every blemish; the hull bore deep scars and gouges with much of the rail still missing, but *Surprise* was seaworthy again, and that, to all of her men, was the joy of the world. On the quay scores of Surprises busied themselves carrying aboard *Eleanor* the stores for transfer to *Surprise* for the homeward voyage. Others assisted those in weakness who were still recuperating to climb, gratefully, back aboard *Eleanor* for the transit to the frigate. All the wounded had been brought to the quay from Metaxata since the dawn and had sat there throughout the morning, absorbing the so wonderful sensation of the harbour and the sea, glorying in the warmth of the sun and the proximity of time and distance to boarding *Surprise*, whilst drinking unceasing weak wine and strong coffee brought from the quayside taverna.

Inside, Pat and Duncan talked with Simon, the three close friends taking refreshment and spending a little time with both Zouvelekis and the harbourmaster, saying their farewells before boarding *Eleanor* themselves. Indeed, Captain Cazzaitti had become a valued family friend; it had been he who had procured the Metaxata house for them; it was he that had supported Sinéad and Kathleen through all their long spells of fear and uncertainty in *Surprise's* long absences, and it was Cazzaitti who had provided them with the resources they had required to care for the first contingent of casualties, those men who had been wounded defending Samos. Pickering came in to make his report, and Pat indicated he should sit and join them.

'You have served your wounded so very well, Doctor Ferguson,' said Cazzaitti. 'You are pleased to be going home?' The harbourmaster failed to conceal the disappointment in his voice; he stared intently at Simon, dearly hoping he would be contradicted, that the surgeon would deny his so obvious leanings.

'I am indeed... and with all my heart. In this moment I doubt anything will ever please me more than boarding that ship, Captain Cazzaitti,' murmured Simon, his morale still at rock bottom. 'It grieves me that we have buried so many of our crew. I attended all of those men with my best endeavours, yet even so the damned vile infection set in.' He sighed and continued, his voice low, brittle, 'I am long a student of the surgical practices of Guthrie: every artery pressed and ligated above *and below* the injury, a dirty tourniquet never used; every wound washed and cleansed with spirit, and that after extraction of even the tiniest of splinter or shot where it can be prized out, and all fragments of clothing and dirty flesh removed with the knife or forceps.' No one else spoke a word, all present stunned to silence as Simon continued his strained litany, his eyes staring as if into the distance, fixed on no one in the group, his words expressed in a quiet monotone and filled with his so evident anguish, 'I endeavour to ensure the saw is cleansed with spirit after every application; I ensure all cut blood vessels are sutured only with silk and sewn within the closed skin of the amputated limb, nothing left outside the wound for the foul miasma to land upon... yet the wretched gangrene claimed them still. I despair so, I do. Do I deceive myself? Am I truly a surgeon, tell? Will I become a cow-leech when I am home... or even a butcher perhaps... when I am away from this damned Purgatory?'

Simon's outburst shocked them all. He was plainly as low in his spirits as he had ever been in all his life. Minutes passed with nothing more said, the silence depressing. Pickering volunteered his customarily cryptic few words, 'Life does not consist of facts, but the storm of thoughts blowing through the mind.'

'And that is the sum of your considerations, Mr Pickering?' exclaimed Simon, his indignation overcoming his customary intelligence, his politeness and his natural reticence. He rose to his feet in considerable anger, flinging back his chair, 'Your inanities are inappropriate, your infernal prating oppressive; you are importunate, sir. You oppress me. Your opinion is not worth a straw. Will you leave this place? Go elsewhere! Go about your business, directly!'

'Simon, please; sit down,' Pat, shocked, stood and pleaded with his friend, 'I venture Mr Pickering was minded to say the right thing, to help... please, be seated.' He gently reached for his friend's arm and Simon, his energy expended, returned to his chair with an audible sigh of despair.

Pickering, still standing, stared at Simon. 'You may rightly say that I am not one of those whose opinions are confined solely to facts, to bleak facts, Doctor Ferguson,' his voice was infused with regret and supplication. 'Indeed, I have no doubt that there are instances when the facts are of precious little use to us and obscure a modicum of good sense. I offer my apology if I have offended you. I will step outside.'

Slowly, Simon stood up once more, the flame of his anger quickly burned out, his white face radiating distress, 'It is I that will apologise, Mr Pickering; for I have been intemperate... impolite... and churlish. Please, I do beg you will accept my apology. I am become disagreeable these weeks since... since...' Eyes met, the proffered hand was seized, the grip held firm, the handshake precious to them both after the flickering moment of disaster.

The flash of altercation diffused to the relief of everyone, the mood settling, all rose in conclusion of the meeting and Pat turned to Zouvelekis. 'Captain Zouvelekis, I thank you for your assistance, for your guidance about these waters these past months. It grieves me so that we could not do more... at Kasos... at Psara. I cannot collect any more frenzied months in all the years when we were fighting Boney, and I despair of the things I have seen, but our time here is come and we must go home. I am truly sorry, I must bid you goodbye.' Pat seized his hand and shook it warmly, his thanks coming from the heart; his eyes met those of Zouvelekis in an enduring gaze, both men staring as if in mutual final assessment.

'News of your service to Greece has reached all across this island, sir, and to every village in all the Ionians. Indeed, I venture it is known now throughout all of Greece. Allow me to thank you, Captain O'Connor; I thank you on behalf of all Greeks.' Zouvelekis stepped forward and seized Pat within both his arms, in close embrace for a silent ten seconds, before stepping back, his deep dismay etched plain on his face. Pat could find no adequate words of reply, and the two men looked to each other, neither speaking further, their intense contemplation unbroken and the onlookers all brought to silence. No one cared to speak until the Greek, plainly in considerable difficulty, asked eventually, his voice cracking, 'Will you return?'

'You are very kind, sir.' A further half minute elapsed before Pat offered his considered response, his mind in turmoil. 'I venture it is presently impossible to say. I know precious little of the position of...' he paused, a reminder within his memory of what little he could reveal, '... of those with an interest in our participation. For sure my own resources are at an end, my men are in want of pay and the barky even now is requiring of very considerable expenditure for repair.'

Zouvelekis persevered, 'And if such matters were resolved?'

'I venture it is conceivable that she will be paid off once she fetches home,' said Pat very quietly, his face reddening, as far as it was possible to do so with the deep tan of his skin. He felt the surge of blood to his face and he realised in that prescient flash that in truth he could not reply with anything more, with any shred of optimism, for the demands on him and his men had far exceeded anything he had ever anticipated. He stared away, into the distance, unfocused, unblinking, avoiding the eyes of the Greek even as he reflected for an instant on the massacres he had beheld on Kasos and on Psara; his mind racing, he considered the great number of his men who had been killed and wounded, many of them known to him personally for long years

174

beforehand and all of them volunteers. He thought fleetingly of the excessive and enduring strain, so self-evident, on his surgeon and close friend, Simon; and eventually, for such was not in his usual circumstances the first occurring thought of the military man that he was, he considered of his wife's distress and his children's anxieties. Could he bear to think of them at home in fear of being without him? No, he found he could not contemplate such, even were he without a single shilling and his potato crop failed yet again. In those occasional days, in the rarest of moments of contemplation in his life when the clearest revelations of purpose, of direction became plain to him, he would make his fundamental decisions, definite ones from which he was forever loathe to depart. He floundered and searched frantically for one such which would not come. No words could he find in his dismay as he strived harder to collect his thoughts, to determine upon his reply.

An observant Duncan interjected, Pat's confusion so plain, 'I believe all will be decided for us elsewhere. I doubt we will have any say at all, for that is the usual way of things. To repair the barky will take all of the winter, if such time is afforded us. I venture ye wilnae see much of the Turk either until the spring.'

'And yourself, Mr Macleod; do you care to share your thoughts?' Zouvelekis' question was asked so plaintively, as if the very essence, the principle, the sum total of all foreign support for Greece all hung on his reply.

'There isnae doubt, Captain Zouvelekis; if there is one thing I will always fight for, 'tis the right for folk to live peacefully in their own homes.' Duncan paused momentarily with thoughts of Harris flashing through his mind, 'For sure, there's many I havnae managed to help back home. I'll be back.'

Chapter Eight

The eagerly anticipated morning had dawned bright, the final transfers from the quay in the hours since of the most fragile and gravely wounded men together with fresh food supplies for the voyage were all completed and *Surprise* was preparing to make her long awaited departure, the mood of the crew buoyant once more. On the quarterdeck all the officers stood resplendent in their finest blue jackets and gold lace. Simon had been furnished by Murphy with a clean tunic, all traces of blood and oil expunged by long steeping in brandy spirit followed by hours in hot water and plentiful soap; the aromatic, vaporous risings perceived by all in Simon's company as a corroboration that the desperate surgical endeavours of recent weeks were all behind them. There was a general frisson of excitement pervading, a grateful acceptance that the fundamental sensation of pleasure could once more be admitted, and good cheer endured within every man and officer aboard the barky. Even Murphy had emerged on occasion from his inveterate whingeing and cross-grained demeanour; indeed, he had revelled in the cleaning of all the officers' uniforms, and it was seventh heaven for him to see the sharp and sparkling plethora of such, all buttons bold and gleaming, on this joyful day of departure.

'Man the capstan,' ordered Pat, the command echoed by Duncan and then by Prosser to Sampays. 'Topsails,' he called out, 'a single reef, if you please, Mr Macleod.'

'The hawser is brought to the capstan, sir,' reported Pickering.

'Very well, Mr Pickering; heave away.'

At the capstan the bosun called 'Stamp and go,' and Maclean began his fife accompaniment to the loud singing of *Round and round we go, step out lads and make your feet tell 'em so* coming from Falmouth's merchant sailors amongst the crew, Royal Navy convention quite absent in the prevailing joy of thoughts of returning home. The men sang the age old tune with obvious pleasure as they stomped on the deck from one turn of the bars to the next, the cable hauled in and coiled below. A short while later and every man gazing intently back towards the town, *Surprise*, her anchors catted and fished, her topsails sheeted home, her yards braced to the weak morning north-easterly *Meltemi* gracefully slipped away from her anchorage, her bow aiming for the town quay to make her farewell salute to the crowds standing all along it before she turned away to starboard.

'I venture we will complete our turn without a kedge if this breeze holds,' said Pat pleasantly. The unmooring had been the most enjoyable and greatly relaxing spectacle, the officers' commands declared by rote and wholly unnecessary, every man of the crew seized with the uplifting spirit, the certainty this time of going home. 'And then we will give them a gun.'

Though the considerable damage had been greatly repaired, much of it remained evident still, for there had been neither time nor resources for extensive repairs. Notwithstanding this, the Surprises had presented their ship with pride and as much decorum as could be mustered: in lines above and below the starboard gunports a rather poor semblance of a Nelson chequer, a particular fancy of Pat's, had been painted, whilst much the same had been completed on the port side until the paint ran out; the missing port-lids were restored and all the rigging made as good as could be with what little was at hand. The battle-ravaged furled main course and the reefed fore concealed the make-do repairs to the shot damages in their canvas. Precious little new sailcloth having been procured, the other sails were patched in diverse grades and shades of canvas. However, on this bright, optimistic morning the mizzen, the staysails and the topsails (the fore topsail reefed) propelled the scarred and repaired frigate to a steady two knots. On the quay, a mere cable away, and within a flotilla of boats of all kinds bobbing near alongside, the local populace of several thousands had gathered from all across the island for the momentous occasion, all cognizant of the frigate's help for the makeshift Greek navy, all knowing of the sacrifices her men had made, and all present were exuberantly waving and shouting their vigorous farewells. At *Surprise's* opened gun ports, men crouched along her length and leaned out; above them others crowded the foc'sle, lined the port side at the waist and even intruded upon the sacred quarterdeck as far aft as the wheel; every man pleased to be so warmly feted and reciprocating the display of amity with bountiful enthusiasm, the customary restrained protocol for departure thrown with utter abandon to the wind. The Surprises had become welcome guests in the small town, and although the ship did not display colours of any kind whilst within Ionian waters her true purpose was understood by all. The many months of *Surprise's* intermittent stay had provided much time for cordial acquaintanceships to be made and more serious friendships to be formed, some extremely personal ones included. The Surprises had embraced the very nature of the Cephalonians, had appreciated their dignity and reserve, had enjoyed their wit and sagacity. Many and varied tales from the crew of their maritime exploits and service, some with only a very little of exaggeration, had found a very receptive audience. Indeed, such was the reservoir of local goodwill that a dozen or more women had long volunteered their services for many weeks to help nurse and comfort the wounded at the Metaxata household, whilst others of particular benevolence had rendered the most agreeable of individual favours to a goodly number of the crew, many of whom were looking back with no little anxiety and fond recollection to the ladies on the quay.

'Bring her about, Mr Macleod; helm hard a-lee,' shouted Pat.

'Aye aye, sir; helm hard a-lee, Mr Prosser,' echoed Duncan. Gracefully the bow swung through a ninety degree arc and the frigate settled upon her new bearing, directly north for the tip of the peninsula, close to the wind, her port beam parallel with the crowded quay, the tiniest of wash along her side. Nearer she came to the thousands of excited people all along the sea wall, many shouting, screaming farewells, their waving an outpouring of exuberance for many and sad dismay for others.

'Farewell dear Cephalonia, farewell Metaxata, farewell our blessed refuge, our sanctuary from strife; farewell our friends, our nurses, our helpers; for we are grateful for your attentions, your kindnesses. Fairwell... we are, all of us, greatly in your debt,' the poignant words were declared very quietly by Mower, sitting by himself on a sea chest on the foc'sle and savouring the sea air, but he was still much too weak to stand.

Surprise herself did not bear close scrutiny: to even the most careless observer the evident damage to the ship, despite hurried local repairs of a temporary nature, was strikingly obvious and could not be concealed, yet the authorities had turned a blind eye; the Resident's Secretary, Kennedy, referring in a recent communication to "storm damage"; though what manner of storm would pierce and scar the hull in numerous places and gouge the masts in such obvious fashion was not a subject which ever arose whenever Pat had occasion to speak with him. At least, on his order, a modest replenishment of rope and canvas had been procured. However, despite this *Surprise* was in a truly sorry state: her paintwork was shabby in the extreme despite the repainting of most of the chequer whilst the mizzen and tops'ls all boasted fresh patches. The carpenter's replacement fore topmast appeared of very doubtful standing to the experienced eye of any shipwright or navigator, for it fell a considerable way short of the customary length of three fifths of the foremast, no proper reserve mast being available. Indeed, when first presented with the overall visual appearance of the short fore topmast Pat had lamented that she might be taken to be a Spaniard, and furthermore, he cursed, it was doubtful that the single reef of the fore tops'l could ever be let out because of the inevitable deficiency of separation in height between the foremast yards. The main yard, its defects less noticeable even to the keen eye in its horizontal orientation, had been strengthened by the resort of a spare topgallant yard, attached with plentiful strapping fished about its starboard inner part, all of which was plainly visible. Of this deterioration not a soul on board gave it any mind, for the mood was jubilant, the men anxious to begin the homeward bound voyage; the essential purpose of their departure was so fundamental, substantially overriding any and every concern, save perhaps for the surgeons, ever mindful of their many wounded charges, many still suffering below.

Captain Zouvelekis was on board the escorting Greek *polacca* of the harbourmaster, Captain Cazzaitti. Both men were watching the events in silence, their own mood far from jubilant whilst reflecting on the loss of *Surprise* to the Greek cause. Despite this both men were minded to make their own final farewells endure for as long as possible. 'Will we see them again?' ventured the customarily voluble Cazzaitti, his question uttered very quietly.

The softly spoken reply from Zouvelekis was immediately forthcoming, 'Mr Macleod has pledged to return, and I have no cause to doubt his word. I have been privileged to be in his service and his company these four months.' His considerable respect for Macleod was plain in his voice, its timbre one of pride. 'I have a great admiration for all those men,' he declared. 'They are not Greeks, they have no interest in this war... yet they fight as if they too were defending their own homes, their own wives and children... and they have suffered great loss... so many of them killed and wounded...' his voice tailed off.

A few minutes passed in reflection. 'Perhaps that is the measure of truly great men,' offered Cazzaitti, turning his head towards his countryman, 'to make the difficult and moral choice, and then to act in its interest, whatever the personal cost.'

'There are certainly many who are untroubled by hiding behind others, indolents who flow with the tide, possessing of no moral compass, who choose to do nothing if it will bring them the smallest of advantage or cause them the least tribulation, odious and contemptible as such conduct is.'

Cazzaitti wondered momentarily whether Zouvelekis might in his principled opinion be referring to himself, living in safe Cephalonia, and he could offer no reply. His thoughts shifted to the many distressed and wounded men who for many weeks had been accommodated in Metaxata, tended by the families of Pat and Duncan, aided by a score of local women. He shifted his gaze back to *Surprise* and looked to her men at the rail, to others looking out from the open gun ports. 'I will offer prayers for the Englishmen tonight,' he murmured.

'They are truly men,' whispered Zouvelikis.

'Let us pray to all the saints that they will come back,' said Cazzaitti plaintively, the hint of tremor, of wavering in his voice belying his stated conviction of an assured return.

Kennedy too had turned out to say goodbye to Pat on the quay and remained there, unmoving, staring, immersed in thought. Indeed his superior, Napier, the absent Resident himself, was a Greek sympathiser insofar as he confided in his closest colleague, though the subject seldom arose between them. 'I doubt we shall see her like here again,' he spoke quietly and to himself. Slowly and with infinite deliberation, Kennedy raised his arm high and waved his hand in farewell, the gesture observed from afar by Duncan, gazing back to the quay, his own mind in considerable turmoil, his feelings mixed.

Pat and his officers, sweating profusely in their heavy uniforms of black hats, blue coats and white breeches - every item pressed to perfection by Murphy that morning - stood on the overcrowded quarterdeck, as did the surgeons: Simon and Marston accompanied by Jason, the spectacle a precious relief from their enduring burden below. The excited families of Pat and Duncan were also present, women and children, delighting in the event, in the bustle and activity of their departure; but relief was their pre-eminent feeling, relief in the realisation that at long last they were going home: their long and many sleepless nights of anxiety and days of fear were all behind them.

'I believe last night you spoke of returning,' murmured Simon, observing his friend's introspection. 'When all is said and done, you and I will have little say in such matters; greater powers will determine that, and there are doubtless many things to attend to at home; would you not agree?'

Duncan turned to look at Simon, a short pause elapsing in thought before he replied, 'While Europe's eye is fixed on mighty things, the fate of empires and the fall of kings; while quacks of State must each produce his plan, and even bairns lisp the Rights of Man; amid this mighty fuss just let me mention, the Rights of Woman merit some attention... Aye, and the rights of Greeks as well.' Simon stared in bemusement. 'Robbie Burns, so it is,' Duncan declared with a broad smile.

181

'Have a care, Duncan, I beg you. I am inclined to agree with your principles, indeed I am; yet it grieves me so to reflect on our time in this Greek cause, for the cost has been high, very high indeed. We might wish it were otherwise. Be easy in your mind, for we have done our best here, and no man could ask more of us. For my own part I will be extremely gratified to see wonderful Mull once more.'

'Aye, and Harris beckons too with a great appeal; thank ye,' said Duncan rather dolorously.

'You both look uncommon mournful,' said Pat, his attention caught by the murmured discourse, 'Homeward bound, ain't that reason to delight? Falmouth bound we are, and you cannot say fairer than that, eh? Murphy, Murphy there; where is that accursed man?'

'We were contemplating on that particular subject,' said Simon, 'and a sounder reason to delight I cannot conjecture. Is that not so, Duncan?'

'Aye, so it is. I long for a boiled cormorant or gannet with a bowl of oats.'

A greatly recuperated Mower had insisted on being present on deck. He had struggled from his sea chest and now stood in bright humour leaning on the taffrail. 'Mr Mower, good morning to you,' said Pat affably. 'Here, come sit down, for all love; over here,' waving towards the wheel. 'Murphy there, bear a hand.' Mower, keen to demonstrate his recovery, handed off Murphy's proffered arm, and Pat again shouted over to his steward. 'Murphy...'

'Oh gawd, what now; no peace fer the bleedin' wicked,' this mumbled very quietly.

'Where have you been this past hour?'

'Well, after washin' the bloody filth off his 'onour the Doctor's best coat...'

'Light along and set a pot of coffee in train; handsomely now, before I set you ashore.'

'Well, here we go; bleedin' anchor's just up an' it's fetch this an' light along that. It'll be madeira an' sunday cake next,' grumbled the steward, but only to himself; for in truth he was lelighting in the day, had greatly enjoyed cleaning and pressing he officers' coats, and he much looked forward to the occasion of the day's dinner, to bringing out once again the silver plate and all the splendid accoutrements which adorned a formal meal at his captain's table.

'The coffee, d'ye hear me, and cease your muttering, ye swab,' shouted Pat, in high good humour.

The invalid Mower hobbled across unaided and sat on the compass housing forward of the wheel, solicitously attended by Sinéad and Kathleen. 'Thank you, sir. I would not miss such a spectacle for all the world,' he declared, 'and it surely merits a poem, one which I shall greatly look forward to reading to you.'

'There is no doubt, Mr Mower, none at all. There is a great deal to be said for poetry,' said Pat, though he could not in the moment think of anything. He smiled and squeezed his lieutenant's uninjured shoulder in kindly fashion, 'You are bearing up famously, so you are; give you joy of this day.'

For many aboard it was an almost surreal feeling: whilst the pleasure in departing for home was considerable, the lingering awareness of the absence of those shipmates who had been killed and the enduring attention to their wounded comrades below, men without the strength to come up to the gun deck, the numbers so great that they occupied much of the lower deck aft of the sick bay, impinged heavily upon the sense of joy and celebration. Putting their best face on things, the Surprises shouted and waved incessantly to the onlookers on the quay and in the boats until their muscles ached and their arms drooped.

'Mr Macleod, we will fire our salute,' declared Pat pleasantly.

Duncan paced forward to overlook the gun deck and shouted down to the gunners standing ready, 'Mr Pickering, fire the salute!' Pickering echoed the command and "BOOM" thundered immediately from *Venom,* followed by *Dutch Sam, Tempest, Hurricane, Delilah, Hell's Mouth, Bill Stevens* and *Heaven's Gate;* all firing their one third charges of the oldest powder, the last scrapings of the magazine, at five second intervals. The ladies and girls shrieked with excitement as the guns fired; the dirty smoke billowed away, sparing them its noxious smell and clearing quickly.

'Sinéad, my love; we are truly going home,' said Pat to his wife with considerable delight, the blissful realisation of that rising within him all morning.

Gaining a little of momentum, *Surprise* headed towards the point of the headland on which the town lay, *Eleanor* astern, two knots bringing her close to the shore and her turn after twenty minutes, another half-mile further west and the rocky tip of the peninsula was abaft her port quarter. 'Mr Macleod,' said Pat greatly enjoying the spectacle and the precious rare sense of relaxation, 'We will bear up, run down the Paliki peninsula before we make our turn, west. Let fall her courses and t'gallants.'

'Stuns'ls too, sir?' enquired Duncan.

'Yes, a capital idea. I am minded we will boom out stuns'ls too; make it so, Mr Macleod.'

Surprise turned south. The feeble wind was now behind her and her speed was increasing. All sight of the town was gone, but the accompanying sailing boats were still all close about her: in her wake, to port, to starboard. From many of them came a continuing fusillade of exuberant farewell shots, shattering any vestige of tranquillity in the morning, their occupants still shouting and waving friendly goodbyes to the Surprises.

'Lord, Simon, we are going home... *home*, and as fast as the barky will carry us. Ain't that the thought of the world, don't you find?' Pat beamed, looking closely at Simon.

'I will be very happy,' murmured Simon without the least trace of happiness in his voice. 'Placidity of mind has been absent for a long time, but I believe I may pass a tolerable day with that precious expectation. It is the world's pity that so many are no longer with us to enjoy it... Forgive me, brother; I remain troubled so, I do.'

Pat, taken aback, stepped towards his friend to offer the only thought he could find in that bleak instant, 'For sure, for sure it is... a pity, a great pity; and neither you or I will ever forget that nor any of the men who ain't with us, but when you come to hink of it, 'tis a rare day too when we ain't pressed for time. We will glory in the moment, eh?'

'I am heartily glad to do so,' murmured Simon, 'and I give you joy of that blessed thought.'

'We will contemplate on the delights of a fine dinner and perhaps a trifle of music later in the cabin.'

'Aye, that will answer for me,' said Duncan, his spirits lifting in contemplation of good food.

'There is a great deal to be said for spending a languorous hour in the simple pleasures, no doubt at all,' said Simon, striving to respond to his friend's efforts.

'Then the matter is settled, gentlemen; you will do me the kindest of service if you would join me for dinner. I collect 'tis a fine griskin, so says Murphy, and Wilkins has promised thick pork chops with crisp crackling and plentiful roast potatoes basted in fat... roasted apples too. I am minded that there never was a better meal served in all of Ireland.'

'I would not care to gainsay your opinion of Irish cuisine,' said Simon with the beginnings of a smile emerging, a welcome change from his customary countenance of duress, of anxiety; his concerns fading a very little from his face in that moment, 'and that will answer very well for dinner; thank you, brother; thank you kindly.'

Tuesday 2nd November 1824   *16:30*   *off Sicily*

Two days of gentle sailing on the steady north-easterly and *Surprise* approached Sicily, the island appearing off her starboard bow in the late afternoon as "*ding-ding*" from the first dog-watch bell resonated throughout the deck. The air temperature was noticeably cooling, sunset nigh upon them, the sun a finger-width above the horizon off the bow. The considerable gathering on the quarterdeck gazed with inquisitive eyes upon Etna, hoping to see some wondrous eruption, some repetition of the activity of 'nineteen and 'twenty-two; but such was not to be, only a thin wisp of rising light grey smoke being visible, becoming white as it reached the cold, higher air. Greek waters being far behind them, it was a relaxed assembly. Simon

had earlier reported, to Pat's considerable gratification, th
general stability of the wounded. Indeed, all were out of danger
Death's omnipresent spectre of recent months was receding
taking with it the constant grip of tension and fear which all ha
lived with for so long; its gradual release giving ground to a slov
incoming tide of normality, of days where run of the mill smal
pleasures could once again be acknowledged and even enjoyed
and that was of the utmost significance to men who had seer
much blood, killing and gory death, men who had long gone fa
past any conceivable threshold of adversity that all had formerly
imagined they could endure.

Pat stared as unobtrusively as he could at Simon who wa
engaged in rather more voluble conversation than Pat had seer
him exhibit since the early summer. For many months hi
friend's face had not shifted one iota from the damnable mask o
strain. 'Was there a welcome shift now?' The precious though
resonated in Pat's mind; he dearly hoped so. He looked across t
Duncan, speaking with the girls. His First, of all of them, ha
better endured the setbacks, the horrors, the distress and th
constant fear; and whilst he could not conceivably have beer
immune to those traumatic feelings and their insidious corrosion
of personal reserves, a burden which had so much afflicted all
certainly his presence, his steadfast support to everyone aboard
officers and men alike, had helped many to tide it over the reef
of mental destruction, Pat included, and he revered his friend fo
that. As the second half-serving of the wine ration was dispense
to the men, Freeman served Greek white wine to the ladies an
generous pannikins of Plymouth gin with Angostura bitters to th
officers and surgeons, for the stores had been replenished ii
Argostoli, the Resident's secretary, Captain Kennedy himsel
generously donating the gin together with a brace of bottles o
whiskey from his personal stocks to Duncan.

'I cannae tell ye what a grand pleasure it is to enjoy a we
dram after so long without a drop,' declared Duncan to the ladie
with great satisfaction, his own anxieties of the summe
campaign fading a little.

'This is a famous gin, a first-rate drink,' declared Pat loudl
and with huge satisfaction as he sidled up to Simon, 'upon m

word, so it is. Do I interrupt you, tell? How are you doing, old friend; what are you about?' The surgeon's face looked haggard, pale, lined; but a little less so than even a few days ago, Pat thought. He had not forgotten Simon's mental collapse after the Bay of Gerontas battle, and he had remained greatly concerned for his friend every hour since.

'Well, *amazingly well*; thank you. I perceive a modicum of recuperation within myself, and I cling so to that precious thought. It has carried me through the day since waking.' A moment more, Pat staring at his friend, and Simon added, 'I believe I observed a puffin amongst the shearwaters this morning when I was taking the air.'

'Did you, so? Pat smiled broadly. 'Murphy there,' Pat whispered to his passing steward, 'is there a splash of gin left for Doctor Ferguson?' He lifted his finger to his lips to preclude any reply and waved Murphy away, not wishing to interrupt his friend's so welcome line of thought.

'I venture I espied a flight of marbled teal...' Simon's voice tailed off as he stared at Pat, his friend never customarily exhibiting such obvious pleasure in his announcements, least of all his ornithological ones.

'Simon, will you take a tint with me?' said Pat gently.

'Thank you.' A pause and Simon spoke again, all thoughts of aquatic birds being forgotten and his face colouring bright red, 'My reserves of fortitude have been much depleted these past weeks, Pat, as you may have noticed... I am no great combatant, I am no Pyrrhus, no Leonidas... as you know... I am mortified to think that you may consider that I might have... have let you down.'

'Never in life, on my oath!' cried Pat. 'God forbid; hold firm, brother; you are tired, that is all it is; so much to endure for so very long, and it has been the trial of the world, so it has; of that I vouch there is not the least doubt, no doubt at all.'

'I have longed so to be at my hearth in Tobermory these past weeks, yet Duncan is minded already to return... to return to that hell, for it is surely such. I marvel at his fortitude, I do, for my own is so greatly diminished; indeed, it is long exhausted.'

'Why, a few months at home and all will be well; to be sure it will. You will find it answers wonderfully.'

'Doubtless you will recall that after the battle I fled the sick bay, left my patients; I could not endure longer after so many deaths under my knife that day... a score or more of men in their agonies in my care. I am in fear that I disappointed you, Pat. Did I?'

'Why, as to that, it was but a fleeting moment of the greatest of anxiety and is of no consequence, none at all, brother. I gave it not the slightest of countenance, none... none whatsoever. You returned below to your charges within a minute or two, no more than that it was, and we are all grateful, very grateful to you. We are in your debt, so we are, every man aboard the barky, every one; I am for sure. You are without any doubt the most uncommonly gifted man any of us has ever met, and we treasure your company, your presence; for without it our own fears would be far, far greater. Pray do not let such anxieties sit longer on your mind, brother. There is not a man aboard who did not have the same doubts and fears, who did not wonder how much longer he could endure, myself included; but that is over, all is done and finished; we are going home... home. We may contemplate on the pleasures of a side of proper hung roast beef, a tankard of ale, a fish from the stream and a frosty winter morning to wake up to; ain't that a fine thought, eh?'

Simon nodded his head slowly, 'You are altogether too kind to me, Patrick O'Connor.' He said nothing more, as if digesting the reassurances, a long two minutes passing before his colour returned to something near normal whilst Pat stared anxiously at his blank expression, in hope that his words had provided some comfort. 'I was contemplating on the prospects for cetaceans.' Pat's face registering no understanding, looking blank, Simon continued, 'Whales, Pat; that is to say, the prospects of seeing them when we enter *the steep Atlantic stream*. How I should like to see our largest mammalian cousins.'

Pat blinked, as if to clear his mind, 'Well, little do I know of whales... such is scarcely my line of country, but I have oft remarked them in the Bay. Plentiful finners abound there in the summer, splendid creatures, but now I venture 'tis a little late in the year for them. Doubtless we have a few men in the crew who have served on whalers and who may care to say more. Have you asked of Prosser? He will know. He is an old whaler and can tell a tale or two about them, no doubt.'

'I have not.'

'I do hope he won't tell of any Jonah aboard the barky; that's the last thing we need in the Bay, particularly in winter; *ha ha*,' Pat laughed, relieved and gratified to hear the tiniest chuckle reciprocated by Simon. 'In little more than a week we shall see the rolling green waters of the Atlantic in all its force, and doubtless you will see your crustasians... your creatures... *whales*; of that I have no doubt.'

'Thank you... thank you,' Simon relapsed into silence.

A discrete cough and 'Beg pardon, sorr; will 'ee have another drop,' came from Murphy who had been listening closely and unobserved to the exchanges, and who had decided another glass would surely serve them well. Both nodded gratefully.

A minute passed, 'Here we are prating away like a couple of fishwives at something or nothing,' Pat remarked, 'but look there now... Mower is coming along admirably, I see.'

'He will do very well. He exhibits the greatest of fortitude. I am minded that he is the marvel of all my patients. I feared so in the early days that he might lose a leg or an arm, or succumb even; but his determination, his courage, I find, has been an uplifting inspiration throughout all the deaths, and when I dwell on that I am the happier for it.' Pat remained silent in his registration of his friend's lifted demeanour, and Simon continued, 'When I attended him last night he insisted I play his grand chess, and when I was defeated again - the queen, the bishop and the castle having an uncommon latitude of manoeuvre - he read one of John Milton's poems to me. He had himself clung to the words when he was laid low and thought he would die. He scribed it for me when I remarked the verse seemed timely. I have it here; will I read it?' Pat nodded, still marvelling at this so welcome turn of events. All persons on the quarterdeck save for the helmsmen edged closer, the turn of

189

conversation intriguing everyone, all other exchanges fading to silence. Simon extracted a rather grimy and bloodstained scrap of paper from his pocket, 'No, that is my list of the men's laudanum drops.' He fetched another greasy note from his other pocket and began to read:

'The star that bids the shepherd fold,
now the top of heaven doth hold,
and the gilded car of day,
his glowing axle doth allay.
In the steep Atlantick stream,
and the slope sun his upward beam,
shoots against the dusky pole,
pacing toward the other goal
of his chamber in the east.'

Simon, glancing to his friend and perceiving Pat's interest waning, read more swiftly to the end of the poem,

'Meanwhile welcome joy and feast,
midnight shout, and revelry,
tipsie dance, and jollity.'

'A capital verse, 'pon my word, so it is,' pronounced Pat, though in truth poems generally escaped his interest and the words had hardly registered whilst he embraced the surge of pleasure in seeing this benevolent messenger of recuperation within his friend.

In the background came the long ululating notes of the pipe blowing the General Call, followed by the bosun's shout of 'Hands to supper.'

'I collect some mention of *welcome joy* in Milton's poem,' said Pat, 'do you begin to feel a trifle of that, do you?'

The reply was hesitant, no more than a murmur, 'I do... I had long thought it lost, gone for ever, the black days enduring so... but now I feel it, a blessed glimmer... and it is the wonder of the world.'

The evening being so calm, barely a breeze in the warm air, Simon's quiet words carried to all the many ears in close proximity, tailing off as his eyes clouded in the overwhelming surge of feeling that consumed him, tears of heartfelt relief trickling down his cheeks as he looked to Pat, the two friends staring intently at each other, and all about them were brought to silence; the men at the helm looking on with unconcealed concern, Murphy in particular pretending disinterest with a shuffling of glasses on his tray. Everyone stared at Simon, all absorbing this unexpected and public confession, for such dialogue was unknown on the quarterdeck, as was what followed: without any word or ceremony, Pat, his own emotions swiftly rising, seized his friend's shoulders in his unyielding grasp. 'Hold firm, brother; stand fast, all will be well,' holding him tight for a half-minute before he released his grip. A pause, 'I collect too a mention of *feast*, and that is what we shall enjoy for supper. Though there ain't no salt beef, not so much as a barren cow to be found on all the island, slow cooked mutton will serve, will be agreeable; and I believe Freeman has discovered a case of claret which Murphy had lost; well, that was his story. I give you joy; I am so greatly pleased to hear what you have said.'

Saturday 13th November off S.E. Spain, approaching the Straits

After breakfast, after his routine inspection of his patients and Pat being on deck, Simon, clutching pen and paper, ventured into the great cabin in search of ink, for he had determined to catch up with his long neglected diary, his record of personal thoughts and medical observations, and too his unfinished correspondence, all of which for some time had been held in abeyance. The feverish activity and his own mind of recent months had never permitted the necessary concentration to focus on such tasks, ones demanding of a long-absent modicum of mental relaxation in which to persevere with any meaningful entries and replies. He walked across the creaking boards, the cabin in rare near silence; he sat down in Pat's comfortable chair behind his large desk and he rummaged through the drawers, looking for but finding no ink, for Pat was not a great one for writing himself. He looked all about the room, a so rare sense of no necessity to rush, no need for haste was dawning upon him, and it was a delightful feeling, almost a revelation, an indication perhaps of returning normality, to what life had once been before all the desperate months serving Greece, and he luxuriated in the pleasure of the moment. The aroma from the bowl of figs on the table registered momentarily with him and he briefly pondered hailing Murphy and sending for coffee or something stronger, but he dismissed the thought in favour of solitude and contemplation, settling back into the chair and allowing his thoughts and his eyes to wander, to delight in the sensation of long-endured mental shackles falling away. His eyes paused on the cases, adjacent to the door to the starboard quarter-gallery, of his viola and Pat's 'cello, and his mind wandered to thoughts of past happy times in the cabin, to musical sojourns, Corelli being a particular favourite of them both. He recalled memories of improvisations becoming extravagances which generally ended in much laughter, and he fought to rein in a rush of sentimentality, to force his mind to return to the present and his letters, but where to start? He looked once more and the ink presented itself within moments. From his pocket he retrieved a particularly leaden Greek bun which he chewed with determination whilst contemplating which letter to begin first. His mind finding a so rare fragment of relaxation in the quietude, his thoughts turned to fond recollections of his wife. He imagined he could smell her scent, her perfume, that he could hear her soft voice once again, and he pictured her with great clarity, in all her beauty before the dreadful wasting and her descent began. He dipped the pen and began to write, *'My dearest beloved, I do not believe in all my years at sea that I have ever felt greater dismay than during these recent months. It gives me infinite solace to be returning home, and I find great comfort in the thought of being once more at your side in our beloved Tobermory. I begin to be minded that perhaps it is time to retire, to always be there with you, my love...'*

He stopped, noticing his silent tears falling upon the letter, the ink running, his words blurring, and he reached for the sand in the adapted salt cellar by the inkpot, a device created by Mower; such blotting paper as had been previously possessed was all long gone.

The door creaked and Duncan's daughter, Brodie, entered, making her bob. 'Doctor Ferguson, sir; we are to be put off the ship,' her words were offered with obvious huge dismay. 'I am come to bid you farewell.'

'Please to come here my child,' said Simon, beckoning, the distraction most welcome at a particularly distressing moment in his personal reflections.

'We are to be cast ashore upon a rock,' Brodie's voice betrayed her uncertainty, her fears.

'No, no, my dear; we seafarers always call Gibraltar the Rock,' said Simon with a self-satisfying inflection whilst gazing with huge affection at Brodie. 'You have misunderstood. You are certainly *not* to be put ashore. I believe you are to be placed in the safe hands of Mr Reeve and Mr Codrington, to go aboard *Eleanor*. She is the swiftest of vessels, a veritable Hermes, and will convey you all to Falmouth at the utmost speed whilst we undoubtedly will labour and languish far behind in this tired ship. It is to be welcomed, my dear; there is not the slightest cause for concern.'

On deck, the wives and Pat's children were engaged in the preparation for transfer to *Eleanor,* the voyage from Sicily to Gibraltar having shown to the most sceptical of observers, the wives, her greater speed in comparison with that of *Surprise*: for *Eleanor* had suffered no damages, had no necessity to husband her sails, no caution was needed for her trim, and neither did she field torn shrouds and sheets, hastily repaired with come what may. Pat had determined that the schooner, a remarkably weatherly vessel and near bereft of leeway - Codrington and Reeve had oft boasted of sailing her as close as five points to the wind - would more swiftly and with greater safety convey home the families, *Surprise* being in such a lamentable state. It was not a determination welcomed by the wives, who had protested loud and long, but nevertheless that was Pat's irrevocable decision, mindful of his own deteriorated charge; her bow caulking in particular was long in need of comprehensive replacement, for the Aegean sun had not been kind to it, and having dried out in the long hot months of the Greek summer much had fallen out, leaving multiple tiny porous holes to admit both rain and seawater. So much so that everything below was damp and the mildew had flourished, the air was foul with its unwelcome odour. The windsails were near completely ineffective and the pumps saw much service. Pat had for a week or more reflected that the forthcoming Atlantic with its customary winter storms was nigh upon them, Biscay and its potentially terrifying tantrums in particular looming large in his considerations. These influences and the sight of the schooner so greatly held back by her companion in the adverse winds and choppy seas since Malta hugely dismayed Pat, *Surprise* at the best she could sail, close-hauled and six points off the wind, and all the time taking in copious water through the shrunken bow caulking. These observations had shaped his reluctant decision to send away the wives and children on the more seaworthy *Eleanor*. Biscay was likely to be exceedingly uncomfortable, and *Surprise*, he was sure, would make prodigious quantities of water. At least *Surprise* had re-equipped to some degree with a supply of additional rope and canvas, provided on the order of Kennedy in Argostoli.

'You must hasten now, my dear,' said Simon gently, a sudden thought coming to him. 'Wait... here, take this.' He stood up, reached within his waistcoat pocket and drew out a tiny Saint Christopher Celtic cross on a silver necklace, draping it over her head and about her neck. 'It belonged to a very dear friend of mine, one sadly no longer with us, and it is deserving of a new owner. It would greatly please me were you to accept it as a gift, a charm... a token of the warmth of our friendship.'

Further words seemed wholly inadequate, inappropriate, the moment so complete; and so without further ado they embraced, Brodie overcome with relief and gratitude, Simon similarly so with a cathartic release quite overwhelming him in the instant that he passed on the precious gift that had formerly belonged to his wife. The enduring hug and Simon's contemplative quietude was broken by the opening of the cabin door, Murphy stepping in without pause to the table and bearing a silver tray. 'Beggin' yer 'onour's pardon,' his voice was calm, steady, bereft of its usual causticity, with no trace of whining; rather it was warm, benevolent, and such was almost beyond belief. Simon looked up from his engrossment, his thoughtful immersion in some little surprise. 'Well, 'ere be coffee, sorr, an' marchpane cakes.' Simon stared in astonishment, speechless: such had never happened before, and Murphy left without another word, a belated and whispered 'Thank you,' from Simon faintly registering as the steward closed the door very gently and passed into the coach.

'I must be away, Doctor Ferguson; mama is waiting. Thank you for the necklace; I shall surely treasure it and always think of you.'

'Bless you. Here, lamb, please to take the cakes.' He wrapped them within Murphy's linen cloth. 'Farewell my dear, go now. With the blessing, we shall meet in Falmouth town within a week or thereabouts.' Brodie kissed Simon on his stubbled cheek and dashed away, turning at the door to look back with a beatific smile before leaving the cabin.

In the late afternoon, both vessels long through the Straits, *Eleanor* hull down and disappearing towards the far horizon, anxious eyes followed her progress. Inexorably, the fast-sailing schooner became a smaller and smaller distant speck as time passed by, a distant Cadiz off the starboard bow. Pat, Simon and Duncan, taking their leave of the quarterdeck, minds troubled by the parting, settled into the great cabin. The weather was clement but cool, the sea state benevolent, and Pat in his chair wondered whether he had made the sensible decision in sending away the families: had it really been necessary? Only time would tell. In the end he convinced and contented himself that he could no nothing save err to caution, for there was no logical reason to do otherwise, *Surprise* so severely deteriorated and profusely leaking. A couple of weeks and the issue would be forgotten; at least he hoped that it would be forgotten by his wife, for Sinéad's irascible temperament had given him considerable grief in explaining his heartrending decision to her.

The Atlantic temperature feeling uncomfortably raw beyond the peak of the day after living so long in temperate Greek waters, the three friends sat drinking hot coffee, dressed in such woollen comforters as could be found in dunnage long since consigned to the hold and thankfully not found by the ship's rodents until, the ship's bell ringing out *"ding-ding, ding-ding"* at the end of the first dog-watch, Freeman entered bearing the toad in the hole, its tempting savoury aroma wafting around the table and stimulating the appetites of all. He was accompanied by Murphy with the wine, near the last vestiges of the liquor locker save for a few cases of execrable quality and uncertain provenance, their identifications long lost to the damp and mould.

During supper, Duncan had strived to sustain flagging conversation with little success; Pat was distracted, his thoughts lingering with his departed family, and Simon seemingly pre-occupied too. His earlier recollections of Mull and of his deceased wife remained very much to the fore in his mind. The plates cleared, Duncan, in some exasperation, his own family also departed on *Eleanor*, played his ace card: one that he invariably called upon, a tried and trusted remedy and usually well received. 'Will we take a wee dram, a brandy perhaps?' On this occasion it failed him; he received only an indistinct muttering from Pat and silence from Simon, and so he fell back upon his last throw, 'I have an inclination for my whistle; d'ye mind?' A mute shaking of heads was the only response. Without further ado, he pulled it from within his jacket. 'I will make my attempt upon Carolan's *Si Bheag, Si Mhor;* aye indeed, that will serve.' With the soft, shrill notes of the whistle filling the air for the next minute, it was impossible for Pat and Simon to do anything other than take heed, their interest becoming engaged. All other thoughts being dispelled, the musicians within them warmed to the tune instantly. 'Now there's a man who didnae ever despair, d'ye know? The blind fiddler he was,' pronounced Duncan at the end, his genuine smile one of simple joy and lifting the mood in the cabin. Without delay, he struck up immediately the cheering notes of *Gary Owen,* and within moments both his companions were tapping their toes vigorously on the deck. An enthusiastic *Galway Piper* soon followed, Duncan looking to his friends with rising pleasure in his eye, for both were utterly captivated, their attention now wholly engaged.

'Duncan, a thousand thanks to you, my dear,' said Simon, applauding, Pat joining him, the cheering fillip provided by the music so welcome to both of them in the glum mood which had descended upon the cabin since the families had left them.

'Simon, will we play?' prompted Pat, his spirits lifting. 'Murphy, Murphy there.' The steward had been hovering outside the door, listening to the music; for he was an Irishman for all his failings, and *the Galway Piper* never failed to capture his interest. 'Light along and pass my compliments to Mr Marston, and would he care to bless us with his presence in the cabin. We are in contemplation of music and would welcome his participation. Whiskey and brandy too, if ye will. Thankee.'

'Good evening, sir, gentlemen,' said Marston a few minutes later, clutching his violin and bow. Murphy, looking greatly pleased, stood at Marston's elbow, laden with bottles and glasses. He poured generous libations without any prompting.

'Here, take a glass with us, Mr Marston; if ye will,' said Pat.

'Thank you, sir.'

'A toast, gentlemen,' offered Pat, 'The ladies having left us, I give you: To wives and sweethearts!'

'Wives and sweethearts!' echoed around the table, the drinks downed in one. 'Aye, and may they never meet!' cried Duncan, helping himself to the whisky.

'Will I freshen your glass?' said Pat to Marston. The chaplain nodded cautiously, for he felt in good conscience unable to concede pleasure to Duncan's jest.

'We are in the spirit for the music of home... *my home*, of Ireland. D'ye care to suggest a tune?' said Pat, the tension that had gripped him all day relaxing a little.

'Why, sir, I am not greatly acquainted with the music of the land, of the Irish country folk, at all,' said Marston, hesitating. 'It may be that I am unequal to the task.'

'Come now; why, I recall your playing with the maestro, Paganini himself, when we was in Genoa, and I ain't heard the like since... that is... I mean to say... your playing is uncommon prime... puts us to shame. Am I right, Simon?'

'Anything you care to play will serve, Michael,' said Simon.

'Anything at all,' echoed Pat.

Marston was a violinist of considerable accomplishment; without further ado he took up his violin and began to play, launching into *Soldier's Joy* with gusto. Simon recognised the tune immediately, bringing in his viola with staccato emphasis, Pat's 'cello joining in, seconding in harmony. Duncan worked in with his whistle, shrilling away with huge gusto and raising the tempo as the tune progressed, the ensemble accelerating every second and only Marston's flying fingers staying abreast of the whistle until after a frantic, wild and animated two and a half enthusiastic minutes with a myriad of erroneous notes the joyous end was reached in great laughter and mutual applause, the chaotic nature of the playing bringing long absent huge cheer to the cabin.

'Once more and a trifle slower, if you will,' cried Pat, a hint of exuberance settling upon him, a blessed modicum of normality - so rare for as long as he could recall - gracing the cabin; and the tune was repeated with a degree of competency wholly absent the first time, to the repeated delight of all present, Murphy dancing a reel outside the cabin whilst clutching the anticipated but diminishing next bottle. Loud congratulations and hand-clapping at the conclusion were followed by Pat's shout, 'Murphy, Murphy there... light along another bottle if ye will.'

'Well, here 'tis, sorr,' announced Murphy with smug self-satisfaction, losing not a moment in placing the tray with bottle and beakers on the table with a flourish and an exaggerated bow; the theatre of it, as Murphy intended, diverting Pat's gaze from the absent top quarter of the bottle's contents, at least until he had left the cabin in unprecedented haste.

Chapter Nine

*Monday 22nd November 1824   12:00   20nm SW of Ushant,
wind SSW, FORCE   7, 25-35 knots, moderate gale, waves
streaked with foam*

Finisterre had been left far astern in the twilight after the sunset
two days previously when *Surprise* had begun her transit of the
Bay. Many hours of uneventful sailing since and the prior night
uncomfortably choppy, the new day had offered a cloudy sky of
unceasing grey which had scarcely lightened since an
unpromising dawn. The sea, with the long Atlantic fetch behind
it, boasted a strong swell whilst the wind had strengthened during
every hour of the day. Before Finisterre, *Surprise* had seen only
the occasional Portuguese bean-cod; after the cape not a single
vessel had been sighted. A distant Oleron lay far beyond the
starboard quarter. *Surprise* was, by Pat's reckoning, closing on
Ushant, the island perhaps five or ten leagues ahead on the
starboard bow. The south-south-easterly wind of the night had
long been near imperceptibly veering and now blew from the
south-south-west even as it grew noticeably stronger, the rigging
everywhere rattling, the yards creaking and their sail edges
whipping to yield the most discordant sharp cracking noises as
the wind gusted. *Surprise* fairly tore along at ten knots, her
plentiful spread of canvas holding her firm and far over to
leeward with little rolling, her lee rail dipping occasionally into
the white water, the frigate's turbulent wake stretching far behind
in unwavering linearity until subsumed within the general
turmoil, the sole discomfort to all aboard being the shuddering
and pitching as she encountered successive wave crests. The long
months of summer Mediterranean heat had made the oakum
brittle, and her return to the pounding of Atlantic rollers shook
the hull hard and dislodged the pitch in the seams, *Surprise*
making water in a thousand small leaks, particularly so at the
hard-pressed bow which was taking the full brunt of the

repetitive slamming of hull into unyielding ocean. The cold air was filled with moisture, although it was not raining hard; it was more a constant light drizzle with short shower flurries. The unshaven stubble of all on deck collected water in tiny droplets, the exposed skin of every man remaining perpetually damp; rivulets of ice-cold moisture ran down every face, the salt taste ever present on the lips. The rain had spattered all over the remaining glass of the cabin, and Pat sat alone in the gloom at his table, in his damp clothes, cold. He was thinking of his family, away on *Eleanor,* and he was in some trepidation of what Biscay might yet serve up as *Surprise* slipped away from its grip and hauled ever closer to home. He shivered as the bell rang its resonating *"ding-ding"* to announce two bells of the afternoon watch. For once he thought it obtrusive as he studied his chart whilst he pondered his predicament. The murk did not allow him to know precisely how close they were to Ushant with its perilously dangerous reefs. In the normal course of things Pat had no inclination to venture close to any coast, save for the approach to harbour, and much preferred the uninterrupted vista of sea, plenty of it, all the way to the horizon. The Brittany peninsular lay ahead of them, and that was a potential disaster in the making, for he had no means of knowing how much sea room he was afforded without she was blown on to a lee shore, nor how long *Surprise* could endure in the storm that his experience told him was coming; for the glass had never in all his years fallen lower and faster, so much so that he could scarcely believe his eyes. He called for reviving hot coffee and sat drinking through a whole pint of the strong, bitter brew, deep in thought, considerations of the plainly now dangerous approach into the Channel and on to Falmouth weighing heavy on his mind. His coffee finished, he determined to return on deck and speak with his lookouts, his mind filled with worry.

In the corner of the coach, Simon sat hunched over the purser's desk, similarly cold whilst writing with intense concentration, ignoring Murphy's occasional enquiry as to whether he wished for dinner.

As far as straining eyes at the tops were able to see into the gloom, scarcely a mile or two, nothing was visible in any direction save for endless water in turmoil. The sea state had developed from the benevolent near calm of the prior few days' gentle swell into turbulent wild green rollers, flecked everywhere with white horses, and the temperature, already cold, was falling discernibly. The ever-darkening sky filled the anxious thoughts of all the men on deck, uneasy eyes staring all about them, heads filled with fretful apprehension, for they too had observed the wind strengthening consistently since first light. Despite his leanings towards the shortest, the most direct passage home Pat could not dispel his personal forebodings; he had slept little the prior night and he weighed again in his tired mind whether *Surprise* should hold firm to her north-easterly heading to shave the coast around Ushant for the swiftest passage or whether to strike off on a more north-westerly course so as to keep plentiful sea room until she had rounded the Brittany peninsula without the least doubt in the poor visibility. He gazed all about him through the cabin lights into the distance before the murk closed his view, and he concluded that the rollers were bigger, the wave heights rising. Putting on his oilskins he stepped up to the quarterdeck. *Surprise* made little leeway in the strong southerly influence of the wind, and for that at least he was profoundly grateful, for the potential presence of a dangerous lee shore, the ultimate fear of every mariner, was prevalent in his thoughts. He stared all about him: dense cloud banks, dark grey in colour, obscured the view in every direction, falling like irregular curtains to converge with the darkness of the sea. In the meantime Pickering had been tasked with several larbowlins in constant soundings with the lead line, the utmost caution adopted in the uncertainty of her position, but no bottom had been reported all morning.

'Why, Simon,' said a deeply fatigued Pat, immersed in thought, yawning and surprised to see his friend appear at his side on the quarterdeck with the weather so inclement, 'What brings you up here?'

'I am come to stand by you for a while, if I may,' Simon's face indicating a profound wish for the company of a friend.

'I should be very happy.'

'I feel the pressing need for bountiful fresh air. Marston and Jason are attending the men, changing dressings and suchlike. It is tolerably foetid below, and as a medical man I abhor the necessity for the sick to languish so long in the noxious airs. I am come upstairs to reassure myself that the end of such squalor is nigh upon us, that we are nearing home, blessed home... that I may report such to anxious ears when I return downstairs.'

There was a long pause before Pat responded, 'We are approaching home, sure; though in this damned murk I cannot know to within ten leagues where we are... still in the waters of the Bay of course.' Silence endured for another minute before Pat resumed, 'I venture your patients will be tolerably pleased with whatever you care to report, for without you I doubt that many of those men would be here to see their families again, whenever we fetch home, and that is blindingly obvious even to a deaf man; that is to say, it is known to every man aboard the barky; of that there is no doubt in my mind, no doubt at all.'

'Pray do not speak of such, of obligation, of my own contribution, brother. Where are we, tell? You spoke of the Bay; do we near the top, the northernmost regions? In such wind as this we must be moving with considerable celerity... *cracking on* as you would put it.'

'Yes, we are nearing the Channel,' roared Pat, his words whipped away by the wind. 'And look... there has never been such a display as the present to see the barky, how well she sails... to see what she can do when she is put to her shifts - indeed, she is flying!'

'She is most assuredly moving at a considerable velocity, that is plain... the floor is canted to an exceptional degree,' shouted Simon, the wind blasting his face, spicules of spray burning in their flying force.

'She is truly a treasure,' cried Pat, 'and it pleases me that we... you and I... can enjoy her at her best, a delight to behold.'

'Certainly it is,' shouted Simon, striving to conceal a plentiful degree of reservation.

'But I have no doubt,' said Pat gazing at the blackening sky, 'that it will most surely come on later with a mighty blow.'

'Is it not blowing so already?' ventured Simon, concern and disquiet creeping in.

'I would not swear to it but I venture we are nearing Ushant,' declared Pat, hesitancy plainly audible in his voice. 'I am minded that Brittany is five or perhaps even ten leagues off the starboard bow or thereabouts, and the next hour or so will see us reaching our turn, our change of course.'

'Almost home, eh? I rejoice, I do.'

'And thence thirty-five leagues to Scilly,' this said without a trace of the levity of the song.

Perceiving Pat's own uncertainty, his tone far from rejoicing, a suspicious Simon persevered, 'What is on your mind, old friend? It is the weather, no doubt? Allow me to ask: will the remainder of our journey be perilous? I am contemplating on your mention of Ushant, on the doubtless presence of rocks, of reefs and shoals, of the perennial dangers of the marine kind whose proximity the navigator may find difficult to discern in these lamentable conditions. Is it near, at all? I had great hopes that we had done with watery hazard and sea-faring jeopardy; I am exceedingly sorry if that is not the case.'

Pat sighed; he had since many years reconciled himself to Simon's inability to grasp the bare fundamentals of the mariner's navigational awareness. 'You hit the hammer square on the nail... on the head. With the light so bad and this wind strengthening by the hour it will be damnably difficult to negotiate Ushant in safety, and neither - *God help us* - when we are in the darkness of the night would I care to follow Shovell on to the Scillies. Are you acquainted with the story?'

'To what do you refer?'

'Admiral Cloudesley Shovell, in the year 1707; a great storm... some say it was a tempest. In November too it was, *may Saint Patrick preserve us*. He was lost with four ships on the outliers of the Scillies. Of the three largest of 'em, of the crew only the ship's butcher, *Lawrence* - if my memory serves me - survived; the admiral was murdered even as he fetched up half-drowned on the rocks, battered by a local woman, a vile fiend, and then his ring was stripped from him; so the tale goes.'

'A harpy indeed,' murmured Simon, gloomy thoughts and fears flickering once more in his mind.

The resonating three bells jolted a thoughtful Pat from his historical reflections, 'In the customary turn of events I would be minded to bear down for Falmouth directly... run before the wind... and so swiftly to home.'

'That would seem to be an admirable notion, dear.'

'... but that is to say *if* I knew where we were to within a league or two *and* in the prospect of arriving in the light of day... and with too no more than a fresh gale astern...'

'Will we not, as you say, bear down directly for Falmouth... and whilst we have light enough?'

'No... no, I venture we will stand off a trifle more to the west, to linger for a watch or two, and we will see if the weather improves before we venture into the Channel.'

'The weather, brother?' the rising flickerings of alarm registered in Simon's mind, which he strived to suppress.

'Alas, by God, there is no knowing how long we might be out here. I fear for the worst. The mercury is falling damnably fast - and that is a pretty... *a scientific* kettle of fish, to be sure. In all candour - and I would not say this to anyone but you - it is tolerably worrying, so it is.'

'And now the mortal rain is falling again,' Simon sighed, large droplets spattering his face and drumming audibly on the skylight glass of the great cabin just in front of them.

'Barton, light along to my cabin and fetch the Doctor my griego if you will; thankee. I think we will bear up a point or two to gain a trifle of westing. I am minded it will not serve us well to press on as best we might for Falmouth,' Pat declared. Another thoughtful minute, 'And there is too much of south-west in this wind to find any shelter in the lee of Ushant... or indeed in the lee of any land on either side of the Channel.' Simon stared, Pat engrossed in his deliberations. 'Neither do I care to consider of lying-to when the wind may shift more to the west... and we may be reduced to precious little sail. The weather will doubtless worsen... better an egg today than a hen tomorrow.'

'Do you perceive this is a chicken and egg situation?'

'Oh... for sure; any certain progress at all will be a prodigious tough egg to crack; it looks precious like a lee shore, and the infernal storm of all time is surely coming; you may count on it. We have a damnably large bridge to cross before we fetch home. I am in contemplation of a blow akin to a hurricane. There, I've said it now.'

'A hurricane?' Simon paused for a mere moment, adding 'Do you mean tomorrow our chickens will come home to roost?'

Pat stared in suspicion at his friend, a titter escaping Simon's lips, 'Eh?'

'So we will not count our eggs before they are hatched or our bridges before we have crossed them?' Simon was laughing loud now, his laughter producing a scowl and ultimately a smile from Pat; the helmsmen too were all sniggering and grinning broadly.

'Have a care or I will send Barton to fetch the cat, the rope kind that is.' Pat decided the time had come for a concession to sail reduction, 'Mr Macleod, a single-reef for the tops'ls if you will.'

'Aye aye, sir.'

On they sailed, rising uncomfortably on the succession of ever-rolling crests and frothing foam caps before descending into the troughs, the formidable waves all about them beginning to build to greater heights, the roll of the ship increasing and the eerie moaning of the wind changing its note to something increasingly sinister, an audible harbinger of things to come; unpleasant things, thought Pat, his eyes drooping, tiredness creeping up upon him.

'A hurricane indeed? I had always supposed that after all these years, after our passages over a plethora of oceans, that I had become accustomed to the shifts of the vessel, to the forceful billows and the extreme aqueous powers as we have oft experienced, but such violence as you conceive this portends, I confess, is a trifle disturbing, despite my customarily being downstairs.'

'The mercury is falling like a stone, an extraordinary swift fall, so it is, and for sure that means this will be as great a storm as we have ever seen. A most uncommon severe blow is coming, of that I have no doubt, and we are perilously short-handed. I will tell you frankly that the chops of the Channel will seem like the smallest of ripple on the water after this night.'

'I speak as one who is unaccustomed to the navigator's perception of these extreme nautical conditions, these challenges, but would you have the great kindness to explain: are we in peril, so?' asked Simon, wondering to what precise extent Pat was concerned, for his face expressed deep lines of worry.

'I suppose it is of no use my speaking of the necessities of sea-room and the exigencies of our navigational circumstances, of the directions she will tolerate in this fearsome wind?'

'I am afraid not, my dear. Is there a particular exigency to which you refer?'

'I am minded, the wind blowing from the south-south-west that it is, that if we remain Falmouth bound then we should gain what westing we can before the wind reaches its coming ferocity; for when that besets us we may be reduced to bare poles in the worst of things, and that may leave us in peril of wrecking upon a lee shore without we are far beyond such dangers.'

'*If* we remain Falmouth bound?' Simon stared at Pat, horrified, 'Wrecking, for all love? Did you say *wrecking*?'

'It is conceivable that we would gain some respite were we to shift into the lee of Ushant and the peninsula... into the Gulf of Brittany... and so wait out the coming storm there. I am considering of these prospects.'

'Good Lord,' exclaimed Simon, the alarming, frightening realisation striking him hard, 'so we are not assured of reaching Falmouth at all?'

'Oh, I should never say that; I would never tempt fate, no... but I venture we shall see a busy night, for sure.' Pat shouted across to Duncan, 'Mr Macleod, with the wind strengthening so, I doubt she will long bear everything she has aloft.' Duncan nodded his agreement and Simon looked aghast, staring anxiously all about him. He reeled back on his feet as the ship heeled violently over in a particularly fearsome momentary combination of wind gust with a rogue wave striking hard on the beam, the spray cascading over all on the quarterdeck. Pat glanced up, increasingly anxious for the topgallants.

'Simon, I venture you may care to prepare your patients for the worst... that is to say, this night will surely be uncomfortable for all... and perhaps a draught will serve them well,' said Pat, adding in a tone of encouragement which did not quite ring true in Simon's ear, 'With the blessing there is no doubt that we will endure, though the coming hours will certainly be... be a trifle uncomfortable.'

Simon started, blinked, Pat's pronouncement not at all what he wished to hear, a long, contemplative moment passing before he spluttered, 'With your leave, I think I will go downstairs to my station. I find I must shift my sodden clothes before I attend my patients; and laudanum, a heavy dose, must be considered for several of them and without delay.' Wiping his dripping face and spitting out the unpalatable salt, gingerly he groped his way to the companionway and left the deck with an overwhelming sense of disquiet, extremely uncomfortable, gravely concerned for his charges, his mind already calculating how far his greatly diminished stock of the laudanum narcotic would go round for the more severely wounded of his patients.

12:30   15nm SW of Ushant, wind SSW, FORCE 8, 35-40 knots, Fresh Gale, spindrift and much foam, "Treble-reefed topsails, or that to which a well-conditioned man-of-war could just carry in chase, full and by"

Looking astern, Pat watched with no little interest a distant squall, a darker patch beneath which the sea exhibited great turbulence as evidenced by the white tops raging below it. The wind, he was concerned to note with a sinking feeling, was blowing it their way. Dalby rang the solitary bell to announce the Afternoon watch.

'Mr Pickering, I venture we will rig relieving tackles to the tiller. Mr Sampays, all guns are to be lashed fore and aft.'

Pat fretted more as the wind strengthened further and he called for every precautionary measure he could think of: rolling tackles, preventer-backstays on the lower and topsail yards; the top-gallants' yards to be struck down to the deck. The pumps were readied, the hammocks brought out of the netting and struck below, a lifebuoy was made fast to the deep sea lead-line and the reel stowed aft - a last, very slim chance for a man washed overboard. He gazed with unease at the much repaired canvas of the sails, for there was precious little, a mere half of a bolt of greatly mildewed number four of doubtful provenance left in the orlop as reserve. 'Mr Macleod, we will rig lifelines on the quarterdeck, waist and foc'sle, one each side.'

'Aye aye, sir.'

'Mr Pickering, preventer painters to be clapped on the anchors, if you will. Mr Sampays, secure the boats with double gripes and check the drain holes are free and clear; all hatchways and scuttles are to be covered with tarpaulins, ready to be battened down. Mr Macleod, two more hands to the wheel.' Another ten minutes of thought and Pat spoke once more, 'Mr Macleod, the spritsail yard is to be swung round and triced up to the bowsprit, the jib-boom run in and made fast. Mr Sampays, will you ask cook for a bucket or two of slush and set a dozen hands to paint it on the lower shrouds where they cross over the yards - it will reduce chafing and may preserve them when the blow comes on to its full force. Set axes at hand at all masts, if you please.' His officers blanched.

After one particular blast of fierce strength and *Surprise* heeling violently, the fore course, which had been torn in several places by shot in the Gerontas battle and damaged when the topmast came down - the repairs made in Argostoli - ripped from top to bottom and billowed out, the two segments wild, flapping and cracking.

'Clew up! Clew up!' shouted Pat.

'All hands on deck!' Macleod bawled, the shout echoed by the bosun on the gun deck, the men leaping hastily up the companionways from below and clambering swiftly up the rigging.

'Man the clew garnets! Man the buntlines!' shouted Macleod, 'Man the leech-lines! Hands to the sheets and bowlines!'

'Mr Prosser,' said Pat to the master at the helm, concern and urgency plain in his voice, 'steer two points to leeward, let us spill a little of the wind and take the load off the sail a trifle.'

'Ease the tack!' cried Macleod, and a minute later, 'Ease off the bowline, handsomely there!' An anxious minute, all eyes staring at the men standing precariously on the yard, clinging on with all their strength, the ship rising and falling fifty feet, and in the wave depths the lee heel swiftly falling off her to give a vicious roll as she righted. 'Ease the sheet!' shouted Macleod, his own deep anxiety plain in his voice.

'Mr Sampays, the fore staysails will serve to protect us, a last resort to save her from broaching if the tempest acts on her quarter. The main and mizzen staysails are also to be hoisted. All staysails must be preserved as best we may and will be set with double sheets.'

'Aye aye, sir.'

'And we will slacken the jib-stay just a trifle.'

'Aye aye, sir,' the bosun nodded his understanding, for the jib-stay was ordinarily taut as a bar of iron and would tighten further in a blow, the rain acting upon it, when it would dangerously work the bowsprit.

The fore course braces were seized, the yard swung round to relieve the strain on the remaining sail remnants, and men prepared to take it in; others hauled up the weather clewline. In that stark moment Pat realised he must further reduce his square sails before much more time passed by and his eyes wandered towards the single-reefed fore topsail as if in assessment of how well it was holding up on its repaired mast.

'Sir, will we close-reef her tops'ls?' ventured a like-minded Duncan.

It was a timely intrusion, thought Pat. He immediately concurred with the concerns of his First, 'Make it so, Mr Macleod... and thankee.' He smiled at Duncan. Standing near the wheel, he could see no further than a few hundred yards. The waves were streaked with foam, flying in the air. Even across the quarterdeck the blown spray was thick. The protesting creak of the yards was plainly audible despite the roar of wind and water, the braces under such tension, and over all was the predominant whistle in the rigging: the whole of the aural barrage pressing heavy on the senses. He rarely spoke to the men at the wheel, for conversation was becoming difficult, gesticulation the only sure way to communicate with even the men standing alongside him. A more extreme series of rolls, every man thrown to clutch for support, and Pat turned away from the wind and cupped his ear to listen to the master's shouted words.

'Sir, 'tis a proper worry, the glass falling so. I greatly fear the approaching tempest, for with no sightings of any coast to be had we cannot know on this course whether we are nearing Ushant or Brittany's coast itself. We will never know in the night if we may be entering the approaches to Brest or closing on any lee shore,' Prosser's face displayed his consternation.

Pat nodded; the situation was becoming more worrying with every turn of the glass, the air temperature falling perceptibly. 'For sure, I am singularly mindful of that, Mr Prosser, that danger. In these conditions I doubt we will see anything of the Stiff light. I am coming to the view that only gaining more westing can help us,' he shouted. 'We will keep her firm on this course for one more hour, no more, to see if we can gain a sighting of land or light, and then we must turn away.'

Below deck, Simon returned to the sick bay from the medical storeroom, greatly concerned with the prospect of the approaching hurricane, his huge dismay showing plain in his face. Were the crew to suffer further injuries very little of laudanum remained to him, and this added to his anxieties. The temperature on the lower deck was also turning noticeably colder, and from hundreds of tiny gaps in the deck above - the caulking having perished in the Greek summer heat - myriads of water droplets dripped down to create the dampest of environments; the air was foetid, the constant dribble soaking the blankets of the wounded in their hammocks. The most severely wounded were lying in the officers' cots within the tiny cabins off the gunroom. 'What news, colleague?' asked Marston anxiously, 'I should very much like to hear from you the Captain's appreciation of our circumstances, our prospects; if you will.' Ears pricked up all about them and the hubbub of shouted dialogue and the murmurings of the sick subsided as a score of men waited expectantly for the reply.

Simon surreptitiously glanced all about him, noting the undeclared interest of numerous anxious faces within earshot. He observed the quietude extending aft like a wave as men further away perceived the silence descending on the sick bay, the change noticeable even as the hull pitched and rolled and the ship continued to be pummelled by the turbulent sea. 'Captain O'Connor is assuredly sensible of our circumstances; that is to say the great wind and our necessary direction to accommodate it, mindful of our intended destination.' This manufactured and meaningless reply was said with some degree of hesitation which did not help to dispel Marston's worry, grave concern showing on his face.

'Forgive me, but when is it anticipated that we will reach home, dear Falmouth town, that precious sanctuary?'

'Oh that cannot be made plain without a very great deal of time and with recourse to the onerous jargon of the mariner, and that is patently tedious in the extreme.' Simon's nervous equivocation was reflected in his wavering voice, plain to all.

'But are we in danger? This is the most frightful of storms.' The chaplain pressed, unconvinced, dearly hoping for a more sure and positive prognosis.

'The Captain is making all necessary preparations in view of the remote, *the exceedingly remote* danger of an unforeseen landfall. I believe he referred to a lee shore and the desirability of sea room, of attaining more of it... or perhaps less; something along those lines.' Simon's report was uttered with an audible degree of uncertainty. 'Though I am accustomed to the principles, of course, I make no claims of proficiency as a navigator.'

'Pray forgive my enquiry, doubtless ill-considered it is, but is the Captain possessed of a sufficiency of knowledge of our precise circumstances, of our present situation vis-à-vis the coasts, the promontories and those shoals which doubtless abound all around us?'

211

'A plentiful sufficiency, a very considerable one, I am sure. I dare say he is tolerably accustomed to these situations, and doubtless such consideration is at the forefront of his mind.' Simon was bridling now, his irritation founded on his own fear, uncertainty creeping in to his thoughts. He sought to change the subject, and in the practised and authoritative voice of the medical profession, wholly intended to dissuade further question, pronounced his diversion, 'Now colleague, let us attend to our patients; I have a modicum of concern for young Trevenen here, for his breathing. I do not care for the sound I have detected this morning within his chest.'

Monday 22nd November 1824   13:00   10nm W of Ushant, wind SSW veering SW, FORCE 9, 40-45 knots, strong gale, overhanging crests   "close-reefed topsails and fore course, the wind a scream in the rigging"

Five bells and the wind had strengthened further, the sound of its all-encompassing presence a low thrumming noise in the rigging; the flying spray had greatly thickened and blew all across the ship as a soaking white spume, the clothing of every man on deck utterly sodden, every man chilled: duty had become a misery. Visibility was poor, perhaps a mile but often reduced to little more than a few hundred yards or less. On occasions only the foaming white crests of the nearest waves could be made out. Pat observed with dismay the rising wave heights and he sensed with growing alarm the latent power of the swell increasing with the long fetch all across the Bay. In the much restricted clarity of view, he could better feel and hear than see. Another shuddering "WHHUUMMP" was followed by the repetitive surge of water over the foc'sle as *Surprise*, sailing large with a quartering wind, smacked down from the crest into the trough of the ever more steeply rising waves, overhanging but not quite breaking, though perilously close to doing so. That thought frightened him a little, for as every seaman knew: a ship would not founder in a wave which did not break, but once the towering summits cascaded their angry white spume down their face, the converse became ever more likely, the danger of being pooped rising considerably.

'It's time to pray that this gale does not strengthen further, Mr Prosser. Would you care to venture your thoughts? I am mindful that the lee shore of Ushant and the Brittany coast are near directly on our bow,' Pat shouted. 'If we could but gain a scrap of protection in the lee of Ushant from this long southerly fetch then we may cling to the hope of some relief,' this was said in the most uneasy of tone, with considerable uncertainty in his voice.

'I would not care to counsel that, sir,' the master volunteered gravely, 'These waters are familiar to me since I was eight and fishing out of Lyme, and were we to round the cape and the wind to veer to its customary south-westerly... well, in the likes of this blow we would be set fair for the Channel Islands and a lee shore mighty close; and, sir, though we may take soundings, without any sightings and precious little helm, 'tis sure the Minkies will not allow us any safe haven inside the Gulf.'

Pat stared at Prosser, digesting his bleak advice, all of which was loudly ringing true. His anxiety increasing he concurred wearily, 'Mr Prosser, pray let us not tempt fate.' He determined to go below and eat earlier before the weather worsened further and mandated his constant presence upon the quarterdeck, as he anticipated it surely would. 'Carry on Mr Macleod.' He stepped down the companionway, his mind whirring frenetically with weather and course calculations.

In the great cabin, Murphy fretted around his pre-occupied captain, bringing unbidden a steaming dish of lobscouse which was of fortunately glutinous consistency, as for ten minutes Pat's plate lay untouched before him; precariously so in the roll and the pitching of the ship, both since several hours extremely severe. Ultimately it was Duncan's very wet entry to the cabin, sodden and dripping, nearly an hour after Pat had left the quarterdeck, which prompted Pat to the necessity of eating; he had already sensed his time at the table would be short. 'Sir, I beg your pardon for barging in.' Pat looked up from his meal, his appetite diminishing by the second and the Lobscouse near cold as his First expressed concerns about the topsails staying atrip whilst the strain on the jury-rigged repair to the main course yard was considerable: it was flexing to an alarming degree, and would Pat care to see for himself.

'Hell and death, Mr Macleod. I will attend in a few minutes after I bolt down this dinner,' declared Pat with despond in his voice. 'Murphy there, light along a dry shirt; I may be some time on deck.'

'Well, there is a puddin' comin' along, sorr,' exclaimed the steward with considerable indignation in his voice.

One hand holding firm the bowl, the other the spoon, the spicy lobscouse was swiftly devoured, although its peppery full flavour, succulent and rich in fat, barely registered with Pat in his renewed haste, his mind filling with heightened concerns. He had put on his dry shirt and was reaching for his oilskins when an indignant Murphy re-appeared, his face incandescent in glaring disapproval, 'Well, if yer please sorr, ain't you a'wantin' cook's spotted dog... 'tis yer favourite?'

In the same instant Simon entered, his steps hesitant, his body swaying with the ship until he gratefully clutched the table. 'I am come to tell you that the roaring profusion of noise is utterly intolerable and water is pouring in from outside, into the sick bay through cracks which have opened in the wall... the bulwark would it be?'

'Sprung caulking in the bow,' added Duncan, his tone resigned.

'It is soaking those of my patients on the floor who cannot be accommodated in a hammock, and I am minded to shift those men to the gunroom, to the officers' cots; with your concurrence that is.'

'Of course, without delay,' an exasperated Pat replied, 'Mr Macleod will assist you directly.'

Simon, mollified, stared at the food, the pudding particularly, and sniffed the tantalising aroma of cinnamon which filled the cabin, 'Ah, such a striking aroma... I am reminded of the admirable Doctor Sydenham, specifically his laudanum; the cinnamon it is he added. Laudanum... that precious substance is proving of the utmost value to my discomfited patients, little that there is left to me.' This producing no response, he continued, 'I m exceedingly concerned for those patients with fractures. Though splinted, the extreme movement of the vessel presents considerable difficulty for them.'

Pat merely nodded absently, continuing to pull on his sea boots.

'Brother, if you are going on deck again, perhaps I will take his splendid pudding with me? Marston is greatly partial to a sweet morsel.'

Pat stared ruefully at the pudding, nodded again, said nothing and started for the door.

'I will return to my patients and lose not a minute - as you might say,' muttered Simon, seizing the pudding.

Pat, at the door, looked back to Murphy and again to the steaming spotted dog with a great feeling of resignation; he sighed, 'I may return for my share if all goes well, when this storm subsides.' This plaintive hope was offered without conviction, without confidence in his voice, with little faith, its foundation plainly mere optimism, all present gaining that feeling about it. Sighing, they resigned themselves to the general mood of gloom and apprehension.

On deck once more, the darker clouds with the fading of the light had further reduced visibility. Whilst in the cabin Pat had heard the increasing force of the wind, felt the greater rise and fall of the ship within the waves, but notwithstanding that he was overwhelmed by what he saw: under an unrelenting dark grey sky, the sea had become white, was now a boiling maelstrom of violent turmoil which stretched to a dimly visible confluence. His eyes blinking, his face stinging as unrelenting water blasted with violent force in the unity of spray and rain combined, his concerns for his ship soared; for he knew her sea room must quickly diminish once she neared the channel and he had only a hazy knowledge of the frigate's proximity to any coast.

He stared for long minutes at the topsails, thinking hard, before his mind shifted fleetingly to other concerns. He shouted to the bosun who was standing with his Second near the helm, Mr Sampays, let the hatches be battened down whilst we still have light enough.' Pat cursed the weather whilst contemplating his precise position, no sighting possible through the dense, grey black cloud which filled the sky, not the least glimpse of the sun nor any bright shard of sunlight evident anywhere. Doub gnawed at his mind for he had kept *Surprise* on her course fo longer than perhaps he should have done, his indecision founded in the dwindling hope that it did at least provide a chance, albei a slender one, of a valuable sighting of land.

From time to time, cold, wet and standing with a degree of trepidation near the wheel, clinging now and then to the mizzer mast to steady himself, Pat gazed in hope but without expectation through his telescope, hoping beyond hope to catch a glimpse o the coast, any coast, anything at all, but his efforts proved fruitless; from the depths of the wave troughs all around the only thing visible was water: thrusting, powerful, energised. From the brief seconds atop the crests nothing at all could be discerned through the dense spray which coated the glass immediately and rendered it quite useless. He called for four more men to relieve those already at the helm for some hours, for the powerful wind and rising seas made their task particularly difficult and tiring He cast his eyes all about the heavens, looking for some small relief from the enduring cloud, but he could see none. He gazed aft for long minutes, the sky blackening perceptibly just a few miles in their wake, white wave tops a thin line all across the southern horizon, perhaps as little as two miles away, which wa as far as he could see, his gaze enduring for a long and anxious several minutes until another dense, dark cloud overtook them. I was coupled with a huge and sudden increase in wind strength. In an instant a further great load was imposed upon the sails and rigging, *Surprise* heeling violently to starboard; massive raindrops blasted down around them with great force, the ai carrying a huge saturation of moisture, so much so that mere breathing necessitated deep gasps and the sensation was akin to drowning, all visibility gone. Hopes of a swiftly passing squal were extinguished after twenty minutes by more dense swathe of heavy rain pouring down without let up, every man on deck swiftly reduced to shivering, wet wretchedness.

For the past half-hour a deeply tired Pat - for his anxieties o the ship's state and the families away on *Eleanor* had meant tha e had slept little during the previous night - had hoped with all is heart that the storm would relent and he could gain the mallest, the briefest sighting of land, make any necessary ecision and then return below for the briefest of naps, an hour of ecuperation; but it was plainly not to be: as far as the eye could ee to the horizon, that is when the low cloud thinned nomentarily, green rollers stretched away to infinity; furious vhite tops and interminable spray were prevalent everywhere; wiftly moving black clouds extended in every direction. The nen aloft were increasingly uncomfortable, so exposed to the nexorably strengthening wind whilst clinging desperately to neir dangerous perch.

Simon had re-emerged on deck, and he hurried across to Pat, lutching his coat about him, the cold, ferocious wind near earing it from his grasp. Reaching Pat he grasped the mizzen nast tenaciously in a hug of his left arm, fearing he might be imself plucked bodily up by the gale. On the flooded uarterdeck men all around him crouched at the carronades, trapping the stubby guns tighter within their slides. He blinked o clear the spray from his eyes and stared all about him: huge rey rollers stretched away to infinity, white crests foaming. A ong fetch sea from the south west and running with the frigate's ourse imposed absolute control over her, Simon was sure, for he ould not comprehend how she could conceivably bear away in ny different direction, nature's force exhibited in all its towering omination. At times the crests towered far above the ship, a undred yards or more between them, the waves coming fast om astern and sweeping past the frigate with a perfect onstancy, effortlessly lifting her stern before raising her bow in assing, *Surprise* rising on the peaks to fall back in the troughs, ails alternately filling with visible great strain upon them before eflating like a burst paper bag as she fell, down, down, until nere was nothing but sea visible about her, and Simon gazed bout him in awe, a silent minute elapsing before he shouted, 'It s a wonder any man can endure up here, within this... this empest.'

'It is impressive,' cried Pat, 'and I do greatly love a blow.' his was said with the intention of cheering his friend, but with

too a resigned acceptance of *Surprise* being an utterl
insignificant entity amidst the raging titans of wind and sea. An
so she was, for the whole ship seemed possessed: the riggin
sang, a resonating discordant note fluctuating up and down wit
the rise and fall of the ship; the deck vibrated with a lov
frequency, a shiver pulsing through it, and nothing held at ba
the ferocity of the wind whilst the cold saltwater swept over th
deck in conflicting switches of direction, quite impossible t
shelter from, *Surprise* thrown bodily up and down, over an
back, heeling far over before coming up, not hesitantly bu
stridently, emerging like a cork from the wave troughs. On sh
went, her topsails and courses all pushing her on, ever faster a
the wind strength inexorably increased, holding firm to he
course.

All the time Pat's roving gaze studied his ship and he
responses to the great forces she was being subjected to; and a
the ship bucked up and down on successive waves, pushed fa
over on the crests to reel violently back again to something nea
upright in the depths of the troughs, his eyes shifted towards th
sails, wondering how well and for how long the old canva
would hold up when the full power of the gale repetitivel
pushed her lee side far over, when the rigging would be takin
the full load. Already her masts were straining, her yard
bending, hugely stressed, the wood and hemp all vocal, groanin
and squeaking. Sheets of spray, great waterfalls of it came flyin
constantly all over the ship, thrown up from the bow as sh
plunged into the rising wave wall before her as she strived t
emerge from the troughs, the wind from astern briefly blocked b
the succeeding wave; and then flung up from astern as she rose
the next blast, the fierce wind from aft, from the south wes
water, water everywhere, passing overhead, striking the mer
flooding the decks, never clearing before the next torrent deluge
down upon them to drench every man on duty, all suffering th
cold chill.

'It is a trifle frightening,' shouted Simon in a voice beggin
for contradiction.

The bosun was struggling along the gun deck from gun t
gun with his men, strapping preventer-breechings to the grea

218

guns, all of which had long been turned ninety degrees before the worst of the storm arrived, the additional ropes to secure them more surely to the hull, to hold them against the flood tide of water that threatened to tear them loose and send them rolling, crashing through the flimsy side; for nothing would stop their half ton of iron weight were they to break loose. Barton was struggling to safeguard the boats, suspended amidst and below the yards. With three men clinging to whatever was at hand whilst affixing more straps, men everywhere were doing what they could as precautionary measures, no commands given or needed, every man a veteran, all familiar with such necessary steps; and from time to time whilst they worked they shouted an occasional word to their shipmates, darted a momentary glance about them to see what was happening, to check what their fellows were doing; they nodded to their few officers, whilst they in turn shouted encouragement, returned many a nod, the wind too strong for words to be audible beyond the nearest man, all hands looking anxiously to the sky, to the upper yards, praying for the sails, that they might endure in the raging ferocity of the wind.

'The barky is cracking on,' shouted Dalby, pulling hard on a preventer-stay at *The Smasher*.

'Sure, and the canvas will be tearing away - any minute now,' bawled Mason, spitting a mouthful of saltwater away, 'if it ain't taken in mighty quick.'

For the past hour or more all the crew had been expecting the order to reduce sail, perhaps to lie up whilst she still possessed her canvas, every man sure it could not endure for much longer, the strain upon everything above the deck so great, the fury of the rising wind strength sure to tear away every scrap of canvas - if Pat did not give the vital order; yet still he delayed. In his mind he was exceedingly conscious that he wanted to gain the full breadth of the south western approaches to the Channel, to shift far, far away from any French coast - Ushant most particularly - before darkness settled upon them. He wanted every knot and every mile out of the remaining daylight, the few hours left so short; and although he possessed a great sense of foreboding for what he believed was coming, the frigate's racing progress gave him a tiny degree of reassurance that *Surprise* could yet gain greater safety; indeed, she must if she was to leave the scene of any potentially calamitous crash onto a lee shore in the darkness of the night, for in the present weather and sea state there could not be even the tiniest prospect of surviving such. He strived to keep his concerns from his face, although his behaviour was increasingly sharp, his orders barked out and somewhat severe; his thinking, his careful deliberations completely fixated upon his ship and her position, her prospects increasingly uncertain - unless she could gain more sea room. He had remained for hours on the quarterdeck, all the time studying the ship, its responses to the extreme weather, yet concurrently considering his men, how they were coping, the wounded below particularly.

'Will the weather worsen?' Simon ventured his concern in a fearful voice, his trepidation plain.

'Yes,' shouted Pat after the briefest reflection. 'Come the night and it will be... it will be...' He stopped, realising his friend was alarmed. 'Gales ain't in it. The glass has been dropping all day, and... and when this sea starts to throw her about... well...' he looked away as if his expectations, grim that they were, should not be shared. 'Mr Pickering, four fresh men to the wheel, if you please. And we will get cook to serve the supper; the galley fire will be put out before the night.'

'Aye aye, sir,' Pickering hastened away.

Thus far the scene had not reached the extremes that Pat had experienced in the distant South Atlantic, where a wholly unimpeded fetch of several thousands of miles and no land to break running seas building over several weeks created waves of monumental height and gargantuan force. He shuddered at the recollection, but the uneasiness in his mind had strengthened with the increase in the wind, and he suspected, indeed feared with rising foreboding that a storm of similar strength was approaching. In that instant a fearsome gust blew Simon away from the mizzen, and he stumbled forwards to plough into the men at the helm, pushing the two on the lee side away from the wheel, the other two hauling hard with every sinew they possessed to stop the beginning of a turn, the tremendous force acting upon the rudder and transmitted to the wheel demanding an incredible effort from them, their muscles straining every sinew as they struggled.

'Seize hold,' shouted Pat, leaping forward to grab Simon. 'Take both hands to the lifeline.'

Simon picked himself up with difficulty, the wind pressing him down, a huge surge of spray soaking him to the skin. His eyes caught the reproachful but understanding look from all the men at the helm, for all were aware he was no sailor. The two knocked away had recovered, and they too were holding firm the wheel, staring at him, not the least ill will in their gaze. He shouted his apology, the words whipped away, nods returned by the men.

The master came up from the gun deck; he stood alongside Pat and Duncan near the mizzenmast. 'Here is your tempest, Mr Prosser; how long will it endure, I wonder?' shouted Pat. 'The glass is falling still and your fears are all come true.'

'I have never seen its like, sir; I venture this wind is veering, a little more westerly is creeping in, as I feared; and if it comes to a south-westerly, then may God Almighty help us, for we are exposed to the full force of Biscay at its worst and rollers from beyond Finisterre. I am sure you are in the right of things; without we gain plentiful more westing, we have precious little sea room in this tempest; and if we pass close by Ushant - no report of the light and none likely - we will be blown right down the length of the Channel, and who knows where; that is if we escape the Wight and its Needles.'

'I am greatly mindful of that, Mr Prosser; let us pray to all the saints that the wind drops.' The words were uttered but wholly lacking in conviction. 'I am minded 'tis time to turn north-west... to gain plentiful sea room,' added Pat, his face a study in concentration.

'Aye, sir,' the master replied, rather circumspectly as if in his own agony of indecision. He stepped away and returned to stand near the helmsmen. It was fully five minutes before, his anxiety getting the better of him, Prosser returned to Pat and shouted loud, the wind near sweeping away his words, his voice filled with considerable agitation, 'Sir, she's taking plentiful water on the gun deck and rolling something awful in the trough twixt crests.'

Pat merely nodded: perhaps it was because he was severely chilled that he could see no significance in the master's words, for such had been plain for many an hour. More likely, he recognised on reflection within mere moments, that it was his lack of sleep, his powers of reasoning at such low ebb. Sleep, blessed sleep; he so desperately craved for it. He could not summon in his weariness the energy to reply and simply stared at Prosser.

'Begging your pardon, sir,' the master shouted again, 'Will you consider of lying-to? It will spare her a deal of strain on the sails and yards.'

Pat had the greatest respect for the master: the man had sailed with him for years, and they had experienced the most severe of gales in the South Atlantic, in the roaring forties aboard *Tenedos*; and so, his considerations crystallising to a determination, he was measured in his reply, 'Mr Prosser, bring her round to wind and with so little of sail? Why, I venture we could not be sure she would come round without falling in irons, and then - *God forbid* - were she to settle beam on to this tempest... where would we be for all love?'

'Head to wind, sir; that's how we endured in *Tenedos*; two days and a night it was.'

'I don't doubt that there is something in what you say, that such would serve well in the normal course of things,' shouted Pat, 'there is no doubt at all, but...'

'Lie-to, sir, 'til the wind drops.'

'You are to consider... what if she does not hold firm her bow to the wind, if she does not lie-to... what if she cannot?'

'For a few hours, sir,' the master persisted.

Pat continued, 'I believe this wind will yet strengthen, and I doubt she will then keep her canvas.'

Prosser, clutching the mizzen fiercely and leaning into the gale, seemed to be about to protest. He hesitated only for a moment and after the short pause he persevered once more, 'Keep her facing it, sir.' This was shouted in a firm tone of voice, no trace of query in it; his determination to press his concern was evident, emphatic. No one in all their years of service together had ever heard him or anyone else make such a blunt suggestion to the captain, and the helmsmen's staring faces betrayed confusion and alarm. Prosser stared, mute, waiting, blinking away the rain from his eyes. The attention of everyone at the helm including Macleod was wholly captured by the master's opinion, for never before had he appeared to contradict his captain. All waited in some small state of shock to see if Pat would countenance his contrary perspective.

A general expectancy, a common anxiety endured for ten long seconds before Pat shouted his reply, no trace of anger in his voice, 'It was said Saint Brendan sailed his currach against wind and tide, so the story goes, but I have never done so.' His attempt at a humorous rejoinder fell on wholly deaf ears: this was evidenced by Prosser's grim, blank face, and Pat pondered his further response. A further half-minute and he added, in his considered respect of the man, his explanation, 'The glass is falling still, Mr Prosser. Twenty-nine inches bar a hair.'

'Is it so?' The master took a sharp intake of breath, for the first time a note of uncertainty, fear even within his voice.

Pat decided upon explanation rather than admonishment, 'I am mindful that if the wind strengthens further, as I expect it will, then she will not long bear the smallest of sail without it is torn away. And what then, eh? She would no longer lie-to, and with so little sea room we will be scudding without the slightest of control and in a dire predicament. I venture when you have reflected upon that you may come into my way of thinking.'

Prosser, no fool, plainly realised that his captain was striving hard to avoid remonstrating with him; he nodded cautiously.

'I am in dread of the rocks of Ushant... of the wind strengthening, of any lee shore along all the coasts within the Channel... no sails aloft and the barky under bare poles, unable to answer her helm; there it is, Mr Prosser,' Pat concluded his explanation, 'What do you say to that, eh?'

The master's face showed the dawning of his understanding, and he felt a rush of regret for his outspoken opinion. He offered his consensus, 'Bear north-west, sir, and keep out of the Channel; we will have all the sea room at its mouth.'

Pat, with relief, his decision evidently accepted, looked to his veteran shipmate, 'Just so, Mr Prosser; we will keep the wind off her larboard quarter and her heading north-west for as long as she will bear canvas.' Pat nodded his emphasis as he shouted the words.

'Aye aye, sir, north-west it is,' said Prosser, acceptance flooding his anxious mind; the prior frustration and anxiety which had filled his lined, weary and soaking face was once more replaced with his customary steadfast expression.

The helmsmen, who had all heard the exchange, settled again to their task, their confidence in their captain flowing through them again like a warming drink on the coldest of days, their faith in him undiminished; they were grateful for that and looked to him with covert glances, their minds filled with respect, with admiration, and they pushed back their fears, their doubts and nodded thankfully to each other, drenched and cold that they were, settling to their task with a rekindling of determination and purpose.

Pat turned to his First, the exchange with Prosser thankfully concluded without argument, no anger or remonstrance on either side, 'Mr Macleod, hands to the braces; I am going to bring her round to larboard, to bear north-west.'

'Aye aye, sir,' Duncan nodded.

'Mr Prosser,' Pat shouted to the master, now standing alongside the wheel, 'We will wear ship. Put her helm down; handsomely if you will, our course is north-west.'

'Aye aye, sir. Helm down, handsomely does it, course north-west it is.'

'We will see how much helm she will bear without she rolls on her beam ends.' Pat's words were spoken in a tone of determined inevitability though his decision was made with a deal of trepidation, for north-west was the inevitable course he had been considering for some hours. The bow swung round circumspectly, *Surprise* heeling more to starboard. 'Give her more helm,' Pat shouted again, gritting his teeth, his thoughts filled with apprehension about his decision. The men hauled hard on the braces to swing the yards round to *Surprise's* new course, a leading wind on her port side, oft near abeam as it gusted. 'Mr Prosser,' bawled Pat, 'keep her steady.'

'Aye aye, sir, steady as she goes.' Uncomfortable minutes passed, her bow turning, turning so slowly, and then she settled, like an energetic dog fighting the leash until brought to heel.

Another half-hour passed by, Pat staring nervously aloft. 'Mr Macleod, we will reef the main course, if you please,' he shouted though Duncan was standing a bare two paces away; such was the necessity with the combination of thunderous sea and shrieking wind sounds.

Once more the helmsmen, four still needed to hold firm the wheel, eased her to leeward to take a little of the wind force off the sails and yards as the topmen were called up from their shelter below to haul themselves up the rigging once more and so to the yard. Soaked, wind-blasted, clinging perilously to anything at hand in the tempest, they pulled up the canvas with the greatest of effort and fortitude, and clewed it up, fingers freezing to numbed insensitivity as they struggled with the knots.

The practice of casting the log now ceased after the man on the line at her side was judged to be endangered by the strong waves which surged over her beam, over the foc'sle and all along the waist as far as the fore part of the quarterdeck; the gun deck below was flooding to nearly a foot of water when the surges pressed back and on in a flood tide, through the partition to soak Pat's cabin and everything within it. With the change of course and the reefing of what sails that could be there was a noticeable diminution of *Surprise's* speed through the water, the leading wind pressing hard at her port quarter and the frigate adopting a constant and greater heel to starboard in the severe wind force.

'Mr Prosser, how do you fare?'

'I confess I am... that is to say... well, I am ill at ease, sir,' admitted the master with his reluctance to say more evident on his weather-beaten face.

'Let us hope that this wind stays constant, broad on her larboard quarter, and that will be a comfort to all below,' shouted Pat, the master nodded his understanding, his words whipped away in the wind.

From everywhere came a barrage of sound: the deep resonating thud of the hull falling off the top of the wave crests, the "WHHUUMMP" of a confusion of wild waves breaking from all directions: over the port bow, athwartships and even occasionally over the stern when the thump and shudder was followed by a cascading deluge of suffocating white spray, and then the hiss and surge of water flooding along the deck and sides. All the time the constant wild shriek of wind through rigging assailed the ears, as did the groan of stressed masts, the creak of ropes at the very limit of their strength holding the staysails, truly stressed far beyond their intended load. The tumultuous racket had somehow settled into Pat's mind as the norm, a stultifying barrage which pressed down on the senses, suppressing all thinking within a general and stupefying melange of fear, of tension, of expectancy of the worst.

In many years at sea, several of which were winter spells in the South Atlantic, Pat had seen nothing akin to the roaring furies of the southern ocean; even as a young boy living on the western Irish coast, where the far peninsulas of Galway were exposed to the North Atlantic storms at their very worst, he had stood on clifftops and gazed in wonder at the power and force of the wind and waves, but the Atlantic that he had experienced, north and south, was as nothing compared to what he was looking at; indeed, had he never before been subjected to great storms he considered he might be rendered mute in complete stupefaction by the scene which he now beheld. The earth in its entirety was moving before his eyes, for that is how it seemed: its very substance folding at incredible speed, crests and troughs in the watery firmament appearing and disappearing; the world itself was in perpetual, violent motion.

His unease was rising with the awareness that the storm had yet to truly reveal itself, its present demonstration a mere introduction and no more. The ship herself had become flighty in the rising swell, her pitching and rolling increasing once more, as

226

if bereft of all ballast, *Surprise* rising and falling over the wave crests like an anxious horse amidst the tumult of the pack leaping over tall hedgerows.

At eight bells of a cold and wet afternoon watch Murphy appeared on deck clutching a flask of brandy and a box of biscuits, much to Pat's surprise, for his steward customarily volunteered for nothing save with great reluctance and where compelling direction was called for - unless it involved a trip to the liquor store. Pat nodded appreciatively, 'Thankee, Murphy; how very much I would enjoy hot coffee.'

'Well, there ain't no more hot food, no coffee... no galley fire, sorr; 'tis flooded out,' shouted Murphy. Pat merely blinked tired eyes and nodded his disappointment to his steward who scrambled below in haste, inundated and cold in the brief minutes of his delivery and report.

Most of the hands still on watch sheltered from the wind and the constant wash of water on the gun deck as best they could, all huddled around the cooling galley stove; more in hope than expectation of warmth for all were cold, soaked and increasingly despondent. They awaited with no little dread the next order to climb aloft to furl the topsails to their yards; it was eventually given at eight bells whilst light enough remained. Pat studied the demeanour of the men; he could see no overt signs of fear present; he considered the wind strength and direction, fretted over the growing height of the surrounding waves and he threw an occasional glance at the compass, to the chronometer and with trepidation to the mercury; the latter falling still, to his great consternation. Pickering and Mower were below, the first striving to rest before his return to duty to spell Pat and Duncan, whilst the latter was still too weak in his recuperations to stand his turn on deck.

The bosun and a handful of men still moved about the great guns. Between the water surges flooding the deck they strived to attach a second round of additional braces to their carriages, the carpenter tapping chocks behind their wheels in the brief moments when the roll of the ship and the descent down the wave face cleared the water momentarily and they could see what they were doing. After every violent plunge, *Surprise* reared up once more, rising from the watery avalanche in which her bow was subsumed and fighting her way to the next crest. For an all too brief moment she rode the wave at its zenith, the wind unceasing, screaming through the rigging, solely her courses remaining unfurled, the wind forcing her further over until, plentiful weed-encrusted copper exposed on her windward side, the roll back began as soon as she was past the crest and descending once more.

Although the reefed main course and mizzen still held firm despite a measure of fragility for them both after the holes and rends suffered in the summer battles (though since repaired by the bosun and his men), their endurance was of the utmost importance in preserving the frigate and all aboard her, for if they were lost there remained only the last resort of the solely fore and aft rigged staysails to save them from the worsening storm, and several of those were held up by the replacement fore topmast which was of uncertain strength. In such an eventuality Pat harboured grave doubts as to how long those small sails could possibly last, but without them there was little to aid the helm, to maintain some control of direction, to stop the ship turning in some capricious gust or rogue wave and broaching-to on her beam, and that was sure death for all in the blink of an eye. The storm was developing into something more severe than he had ever experienced, and for the first time in his life the vague thought crossed his mind that he could not be sure that *Surprise* in her present depleted state would prevail. He dismissed the foolish notion instantly, angry with himself for allowing it.

A little later Pat recognised the inevitable and gave the order to further reduce sail, 'We must furl her main course before it is ripped away, Mr Macleod.'

Duncan bawled out the order, 'Hands to furl course,' but it was doubtful that anyone heard him, for the aural and physical commotion was overwhelming. The order was passed from man to man, from quarterdeck to gun deck; until the men, cold in saturated clothing and at the limit of their strength, hauled themselves aloft, every man on the rigging and along the yard in imminent peril of being blown away in the tempest and without any prospect of salvation. Pat stared at his men in admiration of their courage and willingness to step up to the desperate task. Doubtless every one of them was aware of the necessity for it, their faith in their captain unlimited.

'Ease her a trifle to larboard, Barton, into the lee,' Pat shouted to his cox'n. Barton had long proved beyond any doubt the most capable of helmsmen, and Mr Prosser, the master, had conceded his authority at the wheel whenever the task called for exemplary aptitude. Barton and his mates nodded; they brought the wheel round as she neared the wave crest, *Surprise's* attitude shifting near imperceptibly before she plunged once more into the trough. The men on the yard struggled valiantly, no lifeline available to them as they fought against the wind, plucking at them with huge force, threatening to tear them off the yard. They clung on perilously as cold hands struggled with the knots. *Surprise* rolled hard over each time as she climbed on the wave crests, her return roll vicious as she descended once more. Frozen hands everywhere were burned, blistered and bleeding copiously as, their task done, the main course furled, the exhausted men clambered and slithered rapidly back down to the deck, near all nursing finger nails which were broken, torn and ripped, blood dripping from them.

'To the Doctor directly!' shouted an appalled Pickering, for he had never before seen such severe injuries inflicted aloft. 'Go below, without delay!'

Pat, greatly embarrassed for sending his men aloft so late to take in sail, necessarily so as he saw things, to suffer such injuries in consequence, averted his gaze and looked down towards the compass, his thoughts a tumult of conflict: *Surprise* had had great need of her canvas, as much as she could bear whilst striving to escape the imminent onslaught, but it did not sit well with his concern for his men. He became aware of how greatly tired he was.

The sun, indistinct behind the murk of the spray and the low black cloud which covered every inch of the sky, had long passed its zenith, and as it had descended so with it had the mood of all aboard, the shipboard consensus now become one of deepening uncertainty, every man wondering how much stronger the gale would blow and for how long. Already *Surprise*, holding her course, a steady north-west, was reduced to her mizzen and staysails, whilst the wind noise had risen alarmingly to a raw screaming in the rigging. A bold venture to try the line once more revealed nearly seven knots, and this speed despite the paucity of the depleted sails was greatly encouraging to Pat, for with such progress *Surprise* gained valuable westing every hour.

The winter days being so short, there remained precious few minutes of daylight left. In the prevailing conditions such a prospect also represented an ever-increasing danger were *Surprise* to find herself lacking sea room, but as far as the anxious eyes of all on deck and at the tops could see, all that was visible was the thundering and primeval force of powerful grey-green rollers. The awesome sight was compounded by the roaring crash as seemingly errant waves smashed against themselves and broke against the ship, the force so powerful as to send *Surprise* rolling far to leeward until she lay over at forty-five degrees, the violence of her roll making movement in any part of the ship quite impossible.

'My God,' gasped Pat, 'much more of this and I doubt she will keep her masts.'

For an hour the helmsmen, their hands and faces white with cold, had been strapped to secure them to the helm. The occasional severe force of the rudder, pushed over by a rogue wave, would sweep one or more of the men off their feet with the wheel rotation until the four of them, exerting all their strength together, could bring it back. All the while the wind pushed at their faces, at their bodies; it was a cold, bone-chilling wind which sapped their energy and strength, yet changing the men at the wheel represented a grave danger in itself, and only one man at a time was ever relieved, his three colleagues holding firm at the wheel in their feel for the rudder until the new man was accustomed to the trial of strength that the helm dictated.

A little later Pat considered further the destructive load on her masts and sails and reached a most difficult decision. 'We will furl her mizzen, Mr Macleod; it will not long endure if we do not.' The task was accomplished only with the utmost difficulty, the shattered men struggling with the knots, fumbling with frozen hands, white-faced, trembling with fatigue. Only the staysails now preserved a slender modicum of control and stability.

Pat closed his tired eyes momentarily, the need for rest, for sleep pressing upon him more than ever; he inhaled a huge breath which he released very slowly; he prayed his decision was sound, that she would not be overwhelmed by the still rising wind and huge wave heights before the storm relented. He weighed in his mind the considerable experience of the master, for Jeremiah Prosser was a legend in Falmouth. He had served for many years aboard whalers only to be pressed on his return home after ten years in the South Atlantic, and had then served eight years aboard Royal Navy frigates, the last two of them during Pat's command of *Tenedos*. There was little that he had not experienced in the line of weather and how to respond to it. It was the low pressure, still falling, which had swayed Pat's decision, but there were surely many aboard who would hold as true everything the master said, and their difference of opinion, although resolved, would surely be the subject of much gossip on the lower deck. Pat's eyes closed again and he blinked vigorously and rubbed them with the water streaming over his face. He looked all about him: to all the men struggling at the helm, to the foc'sle - subsumed in water coming over the bow - and then further beyond, to the darkening skies: the end of daylight would not be long in coming, and that would exacerbate their difficulties considerably; he shivered.

The approaching sunset brought with it a palpable sense of foreboding, the light significantly diminishing, but there was no let up in the wind and, if anything, the wave heights all about them had further increased. Dalby rang the bell vigorously to announce the end of the afternoon watch; the sun, sinking away to the horizon off the larboard bow, was barely discernible through the murk. All about them raged the unceasing vista of wave after wave after incessant wave: rising, descending, approaching, surging past, breaking against the ship with a thunderous crash, spray cascading over the ship from every direction, the magnitude of the spectacle imposing an overwhelming sense of the sea's unlimited power. Even to the veterans of *Surprise*, all of them accustomed to the very worst of the South Atlantic, it was becoming increasingly concerning, and a growing apprehension filled the minds of every man on deck. The former, roaring resonance of the wind through the rigging had become a louder, shrill and penetrating scream, greatly more unsettling to all.

The sun was in the final minutes of setting and its light, weak and feeble as it was behind the dense clouds and obscured by the gigantic waves when *Surprise* was deep within the troughs, would sorely be missed; its absence almost represented a closing of God's door, an extinguishment of slim hope in their most perilous hour, heralding the end of their prospects even as its rays were subsumed by the boiling seas between it and them. As the last feeble gasp of sunset petered out, the sun's rays totally obscured behind dark clouds and twilight beginning to settle upon them, the very day itself seemed to succumb to exhaustion and the morale of every man on deck sank just a little further. In the coming darkness every task would be harder, would demand more from bodies and minds intolerably drained by the sustained physical and mental assault of the tempest. If tired men could count on the sanctity of the ship, if the caulking and the hatches endured, if she did not broach on her beam ends, if the pumps did not block and they held back the rising water in the bilges, if the shingle ballast did not break out of the battens nailed athwartships to restrain it and slide too far when she rolled, if the masts held up and none fell to drag her over with their weight and leverage when rising from the troughs and pressed down on her lee side, if all of these things remained in her favour and her men still clung to the remnants of their fading strength and hope, then perhaps she would survive... *perhaps.* All these thoughts pre-occupied the mind of every man aboard and they endeavoured not to reveal it, for such was an admission of defeat, of fear, and not a man was minded to show such. Men all about the ship looked to their comrades, to their immediate petty-officers, to their few commissioned officers, and all sought to find strength and courage to persevere in doing so.

The weak remnants of twilight began to fade in the most dismal end to any day, the last vestiges of light indistinct beyond the dense clouds, no reminder of the sun remaining; its final demise, its exit bestowing a soul-destroying sensation of extinguishment of all hope, of infinite loss; in its disappearance taking with it the remainder of the crew's dwindling confidence; for all about them was the darker ambience of the dusk; the white spume of the spray which had filled their vision all day was visible only for the shortest of distance, its alarming replacement being the overwhelming noises of the fear-inducing cacophony: the thunder of the swell itself, of wave crashing against wave, water smashing against the hull, the surge of the sea flooding over the foc'sle and along the gun deck before came the sucking noise as the water drained out of the scuppers as she rolled. Above all these noises was the screaming pitch of the wind in the rigging, unnerving in tone and frightening in its unrelenting intensity. Pat, for the first time feeling bitterly cold, stood near the helm and looked all about him in the gloaming; his eyes were well-adjusted to the last vestiges of the feeble light remaining, but he could see very little. He trembled, feeling the warmth desert his body.

'Mr Macleod, I am frozen to the bone,' declared Pat, 'I can barely feel my fingers and toes, and I am going below; it is my most earnest hope that I may gain a trifle of rest, an hour perhaps, before the night proper sets in; doubtless it will present its troubles.' Clutching the handrail to steady himself as the ship rolled violently he stepped carefully down the companionway and gazed forward the length of the gun deck which was awash; the cold, grey surge flowed aft and away to starboard, flooding under the doors and into the coach. Stepping through into the great cabin, the deck was sodden with three inches of water. Despite the deadlights long being affixed one of them had been stove in by a following wave, and the ebb and flow of the water across the deck was visible as Pat, shaking his sodden oilskins, stared in dismay at the huge disarray of his shipboard home. The disorder was illuminated by the pale light of the solitary flickering lantern. Everything previously on the table - his books, charts, pen, his reading glasses - had all been thrown to the flooded deck; the books and charts were sodden in the water swilling everywhere, his chair fallen over. He peered again at the barometer next to the door to his quarter-gallery, rubbed his eyes in disbelief, the reading so low, lower than he had ever before observed, and his heart sank with the frightening realisation that the worst still lay ahead. He tapped the glass as if to correct some inherent fault, but no change resulted. 'May God and Saint Patrick be with us,' the heartfelt exclamation his verdict on the shock of the low. Indeed, worse was surely to come, as he had feared and as he had explained to Prosser to the evident dismay of all at the helm. Nothing like this barometer reading had he ever seen before: twenty-eight and three-quarter inches. It was shocking and greatly perturbed his anxious mind. He tapped the glass once more as if by doing so the mercury might rise a very little and his fears be confounded. His stomach turned when his thoughts wandered towards his wife and children, to Kathleen and Brodie, all of them away aboard *Eleanor*, and he fretted about the little craft and her crew. How was the small schooner managing in the maelstrom? Codrington, Reeve and their ten men were all exceedingly capable, of that he had no doubt, but where was the little vessel, how would she fare, was she sure of surviving this night? He looked about for a biscuit, a pang of hunger reminding him that he had eaten nothing since his early dinner before noon, but there was nothing save for a half-dozen of biscuits sluicing about in the water as each fresh wavelet gushed along the deck. He picked up his chair and sat in it; he stripped off his sea boots which pinched his feet, struggled out of his oilskins; his feet were wet already in their sodden socks, as were his clothes, but he gave that no mind. His thoughts were wholly preoccupied again with *Surprise's* dire predicament, her grave prospects; and in the gloom of the cold cabin, despite the roar of the wind and the audible crashing of waves against the hull, he was grateful that he was alone, that there was no companion to see his fears, plain in his face. His eyes closed involuntarily, his fatigue so overpowering, his mind slipping into the vacuity of absolute exhaustion.

An interminably slow quarter-hour passed by, rest let alone sleep entirely eluding Pat in the raging tumult that was all about him. Many years previously, in the worst of the north Atlantic winter, as a lieutenant aboard ships bucking in the most violent of storms, he had, during many a night of discomfort, taught himself how to allow his mind and body to slide quickly into sleep, yet that blessing was now beyond him. 'Perhaps it is the loneliness of command responsibility?' he mused, 'More likely the severity of what was about to beset them,' he concluded. The solitude was strange, for rarely if ever did he sit mute in his own company in the gloomy near darkness of the cabin and amidst such huge danger without the presence of one or more of his officers, without his steward standing ready at his whim and invariably listening closely for the tiniest shred of news to disseminate in gossip to his cronies; and despite his craving for rest his grave doubts could not be dispelled: could he save them all? Could he preserve the ship, bring them through this cataclysm? 'I do not care to linger on such thoughts,' he muttered to himself.

Another five minutes slipped away, Pat drifting in and out of consciousness; he slumped a little within his chair, deep fatigue overtaking him, and to his mind it appeared as if time itself had halted: the furious screaming of wind, of smashing of seas against the hull had faded a little from his conscious thinking, from his awareness; and a picture of his wife crystallised within his thoughts: bright-faced, smiling, extending a hand to him. He blinked to clear his eyes and he determined in that profound moment that he would ensure that the ship pulled through, would endure. He sat up and declared aloud and with conviction, 'Damn you for your doubts, Patrick O'Connor; the barky will survive; we *will* endure.'

Extremely tired, he hauled himself across and into his cot. He did not undress, simply lay back, settling in some discomfort amidst the crescendo of noise all about him, ignoring as best he could the barrage of waves crashing against the hull, closing his mind to the water surging from forward all along the deck and under the doors through the coach and into the great cabin. Accustomed as he was to the violent lift and roll of the ship, he closed his eyes: not to sleep, for that was plainly impossible, but to gain some small modicum of rest, of recuperation before he returned to the quarterdeck. He lay awake, listening, thinking, eventually slipping into a semi-conscious daydream-like state, his mind filled with fears for his wife and children.

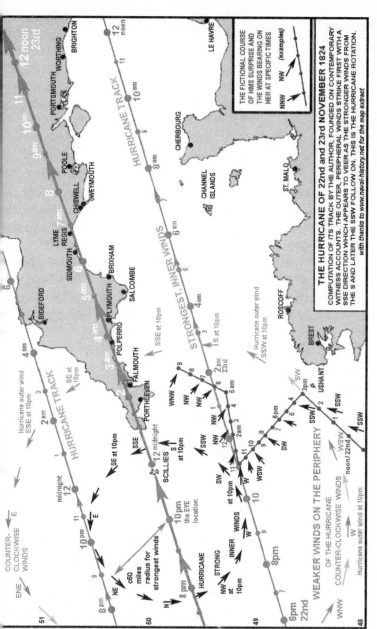

The path of the 1824 hurricane and Surprise's course within it.

Chapter Ten

19:00   31nm NW of Ushant,   wind SSW veering SW, FORCE 10, winds 45-55 knots, storm, sea completely covered with foam, "or that which she could scarcely bear close-reefed main-topsail and reefed fore-sail, the wind a shriek in the rigging."

It was neither the tolling of the bell during the last dog-watch nor any of the vigorous movements of the ship responding to the turbulence of the storm which awakened Pat, rather it was a growing awareness of the wind strengthening which settled insidiously within his subconscious thoughts. Little more than a half hour of dozing had elapsed and he did not feel refreshed in the slightest. His semi-conscious mind had strived to disregard the crash of the boiling seas smashing repetitively against the hull, but the wind had changed its disturbing note once more, and that had subliminally registered within him. The cabin was in near total darkness save for the flickering, yellow light of the solitary lamp, but the noise of breaking glass alerted him to shake his mind from its fretful doze; indeed, to sharp wakefulness. The sea had smashed against the lights, the panes of the stern windows, much of which had been shattered in battle many months previously and been boarded over, and now a half dozen more were swept away by the sea which poured in, soaking the bench against the stern. Pat bowed to the inevitable: he sat up and rose from his cot. In haste he drew tight the cords of his oilskins and pulled on his sea boots, dragged himself across the violently pitching and rolling deck of his cabin to stare in the gloomy light at the barometer; he gasped in disbelief, 'Twenty eight and a half inches! God and Saint Patrick preserve us. Murphy, Murphy there!' he shouted, stepping quickly to the door. Murphy was already there. 'Pass the word for the carpenter,' cried Pat as his dismayed steward stared past him and into the cabin. 'The lights are all to be boarded over.' He continued up the companionway steps towards the quarterdeck.

His brief, all too short absence from command in what was undoubtedly *Surprise's* most desperate hour pressed heavily on his mind and he greatly feared what he might find on his re-emergence on deck. The scene which greeted him was infinitely worse than he had feared. He realised in a frightening instant that the weather had further deteriorated, and his former perception of *Surprise's* enduring stability was much diminished; he instantly regretted his brief respite for recuperation below. In his absence the twilight had faded and with it near all visibility had gone save for an immediate few yards about the ship. The faintest glimmer came from a rising pale moon, hovering low in the sky and struggling to bestow its benevolent light, but it was weak and often behind the darkest of clouds.

It did not surprise him to feel the strengthened wind, tearing the white tops off the waves and throwing a horizontal fusillade of spray at the men on deck. The intermittent moonlight afforded a view of taller waves, ever steeper walls of water before them, the frigate bodily lifted up on crest after crest, *Surprise* heeling ever further over as she was exposed to the full force of the wind, the waves breaking over her stern as she slid down into the troughs, her steep heel relenting, the ship near pooped once or twice by irregular rogue waves contradicting the regular flow of their fellows.

His ears were assailed by the sound of mountainous rollers all about the ship, crashing together and against the hull, and by the piercing shrieking all about the rigging, immensely loud, frighteningly so, reverberating above everything else, assaulting the mind, so terrifying in its intensity. The wind, unlike anything in its terrifying force that he had ever experienced - so overwhelmingly powerful - threatened to sweep away everyone on deck, the helmsmen struggling more than ever to endure. Before his brief and unsuccessful respite *Surprise* had been heeling fifteen degrees, but now, in the gusts, it was more akin to thirty, the forecastle alternating above and below water.

If the beam seas were to become more violent Pat understood that he would no longer be able to hold *Surprise* to her north-westerly course, when he must wear ship and run before the fury else she would surely broach. He hoped to postpone that change for as long as he might in order to gain his cherished objective: more sea room and a subsequent, safer course in the middle of the Channel, but he knew in his heart that the moment was swiftly coming when he would have not the least control over his ship, for the storm was undoubtedly growing worse, not long remaining to him before he would have to put *Surprise* about to run before the raging fury.

Surprise was being hurled along, flying like a tiny piece of flotsam in the strongest of currents, now hard-over and fighting to rise up, her bow subsumed within the confronting avalanche of freezing water, the deck ever awash, the forceful torrent flowing three feet deep, topped with foam and flooding back all along the length of her deck, blinding white spray everywhere. Up, up she rose to the crest, hanging for a mere momentary fragment of time at the top, water pouring off her, before plunging down, sliding through the enormous wave, falling, falling, rolling violently back from her lee heel to larboard when the trough for a few seconds shielded her from the tempest, only to viciously reverse the roll within moments. The senses - sight, sound and feeling - were all violently assaulted; all balance, all equilibrium was utterly overwhelmed.

At the helm, Duncan on duty, Barton and three others struggled desperately to hold the wheel, to avoid unwanted swings as the ship crested each wave. Pat tried to stay upright as he stepped aft from the companionway, past the mainmast and the gratings; he gave the men a half-wave of his arm as he approached closer, one hand clinging tenaciously to the life-line. All about him the sky was black cloud, unrelenting black. 'She is making water, sir, down at least five strakes,' declared Duncan.

'Damned grim, Mr Macleod,' shouted Pat. 'I venture we are in for a proper thunderstorm, eh? Did I hear a thunderclap just now?'

'Aye, 'tis here now. Look behind ye, sir,' Duncan pointed towards the port bow. Pat turned about. In his frightening contemplation of the weather, of the sea state, of the ship's prospects, he was awe-struck and rocked to the core of his very being by the most violent lightning flash he had ever seen;

240

immediately followed by another and another, the flickering blue-white daggers casting away the blackness and lighting up the sky for one successive instant after another, and then came the near immediate and loudest thunderclap he had ever heard in his life, followed by a second and a third in rapid succession, a heavenly drum roll roaring to announce the end of time itself, the crashing of the sea against the ship its ferocious chorus, 'Oh, dear God,' his horrified exclamation. The light spectacle blazed on and on, not a man on deck had ever seen its like.

'I venture 'tis near the eye of the hurricane,' shouted Macleod.

The rain thickened, became torrential; so much so that even the rare light afforded by a weak moon - when not obscured by clouds - was near non-existent save for the lightning bolts, still flashing spectacularly. Water everywhere: ferocious spray, driving rain, waves crashing over the bow, a torrent rushing along the decks; no respite in any direction; water, unlimited tons of it: bitterly cold, in the eyes, in the nostrils and filling the mouth. All on deck had long been soaked to a miserable, cold and frightened existence.

Patrick O'Connor was not a particularly religious man but there had been times in an oft turbulent life, times generally at sea and against French opponents during the long struggle against Boney, when he had uttered words of supplication to heavenly residents, daunting moments when great forces appeared to be aligned against him, anxious times, desperate situations, the ship damaged or plentiful casualties all about him, but worse than such as those were the rare instances when he knew, when he felt - deep within the pit of his churning stomach - that things were about to get very much worse; and this was certainly one of those times - without a shadow of doubt: something enormous, some huge obstacle, an impediment of the utmost severity was forming before them. The signs were in the sky, in the seas all about them, in the crash and boom of the waves which hurled huge cascades of water high into the air above them, in the violent motion which beset the ship; and his stomach turned over when he thought of its implications. Its forbidding presence was foretold in the still falling glass, the lowest reading he had ever observed, and with difficulty he choked back his anxieties, accompanied as such always was for him by bilious acidity rising in his throat.

The wind whipped at his oilskins, tore at his exposed head and hair which thrashed about his face. He looked all about him: to his helmsmen and to Duncan, who was still valiantly standing alongside the wheel, though lashed with rope to the mizzenmast. He forced his thoughts back to focus on his determination to persevere, to lead his men and his ship to salvation. He wiped away his face and, stooping against the ferocious wind, stumbled closer to the wheel, nodding to his men, striving to present a thin smile. With difficulty and freezing hands he struggled to tie himself alongside his First, Duncan seizing him tight in his grip as Pat, buffeted wildly by the wind, struggled with the knot. More lightning flashes, more thunder, on and on for twenty minutes, only gradually diminishing, but the wind and rain as fierce as ever.

Even at the top of the precipitous wave crests, the ship hoisted high within the sea's irresistible grip, the gloaming afforded only a perception but little view of the gigantic waves, four hundred feet or more apart, the wave tops over sixty feet in height from the troughs. The frigate rose steadily on the rise of each successive one, subsumed within the flying foam, every eye staring, praying that the wave face would not break, anxiety general as the minutes passed until the ship pitched steeply to leeward at the watery pinnacle and toppled in frightening manner over the crest. A huge crash followed every time, the masts quivering as everything adjusted to the extreme of the fall, before *Surprise* slid down, down, down to the trough once more. A too brief few minutes of near normal angle ensued before the rise began once again, the repeating sequence interminable, time after time. Consternation had long since replaced foreboding in the minds of all.

Surprise battled on, ever north-west, her staysails alone on her diminished canvas to take her up and across the mountainous slopes of the huge waves which she tackled at the oblique angle allowed by the turbulence of her track, by the storm force winds abaft her beam and the monstrous high seas abounding. No line had been cast to measure her speed for hours but Pat estimated she still maintained six knots or even more. Within the occasional glimpses afforded by moonlight the vast waves were akin to mobile mountains, stretching away into the indistinct grey darkness of the horizon, the crests wild, raging, disgorging vast fountains of foaming spray, the shocking sight more extreme than anything anyone had ever seen before.

Each time her pitch steepened as she approached the wave tops, the frigate's roll becoming far more pronounced, when all the lee gun ports were deep under water, the sea bubbling even through the hammock netting, water surging back the length of the deck as she rose to the next peak, near miraculously, for so it seemed, and the water flooded out from the scuppers.

"WHHUUMMP" the frigate, rising from a particularly deep trough smashed her bow into the wall of water of the thundering, roaring rogue wave looming high and breaking before her, conjoined in confusion with its regular fellow, the forecastle subsumed as if within a tidal wave; no longer solely the constant and driving white spray spicules flying into the eyes of the helmsmen but a torrent of airborne solid water assailing them intolerably even as the wind pressed them hard from abeam, the violence of the water, the spray making visibility impossible and breathing difficult; heads turned away to gain some tiny respite, the sensation akin to drowning; so much so that the arrival of another downpour of heavy rain went unnoticed in the hail of water from the bow. For interminable seconds the foc'sle remained submerged and *Surprise's* wild roll continued, over, over, all on the quarterdeck staring with horror, fearing she might not pull up, for the rogue wave had pressed down upon her with hundreds of tons more of weight and still the waves crashed violently all about her, and then up... up... *Surprise* fighting like a wild thing for her very existence; up she rose as if bearing all the burdens of the world upon her deck, vast streams pouring off her and the foc'sle appearing once more, emerging from within the deluge, to huge exhalations of breath and floods of desperate relief all round.

The cloud had thickened, become so dense that all moonlight was extinguished, the darkness frightening, exaggerating the fears engendered by the sounds and forces of the raging tempest all about *Surprise*. The torrential, wintry deluge made life a hell on earth for all on duty. Clinging precariously to their positions on the quarterdeck, there remained only the four helmsmen with Pat and Duncan. Just ahead of them stood Clumsy Dalby, fiercely gripping the rail overlooking the gun deck. Even his mighty strength was beginning to ebb, though he gave it no mind. The wind had veered to a south-westerly, directly off the port beam - a soldier's wind - its ferocity constantly threatening to tear men away from their stations. Only the cords by which they were tied on, the helmsmen to the wheel and the officers to the mizzen mast, preserved them from being blown away like so much leaf chaff in the tempest.

Every man was cold in the extreme, periodic bouts of shivering impossible to hold in abeyance, all drenched by the torrential rain and soaked to the skin; the pelting spray assaulted them from every direction, and within its ferocious intensity it was near impossible to breathe. Their frozen bodies shivered in the blasting, wintry savagery of the hurricane, not the shortest respite to be found whilst on deck; no man could endure there beyond an hour. The ship was thrown about violently, like a toy, rolling and pitching such that without physical bracing it was impossible for men to stay on their feet at their position. The stronger gusts tore at their oilskins, plucked at the sou'westers strapped to their chins, the violence of the assault pushing men to a lively dance and knocking them back with huge force, time and time again, the lifelines being the Godsend which preserved them.

The former scream of wind through the rigging had become an enduring shriek, a near constant tone, occasionally ululating in volume but always shrill and quite unlike anything any of the Surprises had ever heard before, the implied violence of it deeply disquieting even above the thunder of the waters smashing against the ship. It was a wind noise which even the veterans of the South Atlantic winter found gravely disconcerting. Still the wild waves persisted, raging all about them: crashing in one sickening blow hard on the port quarter and next on the starboard bow; so diverse and so varying was the direction of the forceful smashing that it seemed as if the sea itself was in conflict: the ferocity of force, the savagery of the strikes so threatening in their terrifyingly random nature; the primeval roar of sounds accompanying it periodically falling in pitch to a threatening, lower, deeper moan, a mournful sound which in the superstitious and frightened minds of the helmsmen presaged eventual and inevitable calamity and struck fear into all those men struggling against all odds to remain on deck, to hold firm the wheel and thence the rudder: the slightest variation of which, as they knew well, would lead swiftly to catastrophe. The stifling blasts of the windborne foam and icy water spicules assailed their hands and faces until they were frozen, numbed, all feeling lost; so much so that it was impossible to hunch in the least illusion of shelter for even a moment. The combined physical battering inflicted upon the men was profoundly overpowering, more so than any man had ever previously endured; it sapped their dwindling energy, leaving them weak, precious little of their greatly depleted reserves of strength and fortitude remaining to them.

The four men strapped to the wheel, including Barton who had refused relief at the last change of helmsmen, struggled hard to control the ship, the force exerted through the rudder on the wheel was so extreme, so powerful, the four requiring every ounce of their failing strength to halt the mere beginnings of any turn before such could tear the wheel out of their hands. The wind force was similarly beyond human imagination, so much so that any thought of sending a man aloft for sail handling was patently absurd, for no human could survive for even seconds the ferocity of the hurricane without they were tethered securely to some robust fixing. All above them the night was become so black that the paltry moonlight, such as it was and when it occasionally deigned to break through the dense cloud, hardly illuminated the deck immediately about them.

A little ahead of the struggling six was Dalby, persevering with his own duties as he saw things, turning the glass as the sands ran out and striking the bell as hard as could be. Dalby, lashed to the belaying point near the mainmast, his huge bulk and strength still serving him well in his struggles and his determination to remain on deck, rang eight bells at the end of

245

the last dog-watch, the noise only audible in the overpowering roar of the wind's fury to the helmsmen. For Dalby it was a matter of pride, for he had no illusions of learning or great intelligence, and his participation aboard *Surprise* was generally confined to matters requiring of his great strength - which he dimly perceived - and staying on deck mattered to him a great deal. He had imposed himself in front of his captain when Pa had been recruiting in Falmouth, and his acceptance had been an immense relief to him, for his nickname - Clumsy - was fully deserved and no merchantman owner or captain in his home port would consider of hiring him. He sought in his own way to make his contribution to shipboard life as best he could on those few occasions when opportunity presented itself. Fleeing before the Turk invaders of Kasos, months previously, he had rescued and carried Simon Ferguson on a desperate trek across the island to the safety of embarkation aboard the waiting *Eleanor*, and consequently his stock amongst his shipmates had risen hugely The officers too had taken to him in a way that he had no observed in all his previous years serving aboard *Tenedos*, and Dalby held that feeling of acceptance very close to his heart. He shrugged off the cold torpor settling upon him and he determined in his own stubborn mind that he would not leave the glass and the bell unless the tempest swept him bodily away.

21:00   52nm NW of Ushant,   wind SSW, FORCE 11, 55-6. knots, great storm, air filled with flying spray, "or that which would reduce her to storm staysails, the wind a moan"

Surprise had struggled for six hours on her north-westerly course striving to maintain her stability in massive beam waves propelled by the hurricane wind which had now veered further round to the west-south-west. She was holding her course with only her staysails to aid her, but as she neared the next looming crest, huge volumes of water cascading over her foc'sle and the bow biting into the very pinnacle of the wave, disaster struck from the mainmast just ahead and above them came a piercing CRACK and then a thin tearing noise as the fore topmast staysai tore itself free of its brails and hanks, its block flying down and carried by the wind far off into the leeward darkness; the canvas streamed forward, flapping madly until - after mere seconds - it tore itself clean away and disappeared into the murk. Only the fore, main and mizzen staysails remained; 'For how much longer would they survive?' the question in the thoughts of every man on deck.

Near the helm, Pat, besieged by his abject feelings of utter helplessness and by the insidious cold which numbed his fingers and his feet, strived to make sense of the sounds all about him; for he could see near nothing in the inky blackness. For most of the time he squeezed his eyes closed tight to keep out the salt spray and the chill, and he heard more than saw the constant loud, surging wash and strike of the waves, the drumming reverberations of wild seas battering the ship from all directions, and he struggled, bereft of any visual aids, to determine how *Surprise* was coping, fighting to right herself before the next wave of the onslaught. He felt as much as heard the huge avalanches of water boarding his ship as it rose and fell over each successive crest, exaggerating his perception - for it was unseen - of endless walls of waters before them, and then *Surprise* crashed down again into the following trough and lurched violently sideways, every man clinging on to fragile support as the ship shuddered. He could see nothing below on the gun deck which was constantly awash, and every time the bow pitched down, down into the trough he feared she would never clear her watery burden before striking the next wave head on.

'Ease the helm up a point, Barton. Handsomely does it,' shouted Pat with all his voice, 'We will lift the burden on the stays'ls a trifle. Gently does it, lads, hold firm; if she escapes our hands and we are brought by the lee 'tis sure we will never see Falmouth again.'

The loss of the fore topmast staysail for stabilisation had been immediately felt: the ship's rolling on the wave crests was accentuated, and as she descended the wave she whipped back much closer to vertical with a vicious lurch before the cycle repeated itself. The ship was blown over to her lee side in excess of thirty degrees as she climbed each succeeding wave, her bow carving into the water, all present struck dumb and wondering if she would ultimately emerge at the crest. The repetitive motion was quite appalling and very debilitating for the helmsmen every man was drenched and numbed with cold, the ever-present spray which near suffocated them forcing their eyes to remain closed even as with clenched hands and frozen fingers they clung desperately to the wheel.

On the quarterdeck the helmsmen were finally relieved as Dalby frantically rang the bell, *"ding-ding"*, four men crawling on all fours from the companionway to the wheel, and one by one substituting for their exhausted shipmates, even Barton conceding to his replacement without protest, scrambling to the steps with what little energy he still possessed. Duncan too acceded to Pat's order to go below, out of the wind for some small respite, however brief, and perhaps something cold to eat Pickering took his place in silence, no offerings of levity made on this occasion.

Pat looked about him to all his men in searching assessment of their morale. Shielding his eyes from the torrent he could make out Dalby, standing at the main and near the bell, clinging to his station only with great difficulty. He grappled again unsuccessfully, with the towel tied around his neck in another fruitless attempt to keep out more of the icy water which ran down his face and which had already saturated all his clothes, the cold stream running down his back and his chest until he finally reconciled himself to try to ignore it. In his bleakest despair and ebbing strength he forced his mind to thoughts of his wife and children, in a place unknown within the maelstrom, but in the safe hands of Codrington and Reeve; both of whom he knew were very competent and experienced seafarers, and he found that a considerable help in bolstering his determination to persevere, to keep going and not to let his fears show to his men as he resolved for the hundredth time not to give up.

Four bells rang and four fresh men came up from below for the half-hour rota to spell the helmsmen, Pickering going below for some respite. Prosser lashed himself to the mizzen mast close alongside Pat who greeted him with a nod even as he accepted the proffered flask of Greek brandy. He took a long, warming slug and passed the flask on to the retiring helmsmen, one at

ime being replaced as each of the new men were lashed in turn
o the helm so as to maintain a constant grip of the wheel and
ontrol of the ship.

nexorably and inevitably, *Surprise* was being ground down by
he hurricane: the mizzen staysail had gone the way of the main
taysail; the boats had gone over the side in a crashing, smashing
rgy of destruction, ripping away swathes of the standing rigging
nd the hammock netting, breaking themselves into splinters as
hey pushed through the rigging whilst being battered on the
unwhale until the fragments tore themselves away in the force
f the tempest, the men on the quarterdeck watching helplessly.
he men at the wheel put the helm down a spoke, necessarily to
djust for the tendency to swing downwind consequent to the
oss of the mizzen staysail, only the fore and main staysails
olding on, and Pat praying with his every fibre that they would
ontinue to do so. Her course was now north-north-west; she was
nable to hold more westing in the face of the wind, now further
eered to a consistent west-south-westerly. *Surprise* was rising
bliquely into the waves and clawing her desperate way towards
he crests, her foc'sle more often than not subsumed within the
vall of water she strived to ascend. Up, up, pitching over at thirty
egrees, sometimes more, labouring hard, until at last the summit
vas attained and *Surprise* plunged once again into the most
iolent of pitch as she literally fell down the wave towards the
ough, ferociously whipping back to less heel, the wind relenting
trifle, but the spray hitting the faces of every man with hammer
low force as she reached the bottom of the trough, exploding
nto the wall of water before her; and then up, up again, on and
n, the cycle repeating itself every few minutes. Every time, in
very trough, Pat feared the ship, far below the oncoming,
olossal wave, its crest seventy feet above *Surprise,* would be
ngulfed if it broke, but he could no more look up as fly to the
noon, for his strength was fast failing him. He fought back a
leeting instant of panic, the petrifying realisation striking him
hat all aboard were without doubt fighting for their lives in the
ery worst of the maelstrom, and it was by no means certain that
hey would endure.

'What more could be done?' Pat wracked his tired brain fo the least thing. 'Mr Sampays,' he shouted glumly, 'All shot is t be thrown overboard.'

'Aye aye, sir.'

Pat had been considering lightening ship for several hour she certainly would no longer need such shot as remained afte the Greek battles. He stared briefly at his Second before issuin his next order. 'Mr Pickering, the carronades are to go overboar directly. I think the men can lever them off and push them ove from their slides.' The words, which he had held back through most painful hour of deliberation, were uttered with the utmo: reluctance, his conclusion being that it was their last hope wit the bilge water rising so; it was the last resort for a sinking shi with not the remotest prospect of any respite in the storm and a his men, every one of them throughout the ship, being patentl exhausted. His Second's face flickered between horror an dismay; he nodded his understanding and struggled to mov away, bent double with the wind tearing at his back, pressing hii with huge ferocity. Within minutes a gang of men appeared c the quarterdeck, slashing at the restraining ropes of the portsic carronades with knives and axes, levering them one at a tim with handspikes and all their strength up and out from their slide during the time whilst *Surprise* was in the wave troughs an experiencing a less severe roll, and then with a shout of 'Heav away!' from all present furiously heaving and pushin jettisoning them overboard.

On the starboard side the same process was followed, a sco of men exerting themselves hugely to manoeuvre the leewai carronades with the utmost care up off their slides and ou overboard. All the time every man was smashed by the hug weight of water cascading over the ship and surging all over th quarterdeck. Pat considered for some minutes cutting away th anchors too, for such was all that was left to him, for it was fi too dangerous to contemplate cutting away the long guns fro their restraining ropes - two tons sliding about on the deck was horrendous prospect, a likely fatal one. He determined again abandoning the anchors: it seemed much akin to throwing in th towel, the end of all hope, and he could not countenance that.

Prosser stared with great concern at his captain who, until his order to jettison the carronades, had been silent for a half-hour. He was now slumped against the mizzen mast, his debilitating fatigue so very evident to all. The master shouted to Pat, his vocal chords straining despite being no more than four feet away, 'Go below, sir; there is nothing any mortal man can do here save grip the helm; go below and rest. We will surely have need of you later.'

Pat nodded wearily in resigned acceptance of the truth of Prosser's call; he had not the energy to shout any reply; it was all he could do to untie his safety-belt, and he started for the companionway. As he did so, the breaking of a massive wave over the port beam dumped a heavy waterfall upon him, and in the shock of the concussion his exhaustion overtook him after two steps and he fell hard to the deck, utterly incapable of rising, winded, his throat and windpipe engulfed with water, the helmsmen horror-struck in their awareness of the impossibility of leaving the wheel to help him.

Another cataract, a drowning massif exploded upon the deck, the men at the helm similarly subsumed within it, flooding mouths held open in shock, the water filling ears, flooding into eyes and nostrils, every man's heartbeat leaping to a fast fury, their captain in danger of being lifted bodily and washed away. Such was the force, depth and fury of the water that had the helmsmen not been tied to the wheel it would undoubtedly have washed them all to the bulwark, conceivably away atop it and overboard. As it was, legs were knocked aside, the wheel beginning a perilous turn for several seconds, the men violently turned by their hands tied to the wheel such that those on the windward side were lifted off the deck, and all about them the suffocating white foam surged. Pat, too weak to raise himself from the flood, perceived his consciousness fast slipping away as the water dragged him bodily towards the scuppers, *Surprise* heeling violently, helm control momentarily lost as she began the disastrous turn which would destroy her.

Prosser, petrified with the scene before him, screamed with all his voice, 'Dalby! Dalby there!'

251

At the mainmast, Dalby, tied to it, became aware of the master's shouts, faint in the scream of the wind all about him; he turned, tightly gripping the mast. He saw instantly his captain lying prone on the deck, the water a foot or more deep and carrying him within its unstoppable force inexorably towards the side, Pat about to go overboard. He strived to untie his own lifeline immediately, his numb hands and fingers struggling but failing to undo the knot. In desperation, from his belt he pulled his knife and slashed the rope; he bent down precariously into the teeth of the hurricane and crawled, only his head and shoulders above the water, towards his captain, spitting water and shouting, 'HOLD ON, SIR!' Pat was now near completely unconscious, his residual strength, little that it was, fast slipping away in striving to keep his head out of the flood. Once more Dalby rose to the occasion despite his own energy near gone; bracing himself as best he could against the hurricane, he knelt down behind Pat, seized him under his arms - desperation lending power to his grip - and bodily pulled him up to his knees, and then, with a gargantuan final effort which called for the last ounce of his strength, he hauled both of them to their feet. 'HOLD ON, SIR!' Grunting with the intolerable strain of the exertion, Dalby fiercely grasping his captain, the two of them staggered feebly together to the companionway. As they reached it, the roll of the ship smashed Dalby's face into the woodwork, no hand to save him, and a brief and bloody red torrent flowed all over his face before it was washed away in a second. Together they tumbled down the steps, two men with faces aghast hastening to their aid at the bottom. On they struggled with fresh assistance, directly astern and into the great cabin, the newcomers heaving Pat into his cot.

'Thankee, Dalby, thankee,' whispered Pat, struggling even to utter the words, his strength all gone.

It was more than Dalby could do to stand longer himself; the realisation that there was no question of any return to the quarterdeck was plain to him. He wiped his face with his necktie, nodded to his captain and determined to go below, to the lower deck, to inform the Doctor of Pat's needs, no concern for himself in his own mind.

Murphy arrived unbidden and immediately, bringing the brandy flask and biscuit. Glancing at Dalby as he staggered into the cabin - a particularly severe roll throwing every man standing off balance - he made the tiny concession to the seaman's bloodied face of handing over the cloth he was carrying before he shifted to fuss about his captain. 'Well, an' what's to be done 'ere? Murphy's help is nearer than God's, so it is.'

No one in the ship's complement had ever before experienced a hurricane; no one had previously been aware of precisely how debilitating the extreme wind was to the ship let alone the human mind and form, Pat included. Those crew members who had served at the helm for an hour had all succumbed to physical collapse and they lingered in the comparative shelter of the lower deck near the sick bay. By the gloomy, feeble light of the lanterns utterly exhausted men languished in their hammocks, bereft of any vestige of energy. Slung fore and aft they enjoyed some limited degree of relief from the rolling of the ship, but were at the mercy of the extreme pitching as *Surprise* ascended and then crashed down from the wave crests, juddering so violently that men wondered whether she would shake herself apart. It was a very unhappy and frightened gathering: infinitely preferable to being on deck but uncomfortable still in the extreme, and even veterans of many years at sea in the most inclement of conditions succumbed to sea-sickness and vomiting. At each wave crest, the sense of hovering before the steep pitch downwards brought a crescendo of voluble complaint from the most vociferous of the men whilst others, resigned to the discomfort and some even doubting their survival prospects, simply huddled in their own hammocks for what little comfort, what rest, what privacy they could find. A few pessimists were resigned in their thoughts to the prospect of the barky sinking, but that was not a subject that any man cared to speak of, no one wishing to tempt fate. Those formerly wounded in battle were particularly susceptible to the extreme violence of their hammocks swinging and pitching, and they moaned as the leaden weight of their bodies, quite beyond their control, was thrown on to strapped wounds, their body mass thrust atop broken limbs, many of the men quite incapable of protecting themselves or refraining from anguished screams in their pain.

With the greatest of difficulty Simon, Marston and Jason fussed all about the distressed casualties, assisted by a still-persevering Freeman, the surgeons dispensing the dwindling stock of laudanum with words of reassurance, of comfort. It was into this clamorous scene of discontent that Dalby had stumbled, and he quickly described Pat's exhausted condition to Simon. The surgeon entered the great cabin and hastened to the cot. 'Listen, my dear,' said Simon, 'Do you hear me?'

Pat was conscious and staring at his visitors. He was lacking in all energy but otherwise alert. He nodded, strived to haul himself up, but it was quite beyond his strength. 'I am fairly wasted. How I would value coffee,' he croaked, his face ashen; 'Fat chance, eh?'

The ship lurched wildly to port once more, the several inches of water on the deck washing with it, and a loud and anxious shout came from the man at the door, 'Beg pardon and chaplain's compliments, Doctor; and can 'ee come below, d'reckly; a broken arm it is.'

'Pray tell Mr Marston that I will come at once... in but a moment,' shouted Simon. 'Pat, you are to rest in this cot for at least a half-hour. I caution you against any intention of returning to... going upstairs; haste will not be wise. A half-hour here may restore a modicum of strength, and it will serve you well were you to eat... anything at all will be beneficial... sugar is of the utmost benevolence. Are you cold? Murphy there... fetch a dry blanket and a comforter, and do you have any sugar at hand? A quarter cup mixed with goat's milk will serve, will answer exceptionally well. Will you attend the Captain? I must hasten downstairs.' Murphy nodded, and with that Simon was gone.

'Murphy, bear a hand here. I must return to the deck without delay.' Pat strived to rise from his cot but fell back near immediately, his legs giving way beneath him.

'Well, there 'tis,' muttered Murphy bleakly, in reinforcement of the Doctor as best as he could put it, 'As any proper Galway man will know, an empty sack won't stand.'

254

Monday 22nd November 1824   23:00   66nm NW of
Ushant, wind WSW, FORCE 12, over 65 knots, hurricane, "that
which no canvas could withstand, the sound a deep vibration"

Duncan stared all about him: the lessening of the interminable rain was a huge relief, but it was scarcely less wet as *Surprise* continued to plough through huge seas, time after time smashing her bow into the boiling cauldron that was every wave as she fought her way to its crest amidst vast, soaking torrents of white foaming water, every man on deck remaining perpetually drenched after a few minutes of returning to their station. No one had replaced Dalby at the glass and bell, and time had become an indeterminable in the half-hour that the quarterdeck duty had been limited to; the men waiting below for their turn being governed by Simon's watch, loaned to the duty lieutenant.

Shifting between the lower deck, the gun deck and Pat's cabin, Pickering on his rest rota checked the barometer every half-hour. He had observed twenty-eight inches at eleven o'clock, a low of which he had never seen the like, and it frightened him so much that he did not deign to report it.

In the bilges, the movement of the ship's shingle ballast was alarming, the ship's roll sending many tons of gravel sliding from one side to the other and pressing on its restraining battens, springing the temporary floor nailed above it, making accompanying and disquieting sucking noises as it shifted, visible wavelets upon the bilge water above it. The pumps ejected many tons of water every hour but struggled to keep up with near four feet of water aboard and rising. The bow caulking had taken a dreadful pummelling, and as *Surprise's* bow forced itself into each wave the water pressure forced in numerous rivulets of seawater through minute holes where pitch had been shaken out of the seams between the planks by the repetitive smashing of hull into unyielding water. The men at the pumps were replaced every fifteen minutes, those who gratefully ceded their position slumping exhausted, no desire for food; only the desperate need for rest and sleep pressing hard upon them. Despite all the determined efforts it was clear that the battle was being lost: the water was gaining six inches every hour. The carpenter and his men struggled unceasingly to squash tiny wedges into the largest of the gaps where the caulking had been drummed out by the incessant pounding, but more holes were proliferating every minute.

On deck, visibility remained near non-existent; the ferocious wind and the constant breaking and wash of wave over the decks meant that nobody could endure near the ship's side, and nothing beyond twelve feet could be seen; hence there was no means of understanding their speed or knowing their position; the nightmare had become simply a test of endurance; which would endure the longest: the men, the ship or the hurricane?

The hours had passed with no perception of time moving on; the intolerable physical burden, interminable mental fatigue, frightening uncertainty and fundamental doubt about their survival all filled the minds of every man; all these adverse factors weighing heavily on the most determined of men: numbing their reactions, slowing their thoughts, suppressing their lingering remnants of morale and dashing their hopes; until time ceased to hold any meaning, until existing, holding fast was all that remained in their thoughts. The helmsmen, tired and shivering, contemplated the next half-hour, fifteen minutes, five minutes more until they would be relieved, could go below and get out of the torment, the torture, the numbing maelstrom of chilling hurricane wind, of huge torrents of icy, soaking spray. Cold and drenched, miserably existing in sodden clothing they stood firm: every man had long been resigned to the absence of any alternative. Hunger, tiredness, exhaustion, all pressed heavy upon them. The cumulative effects of many hours of these adversities had dashed their hopes, crushed their spirits; doubt was seeping into every pore of their minds; rising anxiety was overtaking every man, stripping away all lingering hope and substituting a rising abject fear.

In the cabin, Pat had been somewhat revived by sugar in milk and a cold beef sandwich. He lay back in his cot, attended once again by Simon. The Doctor said little but studied his patient carefully, in assessment of his mental as well as his physical status. 'If I am not mistaken entirely, that is to say far wide of the mark, we may believe you are bearing up,' remarked

256

Simon. Pat's dialogue since twenty minutes had been more coherent but his anxiety was loud in his voice, his concern for his ship and men stark in his face.

'Very happy,' Pat offered, although the phrase tripped from his lips only in convention, for he had never felt less so. A little colour returning to his face, his strength restored from its low ebb, he enquired, 'I have no clear notion of how things are below. How goes it? The injured, how do they fare?'

'Will I say there are many much given to lamenting our present circumstances,' said Simon with the weakest of smiles, his feeble foray into humour intended to deter Pat from leaping from his cot. 'There is a plentiful surfeit of water downstairs, and the carpenter and his men are long beyond frantic. Will we endure, Pat... will we, tell?' his voice betrayed his huge anxiety.

'As things stand, if the men continue to attend the pumps and they do not block, if the damned water can be held at bay, then yes, we will endure. Will that answer?' offered Pat, his own deep fatigue betraying his customary cordiality, his tone verging towards intemperate despair.

'Thank you,' said Simon with a sinking heart.

Pat was well aware of his own exhaustion, yet he regretted his sharp response, recognised that he had not assuaged Simon's concerns in the least, and he felt huge guilt for that; so much so that he did not hasten to return on deck until he had settled his friend's anxiety and, as Pat admitted to himself, ameliorated his own remorse a very little. Even in the relative sanctuary of the cabin, unstable as it was, all about them the sounds and forces of the raging hurricane were acutely felt. Water continued to pour in through the shattered and hastily boarded cabin lights whilst the solitary lantern, swinging vigorously, struggled to cast its pale light upon them as the sea crashed thunderously against the hull on every side: "WHHUUMMP" followed by the "whoosh" of water.

Another quarter-hour and Pat decided on returning to deck to show his determination, his perseverance, which he perceived was the essential thing that he simply must continue to do. At least his men would see that their captain was not despairing, had not given up. But before he did so, before he submitted his mind and body once more to the excoriating effects of the cold and the wind, he endeavoured to think through some calculation of their position. Failing to reach any firm conclusions at all, he sat up in his cot, 'I must go out there again.' He stepped out, took a swig of the brandy flask and passed it to an anxious Simon, still present, with a grunt and a nod, his mind still whirling in preoccupied computation.

'Brother, if you mean to go upstairs... into the maelstrom have a care up there and do not linger beyond the half-hour,' said Simon in a tone of deep concern. 'It is of the utmost importance that you do not exhaust yourself once again, the very utmost; am I plain?'

'Thank you, Simon; you are very good. I am greatly obliged to you, but I must return to deck without the loss of another moment.' Pat had estimated that the hurricane was sweeping *Surprise* along at about seven or eight knots despite the paucity indeed the near absence of sail. In such wind strengths, he knew that the masts themselves and her broad hull would act as sails of a kind. In the circumstances he considered that *Surprise* had surely achieved a considerable westerly gain even before the loss of the fore topmast and mizzen staysails, and hence by now would likely be south-west of the Lizard and north-west of Ushant by a considerable margin; indeed, it was likely that she was somewhere midway between the two. If only she would stay afloat then perhaps she could see out the hurricane. It must surely pass them by to leave *Surprise* to struggle in its wake. There was at least now little likelihood of his greatest fear: crashing and drowning in a catastrophic fury of destruction on some rocky lee shore, but whether she would sink or swim was less clear. He rose from his cot, Simon scrutinising him closely, and he peered at the barometer: twenty-seven and three-quarter inches! The observation alarmed him; the unpleasant sensation was akin to a cold hand clutching his heart even as he felt it surge, pulsing ever harder within his chest, his breathing coming faster; his mind raced in fearful contemplation of what worse misfortune might beset the ship, *his* ship, *his men*. He donned Murphy's proffered dry shirt, hauled on his oilskins and stepped to the door with a burning determination to see out the raging fury, Simon shouting to his back, 'Have a care, I beg you; a half-hour upstairs and no more!'

On exiting his cabin into the coach Pat seized upon the four men in oilskins waiting to take their turn at the helm. The Penningtons, father and son, together with Timmins and Green were all veterans, all reliable men and practised at the helm. Beckoning them to follow him he stepped up and emerged from the companionway ladder with great trepidation to look aft and up, his attention caught by the whipcrack of a sail. Amazingly the fore and main staysails remained intact, still affording a bare minimum of lateral stability for which he gratefully praised the Dock sailmakers to the heavens. His gaze turned from the main staysail and he stared all about him as if struck dumb, shocked to immobility, for that was the measure of it: his eyes were gripped by mountainous waves, far higher than any he had seen before on all his voyages, and the raging wind strength was yet further increased - far stronger than ever he could recall.

The low illumination of the moon affording only a dim perception of the raging seas all around the ship, any sense of situation was by feel, by the motion of the deck and by hearing - at least as far as anything could be heard within the tumult. Pat looked aft, a huge wave dimly visible, towering above the stern as *Surprise* struggled to rise from the depths, the looming crest a boiling waterfall of white - such was plain even in the weak moonlight - pouring down into the trough as if seeking to seize and subsume the ship in an aqueous avalanche.

The ship kicked out her stern as the downpour broke all around her, flushing hundreds of tons over the quarterdeck, the helmsmen clinging on for dear life, the water at waist level for several seconds before the worst of it passed, when slowly, painstakingly slowly the frigate hauled herself up, rose on the face of the wave, rising, climbing as if in desperation from engulfment within a closing watery grave. The helmsmen shouted with all they had, roared out as if to assure their shipmates that they were still there, and Pat spat out the cold saltwater and shouted with all his own voice to them, though they stood a mere few feet in front of him. The curve of load on the

259

masts and the strain on the rigging increased as she rose to face the full force of the wind again, and the shrill, shrieking high-pitched resonance of the rigging rose once more.

The prevalent, the all-consuming feeling was that *Surprise* was adrift, akin to a wholly inconsequential twig thrown into swirling chaos and bobbing along on a huge river in spate, and then, quivering, she plunged once more into the trough, pitching forward, and Pat gripped the lifeline with all his strength.

The ship rolled violently, possessing only the two staysails as stabiliser; the deck pitched up and down as *Surprise,* heavy with much water below, battled to stay afloat within her element; never less than a foot of water rushing about the deck, often two feet and even more as she crashed into the successive wave walls, the shock so violent that men all about the ship wondered whether her bows would be stove in. At their crests she shuddered violently before commencing the steep pitch down into the deep trough, down, down, sixty feet down; so far down that nothing but water could be perceived in every direction; water, a sense of gigantic power and force, towering all about and above them as every man lifted his gaze fearfully, the spectacle frightening, terrifying. Only water, everywhere, and the helmsmen were wrestling every second to maintain their stance at her wheel, her bow constantly seeking to turn, to wrest the wheel violently from their hands; only their strength was holding disaster back, resisting her turn - a catastrophic swing until she was beam-on to the seas when the next wave would be her destruction. The endemic feeling of every man was a deep, burning dread, a numbing fear: how much longer could a near flooded *Surprise* survive?

Pat turned at the top of the companionway and stared forward, his senses detecting a change very much for the worse; the closing wave, its white foam all along its curling crest more visible than the wave itself, loomed high over her bow: forty, fifty, perhaps even sixty feet above the foc'sle. He blinked to clear his eyes and looked aft: the receding wave, much less distinct in the weak moonlight, dimly stretched away to similar heights. He turned about once more and stared again through the murk and the spray at the now imminent onrushing wave, its massive presence terrifying and emphasised by its white, breaking crest, very visible and far above the foremast topsail yard. In that stunning moment of realisation, in the instant of *Surprise* being smitten by the most violent of wave, he knew in one horrifying flash and with a thought that struck him like a hammer blow that *Surprise* could not endure her present course, smashed on her port bow by the unceasing stream of aqueous juggernauts, yet held so by only two staysails; and the wind, he sensed, had veered further, a glance down to the compass confirmed this: it was blowing from a little north of west. *Surprise* was facing a wind from just before the beam, too close to the beam, far, far too close now; Pat realised her end was near upon her without she turned away, and she would have to turn swiftly before any further veering put her by the wind and perhaps brought her by the lee, but he could not simply allow her to fall off, for to tarry with a beam sea of this magnitude would swiftly be fatal. She must begin her turn at best possible speed for her course change so as to flee before the wind, to bring the combined furies of wind and sea astern, make her turn and bear away whilst she still possessed a scrap of canvas and before she was destroyed in a calamitous, uncontrolled roll.

Pat was thrown back on his heels as the steep climb began again, *Surprise* ascending the colossal wave, rising valiantly, shedding vast quantities of water out the scuppers, her natural buoyancy fighting the calamitous, leaden burden of hundreds of tons of water seething ferociously across her decks and weighing her down. The wind with titanic force continued to reverberate all around the men, its presence also felt as a deeply resonant low vibration: unnerving, frightening even, although every man existed already, had done so for hours in a state of controlled terror.

He braced his body against the wind; clutching the lifeline he staggered to and tied himself on to the mizzenmast before wiping his face, and he shouted greetings to Duncan, Prosser and the helmsmen. The men at the wheel were a team who had toiled hard several hours previously and who had returned to the wheel a bare ten minutes beforehand. Accustomed to their task they bore the huge physical burden with considerable stolidity, measured and steady in their tiny movements of the helm, each man acquainted with the contribution of his fellows, careful deliberation in their control, fresh strength facilitating their economy of movement.

'MR MACLEOD! MR PROSSER!' shouted Pat. 'SHE MUST BEAR AWAY... AS SOON AS SHE IS OVER THE CREST. LADS! HEAR ME! WE WILL PUT HER BEFORE THE WIND... STAND BY... WAIT FOR THE CREST!' Every face instantly filled with a look of horror, every mind instantly flooded with foreboding, with doubt. Turn away and present her beam to the wind, to the raging sea? Catastrophe was certain, capsize guaranteed, the quick death of them all was assured. The ferocious sounds all about them, crashing, screaming, shrieking, mandated nothing but orders; there was no possible scope for discussion, for contrary opinions, for argument. Catatonic fear struck every man immediately, their minds stunned with the prospect: hearts and pulses raced, breathing accelerated and eyes widened as each man strived to come to a comprehension of what they were about to do. They could see nothing else save that death was now upon them; the barky would never endure such an extreme manoeuvre, never; it was surely impossible and madness to try. Horrified minds were jolted back to immediacy on Pat's next shout, 'STAND BY!'

'Oh my God!' uttered Prosser. The less prosaic exclamations of the helmsmen could not be discerned amongst the fury of noise. Up, up, *Surprise* rose on the rising face of the wave, great cascades of spray flying all about the deck, in the air; the bow crashed through the near breaking crest and the ship tilted down into its descent.

'HELM UP! HELM UP! HARD AWEATHER!' screamed Pat with every vestige of his voice, 'HELM UP! HARD OVER!' Not a man hesitated, the reaction automatic, eight hands gripping the wheel, four men lashed to it; all heaved with every fibre, with every sinew of their body; the windward, port side men pushing, heaving the wheel up and the lee side men pulling, hauling it down, hard, every ounce of energy applied to the task, swearing, grunting, sweating heavily with fear even whilst flensed by the freezing cold rain blasted by the hurricane wind.

262

The bow resisted momentarily before responding sluggishly for the first minute before *Surprise* started her fall down the long wave, and then began the substance of her turn, her bow swinging, turning. Pat had chosen the crest for the turn, the last of her sails would gain the maximum of leverage before she fell into the relative wind shield of the trough. He stared at the staysails, praying fervently that they would hold, at least for the next five minutes.

At the helm the windward men had been bodily lifted by the wheel, lashed to it as they were, whilst on the leeward side those men were being pulled down to the deck, the wheel turning now inexorably, the bow pushed hard by the wave, pulled by the vast force on the final two fragile sails, huge forces acting on the rudder.

Frantically Prosser's knife slashed at the restraining ropes at the helmsmen's wrists, the men to wind tumbling to the deck, the leeward men released from the crushing force threatening to break their wrists and arms; they rolled bodily away from the helm, water surging above them, and immediately returned to seize the wheel.

Duncan had stepped across to grab the helm in the moment that several men were released from it by Prosser's slashing knife. He fought with all his strength to stabilise the wheel's turn; it was impossible to gain the tiniest cognisance of the relationship between the rudder and the bow; he stared, fascinated, fighting the fear that threatened to overwhelm him, freezing spray blasting every man, suffocating in its relentless barrage; he looked forward and then to his left, gauging the progress of the turn.

Pat did not move; his presence could only be a hindrance at the wheel; six men did not need another. Heart pounding, he stared again to the bow, to the beam, to the last two sails, and he fought to hold back the tide of terror that threatened to engulf him.

The ship heeled further and further; she was far over now, sixty degrees or more, the lee rails totally subsumed within the water, *Surprise* appearing to skid down the wave. In that moment came the sound of a whiplash crack as the main staysail tore itself away from all restraints, the canvas flying away in a second, only a momentary glimpse offered before it was gone into the murk.

Surprise shuddered bodily and continued her extreme roll, the boiling black water completely covering the lower deck, just the foc'sle and the tops of her port side rails still evident. Every man stared in horror; the sea seemed to be rising to take them; the quarterdeck was washed by the flooding water coming at them from all sides, beating them, every man chest deep and struggling to stay upright, no let up in the shrieking fury of the wind. The men at the wheel clung to it in a horrifying panic, fighting hard to gain some semblance of understanding of where the helm lay and how it was acting upon the ship, now near wholly over on her side.

'PENNINGTONS!' shrieked a frantic Pat, horror overtaking every man present. 'AXES! THE BINNACLE THERE!' Pat pointed to the compass housing, underwater. The ties were cut and the axes were seized up by Old and Young Pennington. 'CUT DOWN THE MIZZEN!' This was shouted with the utmost urgency and neither man hesitated, the axes swung with desperate strength, biting into the mast just above the boiling water. 'TIMMINS, GREEN!' cried Pat, 'CUT AWAY THE WEATHER SHROUDS!' The men struggled on the impossible slope of the deck, with huge difficulty escaping from the water to clutch the shrouds before the wind swept them bodily away. They cut and slashed manically at the thick, frozen ropes. The wind whipped away oaths, curses, shouts, screams; nothing audible whatsoever save for the shrieking of the wind and the surging, frightening crash of water against the hull, rushing along the deck, white foam spicules flying over all and cold freezing spray immediately soaking and chilling the new arrivals.

The next wave smashed into them with furious force, surging down the deck, the men wholly subsumed for seconds before heads emerged, men gasping for breath, spitting, coughing, taking great gulps of the spray-sodden air. And still *Surprise* continued her catastrophic roll.

264

'HOLD ON!' screamed Pat, the water forcing him under from a precarious footing, his feet slipping beneath him, the weight pressing him down. He swallowed great gulps of water, and he felt his strength failing even as he seized ever tighter to the lifeline and pulled, pulled hard; it was an automatic reaction, for his mind was fogging, he could not breath. He sensed his life was failing, could not long endure, and then a hand seized his collar and pulled, pulled him up until his head came out from the water, the pressure was relieved, and he spat like never before, coughed, coughed until his lungs were on fire. He looked round, Dalby it was, with superhuman strength who had seized him up from drowning; the big man had saved his life again.

Pat stared frantically at the men still fighting with the axes to liberate *Surprise* from the weight dragging her over - if only they could endure. His strength near gone, he clung to the lifeline.

'HOLD ON! HOLD ON!' it was Dalby screaming this time, and again the crash of another wave smashed into Pat, the pressure of water all about him crushing his chest, his lungs squeezed of every last gasp of air, before the wave washed away. Fortunately it lacked the ferocity of the prior one, but Pat felt the frigate slip under a little more: only seconds remained if she was to be saved. *"Thud, thud, thud, thud..."* the axes hammered into the tough, seasoned pine of the mizzen mast, the Penningtons smashing them home time after time, *Surprise* half-submerged, helpless to extricate herself from the water's grip. The men at the shrouds were in dire difficulties, the best Riga hemp of the ropes was hard as iron, unyielding. Duncan, Pat and Prosser struggled through the water to aid their men, all of them fighting the strength of the hemp, cutting, the cord unravelling, tearing under the load and the crushing force upon the mast, the wind thrust putting it under a curve of strain.

At the mast, Old Pennington was tiring, the deep notch cut near half-way through the mast. Young Pennington fought on, finding a primeval strength to sustain the ferocious swinging blows, *"thud, thud, thud"*, his father slower now but still desperately cutting, not giving up, the axes hammering deeper and deeper into the tough timber of the mast.

At the shrouds, Timmins, Green, Prosser, Duncan and Pat, all hands bloodied from many and deep gashes where the knives had slipped and turned on the hard cord, pressed on, more and more shrouds parting, the few still remaining fighting to hold the increasing strain of the mast against the tempest. And then an almighty catastrophic CR..RA..AA..AC..CK, CRACK, the noise clear even in the aural barrage which was the hurricane and all its deafening sounds as the mizzen mast toppled towards the lee side, tearing away the remaining uncut shrouds, crashing, smashing down into the water which covered the lee rails, with all the debris which was the yards and furled sails with it, everything over the side and into the water.

The men at the weather side, the axemen, the helmsmen, all in some state of shock, stared at the great vacancy which the loss of the mizzen presented, an unfamiliar emptiness thrust upon them; they gazed with fear in their eyes and panic in their thoughts as they looked incredulously down into the water, the debris acting now as a drag on *Surprise's* lee side.

Infinitely slowly, for so it seemed to every man, *Surprise* lifted a little, came back from her death roll, resumed turning downwind, shifting inexorably from her precarious beam-on predicament to fall off the wind, slowly, fighting for her very life, her bow swinging, her stern held by the drag of the debris, her foc'sle beginning to point away from the hurricane, a scant wind at her port beam acting upon her hull and her precious, last remaining staysail, the fore staysail. Would it hold for just a few more minutes? Pat prayed like never before, willing the sail to endure, to finish bringing her round.

At the wheel, the four men worked hard, assisted by both Duncan and Prosser, back at the wheel; they now possessed a feel for the effect of the helm, holding it firm, the ship's turn continuing.

Surprise was in the relative shelter of the deep depths of the wave trough now, the marginally lesser wind lifting the pressure infinitesimally off her hull; it was enough: she rolled back a little more to port. Her gun deck was still underwater, but she was turning! Turning! The helmsmen valiantly struggled with all their might, a modicum of control regained, and *Surprise* was rising, rising! Every man sensed it - but would it be in time, or would she be turned broadside on and broach, to roll once more; and if such happened, as Pat well knew, there would be no saving her again, for there was nothing more to be done and her men possessed not the slightest reserve of strength even were there anything that they might do. No, her fate was now in the hands of the Gods: Pat and his tired men could do no more.

She was still heeled far over, still at forty-five degrees at least, but rising on the face of the colossal wave, the wind still so forcefully pushing on every surface of the ship. She was coming up, she was righting herself slowly as her turn continued, now forty degrees of list, thirty-five, her bow turning more, the quarterdeck coming out of the water, the starboard rails rising through the surging foam; round, round she came; she crested the wave and surged forward as if kicked, shaking off the lower deck water through the scuppers, near upright at last. At last!

The explosion of relief in the mind of every man was palpable; every one looked to his fellows in plain astonishment, for not a one had thought she could survive, the turn so extreme, the forces upon her more powerful than anything they had ever experienced, but she fought on; up, over and near upright she came, wind and wave now astern, flying before the wind on the height of the wave, the strength of the tempest at her quarter pushing her on, the ship still heeled hard-a-lee.

Pat was mindful that she could still be pooped, the drag of the mizzen holding her down so, and he shouted - his words carried away unheard - to his men; frantically he waved and pointed to the lee side, now up and out from the water which had been swilling over it for interminable minutes. Summoning their last vestiges of strength, the axemen staggered, bent double in the fury of the wind, to the starboard rail and began to swing down on the starboard shrouds still attaching the mizzen mast to the ship. The axes thudded for five more minutes to cut away the dangerous drag until thankfully the ship was at last prized out of the water's tenacious grip; *Surprise* had miraculously survived her perilous turn; she swam!

The new half-hour watch team came up from below, the departing helmsmen replaced in turn one by one and staggering in their exhaustion to the companionway, near carrying the exhausted Penningtons, and all went below for grateful respite. With no need of command the new helmsmen, shocked to see the absence of the mizzen, bent to their difficult task, for they knew what it entailed, they had already experienced the maelstrom beforehand and they understood the purpose, the necessity for the appalling, the terrifying event which had been *Surprise's* turn downwind. They had endured, the barky and her men; and despite the numbing shock of the near catastrophe they grasped that they had survived. Two hours of rest and every experienced helmsman had answered Pickering's call to return to the wheel. Not to say that they did no longer share the deep-seated fear of their first stint, only that they had learned how to manage it within themselves and without show of the terror that had engulfed them the first time. Pat studied them between his anxious glances all about the ship, and he was heartened by their demeanour of competency, of confidence, unperturbed as they now seemed, and for that he was more profoundly grateful than he could ever recall in his life.

Surprise was running before the mighty south-westerly seas like a fox before the pack, her men with little semblance of control, but all aboard were mindful that the frigate was no longer so much exposed to the risk of a crushing beam sea. The towering, mountainous waves were still hugely dangerous, but just a very little less so: a tiny modicum of the previously all-encompassing danger had been removed. All were aware that there was no longer any possibility whatsoever of altering course, not even by a point, and absolutely no prospect of the master's suggestion of lying-to; in the recollection of it, all these hours on, such seemed utterly ridiculous.

The galley had been cold since the prior afternoon and most of the men below, exhausted and hungry, had resorted to eating the scrapings and crumbs of the last of the ship's biscuit at some point during the hours approaching midnight, the severe fatigue born of their long exertions leaving every man hungry. Most of them, save for the wounded and those who had fallen - breaking or twisting an arm or an ankle - had served several spells at the helm; the experienced helmsmen had taken turn and turn about with many others previously unaccustomed to the wheel, for the task was exacting in the extreme. The severe and energy-draining half-hour was as much as any man could tolerate before the debilitating effect of wind blast and the ceaseless barrage of ice-cold spray firing at them inevitably culminated in severely numbed bodies and afflicted minds; so much so that they became incapable of the swift reaction demanded by the conditions, the extremes of wave peak and trough putting huge demands on the helmsmen as the stern invariably and repeatedly began a dangerous swing which, if not stopped instantly, presented the irrecoverable danger of *Surprise* being swept beam-on to the powerful waves. No one harboured any doubt that such would be the end in an instant, not a man holding a shred of belief that retrospective action at the helm could reverse such a catastrophe.

Chapter Eleven

Tuesday 23rd November 00:00 71nm NW of Ushant, FORCE 11, wind 55-65 knots, great storm, air filled with flying spray, "or that which would reduce her to storm staysails, the wind a moan."

Midnight had arrived and Pickering had returned to the deck to spell Pat, to stand near the wheel with the change of helmsmen. Pat, however, had refused to leave. Pickering tried hard but failed to persuade Pat to go below to rest, his hollowed black eyes screaming his exhaustion. The wind and seas had not relented in the slightest but the cloud, in the moonlight, appeared to be a trifle thinner than earlier and the rain had ceased. Weak indicators, no more, of the young moon could occasionally be glimpsed through broken expanses of cloud, illuminating silvery spray with a brief shimmer of reflection on the turbulent wave surface.

Those men who went below after their short spell at the helm, after an hour of recuperation, of rest, were pressed to join either the pumps, which disgorged torrents like never before, or to pass buckets in a chain that began with men on the sailmaker's loft. Crouching and stooping, tired men filled buckets from just above the hold, five feet of freezing water swilling about below them making standing in it untenable. The constant stream of buckets was heaved up to the lower deck and on to the gun deck where men on all fours passed them on to be tipped out at the lee-side scuppers. Much of the bucket contents were lost en route in the tortuous pitching and rolling of the ship, but without the chain the game would have long been lost, for the pumps could not expel anywhere near enough. The ingress of water through the lost bow caulking had since several hours overwhelmed the carpenter's best efforts, as was plain. Despite this he persevered still, taking neither the shortest break nor any refreshment, even as his shipmates on the pumps - men fit only to drop - plodded from their toils when relieved in a state of abject exhaustion, to find their way to the gunroom where the cook stood ready to dispense the dwindling ship's stocks of biscuit, of Greek cheese and highly spiced *zalzett* sausage bought off the Malta packet. A succession of tired men ate wearily, in silence, to a background cacophony of waves striking the hull, to the unrelenting sound of reverberations from the rigging, the wind in its fury still audible below deck; and when they had eaten or even before they had finished the meagre ration, men who were too exhausted to endure longer slumped down upon the wet deck into a merciful torpor; hardly asleep, for even whilst dozing the violent movement of the ship threw them about mercilessly, true rest quite impossible.

For hour after unceasing hour the hands worked: never a minute was there a break from the tiring task, water by the ton pumped from the rising levels in the bilges, near reaching the orlop, every man cold and soaking in their tiring tribulations; yet on they toiled, in silence, shivering, hungry, every man well aware that if he ceased then he and his fellows were doomed to a wet death by drowning.

Pat was still near the helm, his leaden clothing soaked, his skin everywhere wet, his body bitterly cold, shivering and his teeth chattering when the bosun appeared from the companionway. 'Six feet of water below and shifting terribly as she rolls, the ballast with it, sir,' reported Sampays, his face failing to conceal his alarm. 'The Fish room, the Spirit room and the shot lockers are all under water,' he declared. 'Murphy is attending,' coming as an afterthought.

'I doubt he is in the Fish room,' thought Pat absently, although he said nothing, merely nodded, for even words called upon strength that he no longer possessed.

Duncan, arriving behind the bosun to spell Pickering and overhearing the report, was less circumspect, 'Och aye, I'm sure 'tis nae the fish yon wansonsie gaberlunzie is looking to.' His words raised the tiniest of grim smiles all round.

'Mr Mower is with the men at the pumps,' the bosun added, with noticeably greater reticence in his voice. Mower, as all aboard knew, was barely sufficiently fit to move around the ship without aid and tired very easily; indeed, he had rarely left his cot for much of the voyage before the hurricane.

'Mr Sampays, my compliments to Mr Mower. He is to relieve the men at the pumps every ten minutes; fresh hands may yet save us, and more buckets. Will you send two score more of the men in another chain to the lee side,' ordered Pat. The bosun nodded and struggled away. 'God send we have surely passed the worst of it, Duncan,' Pat shouted to his First as they again exchanged places, a half-hour still as much as any man could endure on deck.

'Havnae fear of that... that damnable turn a-lee it was, nae doubt,' his friend replied, striving to sound encouraging, his free arm steady on Pat's shoulder in small gesture of support, the other clinging to the mast. 'But we've come through, aye.'

'We should be far in the lingering track of this blow by dawn on my reckoning,' Pat shouted, 'I pray it has then relented and we sight land... and with plentiful sea room.'

'How d'ye fare,' asked Duncan, Pat's demeanour wholly one of an exhausted man as he prepared to go below, stooping and with both hands clutching tightly the lifeline, hair whipping all about his face which was a picture of exhaustion.

'I am mortal tired,' the few words were uttered in a deep tone of reluctance mixed with resignation, Pat aware he could stay on deck no longer. 'She is yours.'

'Will I help ye to the steps?' Duncan was well aware of his friend's fading strength, painfully obvious that it was. Pat waived him away; his words were lost in the wind, and he struggled towards the companionway.

For more than nine hours, the Surprises had fought to preserve their ship and their lives; for the first eight of those hours, Pat had strived to gain more westing so as to ensure safe passage beyond the rocks of Ushant, of Brittany and gain the greater expanse of sea that was the mouth of the Channel, but those tortuous hours of hell and the increasing veering of the wind had left him ultimately with no option but to simply set *Surprise* to fall off the wind, to scud before the hurricane and to pray silently for salvation, for a landfall and port before she foundered as the incoming water filled the ship. In the final half-hour whilst Pat had still been on deck, the final staysail, the fore, had simply been torn out of its fixings and been blasted far away to leeward, whipped away, flying on the wind. It left *Surprise* bereft of even that modicum of lateral stability as she rose from the wave troughs and heeled far to leeward in the gusts, her lee-rail subsumed within the foam, before whipping back through forty degrees or more as she pitched down into successive troughs. The fetch of the sea, five hundred miles or more, combined with the hurricane force of the wind had created the gigantic wave heights, the distance between them a quarter mile. The powerful combination resulted in the most violent of movements, lateral and vertical, making all but a very few of the most hardened mariners aboard physically sick. Men who had passed weeks in the worst of the South Atlantic's weather, who had endured the Roaring Forties, whalers many of them, had finally reached their limits of strength and endurance. The lack of any horizon compounded their physiological discomfit, for there was nothing on which men struggling for respite could focus, and the sole benefit of the surging sea across the deck was to wash away frequent disgorgements of vomit. Most of the prior food eaten had been thrown up, retching continuing in the absence of any remaining stomach contents, and now bellies ached throughout the ship, but reminders of hunger were readily cast aside. Murphy, Freeman and the cooks moved about the deck only with extreme difficulty to dispense weak three-water wine in frequent small measures to those who suffered the greatest debilitations.

For the last three hours, below deck only ever for short respite, Pat's legs had trembled as utter exhaustion, beyond anything he had ever before experienced, set in within him, the sensations within his leaden legs alternating between uncontrollable tremors and growing stiffness, a lack of feeling setting in within all his limbs. He strived to kick out to bring back some measure of sensation, some control of his legs; he drank the final draught from the brandy flask gratefully and he struggled back up the steps to the quarterdeck once more.

Shielding his eyes from the vicious stinging spray, he looked aft and upwards as *Surprise* was lifted once more by the following wave. Not that the gloom of the occasional moonbeam allowed him to see the slightest thing save that he had an impression, no more, of the towering wave heights and a glimpse of the slender moon high above through the smallest gap in the cloud, and then it was gone again. Small cheer that it was, he considered that they had endured by far the longest part of the night, and he allowed himself the comforting thought that the day must eventually dawn upon them, and that was greatly heartening; the intolerable blackness would eventually fade and then there might be some prospect of a sighting, at least of the sun if not of the land. For the present there was no let up in the biting fury of the wind or the icy, blinding spray that soaked and chilled everyone within a minute of returning to the deck. Neither was there any lessening of the deafening noises surrounding them: crashing waves pummelling them, the shuddering "WHHUUMMP" of the hull thudding down as she crested each wave and started for the trough, the disturbing shuddering immediately followed by the surge of roaring water overwhelming the foc'sle before racing down the deck in a sweeping flood tide, two feet deep or often more. The over-burdened masts groaned in protest under their excessive load, the bar-tense rigging creaked, and where wood met hemp the tormenting squeal evidenced the clash, the struggle between one and the other. Within the wild furore the incessant wind noises prevailed: whistling, moaning, an uncommon deep throbbing thrum which held the attentions of all; and over all was the constant low vibration, a profoundly disconcerting sound which fluctuated only imperceptibly between wave crest and deep trough.

'Seven feet of water below; will she pull through, sir?' shouted Pickering as he reported once more on the quarterdeck to his captain. The severity of doubt was plain in Pickering's face, a greatly woeful expression. Pat nodded circumspectly even as he felt sure the bald question echoed his own thoughts and those of many of the gloomy men he had previously encountered below deck. Pat stared at his lieutenant; he blinked away the burning saltwater from his eyes, and he was about to shout his reply when spray soused his face once again, filling his mouth, nostrils and ears, and he ducked instinctively as if in doing so he might avoid more. To no avail, the cascade of water kept coming as *Surprise's* bow plunged once more into the water as she toppled off the wave crest and down, down, struggling with the huge burden of tons of water within to haul herself up once again from the trough, staggering like a boxer under the fiercest of assault but picking herself up, punch drunk, to shake the raging water from her decks out through the scuppers.

'Sure, she will... she will!' shouted Pat, but in truth he could not wholly dismiss his own uncertainties, so little control was presently exerted over the ship and there was no sure understanding of her position. Her crew, officers and men alike, could not endure the pummelling indefinitely, even supposing that *Surprise* herself would do so, and seven feet of water in the hold and rising made that extremely unlikely; she was surely sinking and he knew it.

The half-hour seemed to pass interminably slowly, Pat's tired mind striving to mentally calculate the ship's position; unsuccessfully to any substantive degree. His mind was fogged as he grappled with all the unknowns and uncertainties of wind direction, wind speed, the frigate's course and rate of progress. He found his eyes drooping, his attention fading and his thoughts became fixated on a strong yearning for the arrival of the dawn and blessed daylight.

'Will you take a whet o' the brandy, sir?' shouted Barton, espying his captain's decline and offering the flask. Pat nodded gratefully, took a large gulp, the fiery discomfort awakening him.

'Did you ever before see the like of this, Barton?' shouted Pat, the only reply being an emphatic shake of the head. Another ten minutes passed and Pat fought hard to avoid the creeping somnolence settling again within him, his wet discomfort fading as growing fatigue set in; even the shock of the frequent cold showers was lessening as his mind began to drift into the torpor which was insidiously taking him away from all command awareness. His limbs were heavy, his head drooped and he had long lost any awareness of the cold and soaking clothing which stuck to every inch of his skin. The mere ten more minutes before Duncan's arrival seemed interminable, all mental acuity diminishing substantially. Duncan's re-appearance was so very timely, Pat's greeting an indifferent nod, no more; and Pickering, summoned from below and emerging together with Dalby, struggled to assist Pat below for greatly necessary recuperation.

1:00   wind veered more to WNW, FORCE 10, winds 45-55 knots, storm, sea completely covered with foam "or that which she could scarcely bear close-reefed main-topsail and reefed fore-sail, the wind a shriek in the rigging."

Deep in the depths of the ship on the orlop deck, now awash with several inches of flood water - which was still rising - the trio of Simon, Marston and Jason conferred. Having toiled valiantly all night tending to the wounded of the Greek battles and a score more men who had been injured in the storm, they had decided between them that Jason must retire to try for an hour of rest in the tiny surgeon's medical storeroom, away from the enduring cries and wails of the casualties. 'Come, Marston, we will return to our charges,' shouted Simon over the clatter and noise that was the chain gang passing up buckets to try and stem the rising water. Every man in the chain gang was far beyond speech and struggling to pass bucket after bucket to his fellows whilst trying with fading strength during the ship's violent movements to avoid being thrown down into the foul and stinking bilge, the rising water slowly and inexorably filling the ship. A sudden and violent lurch near threw Simon down the steps and into the flooded hold.

'Have a care, there, sirs,' shouted Mower bravely, sodden and mortally tired. 'Take hold here, hands firm on the rail.'

'Mr Mower, I cannot counsel you remaining in this place,' remarked Simon, the lieutenant plainly a man on the edge of absolute physical collapse, his face ashen white, his posture that of a man long beyond complete physical exhaustion.

'I am needed here, sir; thank you,' said Mower. Indeed, the chain gang seemed to greatly respect him for it and redoubled their efforts with the buckets despite their own enfeeblement.

Simon and Marston nodded, and took their leave, struggling up the steps once more towards the lower deck, clinging to the handrail whilst *Surprise* was heeling over and over, and before she pitched violently down the wave precipice.

Simon, when in Marston's company, strived hard to avoid cursing but he did not always succeed, 'Damn this vile scow to hell, and if I survive this tempest may I never set foot in her again.'

'We will pray to our Lord Jesus, dear colleague,' Marston replied, his face ashen, nothing left of his own strength, 'And he rebuked the wind and said "Peace, be still" and the wind ceased... the book of Mark it was.'

Simon looked doubtful and did not reply. Marston persevered, as if in so doing his own fears might be dispelled, 'And I will show wonders in the heavens and on the earth, blood and fire and columns of smoke. The sun shall be turned to darkness, and the moon to blood, before the great and awesome day of the Lord comes. And it shall come to pass that everyone who calls on the name of the Lord shall be saved.' Simon staring open-mouthed, Marston concluded his supplications, 'The book of Joel.' Simon nodded, words beyond his gift in his excruciating personal distress.

Struggling to the top of the steps they gazed forward into the gloom of the lower deck, their ears immediately assailed by the cries of hugely distressed men in their pain and discomfort. The battle-wounded for the most part swung in hammocks from side to side in the roll of the ship whilst lurching backwards and forwards as she pitched, putting an insufferable load on limbs which were splinted and bandaged, re-opening wounds healing since several weeks but which now streamed blood afresh. The men more recently injured in the tempest sat as best they might on the deck, clinging to the benches, nursing bloody gashes or desperately seeking to avoid putting weight and strain on deep bruises and untreated breaks of legs, arms, ankles, fingers, ribs and shoulder bones: all fractures arising from the hurricane throwing men bodily to the deck to strike heads and limbs upon every conceivable danger. Occasionally the surgeons espied amongst the prone men a rat, forced out of the hold by the rising water and up to the lower deck, the ship's cat supremely outnumbered by a dozen of skittish, hungry rodents.

'Lord, in your munificence, grant us relief from this hell,' muttered Marston to himself; the uproar, the misery within the multitude all about him far exceeded anything he could have contemplated in his worst nightmare; indeed, his worst nightmare was now upon him: he had arrived in Lucifer's fiery inferno, and it was testing his resolve, his self-control and his fortitude far, far beyond anything he had ever experienced before.

All about the surgeons men moaned with pain; others had fallen into unconsciousness, weak with struggling for so long in their torments, their fresh agonies an unbearable burden, for such was how it seemed to men who had believed their battle wounds were healing, who had hoped that they were recovering, only to experience fifteen long hours of unconscionable pain as they were thrown about without respite, without attention, whilst the surgeons looked to the newly injured. From several of the suspended hammocks dripped a steady flow of blood, landing on the sodden deck and streaming away into streaks of maroon unless near the steps when the occasional gusher of seawater as someone ascended or descended washed it away. The air was stale, musty, illuminated very weakly in dim light by a handful of lanterns; a similar number had fallen and been smashed to pieces in the incessant rolling. The humid air stank of vomit, of urine and the soil of men unable to shift: helpless men, men wholly incapable of movement, who relieved themselves where they lay. Forward, in the darkness, one man screamed unceasingly, no notice taken of his shipmates' consolations.

'Let us start for'ard,' said Simon wearily, his heart despairing, his strength near gone and his mind fighting the rising tide of horror which had threatened to engulf him since several hours. 'There is a young man, Wagstaff, who troubles me so.' A terrified Marston nodded, dumbstruck.

Slowly and with great difficulty, Simon and Marston stumbled through the throng, every inch of the deck occupied by the injured, by the wounded, by exhausted men striving for rest.

The surgeons looked in passing to each man in brief assessment, giving water to men too weary to help themselves; in a very few cases dispensing the very last vestiges of the laudanum and offering words of comfort, of reassurance to many more.

Jason had returned, deathly tired, quite unable to gain any relief in the wild and violent oscillation of the tiny storeroom. He endeavoured to catch up with Simon and Marston, stumbling and swaying with the roll as he hauled himself through the huddled men on the deck, weaving between the hammocks, offering a nod here and there to anxious faces as he passed by, his own expression equally fearful, apprehensive; yet he determined to throw himself into assisting his colleagues without complaint.

In that moment, *Surprise* tipped bodily forward as she crested the wave as if falling over a cliff edge, throwing the surgeons to the deck, the bottles and tools they were clutching flung to all corners of the sick bay. Down, down she slid, the sensation akin to falling downhill; a score of men called out, a few screamed; Jason shouted before he struck his head hard against a bench, a deep wound opening on his forehead, blood streaming down his face. He lay unmoving, unaided, Simon staring back at him, movement being impossible as *Surprise* compounded their difficulties by rolling forty degrees to larboard at the bottom of the trough; and then she relented, beginning a vicious roll to somewhere near upright just before her bow plunged into the unyielding mass of water, the booming "WHHUUMMP" and deeply resonating vibration as she struck into the mountain of aqueous solidity deafening and felt throughout the lower deck. From everywhere things flew through the air and slid along the deck: tin plates, tin cups, knives, buckets, hats, bandage rolls, bottles, even men who had been struggling to inch their way through the misery of the huddled mass to aid a comrade, to find water, to fetch a bucket for a tie-mate unable to shift. Dozens were sprawled on the deck; some had struck their heads and were dazed and bloodied, their faces streaming; others, less incapacitated, tried to crawl to where they might grasp support.

From all about erupted loud shouting, wailing, as *Surprise* pitched down once again, men everywhere scrabbling to gain a

279

hold, to steady themselves even for a moment, to find anything on which they might grip hard whilst they recovered and before the inevitable next violent lurch.

Marston, seeing Jason tumble, staggered desperately toward his friend, his shrill calls to Simon more akin to screams, the loud commotion of distress, of bellowing all about them making his words indiscernible, inaudible, one small voice amongst a hundred screaming. From everywhere all about him came profanities, curses and pleas of desperation from men who had thought they had previously endured everything that life, battle and the sea could throw at them; but on whom the frightening realisation was dawning that they had not, not by a long chalk, never in their worst nightmares had they envisaged or could imagine the fury, the violence, the frenzy that was a hurricane, a maelstrom of such incredible magnitude, the like of which they had never seen, its frenzy wholly supplanting the thoughts of every man on deck within the overpowering grip of terror, unlimited terror - stultifying and paralysing. Hell had arrived and was upon them, and they knew it. "WHHUUMMP" the hull dropped off the crest into a slide towards the depths of the trough once more.

Marston had been thrown to the deck; valiantly he persevered, crawling past a man lying face down on the deck and crying to himself, past another in distress screaming in the burning agony of his splinted arm which had broken again and which he clutched with his good arm as he lay on his back, and finally to Jason. From his belt, Marston pulled a small, soaking wet towel with which he wiped the stream of blood from Jason's forehead. There was no response, his friend's face was ashen white, his eyes closed, his breathing near indiscernible. Frantically Marston searched for a pulse whilst releasing his anxiety, his desperate fear in a series of pleas, 'Dear God, please help him... God help him. Doctor Ferguson... Doctor Ferguson. help... please... help Jason!'

Simon arrived on all fours, his own left cheek substantially bruised and his eye near closed within the swelling. He stripped open Jason's coat and shirt, pressed his ear to his chest and listened closely to his heart. It was difficult to hear anything at all within the aural cacophony surrounding them, but he found the faintest, the very faintest of beat and at Jason's wrist he felt the weakest of pulse. 'Regular, though a trifle slow,' he pronounced eventually. From his pocket he took a needle and stitched the four inches of wound, halting every minute for the momentary pauses in the ship's oscillation; eight stitches taking him ten minutes to complete before he bound over the wound, wrapping Jason's head gently with a dressing tugged from his other pocket. 'We may believe he will live,' he eventually pronounced, the softly spoken words betraying a will hovering at or near his own limit, his own final and feeble vestiges of physical and mental fortitude fast fading.

'Thank you, thank you,' whispered Marston, supporting Jason's head, the huge surge of relief overcoming all his other senses in hearing Simon's words of reassurance, 'Thank God.'

For Simon, time had ceased to have any meaning. Men passed by all around him, slowly, with difficulty, thrown about by the violent movements of the ship; slumped figures passed him by to seek a brief spell of rest before resuming on deck or at the pumps, others heading aft for a precious crumb to eat, not a man still possessing a shred of energy. For an hour he had been forced to the bitter realisation that there was nothing more he could do for his distressed patients: the last of the laudanum was long gone, the captain's stock of brandy also near exhausted - given to the men in the greatest pain, those for whom the prospect of a moment of respite was beyond them, re-opened wounds or jarred fractures bringing pain to many men. And so he sat, unable to move in his depletion, watching the men trudge by, to the pumps, to the deck, a nod and a word exchanged with several as they recognised him in his miserable huddle.

Several hours still remaining before the dawn he so much prayed for, Simon, still sitting in his own absolute exhaustion on the deck, looked all about him: to injured men who were helpless, to others in the moment of their utter ruin, men in misery who had lost all hope; and in that particular moment, amidst the sink of tormented men, in the anguish of hell that the lower deck had become, he wondered bleakly whether his own efforts would be rendered in vain. As *Surprise* rolled violently

once more to port he knew for certain that precious litt
remained of his own physical strength and he sensed his ment
resources were exhausted too, and that gave him no confidenc
that any of the crew could endure on the deck, for he could onl
dimly imagine how dreadful conditions must be up there. 'If onl
the wind would begin to lessen its ferocious assault...' He s
back in despairing resignation to wait, nothing remaining withi
his heart and mind, no reserve of any kind left to him; wait -
was all that was left to him to do; after all the hours of merciles
and insidious corrosion, his dwindling energies, both physic
and mental, had finally left him.

4:00   wind at NW, FORCE 9, winds 40-45 knots, strong gal
overhanging crests, "close-reefed topsails and courses, the win
a scream in the rigging"

For hour after interminable hour the weary Surprises had clung
their stations: tired, exhausted, cold and soaking in their sodde
vestments, hungry, their sore eyes reddened by salt and hours
rubbing; their last vestiges of strength were failing, their hope
fading. For those on deck, all about them the incessant ra
continued to be blasted into their faces by the fury of the win
stinging in its severity; the freezing water surging about th
decks washed at their legs from their feet to their knees; th
furious waves, boiling with ferocity, as extreme as ever it ha
been all night, tossed them about like an insignificant cork with
a cataract; and the wind assailed their ears and their spirits unti
in that bitter realisation of complete despair when the fin
slender hope has been extinguished, they looked about them on
more, looked to their fellows, first one man and then anothe
man after man sensing the very tiniest degree of abatement, th
smallest diminution in the wind's fury: paltry, infinitesimal b
noticeable, and so immensely significant. Slowly, so very slowl
like a child awakening from its deepest slumber they dared on
more to allow precious thoughts of survival to stretch explorir
fingers into shocked, numbed minds.

On deck, it was plain to the weary men huddled around th
wheel that the wind had indeed diminished in the smalle

degree, yet that small change, the gesture to improvement, that inkling of lessening force was akin to a hand extended to a man slipping away below the water; for it meant the flickering return of hope, a tiny and precious strand of such, which every man had been bereft of for many an hour. Only loyalty to their captain and comrades had brought such tired men back once more to the screaming horror that was the quarterdeck and helm. Digging deep to retrieve miniscule residual remnants of energy, of determination, doggedly they renewed their resolve to stand firm, to hold fast; the minute drop in the wind to men mentally depleted far beyond rational calculation surely meant their salvation was coming. Blessed relief, akin to straws clutched by drowning men, began to flow again in minds long wracked by unmitigated and debilitating fear. Powerful gusts frequently restored the wind's fury to its former full force before easing back for a precious few minutes during which the men revelled in an internal renaissance of mental strength and determination. The helmsmen's flask had been refilled below with the last of the brandy and had been returned with the current short duration watch; it was liberally shared round to restore fleeting inner warmth. All the time Pat shouted words of encouragement to his men between the fierce rushes of wind whilst *Surprise* laboured, continuing her violent rolling and pitching, huge and smashing vibrations still resonating throughout her timbers as she struck hard after cresting the waves, an alarming shuddering of her bow striking water each time following the smash of unbending wood into unyielding water, the crash burying the foc'sle deep within it; and then came the all-powerful tidal wave of water flooding back over the gun deck, over the quarterdeck, into the cabin, washing back as she ascended precipitously once more towards the next crest. During every cycle a dense surge of spray struck the men on the quarterdeck, blasting past them even as the wind, which had veered further and now blew from off the port quarter, dumped cold airborne water on their heads, chilling them, running down their necks and spines. However, the wonderful feeling of hope, cautious but rising, the glimmer of expectancy that *Surprise* would persevere, would survive was taking a tenuous first hold, and that glorious notion heartened men who for hours had concluded that they were lost, that they would not, could not survive, that the conditions were such that no ship or mariner could reasonably expect to endure. Precious hope was flooding back to men who had long decided that they would never see daylight again.

Pat turned to the master who had come over from the wheel to join them, 'Will we change course for Falmouth, Mr Prosser?'

'I vouch we must not, sir,' said Prosser sagely. 'What sails we are fortunate to retain are surely nearing the end of their time and I vouch must not be hoisted until this wind drops, and the rigging and spars too are long past their best days. I venture in this gale, we cannot in good conscience fly a stitch of canvas aloft and turn north-east without we know how much sea room we have.'

Pat nodded his agreement, 'If only the wind would drop further.' He sighed deeply before his next words, spoken with obvious reluctance, 'Very well, we will continue to run before this wind, preserving our canvas, and we shall further consider our course only when the wind drops or after we sight land.'

'Aye aye, sir,' the master nodded, deeply pleased that he and his captain were one in accord on this occasion.

5:00   40nm S of Lizard Point, wind NW, FORCE 8,   35-40 knots, fresh gale,   spindrift and much foam "Treble-reefed topsails, or that to which a well-conditioned man-of-war could just carry in chase, full and by"

Surprise was now heeling much less than when she had sailed with the wind off her larboard beam, and this afforded the men on deck better stability. On the quarterdeck the men at the helm allowed themselves a modicum of relaxation and gratefully released the ties binding them to the wheel, rubbed burned and sore wrists until the circulation came back and painful feeling re-entered numbed and frozen hands.

'Mr Macleod, I venture she will bear a scrap of sail,' shouted Pat, adding 'All hands on deck!'

'Aye aye, sir,' said Duncan, bawling 'All hands, all hands on deck!' at the top of his voice.

'Hoist fore tops'l yard, the sail to be close-reefed,' shouted Pat to his First, the order reiterated by Duncan. From the deck a dozen topmen in oilskins swarmed up the ratlines, more men standing by to haul on the halliards and the braces. Within minutes the yard was hoisted up, hauled round and braced to catch the north-westerly, the topsail billowing out to fill in the gale. Pat observed the immediate diminution in *Surprise's* rolling with the stabilising effect of the topsail, a more constant heel, the ship steadier and much more comfortable to all aboard. He exalted in the return of greater control of his ship, for *Surprise* was tearing through the water, the wind still so strong: Pat estimated eight knots at the least with *Surprise* heeled over at thirty degrees, the lee rail often subsumed within the foaming crests of white water.

'Mr Pickering, I believe she may tolerate carrying her main tops'l,' observed Pat with a cautious smile, 'and perhaps it is time to rig the spritsail.'

'Aye aye, sir,' cried Pickering with enthusiasm.

'Mr Macleod,' shouted Pat, 'I think now is our time; we shall make our turn... our course is directly north-east. With her tops'ls aloft I venture she will hold that line.'

'Aye aye, sir,' cried Duncan and turning towards the helm he bawled, 'Put her helm down, lads; handsomely now, home to Falmouth if ye will.'

'Aye aye, sir,' the master's confirmation was without hesitation, his broad grin automatic, the heavy load lifting from his heart with the sight of canvas aloft once more and the mention of home. Prosser, ever cautious, reiterated the order to his men, 'Helm a-lee, handsomely now, let us see that the canvas will carry the load; we will turn north-east and bear away for dear Falmouth town!'

7:00 wind weakening, FORCE 6, 20-25 knots, strong breeze, large waves

On deck, every man waited with enduring anxiety, staring hard, wishing for the emergence of a faint twilight in the eastern sky. 'Half a glass,' declared Prosser, alongside Pat, 'half a glass, no more, and we will see the dawn. THE DAWN, SIR!' he shouted in emphasis to a Pat who was perhaps not fully listening, not hearing the tone of moderated jubilation shining through the master's voice, though the words did register after some seconds when Prosser's further and entirely triumphant shout of, 'GIVE YOU JOY OF THE DAWN, SIR!' jolted Pat to attention; he nodded wearily, the thinnest of tired smile on his face.

Despite the hopes and unspoken prayers of all on deck, time moved unbearably slowly; endemic hopes were rising: fragile but tangible, and then came the barely discernible lightening of the horizon amidst the enduring blackness; interminable minutes were passing so slowly, the brightening of the eastern sky becoming more noticeable, the weak light presaging the coming of another day; and the spirits and heartfelt thanks of every man soared, up, up to the heavens. Relief! Joy! Jubilation! News of the welcome event was sent down with the retiring helmsmen until every man aboard, long despairing of the hurricane enduring into the next day and for many hours praying with all their heart for the dawn proper to bring respite, luxuriated in the glad tidings, and the faint flickerings of hope of an hour ago were kindled further in minds for hours numbed to any expectations of survival.

'Wind is holding, no shift from north-west, sir,' opined the master to Pat, Duncan and Pickering. All the officers were standing near the helm and awaiting the dawn, fragments of shouted observations reaching soaking, chilled ears to announce the rising realisation that they had endured, they were alive, ALIVE! All about them huge green rollers merged into the gloom of an infinite waste of boiling seas, yet the waves were more ordered, less conflicting; one direction had become common to them all, though atop this aqueous maelstrom *Surprise's* violent gyrations remained, still extreme but more regular.

The high cloud had substantially broken up too, and although the twilight before the sunrise was hardly full daylight, merely the former inky blackness relenting to a shade of dark grey, for the men on deck it was as welcome as anything ever would be; *Surprise* was bathed in pale, diffused light. The low cloud, so low as to mingle with the spume of the waves as far as the limited extent that the eye could make out, precluded seeing anything in the far distance. The enduring waves were greatly diminished in their frightening power though the wind continued with fierce gusts, but at least it blew without its former full fury, its extreme violence had abated; the lessening was increasingly noticeable; the hurricane had left them far behind. However *Surprise* was still in its turbulent trail and still in dire danger, for the hold was filled with water to eight feet deep and rising still. The depressing grey cloud was thinning generally, gaps appearing within it, tiny hints of a paler sky occasionally visible through the overcast as if in answer to many a prayer from desperate men; and with the glad tidings spreading swiftly throughout the ship there was a commensurate and general lifting of the utter despair of the night.

'I could tell you many a tale of storms, South Atlantic furies which lasted for many a day, but never in life did I have any notion of a hurricane, of its full force,' said Pat, cold, soaking wet and shivering, but grateful that his own mental fortitude, near shattered, was beginning to recover.

'For sure, I will pray we never see another, sir,' Duncan replied, his own spirits lifting from the deepest trough he had ever experienced himself. The emergence of a modest optimism within all the men on deck was palpable. Although shouting was still necessary - even with the lessening of the wind - men could once more endure for an hour before relief.

8:00   wind NW, weakening, FORCE 5, winds 15-20 knots, fresh breeze, moderate waves

The glass was turned by Dalby, persevering again at his self-appointed station, and he rang the eight bells of the end of the morning watch, the sky brightening further. The brief twilight had passed, bringing the full dawn, sunrise proper just discernible on the still cloud-filled horizon. Whilst neither brilliant nor calm it represented unmitigated relief for every one of the Surprises; never before had any man been more pleased to see the new day, and the long endured burden of their intolerable

fears and anxieties slipped away to something more nea
normality; for the storm, extreme as it still was, was no longe
terrifying.

From below, a procession of men struggled up to the gui
deck for a glimpse of the day, for a few minutes escape from th
stench, a chance to breathe fresh air once more despite the col
and the freezing rain, still a soaking blast. The sea mist wa
clearing fast, though grey cloud obscured the sun, but not a mai
cared a jot; they had survived; they were alive, ALIVE, and the
rejoiced throughout every fibre of their being. The ship rolle
and pitched as before in the huge swell but, as it seemed to al
less so; the sea still broke over the foc'sle, the cold wate
flooding back the length of the deck and soaking everyone wh
had struggled up from below. No one gave it any mind at all. U
the steps to the waist came scores of men, to lean on the rail, t
clutch the hammock netting and to stare at the scene of rollin
green water, waves so high as to resemble hills in motion; and a
Surprise rose to reach the wave crests the unbroken, unchangin
watery vista could be seen stretching to every horizon, but n
longer the pummelling chaos and cross seas of the hurricane. I
was a more orderly march of rollers, white spume atop ever
wave, the ship still scudding amongst them; and the men revelle
in their unadulterated relief, blessed relief, conversation sti
difficult in the strong wind, shouting necessary beyond tw
paces; but that was no matter, during the night few had expecte
to see this day. The deeply disturbing and resonating vibratio
the shrieking, the screaming which had reverberated and shrille
throughout the whole of the ship during the night had ceased; th
wind was now no more than a fresh breeze, its direction still
constant north-west as the tail end of the hurricane faded. Th
maelstrom had moved east.

9:00   light NW winds, FORCE 4, 10-15 knots, moderate breez
crests break infrequently

Another hour had passed and the wind had lessened a little mor
the rain a lot. The reefs were let out; the long present inches c
flooding on the gun deck were all gone, flowed away out of th

288

scuppers; the lesser water nuisance was now only the cold, flying spray. A grateful belief in restored normality was returning throughout the ship, morale soaring. Duncan went below to rest. The bucket chain gang persevered, Mower still with them, sitting against the bulkhead but fast asleep. The men at the pumps were rotated every ten minutes and the water in the hold was rising no further. The cook, inspired, lit the galley to the accompaniment of great cheers and cries of jubilation.

Little light penetrated to the lower deck despite the canvas now removed from over the hatches, and so there had been little visible indication of the dawn below, but the increasing diminution of the wind was certainly discernible. The most experienced of the men had long felt the change in the seas striking the hull, the cross seas ceding their irregular, violent pummelling to a more ordered, cyclical regularity of the north-west swell; for the past few hours still huge but a movement with which an accommodation could be made, a preparedness found for the more rhythmical nature of the rise and fall as *Surprise* managed the lesser seas of the past hour, the even spacing of the waves far less uncomfortable than the battering from all sides during the hurricane.

'How are you, Marston? How do you fare?' asked Simon, his anxiety still plain in his voice.

'Bearing up, colleague. If our ordeal is coming to its end then I will offer a heartfelt prayer to our dear Lord and I will propose the most grateful of thanks at the table. That is if my stomach will permit the smallest of morsel later.'

'I believe the wind has dropped, the tumult has lessened,' ventured Simon cautiously. 'Perhaps they will take us home.'

Simon gazed round at his charges; the generous dispensing of his laudanum stocks, now all gone, had quieted the distressed, made more comfortable the injured, and the previous screams of agonised men had given way to a background of quieter moans and groans from semi-conscious men. He determined upon venturing on deck himself and signalled his intentions to Marston. The chaplain was still crouching over the prone figure of Jason. He had recovered consciousness after his fall, and he waved away his friends, nodding in affirmation of his weak words of confirmation that he was settled, resting, in no danger. Marston moved to accompany Simon, and together they picked their way carefully through the crowded floor, winding past suspended hammocks and the myriads of silent, exhausted men trying to gain respite and sleep on the deck itself.

'Will we go upstairs, brave the inclemency and see how things lie?' suggested Simon, taking off his blood-soaked apron and throwing an old and greatly worn cloak over his shoulder. 'I have the most pressing desire for fresh air, clean air... to be away from this festering putrescence, even for a minute.'

Clutching each other for support on the pitching and rolling deck, their legs weak, they reached the steps of the companionway just forward of the gunroom, and with infinite care stepped precariously past the bundle which had been the battened canvas, pulled away to admit passage, to emerge under the aftermost covered part of the gun deck. Carefully they edged forward and on up the steps to the quarterdeck, appearing just to the side of Clumsy Dalby who was standing by the mainmast. Just at that moment *Surprise* was at the top of a wave and heeling to starboard in a beam sea, rocking in a violent gust before she descended into the lesser wave trough. Then she rolled back to port, the suddenness of the heeling and the return throwing the two men off balance and towards the port side rail.

'Clap on to the lifeline!' roared Dalby, hurtling across with another great shout, 'CLAP ON, sirs!' He seized the staggering Marston who had fallen to the deck, Simon too already on all fours.

'Bless you,' shouted Marston, picking himself up with the aid of a heave from Dalby. Simon staggered to his feet, shivered the air so much colder than the crowded lower deck.

He stared all about him, open-mouthed, the visual and aural shock so great: *Surprise* was deep within the wave trough but the mass, the infinite substance of moving oceans of green solidity stretched away all about them. Unaccustomed as he was to the situation on deck after so many hours below, the crashing noise of wave and the still virulent wind noise was stultifying. The

290

overwhelming sense of the sea's unlimited force, unremitting and unforgiving, simply overwhelmed his senses. Atop all the waves, gentler now, were white crests, though no longer breaking, with little of the former spume, the wind casting only the occasional spindrift of foam towards those on deck.

'Clap on there, Marston,' shouted Simon, the deck heaving once more under them, 'Belay there, seize the lanyard... the line... that rope!' All in hearing smiled but said nothing, accustomed as they were to Simon's diverse variations on nautical terminology, some of them with an authentic origin.

Surprise, rising up once more on the wave and heeling again to starboard in a roll, threw Simon off balance once more. He hauled himself up with the aid of the lifeline; as the ship reached the crest he perceived a sea that extended as far as the eye could see without interruption; a rolling, seething cauldron of power and energy, quite untrammelled by any opposition in its gigantic procession. He blinked vigorously to clear his eyes, already soaked and stinging in the cold salt spray, the wind instantly chilling him to the bone, for he had not thought to don oilskins and his cloak had been whipped away to disappear in the wind. 'I believe I should be very happy in working again with Cornelius Tripe at the Dock,' he shouted to Marston. 'Here, take my hand, Michael.'

'Thankee,' gasped Marston.

'Hold firm, sir,' shouted Dalby.

Marston, drawing huge breaths of air in his own instant state of shock, clung on to Simon's hand with his own, grasped the lifeline with the other; and he gazed in trepidation as *Surprise* reached the bottom of the wave trough, rolling to port even as her bow rose as if with great reluctance, and then she crashed her bow into the next wave; the much subdued "WHHUUMMP" of the strike a familiar reminder of the former aural fury and shattering vibrations of the tempest as her foc'sle confronted the lesser wave, the shower of cold water flying aft and flensing all warmth from the two men with its chill, soaking the surgeons to the skin. 'And perhaps there might be a vacant benefice?' Marston shouted, neither man sure if his question was in jest.

Pat, still on deck and talking to Prosser, hurried from the wheel to aid his surgeons, one hand on the life line, until, with Dalby standing at their side in readiness to assist, all clung on to the waist rail above the gun deck where the adjacent void below at least provided a little relief from the water streaming intermittently all around their feet. Simon nodded his grateful thanks and, recovering a little himself, looked to his friend with a professional eye, for he had never seen his captain so run-down, so deeply fatigued; his unshaven cheeks and chin greatly exacerbated the deep lines of exhaustion etched into his face.

'It is singularly pleasant to see you, Doctor, Mr Marston,' said Pat with his first smile for hours, steadying Simon with one hand.

'For as long as ever I am blessed with breath and life I hope I never endure another night like that. How do we do? How is our dear *Surprise* in her tribulations?' asked Simon nervously.

'She is carrying tops'ls again.'

'That is most commendable,' said Simon, shivering, his feeble and hesitant voice utterly lacking in any tone of commendation. 'But tell me, what of our position, our prospects for port and shelter, an end to this interminable vile weather, the forceful billows? The vaguest of approximation would serve; in the plainest of words, if you will.'

'Oh, I dare say we will find a landfall as the day passes and perhaps a haven, though which one I don't yet care to say,' offered Pat. 'On my reckoning I believe we are five to ten leagues off the Cornish coast, but I cannot be sure of our longitude.'

'So we have safely passed by that perilous promontory, that infernal cape, the peninsula... an island would it be... Ushant... and, pray tell, we have escaped the dangers of the Scillies?'

'I believe so.'

'Then our physical perils are behind us, would you say?'

Pat looked upon his friend with great affection and it pleased him greatly to concur with Simon, 'Once we do sight the Cornish coast we may be confident of that; perhaps between six and eight bells.'

'And what o'clock would that be?'

'Before noon I venture.'

'Perchance the coast will reveal itself shortly and we can accommodate a change of direction, direct for Falmouth,' said Simon, 'or now perhaps?' all navigational precautions and the limitations of the wind customarily absent from his understanding.

'I hope you do not consider it is improper of me to ask, sir, but will we reach an anchorage this day protected from the storm,' asked Marston tentatively, only his own utter exhaustion allowing him to venture into asking such of his captain. 'That is to say, it will be immeasurably beneficial to the wounded and injured.'

'We will do our best,' said Pat in the kindliest of voice, a little of the fear and anxiety of the past twenty-four hours within him slipping away and relief only slowly creeping to the fore within his tired mind, the gripping tension he had long endured fading. 'How are the men below, the sick, the wounded?'

'Tolerably well; so much the better for Thor's departure, for the coming of the morning and the diminution of the tempest, as am I. Sure, there are broken bones, plentiful strains and the usual afflictions we are accustomed to in such turbulent trials,' said Simon. His professional eye returned to an appraisal of Pat. His friend looked tired, exhibited shrunken and wrinkled black hollows for haunted eyes, his face a ghastly white pallor, 'Will you turn in now, brother; you must surely rest, an hour or two at least?'

Macleod had come back on duty, hauled himself up to the helm and had been listening to the conversation. He added his own voice in support of Simon, 'Sir, I beg ye will take some rest,' this said with considerable emphasis. 'We believe we have plentiful sea room and there isnae any danger now.'

Simon pressed, 'Come, brother; you are quite finished, you must go downstairs.'

Pat appeared to consider the opinions of his friends, and in the surge of comfort that followed the sure realisation that he could rely on both of them in his absence from the quarterdeck he seemed to deflate, his tiny reservoir of energy ebbing away in an instant; his legs turned to jelly and gave way beneath him. He tumbled to the deck before anyone could intervene and he slipped into the merciful unconsciousness of absolute debilitation, Prosser and Dalby moving swiftly to seize him up and carry him below, both the surgeons in attendance.

The distant Cornish coast was sighted far off the port bow at seven bells of the forenoon watch by a vigilant restored topman, sitting comfortably at his station, the wind greatly further abated to no more than a breeze. At noon Duncan prepared for a sighting, serving on deck whilst Pat was sleeping the sleep of utter exhaustion. No precise observations could be made, the great swathes of grey cloud still so thick, but the general brightening of the day with greater illumination through occasional gaps in the cloud coverage enabled a more distant view of the surrounding seas, nothing else visible from the deck.

The wind so weak, Duncan and Prosser accorded on striving for a north-westerly course, tacking for Falmouth, the ship close-hauled, progress laborious and slow. To the veterans of *Surprise*, the situation now was entirely within their capabilities, and men bustled about the ship making small remedy to the many and various damages inflicted during the hurricane. Three score of men on a rota continued to serve the pumps which spewed out a constant torrent of water to port and to starboard. Duncan was able to order the main course unfurled, though there was no replacement canvas for her torn fore course, the sail additions giving *Surprise* more precious stability and speed.

All early afternoon they pressed on, making long boards, the wind benevolently weak, the former fury of the seas itself, it seemed, now exhausted, the surface little more than a millpond with ripples and the sky brightening further as the dark grey clouds of the morning ceded to an ever lighter shade as time passed. At two bells of the afternoon watch a refreshed Pat re-emerged on deck once more. The wind now slackening to little more than a weak breeze, a thin sea mist had developed, shrouding the distant Cornish coast from the tops, though periodically clearing in the immediate vicinity only to settle all about them once again. Every man of the crew save for the wounded was on deck, on the gun deck, on the foc'sle, on the forward part of the quarterdeck, along her sides at the waist; to a man all alive to the possibility of sighting the coast, a precious glimpse of which was anxiously awaited by men who were coming to terms with that which they knew in their heart: they were lucky to be alive. The stark fear of the night had left them, the gloom and apprehension had dissipated, and deliverance, dawning strong, was the feeling common to all, a little of anxiety still present with the nearing prospect of getting home, home to their loved ones, and the excitement was general and rising throughout the ship.

'The bilge water is down to five and a half feet, sir,' announced the bosun. It was a welcome step in the right direction, but *Surprise* still wallowed heavily.

'Well done, sir,' declared the master, offering Pat his hand.

'Well done, sir; you have brought her through,' cried Pickering, every man on deck alive to the improving prospects.

'Aye, my heartiest congratulations,' shouted Duncan.

'It was for sure a close run thing,' murmured Pat, relief coursing through his every fibre, his nerves still shot, and of his strength precious little remained.

From the helmsmen and the men on the forward part of the quarterdeck who had been listening intently to the officers came forth a ragged cheering, the unusual noise alerting men all along the waist, on the gangways and on the foc'sle, reaching the ears of men on the gun deck and others coming up the companionways, all of them joining in with the spontaneous gesture of appreciation as they reached the deck, the heartfelt chorus rippling forward and becoming general, a full-throated roaring, 'Hurrah, hurrah!' On and on it went, unceasing, the men so very grateful to their captain for leading them to salvation. The officers seized Pat's hand in turn, Duncan clapping him on the back without ceremony. In his realisation of the event, the significance of the moment, Pat could find no words; indeed, his own exhaustion rose once more to the fore to near overcome him as he stood mute, gazing all about him at his men, hundreds of feet now stamping the deck in resonating chorus to the enduring cheering. His body beginning to shake, at last he summoned some tiny vestige of strength to raise his arm in salute, and he turned all about him to wave his acknowledgement to all his men, a broad smile across his face, blessed relief in his mind and pure joy filling his heart.

Appendix   Pat's dilemma

It is 3pm on November 22nd 1824 and *Surprise* is 10 nautical miles north-west of the island of Ushant. The wind is a strong SSW, air pressure 29 inches and dropping for hours. What should Pat do? Looming large in his mind is the sense that things are about to change for the worse and in a big way: the steeply falling pressure is a significant clue. There has also been a subtle shift in the wind direction crossing Biscay, from SW to SSW, i.e. it has not veered but backed. He has, of course, some familiarity with the hurricanes of the Caribbean, but who would suspect one was imminently to arrive from the Western Approaches. A strong storm? Yes. But a hurricane? Who would have thought it? Pat is aware that the general track of storms arriving from the SW is NE up the Channel. He has several options to consider but precious few can he choose without facing disaster:

1. The obvious one is to sail directly for Falmouth; however, it is still 100 nautical miles to Falmouth, 10 to 12 hours of speedy sailing it nothing changes, i.e. it means a 3am arrival in the black of night and potentially in a hurricane with *Surprise* carrying no sail and the wind direction unpredictable. This is the point: if the already strong wind both strengthens further to the stage where *Surprise* cannot bear canvas and - as will happen if it is indeed a hurricane approaching - the wind also veers to a more southerly wind then he is in danger of wrecking on the lee shore of Cornwall.

2. He cannot sail directly south for there lies the perilous dangers of Ushant. He could retrace his course SW of Ushant and turn east into the sanctuary of Brest, but the strong wind is already directly against him and were the wind to veer to more of a WSW then the narrow approach into Brest in such formidable winds with a lee shore in near every direction is very far from easy. In any event, to Brest is probably near 50 nautical miles and generally into the wind for the first 20, hence much tacking would be needed, and so it will be very slow even, as he suspects, the wind will strengthen considerably and veer to become a more hazardous WSW.

3. He could continue past Ushant, bear directly south into the relatively open waters beyond Brittany, but that is a considerable distance in adverse winds. If the wind strength further develops, as Pat must consider, then he will have a lee shore for every mile and every hour of that long passage which, if reduced to bare poles, represents a considerable danger, particularly if the wind does veer to a WSW one, for in such circumstances *Surprise* would be hard pressed to avoid wrecking on an ultimate French lee shore.

4. Can he lie to, facing the wind? If, as he suspects, it is wind of a strength approaching a hurricane that he is to face, *Surprise* could not sustain any sails against such a wind force, and she would then be in perpetual danger of turning beam on to the wind and capsizing.

5. If indeed the wind is of such strength that *Surprise* cannot bear canvas and if Pat opts to run before it i.e. to scud into the Channel, then without sails he has ultimately no control over *Surprise's* direction and the entire English south coast becomes a perilous lee shore. If, as he suspects, a hurricane it is which is approaching, Pat knows that it will ultimately overtake *Surprise,* and then she might well be exposed to southerly winds when the lee shore risk of Cornwall and later Devon will be so much the greater.

6. The hurricane which he fears is approaching may yet be some hours away, which represents a chance to gain more westing, taking *Surprise* further from the English south coast which will be exposed to dangerous southerly winds - as the contra-rotational nature of the hurricane winds will become as it overtakes *Surprise.* He can only do this whilst she can still bear canvas. NW is the only option. He cannot sail closer to the wind than NW. Can he gain sea room on the southern fringe of the fiercest winds before *Surprise* in her weakened state is overwhelmed by the power and violence of the arriving hurricane? If he can, *Surprise* might then be blessed by the NW winds of the hurricane on its south-western fringes, winds which would carry *Surprise* further away from the Cornish coast and to greater safety. How much time does he actually have? Very little indeed. There is not a moment to be lost.

Extracts from THE KEDGE-ANCHOR by William Brady
New York, 1847

312. PREPARATIONS FOR A HURRICANE AT SEA.

Endeavour to get sea-room; if you have it, run before the wind.

338. A SHIP ON HER BEAM ENDS.

When the severity of the squall is felt, hard up the helm and let fly everything; but if she goes on her beam ends before she can be got off sufficiently to diminish the effects of the wind, the best way will be to cut away the mizen-mast before the headway ceases, which falling over the lee quarter, will act as a drag, to pay her off... great decision and rapidity of execution is necessary, as the ship must go down a short time after she goes over.

Note: All dates referred to within this book are of the Gregorian calendar. Greek historical texts, using the Julian calendar, are 12 days behind.

GLOSSARY, for pressed shipmates

Bargeman.................weevil (usually in the bread and biscuit)
Blunties ....Old Scots term for stupid fellows
Boggies.....................Irish country folk
Bombard...................Mediterranean two-masted vessel, ketch
Bower.......................bow anchor
Boxty........................traditional Irish potato pancake
Breeks......................Scots term for trousers or breeches
Bumbo.....................'pirates' drink; rum, water, sugar, and nutmeg
Burgoo.....................oatmeal porridge
Captains' Thins........Carr's water crackers, a "refined ship's biscuit"
Caudle......................thickened, sweetened alcoholic drink like eggnog
Clegs.........................Scots term for large, biting flies
Crubeens..................boiled pig's feet
Dreich.......................Old Scots for cold, wet, miserable weather
Drookit.....................Scots term for drenched
Etesian......................strong, dry, summer, Aegean north winds
Felucca......................small sailing boat, one or two sails of lateen rig
Fencibles..................the Sea Fencibles, a naval 'home guard' militia
Flat............................a person interested only in themself
Flux...........................inflammatory dysentery
Frumenty.................a pudding made with boiled wheat, eggs and milk
Gomerel....................a stupid or foolish person
The Groyne..............La Coruña in north-west Spain
Hallion......................a scoundrel
Hoy...........................small (e.g. London-Margate passengers) vessel
Jollies........................Royal Marines
Kedgeree..................a dish of flaked fish, rice and eggs
Kentledge.................56lb ingots of pig iron for ship's ballast
Laudanum...............a liquid opiate, used for medicinal purposes
Lobscouse................beef stew, north German in origin
Marchpane..............marzipan
Marshalsea..............19th century London debtors' prison
Mauk........................Scottish for maggot
Meltemi ....Greek and Turkish name for the Etesian
Millers.....................shipboard rats
Mistico.....................similar to the Felucca sailing vessel
Nibby.......................ship's biscuit
Puling......................whining in self pity
Scrovies ....worthless, pressed men
Solomongundy........a stew of leftover meats
Snotties....................midshipmen
Stingo......................strong ale
Treacle-dowdy........a covered pudding of treacle and fruit
Trubs.......................truffles
Yellow jack..............Yellow fever (or flag signifying outbreak)

I hope that you have enjoyed reading this book in my series
"The continuing voyages of HMS Surprise".

You can find out more about my books by visiting my website:
https://alanlawrenceauthor.wordpress.com/

Alan Lawrence